Long Way Home

By D. Emily Smith

This book is lovingly dedicated to …

The military men and women I have had the honor of getting to know over the past decade.

To Dr. Faith Thomas and her amazing co-laborers in Christ who minister to those broken in spirit.

To Little D. You are loved by a Father who will never leave you. He doesn't hold your past against you. In fact, He's given you a future. It's in His strength - not yours - that you will make it to the end. You WILL see the goodness of God in the land of the living.

Trigger Warning: This book contains mention of suicide and suicidal ideation. This book briefly mentions human trafficking and physical abuse, though it is not focused on in depth. Please understand that while it is included in this book, the goal is to point towards hope and restoration in Christ.

ISBN 979-8-218-89883-0
Book Cover by Kat Schmitz

"I remain confident of this: I will see the goodness of the Lord in the land of the living."

(Psalm 27:13)

1

Jenna Clark smiled as she tucked her cellphone tightly between her shoulder and ear. Her mother gushed on and on about the flurry of activity back home in Deer Creek, New York. The last of the Tyler brothers, Michael, finally gave up the fight for singleness and was now engaged to the love of his life. All of Colleen Tyler's children were now either married or soon would be.

Just the day prior, Jenna received a text while she was at work with a video of the proposal. She never knew her brother could be so romantic. He chose to propose to Anna while he was at the school doing a fire safety demonstration for the students. In between seeing patients in the ER, Jenna cried tears of joy and then burst into laughter at the klutziness of her future sister-in-law. Anna had knocked the ring from Michael's hand, sending it flying. Michael had to retrieve it from under the fire engine. How she wished she could've been there to see it in person!

She and her husband, Ben, were stationed at Fort Bragg in North Carolina, a hefty twelve-hour drive away from their families. Deployment had taken him far away from her, but she had learned to find contentment with the fairly regular video calls. During this last call, he had warned her that their talks would soon be few and far between due to an assignment he couldn't speak of. She was a new wife and new to military life. She wasn't as seasoned as some of the other wives who learned how to cope when their spouses deployed for months on end. However, judging by her work schedule, Jenna would have plenty of work to keep her distracted in Ben's absence.

"How soon do you think you can get home?" Jenna's mother cut into her thoughts. "Anna is anxious to start dress shopping."

"I'm packing as we speak," Jenna chuckled as she folded her favorite sweatshirt and placed it into her carry-on bag. "I took off a few days over the weekend, and I'll check out the flights as soon as I get off the phone with you."

"Let me know as soon as you find a ticket. We'll cover the expenses."

"*Mother*!" Jenna tried to sound stern. "You and Dad can't keep sending me money. We talked about this. Ben and I are doing fine financially. Especially now that I'm working at the hospital."

"I know, but you two are still starting out." Colleen paused, and Jenna waited for her mother's real intent behind the offer. She didn't have to wait long. "*And*… I know you are trying to save up so you can start a family. I don't want to slow that process down any."

Jenna laughed. She debated whether she should tell her mother about the conversation she and Ben had during their last call. Had it really been over a week since she last talked to him? Her heart constricted as she looked at his side of the bed, untouched and empty. Instinctively, Jenna grabbed his pillow and breathed in the fading scent of his cologne as she remembered their last video chat.

He looked tired, but oh so handsome in his desert cammies. His hair was ruffled, and there were bags under his eyes, but his quirky smile still sent her stomach into a fluttering frenzy. They'd been married for over a year, however, most of that was spent apart. Deployment came way too soon after they arrived at Fort Bragg.

"You look tired. Are you sure this is a good time to talk?" she asked.

"Are you kidding? Seeing you is giving me a second wind." Ben gave her a mischievous smile. "All I keep thinking about is taking you away on another honeymoon when I get home."

One of his fellow soldiers made a crass comment and Ben turned to the man, telling him to get lost. Jenna blushed when he returned to the screen. He looked annoyed at the interruption.

"I can't wait until we can have a conversation without an audience," Jenna said wistfully.

"Yeah. You're telling me. There's not a lot of privacy here."

Jenna pressed her lips together, debating whether to ask the question on her mind. Ben had mentioned in their last conversation that he may have news about a possible return date, but she didn't want to push.

"I know that face. What's on your mind, Babe?"

She gave a slight shrug and a cheesy smile. "Is there any news you want to tell me?"

He smiled and sighed. "There's nothing definite, but... what would you think if I'm home by Christmas?"

Jenna squealed and jumped up, dancing around with the phone in her hand.

"Really? Please don't get my hopes up."

Ben laughed, nodding. "That's what I'm hearing so far."

"In time for Christmas?" Jenna couldn't contain her joy.

He nodded again and moved closer to the screen, conspiratorially. "You know how we talked about starting our family in the next year? How would you feel about starting right away? As in, as soon as I get home?"

Jenna blushed and couldn't stop her smile from spreading across her face. "Are you serious? What changed your mind? You said you wanted to save up a little more."

"Remember me talking about my friend Kent? He and his wife are expecting. He found out the other day and... I don't know..." Ben shrugged thoughtfully with a warm glow in his eyes. "Watching him find out just did something to my heart."

"Are you sure, Ben? I mean... of course, I want to, but I also know with deployments..."

"If we keep waiting, it may never happen. I want a little Jenna running around getting into trouble." He smirked.

"What about a little Ben? A perfect little gentleman?"

"Ha! You met me after I found Jesus, Sweetheart. I would rather our kids take after you," Ben gushed. "So... we'll start trying when I get home then?"

Jenna thought her heart would burst as her eyes filled with tears. All she could do was nod. Someone on Ben's end said something that got his attention. He nodded curtly at them and turned his attention back to her. His expression was tender, but quickly turned regretful.

"I have to go, Jenna. It may be a little while before I can call again."

"Why? How long?" She knew she shouldn't whine, but she lived for these calls while he was away.

"Things are just going to be... intense... here for the next week or so." Ben looked at someone Jenna couldn't see off camera and his expression made her curious. It was a mix of trepidation and reservation. "I love you, Baby. Hopefully, when I talk to you next, we'll be planning my homecoming."

Jenna realized she was still clutching Ben's pillow in her arms as her mother's voice kept speaking about dresses and Anna's elaborate plans. She smirked, realizing she had missed several parts of the conversation, but Colleen didn't seem to notice. Jenna caught the tail end of something about Michael wanting to incorporate a fire truck in their wedding.

"But Anna has this thing literally planned to the smallest detail already and it has only been a week or so. She's adamant no fire trucks, but I think she will give in eventually." Colleen chuckled. "You know how persuasive your brother can be when he turns on his charm."

"Oh, I know. I still have the scar on my knee from him persuading me to climb Mr. Benson's oak tree," Jenna smiled, finally releasing her husband's pillow and putting it back into place on Ben's side of the bed. "I bet you're happy to finally have one of our weddings on the farm. I wouldn't change how Ben and I did things, but I *am* sorry I didn't have you with me."

"Well, that's water under the bridge now," Colleen said softly. "You know I'm happy for you. And we adore Ben. So, there's nothing to be unhappy about, is there?"

Jenna knew that eloping shocked her family. Being the only girl in the Tyler family, her mother spoke quite often over the years about having an elaborate celebration when Jenna got married. Yet as soon as Ben learned he was being moved to Fort Bragg for training, Jenna didn't want him to leave without her. They risked their families' disapproval and sought out a justice of the peace.

"How have things been at your new church? Are they taking good care of you while Ben is gone?" Colleen asked.

"Oh, yes." Jenna resumed packing her suitcase for the trip home. "Though I've been too busy to plug into the church the way I wanted to. I am making friends at work and on base. Our neighbors are nice."

"Good. I worry that you will be content to hide away all alone until Ben comes home without any friends around you. You've always been so independent."

Jenna rolled her eyes. She probably shouldn't tell her mother that the closest friend she had was Chase, Ben's best friend. Inevitably, there would be a lecture on how she needed *female* friends, but Jenna was the perpetual tomboy. There was no escaping that, being the lone girl with three older brothers. Added to that, the Tylers were farmers. Jenna spent most of her growing-up years proving she could do exactly what her brothers could... sometimes even better. She'd much rather be out shooting a rifle at a range than talking to the other wives about the latest gossip. Although maybe she should find a few other young friends who were mothers. Especially if she and Ben got pregnant quickly.

Jenna smiled at the thought. It would be nice to have a few girlfriends to talk to and share her excitement with. Christmas couldn't come fast enough.

"Any news on when Ben might be home?" Colleen asked.

Everything in Jenna wanted to broadcast the potential good news, but she knew better. What she *had* learned from her small number of military friends was that the Army could say one thing one day and the next day it could all change.

"No news." Jenna cleared her throat and decided to direct the conversation back to the wedding plans. "So, Anna isn't going to make us wear a hideous color, is she?"

Colleen laughed. "I don't think so. We're looking at a late spring or early summer wedding. I've heard her mention pink or sage green so far."

Jenna cringed. *Pink.* "Maybe I could steer her to a darker color?"

"I doubt it. One thing I will say for Anna, she is taking this wedding seriously. Her first wedding gave her very few choices, remember?"

It was hard to imagine Anna with anyone but Michael. Yet Anna had been engaged once before. The poor woman had very little choice in the wedding decisions. To add insult to injury, her fiancé broke up with her before they could even walk down the aisle.

"Will we be able to pull off a wedding between now and spring? It's already October," Jenna mused.

"Kate and Dan managed it in *less* time," Colleen pointed out. "I think the real obstacle will be the fact she has to testify at the upcoming court case. Michael's friend, Jake, said he wants them to take precautions until after the case is officially done."

Jenna's brow knit in concern. "Why? Are they in danger?"

Anna had quite a penchant for getting into odd scrapes. One of those scrapes included uncovering a crime ring and getting the attention of some pretty high-profile people.

"Jake is taking good care of them and communicating with Detective Jenkins here in Deer Creek. So far, everything seems fine." Her mother seemed confident, so Jenna decided not to borrow trouble.

Colleen changed the topic to her grandbabies, Jenna's nephew and nieces. It was while her mother was in the middle of a funny story about Sean changing his infant daughter's diaper that Jenna heard a car door shut in front of her house.

She moved to the window and looked down as two formally dressed military men stood next to the parked car. She'd heard nightmare stories of men in their dress uniforms showing up unannounced. Jenna saw her neighbor, who was out walking her dog, pause in what looked like pure terror. The woman didn't move for quite a few moments until they passed her on the sidewalk. Then, she let out a visible sigh of relief. Someone was about to get bad news and Jenna's heart twisted. *I wonder whose house they're going to.*

Jenna prayed a silent prayer for the recipient of their visit. Just then, another car pulled up behind the other. This car was familiar. *Chase*! He moved to say something to the other two, and they collectively looked towards her home before moving up the sidewalk. *God, please, no. Not my husband!*

"And then Tessa took baby Evie …" Colleen continued without pause. "And she had to give her *another* bath!"

The doorbell rang below.

"Mom, can I call you back? Someone is at the door," Jenna said numbly, feeling all life drain from her veins.

The call ended, though she didn't remember hearing her mother say goodbye. Jenna slowly moved out into the hallway and descended the stairs. She heard the men's muffled voices from the other side of her door. When she opened it, she saw Chase standing next to a man with several multicolored bars depicting a high rank. The other man, standing slightly behind the first fellow, had a cross on the lapel of his uniform.

"Chase, what's going on?" Jenna asked nervously, looking at the strangers on her stoop. *This isn't real. This isn't happening.*

"Mrs. Clark? May we come in?" the high-ranking man asked politely.

Jenna silently moved to let them pass. Her stomach clenched as Chase took her hand, leading her into the small living room. He guided her to the sofa before the men spoke again.

"I'm Lieutenant Corporal Johnson. I regret to inform you that your husband, Benjamin Lucas Clark, was killed in action…"

The man continued speaking, but Jenna didn't register one word.

"I'm sorry… *what* did you just say?" Jenna looked up at Chase and noticed how red his eyes were. He looked tormented.

"Ben's gone, Jenna. He died helping evacuate civilians from…"

Cutting Chase off with an unhinged laugh, Jenna spoke loudly. “No. There’s a mistake. I just received flowers from Ben yesterday.”

She jumped to her feet. If she could just show them the card from the bouquet, she could prove he was fine. The flowers were blooming in their vase in the center of the dining room table.

“See? He sent these to me yesterday, so there’s no way that…” Jenna grabbed the vase with shaking hands.

“Jen.” Chase approached, but she jumped backwards, her grip loosening on the vase. The glass shattered onto the tiled floor, sending shards of crystal and petals everywhere.

The older man with kind eyes approached her. “I’m Chaplain Thomas, Mrs. Clark. Come sit down here and let me take care of that for you.”

“No!” she yelled. “You’re not listening to me. He’s fine. He’s… He’s…”

Jenna couldn’t catch her breath, and the world started blurring around her. Were they trying to say Ben was gone? *Dead*? No, they were lying. Hot, stinging tears rushed to her eyes, and Jenna felt strong arms circle around her. They weren’t Ben’s arms, though. Only *Ben* was allowed to hold her like this. She tried to push and fight, but the hug tightened as she fell against Chase’s chest in sobs.

“He’s not dead. He can’t be.”

She heard words come from the other men, but she couldn’t make them out. All Jenna heard was Chase whisper in her ear, “He’s gone, Jen. I’m so sorry. Ben is gone.”

2

Seven months later…

"Shh. It was just a bad dream, Babe. Wake up." Jenna heard Ben's soothing voice. She smelled his cologne and smiled in a sleepy haze. *Praise God!* She knew it all had been a bad dream. God wasn't that cruel. Not when the two of them were just beginning their lives together.

The sound of her alarm pierced the air, but she clenched her eyes shut tightly. Jenna could see the daylight dance across her closed eyelids, but she didn't dare open them. She rolled over, ignoring the intrusive alarm, and attempted to put her arm around her husband's frame. Yet, she only felt the cold, flat, empty side of his mattress.

Slowly, her eyes slid open. She wasn't in *their* bedroom. This was the cold, economy apartment near the hospital that she moved into shortly after Ben's funeral. Living on base had been torture following Ben's death, watching the soldiers from his unit return home to their wives and families. Moving seemed like the best thing for her to do.

The smell of Ben's cologne still teased her senses as she pulled his pillow tighter to her face. She caught sight of the almost empty bottle of cologne on the bedside table. Once upon a time, Jenna's nightly routine had been snuggling up against Ben's chest, listening to his heartbeat until she fell asleep. Now, at night she sprayed his pillow with cologne so she wouldn't forget what he smelled like.

Beep. Beep. Beep. Angrily, Jenna swiped at the unwelcome noise that disturbed her dreams. She didn't want to wake up. Closing her eyes tightly, she tried to recreate the last moments of the dream. Ben was with her and held her tightly. Yet, no matter how hard she tried, she could not recapture the moment.

A text cut through the silence, and she reluctantly glanced at her phone.

"Can you cover my shift later this week? I wouldn't ask, but I'm desperate," one of her co-workers had texted.

Numbly, Jenna sent the thumbs-up emoji. She rolled to her back and stared at the ceiling. The more distractions she had that week, the better. That upcoming Friday was her and Ben's anniversary. Holidays came and went. Special events passed. Anniversaries of the silly things they used to celebrate. None of those days were easy to get through, but their second wedding anniversary? Well, that day was going to be a special type of torment.

Her phone hummed with an incoming call. It was her mother… *again*. It was the fifth call that week and – just as she had the other five times – Jenna sent it to voicemail. At some point, she would have to return the calls. Knowing her mother, she would be on the first plane to North Carolina if Jenna didn't speak to her by the end of the week. She didn't want that.

Jenna turned her head to look at her bedside table. The laptop was still open to whatever video she had watched last night to help her fall asleep. Food wrappers and soda cans cluttered the floor. Discarded clothes covered the ugly old carpet of the bedroom. Yeah… her mother could never see this.

Checking the time, Jenna calculated she had managed to get a solid four hours of sleep. *Not bad. That's an improvement.* She had fought with her doctor about the sleeping pills. He pushed them and she tried to avoid them. However, if they helped her to get some sleep before she had to work, maybe they were worth it. The downside? Waking up. Sometimes at night she prayed God would just take her in her sleep, but He wasn't listening to her anymore. Every morning, she opened her eyes to a new day… alone.

Putting her feet on the floor, Jenna forced herself out of bed and into the small kitchen to get the coffee started. Several boxes still lined the walls. She had moved into the apartment months prior, but she didn't have it in her to unpack. Several military families had banded together to help her get settled into her new home. A civilian apartment. No rules or regulations. Just pay rent on time and stay out of trouble. She could've stayed in the house on base. No one was kicking her out, but she couldn't… not with every corner reminding her of *him*.

The people in the apartment above hers turned on their pounding music. It seemed to be their morning ritual. Apparently, her new neighbors didn't follow the same polite etiquette as her old neighbors on base. It was a noisy apartment complex, but it was cheap. At least the noise made her feel less lonely.

Her eyes landed on a box. She should've resisted the urge, but Jenna opened it with a sigh. It contained sentimental items. Old letters. The velvet box her engagement ring came in. A triangular, folded flag. It had draped Ben's casket. The soldiers had taken special pains to fold it and present it to her. She could still hear the sound of the rifle shots as she got lost in her memories.

"But why are they shooting in the sky?" Eli, her nephew, had asked from somewhere behind her. Maybe another time... another place... Jenna might have found the innocent question cute. But with each shot, she felt her body jolt. She stoically stared at the casket resting on the mechanism that would lower the love of her life to his final resting place.

Next to her, Ben's mother and sister sobbed. His father saluted, being a retired Army man himself. Jenna didn't cry. She couldn't. She had already cried herself dry. A warm hand rested on her shoulder. Michael. He was worried about her. They all were. Her entire family took turns making sure she had someone to sit with her the entire week of Ben's funeral.

Returning to North Carolina was appealing to Jenna for no other reason than to escape her family's watchful eyes. Chase stood with the other soldiers wearing his dress blues. He was supposed to be at attention, but she glanced at him to find he was looking at her from the corner of his eye. Just as quickly as she had spotted it, he returned to attention.

Chase had been such a help with everything from funeral preparations to flying back to New York with her. Ben could've been buried in Arlington due to the fact that he died on active duty... a hero's death at that. Yet, Jenna and Ben's parents knew his heart was always in Deer Creek where he was born and raised.

Instinctively, Jenna's mother-in-law reached over and grasped her hand tightly in her own. It was a loving gesture and Jenna forced herself to squeeze in return, though inside she felt numb. Dead. Just like her husband.

Anna's father, Pastor Tim Munson, had given a loving message. He mentioned knowing Ben as a young boy and shared several stories. He spoke on Heaven and how Ben was there now, basking in God's glory. His words fell flat. Ben missed out on being a father. He was missing out on their life together. There was no goodness in Ben's death... no matter how many Bible verses people tried to quote to her. No one would ever be able to convince her otherwise.

The coffee gurgled as the last of the dark brown liquid filled the carafe. Grabbing a shiny, foil-wrapped breakfast pastry from the cabinet, Jenna ate it without tasting. She drank her coffee down hot… a habit she developed while working at the hospital. She had just enough time to take a quick shower, throw her hair up into a messy bun, and jump into her scrubs. Her phone vibrated, catching her attention. *Chase.* She hadn't answered her mother's call because at least she knew her mother wouldn't be there right away if she didn't answer. Chase *would* be.

"Hey, Chase," she rasped out.

"Hey, yourself, Stranger. Where have you been? I left several messages." His tone was caring, but stern.

"Uhh… I don't know if you noticed, but I work at the ER."

"Don't be sassy. You know what I mean."

"I've picked up some extra shifts. Turns out people don't like to work when the weather is nice." Jenna sighed.

"Well, speaking of nice weather. This weekend is perfect beach weather. I thought maybe we could take a trip to…"

"I'm sorry, Chase. I can't."

"Can't? Won't? Or you don't want to?" There was a hint of amusement in his tone. He knew her too well.

"All the above?" Jenna smirked.

"I know Friday is going to be tough. I thought maybe we could spend it together so you're not alone."

"Who said I'd be alone?" she teased as she set about getting ready for work.

"Oh? Is there something you want to tell me? Have you met someone?" She knew he was teasing right back, but even the notion was like a knife in her heart.

"Friday, I will be spending the day with North Carolina's sick population. And maybe a few hypochondriacs for some added fun."

"As enjoyable as that sounds, maybe we can grab a late dinner after your shift. Maybe drinks in honor of Ben?"

"Ben didn't drink," Jenna pointed out as she turned the shower on.

"*I* do and I miss him." Her heart hurt at his admission. She wasn't the only one who had lost someone.

"I'll think about it, okay?" She lied, but if it got him off the phone so she could get ready, she didn't care.

"You better. You're getting pale being inside as much as you are."

Jenna smiled. "Later, Chase. I have to get ready for work."

She disconnected the call only for him to send her a text telling her that he'd call her later to pester her some more. She just shook her head and readied for work. Chase was trying to be a good friend. It was as if he had made some type of oath after Ben's death to watch out for Jenna. The thought was sweet, but Jenna just wanted to get through the week without breaking… and she wanted to do it *alone*.

*****

The emergency room was more active than usual. By lunch, Jenna had helped patients with a wide array of issues. A perforated appendix. Heart arrhythmias. A child who stuck a marble up his nose. By the time her shift wound down, she was exhausted.

"Jenna, did you get that bloodwork on Mrs. Murtaugh in room three?" Dr. Santini asked without looking up from the file he was poring over at the nurse's station.

"I was just going in."

She retrieved the blue caddy with all of the various test tubes and knocked before entering the room. There she found a younger woman, roughly Jenna's age, lying back against a pillow with a pale complexion. The woman clung to a bucket that she must've brought from home.

"Mrs. Murtaugh? Hi, I'm Jenna. I'll be your nurse today. I hear you're feeling pretty crummy." Jenna attempted a sympathetic smile.

"I think I have food poisoning. Or maybe it's a virus? I can't even move without getting sick," the woman lamented from the bed.

Jenna was a pro at finding healthy veins, but she could tell just by looking at her that Mrs. Murtaugh was probably dehydrated.

"Let's get this IV going first and see if I can get some blood from you. The Doctor has a bunch of tests he wants to run." Jenna tapped and poked until she found a hopeful vein. Tying off the patient's arm with a blue band, Jenna set about inserting the IV port and withdrawing blood for the tests. "There we are. This fluid will help you feel better, I bet."

"Thank you. Can someone let my husband know I am back here? He had run out to the car to get something, but they brought me back to a room before he returned."

"I'll see if I can locate him for you."

Jenna smiled gently and left the room. After depositing the blood samples at the drop off, she busied herself with other responsibilities. That is, until she saw *him*. Jenna jumped and stood frozen in place. Just a few feet away with his back to her… was *Ben*. He was dressed in his army fatigues and his hair looked tousled in that adorable way that made her heart pound. She stared in utter shock and dared not breathe.

Slowly, he started to turn. His eyes met hers, and disappointment set in. This man wore glasses and had a mole on his cheek. It wasn't her husband, but oh, how he had looked like him from the back. Jenna's heart constricted as the man approached her.

"Excuse me, Nurse," the man said nervously. "I'm looking for my wife. Do you know where they took her?"

"Mr. Murtaugh?" Jenna asked numbly.

He nodded and visibly relaxed when Jenna said, "Your wife is in room three. She was asking for you."

His smile was wide as he nodded his thanks to her and disappeared into the room with his wife.

"Earth to Jenna. Where are you right now?" Calista laughed as she breezed by her in a blur. "What are you staring at?"

"I thought he was someone I knew," Jenna said softly.

"Hmm. Well, don't tell that fine man that just stopped by to drop these off for you that you're looking at other men."

For the first time, Jenna looked at her coworker. She was holding a bouquet of red roses with a small card sticking out of the top. Calista was a newer addition to the staff and she was clearly not aware of Jenna's grief.

Jenna furrowed her brow. "Who was it?"

"Read the card, Dummy," Calista smirked. "How many good looking men do you have that you don't even know which one brought you roses? Oh, and he invited us all out tonight to that new club around the corner. Something about celebrating a guy named Ben."

Jenna snatched the card and tore it open. It read, "No more hiding away. I'm picking you up after your shift tonight and we're going to have a good time. *Chase*."

No, no, no. Who gave him the right to make those decisions for me? Jenna fumed. She was going to kill Chase when she saw him next.

"Your patient's light is on," Calista pointed out, still smiling mischievously.

With a resolute sigh, Jenna turned back towards Mrs. Murtaugh's room, trying to stifle the rage building up inside of her. *How dare Chase do this to me? If he thinks I'm going anywhere tonight other than home, he's sadly mistaken.*

"Could my wife have a blanket? She's feeling cold," the Ben look-alike requested.

"Yes, of course," Jenna said flatly, turning to the closet in the corner of the room and pulling out a white blanket.

Just as she fixed the extra blanket around the nauseated woman, the doctor came in.

"Mrs. Murtaugh, I have good news. It's not a virus or food poisoning," Dr. Santini announced. "You're pregnant."

Jenna stood still as the scene played out in front of her. Mr. Murtaugh jumped up with an ecstatic look on his face and ran to his wife, who started crying happy tears. She clung to her husband as he whispered soothing words of love against her hair. Jenna felt her throat swell. If Ben had come home, that could've been them rejoicing in the news of a brand new life. But Ben didn't come home and the idea of motherhood was nothing more than a dream out of reach. Jenna needed to leave… and quickly.

Excusing herself from the room, she was relieved that her shift was coming to an end. Her phone vibrated with a call from the pocket of her scrubs. Once inside the women's changing room, she pulled it out.

"Did you get my roses and note?" Chase asked as soon as she answered.

Jenna let out a harsh laugh. "Yeah, Chase, I got them. What were you thinking springing this on me?"

"Don't be mad, Jenna. I just… I want to pull you out of the darkness you're in. Even if it's just for a few hours."

There was something in his voice that caused her heart to thaw a little. He cared about her. And if she were honest with herself, she *was* in a deep darkness. She hadn't realized just how deep until she almost broke down at the sight of that couple receiving happy news. Jenna *resented* them.

"Jenna? Are you still there?"

"Yeah."

Chase cleared his throat. "What if we just *try* to go out and see what happens? If you're miserable and hate it, I'll take you straight home."

What was her alternative? Hiding in her bed covers, watching something mindless on her laptop until she dozed off for a little bit?

"Fine." Jenna sighed. "But you better not be planning on a late night. I'll give you an hour… tops."

"Deal. I'm on my way."

3

Strobing lights pulsated to the beat of the loud music and a crowd of people jumped with their hands in the air on the dance floor. Other than the over-the-top colored light show, the club was dimly lit. If it hadn't been for the tight grip Chase had on her hand, Jenna would've been lost in the throng of people.

"Come on. I see an open booth," Chase yelled into her ear so she could hear.

A few of her coworkers from the hospital had followed them to the club. Judging by the huge smiles on their faces, they found the atmosphere more palatable than Jenna did. Growing up in a conservative Christian home, places like that were an anomaly. Deer Creek had a few bars, but nothing as lively as the club they'd entered. And even then, Jenna had never darkened their doorways.

Chase motioned for her to sit next to him in the booth while her coworkers took the seats across from them. A waitress wearing tight black shorts and a t-shirt sporting the club's logo approached with drink menus.

"I haven't had a good margarita in months," Calista's smile grew wider.

"Just give me the straight tequila after the shift I had today," said the other woman Jenna knew as Becca.

"What about you?" Chase nudged Jenna with his shoulder playfully.

"I… I don't know. I think I just want a Coke." Jenna pushed away the agitation when he laughed out loud.

"That's the drink you want to toast Ben with? A *Coke*?"

"You know we didn't drink much. Ben and I weren't big on…" Jenna paused to look around. "…all of this."

"Well, of all the times you need a drink to unwind, I'd say this week is it. Enjoy life, Jenna. That's what Ben would want for you." His tone and expression turned slightly serious. Jenna, for a split second, wondered how Ben and Chase had become friends. They were wildly different. "I think most women like pretty drinks. Fruity things. Help me out, Ladies."

"It's okay, Jen. I got you, Girl." Calista winked and turned to the waitress speaking some secret code Jenna couldn't decipher.

The waitress smiled broadly and winked at Jenna before turning to Chase for his order.

"I'll have a beer."

With that, the waitress rushed off leaving the small group to talk.

"So, who is this *Ben* person we're celebrating?" Calista asked. She jolted when Becca elbowed her in the ribs suddenly.

"He was a hero," Chase said solemnly and swallowed back emotion.

"He's my husband. He was killed on deployment," Jenna muttered, wondering when the waitress would return so the conversation could cease.

"You were married? Oh, my word, Jen. I didn't know. You're so young to be a widow," Calista said reaching across the table and grabbing Jenna's hand. "How old are you anyway?"

"Twenty-six."

"What happened to him?" Calista asked.

"He was shot when his team was helping the locals get to safety." Even to her own ears, Jenna sounded callus and cold. Bereft of any emotion.

"He died a hero. Thank you for your sacrifice, Jenna."

Jenna's mother raised her to be polite, even in uncomfortable situations, but this tested her limits. Jenna knew that Calista meant well. Of all of the things that Jenna had been told over the past year, Calista's comment wasn't the worst by any means. *God still has a plan.* That particular gem was spoken to her at the luncheon after Ben's graveside service. Even if it was a true statement, a plan without Ben wasn't one Jenna cared to be a part of.

A moment later, the waitress returned. Jenna had no idea what to expect when Calista had ordered for her, but the rolling cart with an enormous science experiment smoking from the top was not it. The cylindrical glass beaker was at least three feet tall filled with a red shimmery liquid. The opened top had sparklers sticking up and dry ice sent billowing white clouds slithering down the sides.

The waitress produced three huge glasses, all rimmed with what looked like sugar. She put one at the bottom of the beaker and pushed down on a spout that Jenna hadn't noticed. The red liquid filled the glass and she handed it proudly to Jenna.

"You get first sip," Calista said ceremonially.

When she didn't immediately oblige, Chase nudged her gently. He leaned in close and whispered, "It's okay, Jenna. You're not going to go to Hell for having a drink."

Then he took his beer glass and raised it. "For Ben!"

Jenna lifted hers, not expecting it to be so full. Becca and Calista followed suit and everyone took a long sip of their beverages. Jenna took a small sip at first, but, when she realized it didn't taste so bad after all, she went back for a longer one.

They ordered food and Jenna felt herself relax as they chatted about nothing in particular. After Becca and Calista finished their food, they excused themselves and made their way to the packed dance floor.

"It's good to see you out with your friends." Chase smiled at her.

Jenna laughed. "Friends? I've said more to those two in the last hour than I have all year."

"Hopefully that will change after tonight. Ben wouldn't want you locked away. I think you know that." Chase took another slow sip of his beer.

"Maybe." Jenna did likewise and drained her second glass.

"No, not *maybe*, Jenna. I miss him too, but we have to live on. I owe it to him to make sure you are cared for."

"Ha! I knew it!" Jenna said a little louder than she had intended. "You've made me into your personal mission or something."

Chase ducked his head down, but she caught his smile. When he brought his head back up, his eyes were gleaming. "I wouldn't call you my *mission* necessarily. Although, I do have a vested interest in you."

It was easy to see why ladies found Chase so charming. He had the most amazing dimples and blue eyes that seemed to stare right into her soul. Jenna had to look away. She was getting lost in them. What was she thinking? Chase was a friend. *Ben's* friend. Her head felt hazy.

"Well, stop it." Jenna slurred as she leaned over to the margarita tower and refilled her glass for the third time.

"Stop what? Being interested?"

"Yes… that." Jenna waved her hand in the air, sloshing her margarita in the glass before guzzling down more of the sweet drink.

Chase looked highly amused and Jenna furrowed her brow. "You need to find a new project. I'm just fine on my own."

He reached over and took her glass from her hand, putting it safely on the table. Then he turned her face towards him using only his index finger under her chin. It was a surprisingly intimate gesture and made Jenna flush.

"But you don't *need* to be on your own, Jenna. Let me in." The words were spoken so tenderly and she felt herself begin to lean into the warmth of his breath as he inched closer.

Ben had been her first kiss and he had owned every kiss since. *What would it feel like to kiss Chase?* Jenna wondered in her heated haze. *If I close my eyes, I can pretend it's Ben.* As his lips touched hers, a jolt went through Jenna, but it wasn't exactly pleasant. His lips tasted like beer. His cologne was too strong. Ben's had been… *perfect.* The arms that were closing in around her were aggressive. Ben was always so gentle in his embrace, not *handsy* like Chase was becoming. All of the sudden, Jenna felt ill. *This isn't right. He's not Ben.*

Jenna squirmed in Chase's arms. "No. Stop, Chase."

"What is it, Jen? Talk to me," he pleaded softly. "You have to know how much I care about you. It is natural for us to…"

"Maybe I overdid all of this…" Jenna moved away quickly and looked over the plates of mostly eaten food and half empty glasses. "I feel sick."

He instantly released her, a look of concern mixed with disappointment on his face. He quickly recovered and followed her out of the booth. "I'll take you home."

Chase threw a large sum of money onto the table and reached over to take her arm. She tried to shake him off, but realized she didn't feel all that steady on her feet. She allowed him to lead her to the car. Her nausea worsened as the car sped down the streets back to her apartment. Chase put her passenger window down and Jenna turned her face into the torrent of air with her eyes clenched shut. Even after she started feeling better, Jenna kept her gaze outside the window. The open window and rushing wind ceased any conversation and that was fine with her.

"Here we are," Chase said as he pulled up in front of the older building. "I'll help you up to your apartment."

"No. I'm okay now. Thank you though." Jenna knew she sounded rushed and awkward, but did not care.

She started ambling up the sidewalk to the double glass doors and realized he had gotten out of his car.

"Jenna, wait. Can I call you later? We should probably talk about that kiss." He walked closer carefully as if approaching a wounded animal that may bolt at any moment. "I don't regret it and I sure hope you don't either."

Jenna looked up into Chase's face. His heart was in his eyes and her own broke a little more. He brought his hand up to her cheek and she backed away, causing him to drop it to his side.

"We'll talk later, Chase. I promise," Jenna said softly before clumsily letting herself inside the building.

All the way up to her apartment, she could hear Ben's voice chastising her in her head.

Come on, Babe. You know better. You've never even had a drop of tequila before in your life and you drink three glasses? On an empty stomach?

"I know. I'm an idiot." Jenna cried into her hands once safely on the other side of her locked door. "I just miss you so much and for one moment… I felt numb. It was nice not to *feel*."

But Chase? He was my friend. You kissed him.

"Forgive me, Ben. I'm so sorry." Jenna slid to the floor and sobbed. "He's not you. No one will ever be you."

*****

The sun cascaded through the blinds and Jenna squinted at the light before throwing the blankets over her head. She was grateful it was her day off, but she wished she could enjoy it without a splitting headache. With a groan, she forced herself up and sought out aspirin.

Memories of the kiss she shared with Chase came back to her reverie and, with it, feelings of regret and guilt. He had tried to call her after he had gotten home, but she had responded by texting him that they'd catch up later. In truth, she didn't know if or when she would talk to Chase again.

Jenna crawled back into bed after she had taken her pain medication, but her phone vibrated on the bedside table, thwarting her sleep escape. It was Michael. Her mother must've enlisted him to call, knowing he'd get her to answer the phone.

With a sigh, Jenna answered.

"Yes, I'm alive. No, I don't need anything. Yes, I am doing just *swell*," Jenna spouted off to her brother. "Tell Mom to stop worrying."

"Good morning to you too, Sunshine." Michael laughed. "You know, if you'd just have answered her call she wouldn't have had to send in the big guns."

"And you are supposed to be the *big guns*, I take it?" Jenna pulled the blanket up over her head to block the light out.

"Hey, just so you know… you are on speaker phone. You have an entire family of people who miss your ugly voice." She could almost hear the smile in his tone.

"Nice. An early morning ambush," Jenna groused.

"Early morning? It's almost noon." This came from her father and Jenna moved the phone so she could see the time. Sure enough, it was 11:57.

"Jenna, it's Anna. We have a new wedding date for you to mark on the calendar."

Jenna clenched her eyes shut tighter. They still wanted her to be a part of the wedding. It had been postponed after Ben's… Well, Jenna had hoped they would just move on without her being a bridesmaid, but apparently they weren't going to budge. *Typical Tyler family loyalty.*

"We're thinking next June. How does that sound to you?" Anna went on without waiting for a response from Jenna. "It's a little over a year and Jake said by then most of the stupid drama from the court case would've died down. Do you think you can get free to come home for a dress fitting?"

Jenna accidentally let out a groan. *Oops!*

"You know, it's enough for me just to be invited. I don't have to be a bridesmaid, Anna." Jenna hoped her future sister-in-law wasn't picking up on her negativity.

"We can't get married without you." This came from Michael. "I want you standing up there with us."

"Hello, Baby, it's Momma." Jenna felt tears sting her eyes. Hearing her mother's voice was usually like a balm, but Jenna could hear the desperation in her mother's voice. This call wasn't just to chat. They were all genuinely worried about her and that caused Jenna deep pain. "What if Dad and I arranged for you to fly home this weekend? I know it's your anniversary, but maybe being with your family would help?"

Jenna shook her head. *Help*? Being around four happy couples at various stages of development? It would be a horrific reminder of what could never happen for her and Ben. Michael and Anna's wedding should be joyous, even in the planning stages. She knew her presence would bring everyone down. As it was, they had already put off their wedding far too long and Jenna's miserable life was partly to blame for the delay.

"I'm sorry. I have to work."

"Well, maybe next week?" her mother prodded.

"You know what? I'd really just rather you all go on without me," Jenna blurted out. "I know you want me there, but I'm really too exhausted to care what everyone wants out of me right now. What about what *I* want?"

There was movement on the other line and her mother's voice came on louder. Jenna assumed she took her off speaker phone. A few sniffles and whimpers in the background cut at Jenna's heart. Someone was crying over her outburst. *Great! Nice going, Jenna.*

"And what is it you want right now, Jenna?" Her mother's question was spoken gently and kindly.

"I don't know. I don't know anything anymore, Mom," Jenna cried.

"You know you are dearly loved, right? You know God won't let you go, even if you *feel* like He's abandoned you."

No, Jenna *didn't* know that. Yet, she dared not tell her mother. If her family truly knew the depths of Jenna's thoughts, they'd be on the next flight to North Carolina to collect her. For her mother's sake, she had to play along.

"Yes. Of course, Mom. This is just a season. I promise, I'll be okay," Jenna forced the words out and lightened the tenure of her voice. "Now. Tell me all about the kids. I bet they're growing so big."

The tears silently slid down her face as she barely heard a word her mother said. For the first time in over a year, Jenna knew her next step. It wasn't going home. It wasn't pursuing a relationship with Chase. It didn't even have anything to do with her career. Jenna needed to be with Ben and finally out of her misery.

4

On Friday, Jenna called out of work sick, though for the first time in a while she felt wonderful. The agitation of her coworker who took the call didn't affect her one bit. Jenna had her day planned down to the minute. She drove as close to the gates of Fort Bragg as she could and pulled off to the side of the road. She remembered the first time driving through them with Ben. They had been so excited to see their new home and meet new people. If she wanted to, she could still get on base to take a final look at their first – and only – home together, but she didn't want to risk seeing any familiar faces. These moments weren't to be shared with anyone else. They were sacred to her as she said goodbye.

After a few moments, Jenna pulled away and drove to their favorite restaurant. She felt a little odd asking for a specific table for just herself. She tried to envision Ben sitting across from her as he had right before he deployed. Jenna ordered her favorite meal and ate in silence, remembering every time they sat in that booth talking about their future.

After lunch Jenna pulled into a liquor store and splurged on good tequila. It worked the other night to dull her, hopefully, it would work again one last time. As she was about to turn onto the road that led home, Jenna caught sight of a big, white steeple.

She turned the car in that direction and pulled into the parking lot. It was mostly empty and she paused a moment as she remembered how kind the church members had been to her and Ben. She really hadn't given them a chance to minister to her after Ben's death.

She regretted that now, but Jenna was convinced there was nothing they could've done, ultimately.

A man walked out of the church towards his car but paused when his eyes met hers. It was the pastor. Jenna sighed as he changed direction and headed her way. She should've pulled away, but instead she reluctantly put down her window.

"Jenna Clark! How are you?" he asked in the southern accent that she'd always found sweet.

"I'm fine," she lied. "How are you, Pastor Richards?"

"I can't complain. Grateful for another day of life." He paused a moment and Jenna braced for his meddling to begin. "We've missed seeing you."

Jenna forced a smile. "I've been busy with work."

He smiled a polite smile and nodded, though she knew very well he saw through her words. Anna's father, Pastor Tim Munson, had been a family friend since she was a little girl. He had often shared some of the excuses and silly reasons people used to keep them from church. She never imagined one day she'd be one of those people. But, then again, she never imagined God would be so cruel as to take away her love.

"Well, I need to go, Pastor Richards." Jenna started her car.

He nodded. "I do hope I see you again, Jenna. I don't pretend to know what it's been like for you this past year without Ben, but you are dearly loved."

Jenna swallowed hard and nodded before driving away. In her rearview mirror she saw him stand still, staring after her as if he knew her thoughts… her intent.

That wasn't possible. No one knew. Just herself and the bottle of tequila on the front seat in the brown paper bag.

Her phone cut through the silence and she saw it was Chase... *again.* She swiped the screen and sent it to voicemail. He had been calling just about every hour. If anyone could ruin her plans, it was Chase. He had managed to confuse and confound her. For a moment, she had actually entertained a man in her life other than Ben. That just couldn't happen.

She felt the solemnity hit as she pulled into the parking spot of her apartment building. In silence, she took the elevator to her floor and let herself into the lonely one bedroom unit. With a sigh, she pulled up the song she and Ben loved to slow dance to and let it play on repeat through her wireless speaker.

From her bedroom, she retrieved an envelope addressed to her parents and put it on top of a pile of other important papers they might need after she was gone. She paused as she grabbed a glass and the bottle of tequila. Was she really going to do this?

The words of the song took her back in time to the honeymoon she and Ben shared on the way down from New York to North Carolina. The way he had held her and spoken to her... She couldn't live without moments like that. Jenna didn't want to know what life could be like moving forward without Ben.

She opened the bottle, scrunching her nose at the strong scent. Pouring the glass full, Jenna took a sip, choking as she did. It wasn't the same effect as the other night. This wasn't the sweet drink she had liked, but a bitter and burning sharpness sliding down her throat. Soon she'd be numb to it anyway. Grabbing the bottles of pills she had collected from the medicine cabinet, Jenna sat on the couch and began pouring them onto the palm of her hand, a mix of medications that she knew would do the trick.

"Take me quickly, God. Just let me go fast and I can be reunited with Ben." She spoke the words through tears.

Don't do it! The words screamed in her head, but Jenna swallowed the first handful, chasing it with the liquor. Then, she repeated the action again and again. It wouldn't be long until the pain was over.

*****

"I'm sorry, Chase. She called out last minute," Calista informed him in the emergency department's waiting room.

Chase had shown up at the hospital, hoping to catch a moment of Jenna's time. There was a growing feeling of unease in the pit of his stomach. Jenna wouldn't do that. She loved her job.

"Has anyone tried checking on her?" he asked feeling panicked. "She hasn't answered any of my calls. Maybe she'd answer if you called."

"Wasn't today supposed to be her anniversary? Maybe she decided to be alone." Calista shrugged off Chase's suggestion. "I wouldn't want to be here either."

Chase scribbled down his number hastily on a piece of paper he found on the registration desk.

"Here. Call me if you hear from her. Please."

Calista took it and nodded before going back to work. Chase stood for a moment trying to figure out what to do next, if anything. He should never have kissed Jenna. It was a moment of weakness and he knew better. She was so vulnerable. For a moment, he thought maybe things would work out well for them both when he felt her reciprocating the kiss. However, if the calls sent to voicemail were any indication, he was sorely mistaken.

He had to see her, even if it was just to apologize. Speeding through the streets to her apartment building he found a spot to park and took off at a brisk pace to the double glass doors. Chase buzzed up to her apartment, but no response came.

An older man entered and pushed in a code. He opened the door, but cast a curious glance over his shoulder at Chase.

"Could you hold the door, please? I forgot the code and I'm supposed to be apartment sitting for a friend." Chase tried to keep his face friendly.

In what felt like forever, the older gentleman assessed Chase, finally nodding approval and holding the door open for him to enter.

"Thank you," Chase called back as he took the stairs two at a time, bypassing the elevator. He didn't have a tangible reason to feel the fear he felt, but something was wrong.

He was winded by the time he made it to her door, but knocked determinedly. He could hear familiar music coming from inside the apartment. Ben used to play that song. He remembered how his friend played it on repeat when they were away on a training and had to share a room. He knocked louder and harder. Still no answer.

The neighbor across the hall poked her head out of her door.

"Have you seen her? Is she in there?" Chase asked the woman.

"She's in there alright. She came home about half an hour ago. I knocked on the door to ask her to turn down that music, but she didn't open up." The woman shook her head in frustration.

Chase put his hand on the doorknob. Ben had been a praying man. Jenna had been a praying woman once as well. For the first time in his life, Chase attempted a prayer.

"If you're real, God, let this door open."

The door gave way and Chase pushed into the room scanning the small living space. There on the couch was Jenna, slouched over to one side. Her mouth gaped open, but her eyes were shut. Her complexion had a deathly pale hue. Around her were empty pill bottles and on the floor was a spilled glass of what smelled like tequila. The large bottle on the coffee table in front of her was half gone.

"No, no, no! Jenna, can you hear me?" he yelled as he rushed to her side, feeling her wrist. At first there was nothing and his heart dropped. He pressed his fingers into her neck. Forcing himself to calm down and quiet his own breathing, he finally felt a slight pulse.

Wasting no time, he called 9-1-1.

"Oh, my goodness! Is she…" the voice of the neighbor came from the doorway.

Chase ignored the neighbor and looked at the face of the woman he had dreamed about every night for the past several months. It worked once, maybe praying would work again.

"Please, God. Let her live. I can't lose her, too."

*****

I finally get decent sleep and I dream about work? It even smells like it. Oh... wait.

The familiar beeping of an IV machine caused her to open her eyes as reality hit. Her head hurt. She was groggy. Her throat felt like it had tried to swallow a toilet brush. And her stomach… It all came back to her in a rush. Apparently, she was still very much alive.

Well, that's just great.

"Hey there! Welcome back to the land of the living," a familiar voice said above her. She made out the outline of a man in a white coat.

"Dr. Santini?" she managed to croak out.

"Your throat is going to hurt for a bit. You were intubated, young lady. We had to pump your stomach. You're lucky to be alive."

Jenna sighed and turned away.

"I think your friend found you before the pills could do real damage."

"Friend?" Jenna rasped. She tried to focus on the doctor and he nodded to the corner of the room.

In a chair sat Chase, looking disheveled and *angry*. His eyes met hers and softened a bit, but he was still unmistakenly upset.

"I'll leave you two. If you need anything … well, you know the drill, Nurse Clark," Dr. Santini said humorlessly, but paused a moment to look into Jenna's eyes compassionately. He squeezed her hand, something that was very uncharacteristic of the dry humored doctor. It touched Jenna even in her sedated haze.

Chase waited for the doctor to leave before standing and approaching her bedside.

"Do you have any idea how scared I was, Jenna?" His voice was pained though controlled. "You could've *died* tonight."

Jenna slurred sleepily, "Duh!"

His shoulders slumped. "Not funny."

"I'm sorry." She was sorry he was hurt, but she was sorrier that he had found her *just in time*.

"Was this my fault? Was it the kiss?" He ran a hand through his military cut. "I'm so sorry, Jenna. It was stupid of me to do."

"No, Chase." Jenna managed to lift her hand and grab his wrist where he held the side railing of her bed. "It's just… there's nothing left."

"That's not true, Jen. There is so much more life left for you." Chase leaned down closer to look directly into her eyes. "You once believed in God. Can't you find hope there again?"

Jenna felt too tired for this conversation.

"I prayed today. I prayed so hard." Chase's eyes filled up. "I don't know if there is a God, but you're alive right now and you *shouldn't* be. I think He heard my prayers. That has to mean He has something for you still, right?"

Jenna slid her eyes closed. She didn't have it in her to argue.

"I called your family. Thankfully you listed them in your contacts as Mom and Dad."

She opened her eyes wide and pinned Chase to the wall with them.

"Go ahead and be mad at me, but they needed to know. I called in a favor to a friend of mine outside of Fort Drum. He's flying them here. He's a pilot," Chase stated in a matter of fact tone. "They'll probably be touching down soon, so you might want to prepare yourself."

He hadn't been kidding. Just mere hours after Chase made the comment, Calista tapped on her door to let her know her family had arrived. Ben used to tell her that Chase had some pretty high up connections, but to get her brothers and parents to North Carolina in record time? If she weren't so mad, she'd be impressed.

"Do you want to see them?" Calista asked. "Dr. Santini said he'll bend the rules on the number of visitors for your sake… just this once. Just for a little bit anyway."

Jenna reluctantly nodded and Calista gave her a sympathetic smile before talking to someone outside the door. *Great. This is what my actions have gotten me. Not relief… just pity.*

Her family entered, all wearing the same look of exhaustion and fear. Jenna's eyes met Chase's and he said, "I'll leave you in your family's capable hands."

There was something so sad in his tone, but Jenna didn't have time to ponder on Chase. She was now the center of attention of three very angry brothers and two tearful parents.

"Promise me right now that you will never do anything like this again, Jenna Colleen!" her mother cried as she wrapped her daughter in a tight embrace.

Jenna wanted to give her mother what she wanted, but she could not. She just returned the hug, catching

Michael's eyes. An entire conversation was spoken between the two of them without a word. He pleaded and she apologized. Would she try again? Did she have it in her? Her mind was too cloudy to come to a conclusion.

One thing was for certain, something would have to change. She remembered the expression on Chase's face as he left and she considered the concerned looks plastered on the faces of her family. Jenna couldn't continue hurting the people who loved her. Maybe surviving was God's punishment for the damage she'd done.

5

Another year later…

The curtains swayed at Jenna's bedroom window ushering in the familiar scent of lilacs. She stood in front of the old mirror on the back of her childhood bedroom door. She never thought she would be living at home again, but there she was. Her bedroom was an odd mix of her younger years mixed with her present. Raggedy, well-loved stuffed animals stared at Ben's fold-up rowing machine that she had decided to pull out of storage. Against a wall was her bookcase filled with old teenage romance novels next to nursing manuals.

Jenna clipped her ID to the pocket of her scrub top and sighed at her reflection. Out of the corner of her eye, she caught sight of the framed picture of her and Ben on their wedding day. She wore a simple white dress and he was in his dress blues. *Could that really have been three years ago?*

"Happy Anniversary, Ben," she whispered into the empty room.

A text lit her phone on the dresser and she smiled slightly. *Chase. Just like clockwork.*

"1-10, Jen. Where are you at?" Every morning for the past year, he had taken her counselor's suggestions to heart and made her give an assessment every single morning. Then he repeated the gesture again at night before bed. The number one meant she was great, no suicidal thoughts at all. Ten meant she had a new plan in place, possibly already engaged. *As if I would ever admit if I was at a ten.*

"At a solid five," she texted back.

She watched the dots appear as he formulated a response. A five was great considering all that Jenna went through over the past year. She moved back to Deer Creek. Said goodbye to Chase. Left her job at the hospital. Went through some heavy duty counseling. Became the object of her family's constant scrutiny and surveillance. Her therapist seemed quite pleased with her progress. *Now if everyone else would just back off.*

"Praying for the day that you get to 0."

Chase was starting to take the church thing seriously. Ben would've been thrilled. He would be less than thrilled at *her* attendance, however. Going back to the church they both grew up in wasn't appealing. Who needed those painful reminders? Add to that the sympathetic faces and whispers behind her back. Once someone attempts suicide everyone starts treating them differently.

"Happy Anniversary, Jen. I'll check in later." His final text came through.

It was a day of two anniversaries. Her wedding anniversary to Ben, but also the anniversary of her suicide attempt. Dr. Crenshaw, her therapist, encouraged her to celebrate it as a day of victory. Jenna wasn't sure she could call it a victory. At least, not yet. Maybe someday. There were still days she wished she had succeeded.

The smell of coffee caught her attention and she gave herself one more look in the mirror before heading downstairs to the kitchen. She stifled a chuckle as she caught the tail end of her parents' conversation.

"You don't have to put these stupid pills in front of me like I'm a child, Colleen," John Tyler groused.

"If you'd lay off the junk food when you're out, maybe you wouldn't have to take these," Colleen scolded her husband. "Cholesterol isn't a joke. Do I need to remind you what your cardiologist said?"

"For heaven's sake..."

"She said that you are on the fast track to clogged arteries."

Jenna walked in and right to the coffee pot. "Listen to her, Dad. Or would you like me to tell you how angioplasty works?"

"Not you, too, Jenna," he muttered.

She smirked at her father, but the smile faltered as she watched her mother collect the medicine bottles carefully. She put them back into a lockbox, latching it shut, and put the key in her pocket after hiding the box in the farthest corner of the pantry.

Her mom caught her gaze and attempted a pleasant smile. "I made muffins. They're on the counter."

Jenna just nodded silently and took a sip of her coffee. Before she arrived back at the Tyler home, her family didn't have to lock up their medications. This was a part of Jenna's *safety plan.* All meds needed to be under lock and key. No alcohol. All guns had to be removed from the home. Thankfully, Dan and Kate were more than willing to store her father's hunting rifles in their gun cabinet at their house. They even locked up the steak knives. *As if I would ever opt for a painful death. Talk about overkill.* She snorted to herself at the unintentional pun.

"Did you say something, Dear?" Colleen asked absently from her place at the table.

"No. Just clearing my throat." Jenna joined her parents at the table. "I'm not going to be right home after work. I have a couple errands I need to run."

"Oh? Would you like company?" Her mother did not have a good poker face.

"I'm okay, Mom. I promise."

Her father cleared his throat. "It's just that… well, we know today might be hard for you."

"*Every* day is hard for me, Dad." Jenna reached over and took his hand. "But I'm serious when I tell you that I'm okay. If I get in my head, I promise I'll reach out to Dr. Crenshaw."

Her parents didn't look convinced.

"You know, Dr. Crenshaw mentioned that our appointments can go monthly instead of bi-weekly now. That's a good sign," Jenna asserted.

The fact that her parents still didn't look pleased hurt her a little. Jenna was serious when she said she was doing better. However, it would take a lot more than her words to alleviate their fears. They may never look at her the same again. Even after a decade, they may still look at her with a twinge of grief and apprehension behind their eyes. While she understood, it also reminded her of a time she wanted to forget… to move past. How could she when the pain on their faces was so evident?

"Well, I'm off to work. Thanks for the muffin, Mom." Jenna kissed her mother's cheek and moved to her father to do the same.

She breathed in the fresh air deeply as she got into her car. The dermatologist's office that she worked at part-time was less than ten minutes away and she knew she'd get there earlier than needed. However, Jenna needed space. Something had to change… and fast.

Jenna felt exhausted trying to prove to her family that she was normal. In addition to Chase's check-ins, she had to answer to *eight* other people. Kate and Dan made it a point to give her tasks on the farm to keep her busy and distracted. Sean and Tessa asked thoughtful questions to assess her mental state and get her to talk about her feelings. Jenna normally laughed through those conversations. Tessa called it *deflection*, but Jenna called it coping. Michael and Anna, though slightly more enjoyable, made her go to the gym with them and work out because supposedly subjecting one's body to stringent exercise combats depression. *Who knew?*

And then there were her parents. They watched her every moment she was in the same room. If she was sequestered too long upstairs, they'd seek her out to check on her. You know, just to see if she needed anything. They kept every conversation light so as not to darken her mood… even withholding important information like the fact that Michael and Anna had received bad news about Anna's sister. Apparently, Alexis relapsed after her release from the drug treatment center. They had hoped she'd be at their wedding clear headed, but they didn't even know where she was at that point.

Ugh! The wedding! In a few short weeks, Anna and Michael would have the wedding of the century. Of course she was happy for them, but she'd also be relieved when it was done.

Jenna's phone sounded from the holder on the dashboard. *Skennan Cove Memorial*. Her pulse quickened as she answered. "Hello?"

"Hello, Mrs. Clark?" a female spoke. "This is Cara Smith."

Jenna recognized her as one of the people in attendance at her virtual job interview that she'd had a couple of weeks prior. It had been quite an undertaking to keep the job interview a secret from everyone, but she had gotten good at keeping secrets. Jenna held her breath, praying for the first time in a long while. *If you still exist and care for me at all... please let this be good.*

"After some discussion following the phone interview we had two weeks ago, we would like to offer you the RN position in the Emergency Department."

Jenna sighed a heartfelt sigh and slid her eyes shut tightly as she felt the relief flood over her.

"Mrs. Clark?" the woman asked after a moment of silence.

"Yes. I'm here and I am so thankful for this opportunity," Jenna gushed.

The woman's tone softened. "Your previous hospital had only wonderful things to say about you."

Jenna wanted to ask if anything about her past mental health had been mentioned, but thought better of it. "I'll need a few weeks to settle things here in Deer Creek. I want to give Dr. Higgin's office time to find someone new."

"Let's plan on the first week in July for orientation. Would that be adequate?" the woman asked.

"Yes. Thank you."

"We look forward to working with you, Mrs. Clark. I'll email you the particulars. Have a great day."

It took Jenna a moment to register that it was her own face she was looking at in the visor mirror. She was smiling. Not just the hollow smile that she gave everyone to be polite. Her face glowed for the first time in years.

"I'm bouncing back, Ben. I promise. This will be a new start for me." Jenna just wished he was there to share it with her. *Is this Your doing, God? Or was it a coincidence?*

She didn't have much time to think on it. The gap of time she'd allowed herself earlier to get to work had been gobbled up. She'd have to tell Dr. Higgins her news as soon as she got in. She'd only been there four months so there weren't strong emotional ties. The real issue was: How was she going to tell her family?

*****

Loaded down with roses and her dinner, Jenna pulled up alongside the plot of land where Ben's grave waited. Over the year, she had come to *visit* her husband a handful of times. Most of the visits ended in tears and sadness. Something felt different this time. This visit felt purposeful.

As she had done in the past, Jenna smoothed out a picnic blanket next to Ben's headstone. She started laying out their anniversary dinner and began talking.

"I know it's been a while. I hope you don't think it's because I have forgotten about you. I haven't." Jenna put the red roses on what she imagined would be his chest. "Happy Anniversary, Babe."

Spreading out the Chinese food cartons on the blanket, she started putting some on a paper plate for herself.

"I had to get this from our second favorite place. Did you know they closed down *The Lotus*?" Jenna put a dumpling in her mouth and chewed quietly. "Not bad, but not *The Lotus*."

She sighed as she looked over the well-kept cemetery. The birds chirped happily in the trees. Squirrels played around the base of the huge oaks. Did they even know six feet below them rested the bodies of people who once walked the streets of Deer Creek? People who were loved and who were missed dearly.

"I feel like I did when we had just started dating," Jenna chuckled. "Sneaking out to see you. Desperate for a moment alone. I told Mom I had errands to run just so I could have dinner with you."

Jenna smiled reflectively as she remembered their first date. She had been so excited even though she had tried to play it cool. Ben had been the perfect gentleman that night. He allowed her father to ask all kinds of intimidating questions and withstood the glares of her brothers. Would she ever feel that type of excitement again?

Her brow furrowed. The intrusive thought ruined the moment. She had *no* desire to experience that type of feeling again with someone else.

The sound of tires on gravel caused her to turn her head towards the cemetery entrance. The red truck heading her direction caused her scowl to deepen.

"Uh oh, Babe. I've been found out," she muttered low.

Michael pulled up behind her car and got out slowly. Clearly he was assessing her mental state as he took in the picnic laid out next to her husband's grave.

"Thought you might be here. Mom said you had a few things to do after work." Michael smiled softly at his younger sister. "Mind if I join you?"

Jenna shrugged and motioned for him to sit. He wore a black t-shirt with the fire department's logo on the upper left corner. He must've just gotten off a shift. The two sat in silence a moment and Jenna watched as he stared at Ben's headstone.

"Are you going to say something? Tell me I'm perpetuating my grief? Tell me you're worried about me? To snap out of it?"

He didn't look at her, but she saw a small smile on his lips.

"Nah," was his only response.

"Good, because I was going to throw an egg roll at you if you did." Jenna relaxed a little and took another bite of food.

"Are you going to share or is this sacred food?" her brother asked, finally turning towards her.

"Help yourself, Dork."

She watched him quietly pick up the egg roll and take a healthy bite.

"Michael? Can I tell you something?" Jenna asked quietly. "You have to promise not to overreact or shut me down."

"When have I ever done that?" He playfully feigned an innocent look before once again softening his expression. "Of course. What's on your mind?"

Jenna weighed her words carefully. "I need to live my life again… just not *here*. Not where I can't move past, you know, *what I did*."

"Are you sure you're ready for that?" he asked softly.

"I'm sure. 100% sure."

She didn't know what to expect from Michael. She watched as he sighed deeply and slowly nodded.

"Do you have a specific place in mind? Or are you just talking in general?"

"A specific place," Jenna wondered what he would say when he heard her news. "I had an interview a couple weeks ago with Skennan Cove Memorial. I got the call this morning that they want me."

He let out a breath before nodding. Michael hadn't always been this calm and collected. Once upon a time, he was a merciless jokester. Anna tempered his wilder traits. Yet, he was the one you wanted next to you in a crisis. He had always been able to communicate with people in the worst moments of their lives and even get them to smile. He had a soothing effect on people. It was probably why he was so good at his job.

"Skennan Cove, huh?" he asked. "You'll need a place to live. That's quite a commute."

Jenna forced out a laugh. "I wasn't planning on commuting hours every day. I need to start looking as soon as possible."

"Will you let me help?"

"You've got your hands full with the wedding," Jenna pointed out. "Plus, I don't want you to suffer the wrath of Mom when she realizes you're helping me. Something tells me she won't take it as well as you."

Michael smirked mischievously before reaching over and messing up her hair. "Just trust me, okay? I think I know a guy that can help."

6

Jake Corey got out of his truck and made his way up the sidewalk to his home. Part of him hoped that Brian and Helena Hamilton weren't inside, waiting on the staircase that led to their upstairs apartment. Then again, he *did* want them there so he could give them a piece of his mind. What were they thinking setting him up with Chantille Berkley?

At thirty-five years old, Jake was garnering quite the reputation as a reclusive bachelor. So much so that Helena thought it necessary to show him picture after picture of every single friend she had on social media in the hopes that one caught his interest. Just because she'd had success once – setting him up with his Beth – she seemed to think she could bring about the same miracle twice. Well, she was wrong.

Jake sighed as he opened the front entrance and saw his two friends standing there waiting with expectant faces. Brian was a fellow law enforcement officer through the Skennan Cove Police Department. He was a patrol officer while Jake was a detective with the major crimes unit. He was like a brother to Jake, making Helena like a sister and their two-year-old daughter, Tori – also known as Stinkerbell – like his own niece.

"Well? How was it?" Helena asked, barely containing the excitement on her porcelain complected face. He hated letting her down. Wait… no he didn't!

"What in the world, Helena?" Jake asked incredulously. "What were you thinking?"

Shock registered on her face. "What? She's perfect, Jake!"

"Please tell me you're kidding." Jake let out a gruff laugh. "You and I have crazy different views on perfection."

"You said you wanted someone well-read and able to carry on a fun yet intellectual conversation." A very pregnant Helena waddled down the stairs towards him, waving her hands emphatically. "Chantille checked all those boxes and then some."

"Did she now?" Jake shook his head in disbelief. "Well-read does not mean *Dr. Seuss*."

"That's a bit harsh, don't you think?"

"She didn't have *one* original thought in her head. Every time I asked her what she thought of something she shrugged and asked *what about you, Jake?"* he mimicked in a saccharine sweet voice. "She couldn't even tell the waiter what she wanted off the menu. She literally made me order for her."

Brian burst into a fit of laughter, but quickly composed himself when his wife gave him the evil eye.

"You probably just made her nervous, that's all," Helena rationalized. "If you glowered at her like you're doing right now at me, no wonder! That works for suspects… criminals! Not for sweet women trying to get on your good side."

"That was the last matchmaking attempt, Helena. Understand?" Jake said sternly before softening his expression and tone. "You introduced me to Beth and changed my world. Just because she died, it doesn't mean you need to keep on looking for me, okay?"

"You're lonely and miserable," Helena said softly. "We all see it. We just want you to be happy, Jake."

"Is that right?" Jake looked at Brian who stood indecisively, clearly unable to make eye contact with him. "Do you agree with your wife?"

"She's not completely off base." Brian shrugged.

Jake opened his mouth to protest when his phone went off in his pocket. *Michael Tyler*. He looked up at his friends and pointed a finger at them, "We're done with the matchmaking. Understood?"

Helena raised her chin an inch. "We'll see."

Jake muttered something about raising their rent under his breath as he answered his phone and entered the first floor apartment. "What's up, Tyler?"

"Did you ever find a renter for Trip's apartment?" He could always trust his friend to get right to the point.

"Not yet. Why?" Jake asked as he threw his keys onto the table next to the door before sinking down into his couch. Goose, his German Shepherd, jumped up on the couch next to him and nudged his snout under Jake's hand until he ruffled the dog's fur playfully.

"I might have someone interested, but there's a hitch."

Jake sighed. "I don't like hitches, Tyler."

Michael cleared his throat and Jake sat up a little straighter as he waited for his friend to say what was on his mind.

"It's my sister."

The words were spoken softly and Jake knew instantly why the situation came with a hitch. Jake had been there the day Michael found out that his sister tried taking her own life.

"Go on. I'm listening," Jake prodded gently.

"She's been doing good lately. Feeling smothered by our well-intentioned family though," Michael sighed. "It seems she took a job at Skennan Cove Memorial in the emergency room."

"Ahh. That's a bold move. Do you think she's ready to be away from her support system?"

"I think so. She's always been stubborn. If anyone can bounce back better, it's Jen," Michael said with affection and admiration. "But at the same time…"

"You want her to have a babysitter?" Jake supplied the answer.

"I want someone who knows the situation to be able to let me know the minute something feels off. Does that make sense?"

Unfortunately, it did. How could Jake tell Michael no without hurting his friend? Jake was one of the groomsmen at his and Anna's upcoming wedding. He didn't want things to be awkward.

"You know I try to only rent to fire or police personnel, right? And at that, married couples or single men," Jake reminded him.

"I'm fire personnel."

"Not Skennan Cove. You're not the one living here or paying rent." Jake smirked.

"Actually, I want to cover half the rent."

"What?"

Michael paused again. "My brothers and I decided that we will help pay half of the rent if we could be assured she'd be near someone who could watch her for us."

"And how does *she* feel about that?" Everything Jake had ever heard about the feisty little sister told him that would go over like a lead balloon.

"She doesn't need to know. In fact, she *can't* find out. Please, Jake," Michael pleaded, something he simply didn't do.

"So, you want me to lie to her?" Jake felt uneasy.

"No. Just tell her the amount she will pay. Leave out how much we're covering of the rent." Michael sounded frustrated.

"You don't think she'll catch on when she starts seeing how much rent runs in this area? Especially one with a view of the St. Lawrence?" Jake shook his head. This couldn't end well.

"I'll tell her you're cutting her a break because she's my sister." Michael waited for Jake to answer, but Jake wasn't sure how to. "Look, Jake, either way she's moving out that way. I just want to know she's living somewhere safe. I saw the list of apartments she's dragging me to tomorrow. We're talking old *Broker* stomping grounds."

The Broker. Jake's mind flashed back to when everything hit the fan in his department. His best friend JT's murder. His partner's betrayal and ultimate death. Anna's near brush with danger. How could he tell Michael there were rumors of a *new* Broker? A worse one? It wouldn't ease his concern over his sister's move to Skennan Cove. If it were *his* sister – if he had one – it would drive him crazy.

"Fine," Jake finally said. He hoped this didn't backfire on his friend… or on himself, for that matter. "When will you bring her by to look at the place?"

"Are you available tomorrow? Three o'clock?"

"Yeah… sure. If I'm not here right away, I'll leave the key with Helena."

"Thanks, Jake," Michael said sincerely. "I owe you one."

"You owe me way more than *one*, Tyler."

Michael laughed, knowing full well that Jake had saved his hide several times over the past few years. Before saying goodbye Michael assured Jake, "And don't worry about Jenna. I promise she'll be the perfect tenant. You'll never even know she's there."

*****

"Can we get out of here now please?" Anna cringed as she glanced around the last apartment on Jenna's list.

"Yeah… I guess," Jenna said in frustration. "Why do these people charge so much money for roach infested rat holes?"

"Because they can," Michael replied caustically to his sister. "Are you ready to see my contribution to the search now? I guarantee you'll like it way better than this place."

Jenna nodded curtly. She had held out her highest hope for that last apartment. The pictures online looked amazing and it was in her price range. As soon as Anna started recounting some of the past crimes that occurred in that area, Jenna second-guessed herself. The dead mouse in the bathtub sealed the fate of that unit.

As Jenna sat quietly in the back seat of Michael's truck, she wondered if she was being unrealistic. Was she ready to move to Skennan Cove? What if the pressures of life and grief got to her again? Would she try to kill herself once more? She honestly didn't think so, but then again she never imagined that she would've tried to kill herself the first time.

Her family had been surprisingly supportive of her decision to take the job in Skennan Cove. It was hard to read whether it was because they felt she was truly healed enough, because they needed the space as much as she did, or if they were just too afraid to tell her the idea was ridiculous. She was starting to wonder if it was the latter.

Michael turned down a beautiful water-edged road and instantly Jenna's curiosity piqued.

"How far away is the next apartment, Mike?" she asked.

"Right up ahead on the left. The beige house."

"*House*? Here? But this house is waterfront. There is no way that I can…"

"Remember I told you I knew a guy?" Michael smiled at his sister in the rearview mirror. "Just relax, okay? I think you'll find this one much better than the others."

"I don't doubt that I will. They were scary." Jenna wholeheartedly agreed. "But this looks *expensive*."

"Just keep an open mind." Her brother smirked as he parked in front of the old three-story Victorian and got out.

Jenna looked over at Anna in the front passenger seat, but her soon-to-be sister-in-law had her head suspiciously turned away from her. Jenna's phone chimed and she glanced down to see Chase's text. "How's apartment hunting? Any winners yet?"

"Is that the Chase guy again?" Michael asked when he realized his sister was not making any effort to move.

"Yes. It is Chase." Jen rolled her eyes. "I don't know why you guys say his name like that. As if he's a predator."

“Humph.” Michael snorted and tapped at his watch. “We have a three o’clock appointment, Jen. Tell him you’ll chat later.”

Dan, Sean, and Michael seemed to have some type of animosity towards Chase since their one and only encounter with him at the hospital. Sometimes being the youngest of three older brothers was annoying. Didn’t they realize he had saved her life?

Jenna tapped out a quick text to Chase as she followed Anna and Michael up the porch steps and into the house. She was caught off guard when a pregnant woman stepped forward with a warm smile to greet them in the foyer. A young girl hid behind her legs and peeked out at them with a sweet smile.

“Hello, Michael and Anna. So good to see you again. I hear your wedding is coming up quickly. Congratulations!”

“Thank you, Helena.” Michael smiled before asking, “Is Jake going to meet us upstairs?”

“Yes, he said to go on ahead and start looking around. He had to pick up Goose from the vet.” It was then that Helena’s eyes landed on Jenna, filling with wonder and curiosity. “I’m sorry, I don’t know your name.”

Jenna stepped forward and shook the lady’s hand politely. “My name is Jenna Clark. I’m the one looking to possibly rent the apartment.”

A smile spread across her face. Jenna squirmed awkwardly under her gaze. Why was she looking at her with such interest?

"Really? The upstairs apartment is for *you*?" Helena asked looking from Michael, to Jenna, and then to Anna.

"Jenna is my sister."

"This is amazing. Absolutely perfect," Helena said gleefully.

"I'm sorry?" Jenna asked in confusion.

"Nothing. I just hope you decide to take it, that's all. I would love having another female around." Helena motioned for them to follow her up the two sets of stairs to the third floor. Jenna wondered how Helena could climb the steps at all with her little girl's arms tightly wrapped around her leg, but she managed.

The door was unlocked and everyone allowed Jenna to enter first. The breath caught in her throat. The first thing she saw was a wall of large windows that faced the St. Lawrence river. Her footfall echoed on the hardwood floor as she went to stand before the window in a daze.

"Told you it was better than those other places," came Michael's voice beside her.

"It's too good to be true. No way can I afford this place!"

"I told you already. It's my friend's place and he's willing to cut you a deal on the rent."

Jenna rolled her eyes. "Does your *friend* live downstairs?"

Her brother shrugged. "Yeah, why?"

"Was the idea of this place so I'd have someone watching over me, Michael Tyler? Is that why we're here?" That was the last thing Jenna needed or wanted… someone to report back all her activities to her family.

"It would make me feel better knowing you had someone keeping the bad guys away."

"Bad guys?" Jenna laughed. "You think everyone who even looks at me is a *bad* guy. Chase included."

"Yeah well…" her brother looked at her as if he had more he wanted to say on the issue, but Jenna wouldn't have it.

"I promise you there aren't criminals in every shadowy corner waiting to do me harm, Big Brother," Jenna said emphatically. "I don't need coddled. Not everyone is a bad guy."

"I don't know about that. I think everyone has a little *bad guy* potential in them." This came from behind them at the open door of the apartment, nearly causing Jenna to jump out of her skin.

Everyone turned at the same time to see a man with electrifying steel blue eyes standing in the doorway. A massive German Shepherd sat at his feet as if waiting for the command to rip their heads from their bodies. Jenna glanced around the room to see if anyone else felt alarmed, but they all smiled at the eavesdropper.

“Was wondering when you’d show up, Corey.” Michael moved towards the man and exchanged some male-bonding type of handshake with him. “Jenna, this is your new landlord. Jake Corey.”

7

"Jake Corey … as in your *cop* friend?" Jenna turned to her brother and asked quietly, trying not to let the man in the doorway hear.

Anna's smile was her answer. It all started to make perfect sense. Michael had been so quick to help. Come to find out, he was willing to help because he had a *spy* waiting to be his eyes and ears.

"I *am* a cop… yes." Jake smirked as he approached with his hand extended for her to shake. "It's nice to meet you, *Little Sister*."

Jenna's eyebrows shot up. "Little sister?"

"I thought we were using labels to address one another." Jake shrugged and dropped his hand when she didn't accept it, but his smirk remained.

"Jake owns this house, Jenna, but he's not intrusive." Helena stepped in. "He's a great landlord. Very reasonable."

The little girl who had clung to her mother's leg now inched closer to Jake with a goofy expectant grin. It looked as if she was going to try to sneak up and scare the man. Then as if on cue, he reached down with little warning, grabbed her, and threw her up in the air. Her giggles filled the room. The German Shepherd looked up and wagged his tail as if this was a normal occurrence.

"Don't get her riled, Uncle Jake, or *you* will be the one dealing with her cranky attitude later if she doesn't nap." Helena clearly was trying not to show her own amusement at the exchange.

"You heard your mom, Stinkerbell. Nap time." Jake gave her a little squeeze before passing her to her mother.

"No, I stay here with you." The little one attempted to lean out of her mother's arms towards the tough guy, but Helena was a pro at wrangling the feisty child.

"Maybe later, Tori. We need to let Uncle Jake talk to his friends now." Helena sent Jenna a sweet smile. "I do hope I see you again soon. It would be amazing to have another woman around."

"Goodbye, Helena," Jake said quietly through a forced smile.

Jenna was scrutinizing the interaction when movement caught her attention off to the side. The big dog stood and Anna started backing up. *Odd. Anna is a dog lover.* Jenna put her hand forward, palm side facing up, for the dog to sniff as he came close.

"No. Don't, Jenna! He's not like other dogs," Anna warned as she slid behind Michael.

Jenna chuckled as the dog sniffed her hand before nudging it with his snout.

"You *love* dogs. What's the matter, Anna?" Jenna asked as she gave the dog scratches behind his ear. He let out a grunt and tapped his foot. The German Shepherd had beautiful blue eyes. They matched those of his owner. Jenna stopped petting the dog abruptly. *Stupid intrusive thoughts.*

"She and Goose got off on the wrong foot." Jake smiled.

"That sounds like a story you can tell me on the way home." Jenna turned to her brother and Anna. "Are we ready to go now?"

"Don't you want to find out the details about the apartment?" Michael pushed.

"I've seen it. It's beautiful, but I also know that it's well out of my price range." Jenna turned to Jake then and said, "Thank you for your time, Mr. Corey."

"Jake," the man said softly.

"I'm sorry?"

"Jake. My name is Jake." His smile was kind.

"Right." Jenna forced a polite smile. "I think we both know I can't afford this… no matter what my brother discussed with you beforehand. So, I think we should leave and let you enjoy the rest of your day."

"Don't you want to know what the rent is before you reject it?" Michael's tone skirted the edge of frustration.

"Sure. I'll play along."

Michael motioned for Jake to speak. The man started spouting off all of the amenities of the apartment, including a few that Jenna hadn't anticipated. Jake finished by quoting a laughable price tag. If she were being honest, Jenna wanted to jump up and down and sign her name on the lease right then and there. However, she knew very well it didn't add up and she wasn't a charity case.

She took one last look out of the stunning window at the view of the sun shining high above the St. Lawrence. In her imagination, she could picture herself enjoying a breezy day with the windows open, watching the boats cruising on the water. It was tempting to give in and accept the obvious gift being offered.

Instead, she turned away from the view with a nod and said, "Thank you. I'll think on it."

She could feel their stares on her back as she walked out of the apartment and down the stairs. Michael muttered something testy and Anna did her best to soothe him. "Give her time, Michael."

It was going to be a long drive home.

*****

Brian walked up the sidewalk towards the house as Michael pulled away from the curb.

"Was that Tyler?" he asked Jake as he watched the red truck drive out of view.

"It was. His sister was looking at Trip's apartment."

Jake kept a neutral face as his closest friend turned back around with wide, interested eyes. "Oh? And did she like it?"

With a sigh, Jake turned towards the house and shrugged. "She said she'd think about it. I'm not holding out much hope."

"Huh. Fascinating," Brian commented as he started following him into the house. Did Jake dare question what his friend found interesting? He knew he'd regret it, but the silence hanging between them suffocated him.

"What's so fascinating about it? She looked. She didn't seem interested. That's all there was to it." Jake glanced at Brian.

"Helena texted me that she found your perfect match and that she was touring the apartment. If Helena has anything to do with it…"

"No." Jake paused and raised his hand up to halt the ridiculous direction of the conversation. "She's the kid sister of one of my closest friends; One who is going through something at the moment. Tell your wife to back off… please."

"Helena said you *flirted* with Michael's sister. Is that true, Corey?" Brian smirked.

Jake laughed out loud. "I guarantee there was no flirting. She's a little young for me. Helena is wishful thinking."

"I don't know, Man. My wife has pretty good intuition normally." Brian still sported his intolerable grin.

"Really, Brian? If Chantille is any indication of Helena's intuition, I'd say she'd better leave things alone." Jake laughed as he opened his apartment door, letting Goose enter ahead of him.

"Maybe her pregnancy is causing mixed signals." Brian's smile grew bigger.

"I heard that, Brian Hamilton," came a voice from above them. His smile turned to one of contriteness as he looked up the stairs to his beloved.

Jake ducked his head to hide his smile and excused himself as he entered his own home. Grateful for the quietness, he plopped down on his couch with a heavy sigh. Goose joined him, laying his head on his lap. As he stroked the dog's head, his thoughts went to Jenna. She was definitely a Tyler. Fiery. Stubborn. *Trouble.*

Still, he felt compassion for Jenna Clark. Beth had been gone for four long years. Grief made every day different. Some days, he missed her to the point of tears. Then on other days, he'd remember a funny memory and find himself laughing. Still, Beth was never far from his mind.

Instinctively, Jake looked over at the huge picture window. Five years ago, there had been a recliner positioned right in front of it. Beth would sit and enjoy the seasons on the river as she read her Bible or her latest favorite novel. He had watched her in that chair go from a vibrant young woman to a frail, fragile doll that needed help moving to the bed.

As was his habit, he reached down to turn his wedding band on his finger only to find it gone. He had removed it several months ago when he started entertaining the notion of dating. He felt like a traitor. Yet, as misguided as Helena had been in her matchmaking attempts, she was correct about his loneliness. *Who was I kidding? There's no one that could even come close to my Beth.*

Jake leaned his head back against the couch and closed his eyes. It had been quite the day. Another lead had come in regarding the individual referring to himself as *The Broker*. Jake thought that mess had been dealt with, yet here he was hearing rumors of a man that can access all types of illicit and illegal goods for the worst of the worst.

Maybe the most disturbing piece of information was the description of the criminal. Sure, most of it was the typical vague portrayal. He was six-feet-two with brown hair, and dark eyes. However, it was what the one witness said that stood out above all the others. The man in question walked with a limp and sported a tattoo of angel's wings and the name *Beth* on his neck. Was it a coincidence that the new Broker commemorated someone named Beth as well? Or could it be the other man who mourned her death?

The last time Jake saw his traitorous old partner, Nick Spencer, was the day he had shot and killed him. The images of that day floated back into his reverie like a bad dream. Anna Munson had information that could put many people away. Nick, who had been working for a crime ring while trying to pass himself off as a good cop, had cornered Anna on an isolated trail. Jake had spotted him approaching her location and he did what he had to do to protect Anna. He shot Nick's leg to disable him. The smugness of Nick's voice still haunted his thoughts. His tone. The words. The way he reached for his gun.

"You see, that's the difference between you and me, Jake. You're slow to act. Maybe if you weren't so slow Beth would still be ..."

Jake's final shot was a kill shot to the chest. There was no way Nick could've survived. He had fallen off the edge of the steep rocks into the rushing rapids below. Jake had waited for the search team to recover the body, but they said that the current probably took him too far out. Nick Spencer was never found. *And now there's a monster out there resembling Nick. With my wife's name tattooed on his neck.*

Jake had no answers. Nothing to relieve him of the worst case scenarios running through his mind. If Nick lived… then Jake had failed. *Again.*

*****

The Broker took a long drag on the cigarette clenched between his fingers before flicking it out the car's window. The river's breeze took the butt further down the sidewalk until it landed on the curb before finally dying out. He was on a recon mission only. Had he known three of his main sources of grief would be present in one location, he wouldn't have wasted any time in picking them off one by one with his rifle.

"The hype from the court case is just dying down. Don't do anything stupid, Broker," Damon had hissed into the phone.

"I'd think the fact that several of our clients were put in jail would make you want Anna Munson and…"

"Don't try to read what my intentions are. If we act stupid, we draw attention. Let them continue to think you're dead. That Munson girl is nothing to me now," Damon said calmly. "We are rebuilding."

"But Jake…"

"Drop it, I said. We're moving forward. Keep your vendettas to your own time."

The Broker remained silent, but cracked his knuckles at his side.

"Did you meet with the Captain? Is the shipment on schedule?" Damon asked.

"Yes. Everything is going as planned."

"Good! That shipment is your future, Broker. Remember that."

Even as he disconnected the call and drove towards the rendezvous point for the pickup, he was formulating his next steps. Why was Anna back in Skennan Cove? Who was the other woman with them? Nick knew who he could call for information without giving himself away. He could be patient, but Jake's time was coming. And Nick would gladly kill several birds with one stone in the process.

8

"How are you holding up? Any luck finding an apartment?" Chase's voice was a welcomed distraction from the Memorial Day activities.

Maybe it was because she wasn't as numb as she had been in years past, but the day hit Jenna differently this time. There was a parade earlier in the day. It was followed by a special ceremony at a monument memorializing the local soldiers who lost their lives while serving their country. The local VFW laid a wreath at its base.

How many years had Memorial Day come and gone without so much as a care except for how she was going to spend her long weekend? Even growing up near an Army base, it hadn't ever dawned on her the importance of the day. That is, until she saw a banner with Ben's face hanging from one of the vintage light poles on the side of Main Street. Jenna attended the ceremony with her father, an Army veteran, by her side. She held her composure until they fired shots into the air, much like they had at Ben's funeral. Her father reached over and took her hand in his, giving it a gentle squeeze.

Now as she sat under a tree watching children play tag, she drew strength from Chase's voice. She hadn't realized how much she would miss him. It was as if he was her last link to Ben. Having Chase in her life meant Ben felt a little closer.

"I'm scared to say my best bet is an apartment in the worst part of town. Move in is being delayed so they can fumigate." Jenna scowled at the thought of roaches crawling over her possessions. Yet, it was the most economical and practical choice.

"What happened to the place with the awesome water views?" he asked. "Don't let your frugality put you in an apartment that's not safe, Jenna."

"*Frugality*?" Jenna laughed. "Are you calling me cheap, Chase Peterson?"

His returned laughter soothed her. "Never. But…"

"Oh no. Here it comes." Jenna rolled her eyes. "But what?"

"But, you know very well the benefits you get from Ben can handle a little extra in rent. Where would *he* want you to live?" Chase reasoned.

"That's a low blow, Peterson." Jenna sat up straighter. "Are you trying to turn this into a WWJD thing, only with Ben's name?"

"It depends. Is it working?"

Jenna was going to answer with some witty reply when she saw a truck pull down the Tylers' driveway. Her brow furrowed as she tried to make out who was driving. Then the face registered in her mind.

"What is *he* doing here?"

"Who?"

Jenna realized that she had asked the question out loud and sighed before trying to answer Chase. "The cop. Michael's friend who has the charity apartment."

"Huh. Should I be jealous?" The question was asked in complete seriousness, but Jenna couldn't hold back the laughter.

"One, he's too old for me." Jenna held up a second finger despite the fact Chase couldn't see. "Two, you can't be jealous about something that doesn't exist."

"Ouch, Jenna."

She cringed. People told her often that she tended to speak too bluntly. It had gotten her into trouble in the past. "Am I wrong though? We're not even in the same state."

He sighed. "You're not wrong."

"Anyway. I don't ever plan on dating again."

"So, this guy… he's old and ugly?"

Jenna watched as Jake walked down to where Michael and her brothers stood. Ugly was not a word she would ever use to describe the man. He had a muscular build. And those crazy blue eyes that could go from laser focused to soft in mere seconds… She had seen them in action that day in the apartment. *How old is he anyway?* she asked herself. He had to at least be the same age as her oldest brother.

"Maybe mid-thirties?" Jenna guessed.

"That's old?" Chase laughed.

As if he knew he was being discussed, Jake scanned the vastness of the yard until he spotted her. She looked away quickly and pretended to be engrossed in watching the kids.

"Jenna, help me grab the last of the food please," her mother called as she walked by the tree and into the house."

"I have to go, Chase. Go show them who's boss on the volleyball court." Jenna smirked as she pictured Chase and the other soldiers playing their annual tournament. Ben used to be a part of the fun, too.

"That's a promise. Don't you go falling in love with any old cops."

Jenna guffawed at the absurdity. "That is a definite promise."

A couple hours later, the kids were starting to wind down and get tired. Tessa and Sean ushered Evie to their car. Kate and Dan wrangled their two children down the path that connected to their property. With their friends disappearing, the remaining kids sought out Jenna. Ellie, Sam, and Livi were Anna's nieces and nephew, but Anna helped her father raise the kids as if they were her own.

"Jenna, push me! Push me!" Livi called from the swing.

"Aren't you tired yet, Kid?" she asked as she gave the cute strawberry blonde a hefty shove. Her giggle was Jenna's reward.

"Livi never gets tired." Ellie, her teenage sister, groaned from the side of the swing set rubbing her sore arm muscles.

"Watch me, Jenna. I've been practicing my groomsman walk." This came from Sam who strutted with a swagger that made Jenna burst out in laughter.

"Okay, You! Calm down or every pre-teen girl's heart will flutter."

"Michael showed me how to walk cool," Sam said proudly with the cutest smile. "And watch this."

In a slick move, Sam leaned against the pole of the swing and whipped a pair of shades from some unknown pocket, striking a pose with his arms folded across his chest.

Jenna shook her head. "Of course, Michael showed you that."

"What did I do?" Michael asked from behind his sister.

"You showed me this…" Sam answered and then showed his tricks all over again, earning the laughter of everyone there. One unfamiliar laugh sounded with the others and Jenna turned to see Jake standing next to Anna and Michael.

"Well, kids, I hate to spoil the fun but we have school tomorrow," Anna said. Groans and complaints followed.

"Hey, before you two disappear I wanted to offer something," Jake said quietly. Jenna kept pushing Livi, pretending not to listen in. "I was talking to several of our mutual friends on both Deer Creek's and Skennan Cove's police department. Several agreed to be on guard at your wedding. Just in case. I think it would be good to have them come see the layout of the venue."

"Do you really think that's necessary?" Jenna asked, stopping Livi on the swing, much to the little girl's protests. "The court case is finished. Those who were threats are in jail."

Jenna knew she had to speak carefully around the children. One of those threats she spoke of was *their* father.

"I think it's better to be safe than sorry," Jake smiled slightly.

"It seems excessive to me," Jenna said under her breath.

"It's only excessive until the need arises," Jake challenged and then turned to Michael and Anna, quietly adding, "I have reasons that I can discuss with you later when there aren't so many ears."

Michael nodded. "I trust you, Man. You know that. If you say we need it, we need it."

"Walk with me." Jake motioned to Michael.

The two headed up the incline of the driveway together deep in conversation.

"Kids, go inside and thank John and Colleen," Anna instructed.

They complied, leaving the two women alone. Jenna watched as her friend's eyes followed Michael and Jake.

"I'm sure it's nothing, Anna. Police tend to be hypervigilant," Jenna attempted to comfort.

Anna nodded. "But Jake is usually spot on. If he says it's needed, there's a reason."

Jenna watched as Anna nervously twisted a golden bracelet that contained a heart shaped charm. She did her best to change the subject.

"Any word from Alex?" As soon as the question escaped her lips, Jenna wished she could take it back.

"No. I'm so scared she's back into her old ways. That would kill the kids." Anna twisted the bracelet so hard that Jenna feared it would snap. "She had been doing so good. The kids were just getting used to seeing her again. It doesn't make sense. I was so sure she was on the right path finally."

"I'm sorry." Jenna fumbled uncomfortably as she tried to think of a more pleasant conversation. Thankfully, the kids returned followed by Jenna's parents.

"Tell your father we missed him." Colleen pulled Anna into a hug.

"Yeah, he was supposed to be my cornhole partner today." John scowled, but quickly softened as he embraced his future daughter-in-law.

"Believe me, he would've rather been here than nursing that sinus infection." Anna chuckled, but then grew serious again as the men approached. Michael looked sober as he and Jake spoke under their breath to one another. When they got closer their conversation ceased.

"Ready, Petunia?" Michael leaned down and kissed Anna's cheek. Jenna noticed he whispered something in her ear and she nodded, concern in her eyes.

Great. Everything was just fine until that Jake guy showed up. Jenna looked at him with aggravation.

"Jake, can I send you home with potato salad? Or maybe a few hamburgers?" Colleen offered.

"That's very generous of you, Mrs. Tyler, but…"

"It'll do you no good to say no, Son. And please call us John and Colleen." Jenna's father hit the man on the back, her father's favorite demonstration of friendship to other men.

Anna and Michael said goodbye and the kids followed them to Michael's truck. Her mother and father disappeared inside to grab leftovers to send with the man. This left Jenna and Jake alone in the early dusk.

"So, did you choose an apartment?" Jake asked, trying to make conversation.

"Yes. I'm going to live in the Regency Apartments."

Jake burst out in a laugh and Jenna stiffened. "Is that funny to you?"

"A little. Have you actually gone *inside* to look at those apartments, Jenna?"

"No. I like to rent apartments sight unseen," Jenna spat out. "Of course I went inside to look, Mr. Corey."

He threw his hands up in defeat but his smile remained in place. "Okay. Okay. It's just that we get calls there on a daily basis. There's a lot that goes on in that building."

"I appreciate your concern, but…"

"But you think I'm being *excessive*?" Jake finished her sentence with an aggravating wink.

Jenna tried to formulate a response, but her brain seemed to have stopped working. She blinked a few times and remained silent when she heard her parents approaching.

He leaned in a little too close for her comfort and said, "My offer stands. The apartment is still available if you change your mind."

With that Jake accepted the food from her mother and with a nod, walked to his truck. Even after he pulled away, she remained staring at the place where his truck had been parked. It took a moment to realize she was being watched. Her parents stood staring at her.

"What?" she demanded.

"Nothing." Colleen smiled. "It's just that I haven't seen you look like that since…"

Jenna gave her mother a warning glare, but her father finished the thought.

"Haven't seen you look at a guy so perplexed like that since Ben." He snorted a laugh and patted her on the back before walking back into the house without another word.

"That's... that's..." Jenna stuttered at her mother who still stood next to her. "*Ridiculous*! I don't know what you think you just saw, but I promise you it was nothing."

"Okay, Dear," Colleen soothed. "But if it was something, you know it would be okay, right? There's nothing saying you have to stay alone for the rest of your life."

Jenna shook her head. "Please stop."

"I'll stop." Colleen nodded and turned with Jenna back towards the house. "But he is really cute."

*****

The Broker waited in the moonlight on the edge of the small island's shoreline. Back in the days of pirates and other scoundrels, that island had been used as a hideout and storehouse for all sorts of ill-gotten goods. Some things never changed. Its location – one small island in the middle of thousands – still offered the secrecy and seclusion needed to go undetected.

Under the cover of the trees and hidden by the massive rocks, he pulled up his night-vision binoculars and scoped out the waves. No Coast Guard. No Border Patrol.

"Greenlight," he spoke into the phone.

In a few minutes, he'd have to inspect, then transport the weapons quickly from the Johnny boat to his own vessel with his man. Someone else should've been out there making the hand-off with the dealers speeding out of Canada, but Damon insisted it had to be overseen by the Broker personally. It was beneath him. *Insulting.*

Just as expected, a low hum came from the direction of the Canadian border.

"They're coming, Sir," Scout spoke up from his perch above him on a jetted rock.

"Get ready. I want out of here."

"Yes, Sir."

The boat skimmed close and Scout grabbed the rope thrown by one of the other men, pulling them close. Two large containers were offloaded to the sandy banks. It didn't take the Broker long to open, inspect, and give his nod of approval.

"Pay them," he directed Scout.

"Hold on, Broker. That's not all," one of the slimy men said before calling to his friend. "Grab her."

The other man lifted a woman off the floor of the boat. Her hands were bound and she was clearly sedated. The Broker flashed his light over her young face. Bruises around her eyes and mouth spoke to what she had already endured.

He sighed. "I wasn't here to pick up human cargo this trip."

"She's a bonus. For Damon." The other man smiled a toothless smile.

No wonder Damon made him come on such a menial exchange. His boss didn't trust just any man around his playthings.

"If she wakes up, give her this." The man held out a syringe.

The weapons were loaded onto the Broker's boat and then the girl was lifted in. She stirred and started murmuring her pleas. Though her hands were bound, she grabbed at his jacket sleeve, pulling him down. He watched her eyes trying to focus and then they rested on his neck. In her drugged state, she read the name she saw tattooed there. "Who's Beth?"

Jabbing the needle into her neck he emptied the contents. "Go back to sleep."

With a nod to Scout, they were off, traveling over the waves at high speeds. Damon could get his own toys next time. Hearing Beth's name on such inferior lips was insulting. Beth's face flashed into his memory. Smiling. Sunny. Alive. What if she had chosen him over Jake? What if she had lived? Maybe Nick would've been the hero and Jake would've been the lost one. But he'd never know what that would've felt like. Nick Spencer was dead. All that existed now was the Broker.

9

June arrived in a flurry of activity. Dress fittings. Bridal showers. And a nauseating amount of wedding talk. Jenna grew weary hearing about seating arrangements and assisting her mother and sisters-in-law making party favors to put at each place setting. Yet there she was, the day before the wedding putting tiny rainbow mints into little, white, lace sachets. She sat around the Tylers' kitchen table with the girls while Anna ran last minute errands.

"I didn't think people used these in weddings anymore," Jenna said popping a mint into her mouth. "Kate, didn't you say they were *old school* when you were planning your wedding? And that was forever ago when you and Dan got married."

Kate gave her sister-in-law a look of disdain as Tessa tried to cover her laughter with a well-timed cough. "It wasn't *forever* ago."

"I was in high school," Jenna pointed out with a mischievous smile and popped another mint into her mouth.

"*Nine* years is hardly ancient." Colleen corrected and chuckled at the exchange. "Wait until you all have been married as long as John and I have been then…"

Jenna's mother stopped mid-sentence as if remembering not everyone in the room was married… at least not anymore.

Tessa cleared her throat and grabbed a handful of mints. "Personally, I think rainbow mints are timeless."

"And so does Anna. She wants a traditional *old school* wedding, so we're going to give it to her." Kate smiled as she tied a tiny sachet with the little card sporting a Bible verse on one side and Michael and Anna's name on the other.

Kate was the resident party planner. She had a knack for pulling together all kinds of events at the farm. So much so, they built a wedding barn to host events. Jenna loved her creativity. The farm had always been a typical family farm. Her parents had aspirations of turning it into a place where people could have fun and at the same time add extra income to the Tyler bank account. When Kate came crashing back into their lives, after moving away following high school, she put life back into everyone's dreams. Including Jenna's older brother Dan.

"Has Anna relented yet about allowing Michael the vintage fire truck?" Tessa asked, chuckling as she folded silverware into linen napkins. "Michael asked me to give pre-marital counseling on compromise in hopes of getting Anna to change her mind."

Colleen chuckled from her place at the table. "I think she's softening on the idea. Though his friend Jake is trying to discourage it."

"Jake? As in Jake Corey?" Jenna looked up from her pile of mints. The small tug at the corners of Colleen's mouth irked Jenna. "Why is he interfering in their plans?"

"He said that with it being so soon after such a public court case, it may be too risky." Colleen took a sip from her coffee but regarded her daughter from over the top of her mug. "He advised them to keep things… *low-key*. I think that was the word he used."

"It's *their* wedding. It's kind of high-handed of him to dampen their day, don't you think?" Jenna scowled.

"Oh, like critiquing rainbow mints?" Tessa tilted her head slightly and gave her a look that Jenna imagined she gave all of her counseling clients.

Tessa was a counselor and helped run a shelter for battered and distressed women alongside Jenna's second oldest brother, Sean. They made a great team, even if Jenna had had her doubts about them as a couple at first. She was grateful for how they served the community together. Sean was also the assistant pastor and would be taking part in officiating next to Anna's father, the head pastor of Deer Creek Community Church.

"Speaking of Jake and the guys," Kate said as she picked up on Jenna and Colleen's exchange. "I believe they will be here shortly."

"What? Why?" Jenna looked down at her attire. She had been helping Kate in the wedding barn with last minute touches and had not changed out of her work clothes. "Why are they coming here?"

"Dan said it was to get a look at the land and layout of the barn for security. You know, just in case. This Jake friend is very thorough." Kate smiled before rolling her eyes and adding, "Then they are having Michael's bachelor night at our place while we are out celebrating with Anna. They're grilling steaks and shooting skeet."

"What are *we* doing?" Tessa asked.

"Nails, trying out different make-up for tomorrow, and then we'll meet Anna at that new fancy restaurant in town," Kate supplied.

Jenna sighed and said under her breath, "I'd rather shoot."

The door opened and about five boisterous men entered, one of them being Jake.

"What do we have here? Oh, I love these things!" Michael said as he reached in front of his sister and tried to grab a handful of mints.

Jenna swatted at him, but he still managed to grab a few. With his other hand he messed up her hair, like he had every day of their lives growing up under the same roof.

Normally, the act was just an annoyance. However, when Jenna's gaze met Jake's amused smile she grew indignant. She straightened her hair the best she could, shooting her brother a death glare.

"So, Jake..." Colleen turned her attention to the man standing on the outskirts of the room with his arms folded at his chest. "What do you think? Are there any other precautions we need to consider at the church or barn?"

"No, Ma'am. I think we have things figured out nicely. No one needs to worry." Jake gave Colleen his full attention, but Jenna knew his last line was intended for her. "No need to be excessive."

Jenna rolled her eyes and sat back against her chair a little harder than she intended.

"What's your problem?" Dan asked as he scooted by Jenna to his wife, planting a kiss right on Kate's lips.

What's my problem? Her problem was all the happiness around her that she couldn't share in. Her problem was the endless festivities. She didn't care about getting her nails or makeup done. Her problem was that everyone either forgot her pain or tried to suffocate it. And then there was the irksomely good looking man in the room that thought she was a charity case. Why did she even care what he thought? Jenna didn't know, but she did. The kitchen felt claustrophobic. She needed air.

"Excuse me. I need to make a call." Jenna got to her feet and headed out the backdoor.

"It's not that Chase guy again, is it?" Michael asked.

Her other two brothers all of the sudden looked up from their places next to their wives to stare at her.

"I didn't know you were still talking to him," Dan said in his usual protective, grumbly way.

Jenna shot them a glare before she turned and went through the door. As she closed it behind her she heard Jake ask, "Who's Chase?"

"The guy that pushed our sister to the edge," this came from Sean.

She could've gone back into the room to defend Chase, but she didn't have the strength. The sooner the wedding was over and she could move into her own place, the better.

Just the other day, Jenna drove to Skennan Cove to look at the apartment and take measurements. She had also intended on signing the lease agreement, however, the rental manager was indisposed apparently. As the maintenance man opened the door, a gust of fumes hit her face.

"We exterminated," the man informed her.

Jenna walked through the apartment and her heart sank. The carcasses of many roaches and one mouse were scattered across the floor. However, the most traumatizing moment came when she pulled out her tape measure and moved to pull the curtains aside to get the window's dimensions. The lifeless body of a roach fell onto her hair. Now, Jenna was a country girl… born and raised on a farm. Still, some creatures were *not* okay in her book.

"Dead is better than alive," the maintenance man joked as she danced around like a wild woman to get the shell of the bug out of her hair.

She shuddered at the memory. A text vibrated her phone, bringing her back to the present. Jenna checked her messages. The rental manager texted to confirm her move-in day as *July seventh.*

"No, no, no." Jenna wanted to scream. Orientation was the first week in July. How was she going to commute from Deer Creek, move her stuff into the new apartment, and be in her right mind for orientation?

"Something wrong?" a masculine voice asked from behind her. *Jake.*

She turned as the men were filing out of the house with bottles of soda and water. They headed towards Dan and Kate's property.

"Nothing." Jenna forced a polite smile. "On your way to shoot skeet, huh?"

Jake smiled and Jenna resented the fact that it made her feel warm inside. Up until that moment, Jake's facial reactions had been guarded. His genuine smile – the one she was staring at in that moment – made her want to return the gesture.

"Yes. I hear Michael is a great shot. We'll see," Jake said pleasantly. "I've tried to get him to come with me to the range, but he always seems busy."

Jenna let out a soft laugh. "Ironic."

"What is?"

"Before Anna, he used to complain that no one had time for him after they all started getting married." Jenna smirked.

"Well, I guess that happens." Jake looked at the guys headed down the path without him. "Before I go… I wanted to let you know I had someone interested in the apartment, but if you had a change of heart, I'd gladly give it to you."

Tell him you want the apartment! Tell him, Jenna! She hated when her intrusive thoughts sounded like Ben's voice.

"No. You give it to the other person, Jake." Jenna smiled. "And, please, charge them the *real* rate."

Jake laughed. "You still think I was cutting you a deal?"

"Don't play with me. My parents didn't raise a fool."

"That's obvious. You are *no* fool." Jake smiled and dipped his head. Those dimples. Jenna had to look away.

"Just out of curiosity… why were you willing to cut the rent for me? Just because I'm Michael's sister?" Jenna asked as he started to walk away.

He turned back around with an amused face. "I never cut the rent. You want answers? I suggest you talk to your brothers."

"My brothers!" *Of course!* They probably were going to split the difference on the rent. Those stupid idiots. Those amazing, wonderful, big-hearted idiots!

"You have a family that loves you, Jenna," Jake said softly. "Even if they annoy you now and then."

With that he turned and walked down the path that led to Dan and Kate's house. The loud laughter of the other guys made Jenna smile. Something told her that they were going to have more fun than what she was going to have.

"Jen, come on. It's time to get ready," Kate called out the door, wiggling her fingers with an excited face. "It's nail time!"

Jenna sighed. *Even if they annoy you now and then...* She glanced once more back down the path to the men before reluctantly following her sister-in-law into the house. She would put on a cheerful face and celebrate with her sisters-in-law and mother even if every moment reminded Jenna of her loss… because she loved them, too.

*****

To most people the dark cemetery would've been terrifying at that hour of night. Not to him. He found this place oddly comforting. Peaceful even. Maybe the sweet feelings were because of who was buried there.

Pulling the heavy load behind, he saw the headstone he sought out. *Beth. My sweet Beth.* He should've brought flowers like he did the last several times he visited. Next time. His hands were full.

The tarp-wrapped mass slid easily enough on the grass. He quickly set about getting his work out of the way so he could focus on the more personal reasons for his visit.

Damon wanted a body disposed of. The Broker wanted to send a message. *Win, win.*

He spread the tarp open on a grave a few spaces down from Beth's. Nick arranged the dead man's body nicely in a resting position and smirked at his handiwork. He was far enough away from Beth's grave not to defile her resting place, but close enough to send a message to Jake. He was alive and he was coming for him.

After the Broker was content with his work, he dusted off his hands against his dark jeans and moved to stand over Beth's grave. *Beloved Wife.*

"Yeah, how did that work out for you, Love?" Nick asked softly as he placed a hand on the cold stone.

He remembered Beth alive and vibrant back in the days when she worked as a dispatcher. Beth could answer a screaming caller and always manage to diffuse the situation. At least long enough to calm them until help arrived. Her reputation was well known. Beth was the best in the call center.

Every so often their paths would cross when she came to visit her best friends, Helena and Brian. Nick had heard Helena teasing Beth about some newly transferred cop named Jake Corey. They thought he was *perfect* for her. What were they thinking? Nick did everything he could think of to win her affection. He started attending the church she went to. He ate at the places she frequented. He started up conversations with her when he saw her in the office. And, for a while, it worked.

Two or three dates in, he knew. Beth was the one he loved. If only he could've convinced *her* that they would've been good together.

"Why, Beth? Why *him*?"

Just because Jake Corey made some ridiculous profession of faith… some crazy talk about becoming a *follower of Christ*… Beth's attention dwindled. She claimed she needed a man that loved the Lord.

How long had Nick been forced to watch that inferior man get what was his? Jake Corey – hailed as the department's favorite detective. He won medals for his accomplishments, even though Nick was just as qualified. Jake was praised for being the youngest to make rank as a detective in the major crimes unit. The local high school even had him in to talk to students about a career in law enforcement during *Career Week.* No matter how hard Nick tried to get ahead, Jake always seemed to get the attention and recognition of everyone around them. Including his Beth.

He had attended their wedding, waiting for the day she would wake up and realize it had always been Nick that she wanted. That day never happened. Instead, she was diagnosed with cancer. A rare and aggressive form that spread quickly. Where was her God then?

To make matters worse, her own failure of a husband waited too long to get her care. If he had insisted she go sooner… Beth would've been on the other side of that grass-covered mound she was laying under. Still alive. *Mine, not Jake's.*

The Broker stood straight and turned his attention back to the man he left a few feet away. He smirked at the headstone he had laid the body at. The last name etched in stone was a message in itself. *Jacob*. The message was clear. Jake would know exactly what this meant. He would realize that he hadn't succeeded in killing him. Oh, he may have wounded him, but no one could kill the Broker.

10

"What about the flowers? Did the florist bring them over yet?" Anna asked sticking her head out of the bathroom door for the millionth time that morning. It was a miracle that her makeup even made it onto her face with as many times as she stopped to worry about something.

"Uh, yeah. You mean these black dahlia bouquets over here?" Jenna asked trying to hold back her amusement.

Ellie giggled at her aunt's instant terror, but the enjoyment was not shared by the others in the room.

"What? *Black*! Oh, please no!" Anna's face was as red as her hair as she came out in her robe with the word *Bride* stitched on the pocket.

Colleen, Kate, and Tessa all gave Jenna a stern look.

"Calm down, Aunt Anna. It's fine." Ellie held up the flowers for the bride's inspection.

"Oh… you were teasing." Anna let out a huge rush of air from her lungs and her complexion started going back to its normal porcelain hue. She let out a fit of nervous laughter.

"Black matches everything. It would've been okay." Jenna shrugged nonchalantly at the others in the room.

"Jenna." Her mother used *that* tone. The one that told her she was on thin ice. It was normally reserved for giggle outbursts during church services or when she took a prank on Michael too far.

"Everything's going to be just fine, right?" Anna looked to Colleen for comfort.

"Of course, Sweet Girl!" Colleen soothed her lovingly.

"My mother was always so good at planning these things. How many weddings had she done at this church over the years?" Anna said clinging to Colleen's arms. "Do you think she ever had a crazy bride like me?"

Jenna felt horrible. Now was *not* the time to pick on Anna, even if Jenna had meant it to be funny. Anna had lost her mother years ago, of course the morning of her wedding would be hard for her. Colleen stepped in as the perfect surrogate.

"Are you kidding me? Your mother would be beside herself right now," Colleen gushed. "You are not being a crazy bride."

Jenna resisted the urge to say something, but her sisters-in-law gave her warning glares.

"You and Michael waited so long for this day. You want it to be perfect." Colleen pulled Anna into a loving embrace. "And it will be. At the end of the day, you will be his and he will be yours. And even if your flowers are black or the cake is slanting…"

"Wait! What's the matter with the cake?" Anna lifted her head from Colleen's shoulder, eyes wide.

"Nothing. Everything is and will be just as it should be, Anna." Colleen smiled and kissed her newest daughter-in-law on the cheek. "Now go. Get dressed."

"What time is it? It's getting late, isn't it?" Anna searched the room for the clock.

"Here, Anna. I'll help you," Kate offered and stepped with her into the other room.

Jenna tried to sit down carefully in her silky, sage green, sheath dress. The couch in the parsonage was low and there was a real chance she might not be able to stand back up gracefully without help. Jenna couldn't help but reflect on her own wedding day.

It hadn't been anything like what Anna's and Michael's wedding promised to be. Ben had picked her up from her college dorm and the two went to a mall to find a dress. She tried on about three or four until she saw Ben's eyes light up and she knew it was the right one. Then they were off to the courthouse with the marriage certificate they had petitioned for weeks prior.

The office in which they said their vows was dark except for some late afternoon sun shining through the heavy drapes on the windows. A judge said a few words, they repeated them, they exchanged rings, and kissed. All while laughing like giddy school kids. A smile tugged at Jenna's lips.

"What's that smile?" Colleen said warmly coming to sit next to her.

"Nothing. Just remembering." Jenna swallowed hard at the emotions she desperately wanted to keep hidden. *Not now. Not today. Cry later, Jenna. Don't ruin this moment for them. This is about Michael and Anna, not you.*

"I heard about the apartment Jake had offered." Colleen changed the direction of the conversation and Jenna, though not keen on the topic, was grateful.

"Did you also hear how your sons and their wives wanted to bankrupt themselves to make it happen?" Jenna said loud enough for Tessa to hear.

"It would hardly bankrupt any of us." Tessa rolled her eyes. "You know it's a better – and *safer* – option than what you're considering."

"Maybe you should reconsider?" Colleen prodded. "So what if it's more money? Cut back on those trips you were planning. This place is going to be your home. Will it be a haven for you when you come home from work every night after a long shift?"

Jenna wanted to give in. She really did.

"Or you can just swallow your silly pride and let us help you," Tessa said as she came forward, handing Jenna her bouquet of perfect pink roses and baby's breath.

The bedroom door opened and all conversation ceased. They were rendered speechless. Anna stood before them in the most amazing princess gown Jenna had ever seen. Her red curls were piled on top of her head with pearls interspersed. A few delicate coils strategically cascaded in just the right places, framing her face and those dazzling green eyes Michael adored so much.

"Aunt Anna, you're stunning," Ellie gasped, taking the words right from Jenna's mouth.

"Will Michael like it?"

"Oh, Anna!" Colleen said through tears. "He won't see anyone else in the room but you."

All the women hugged in a huddle until the front door opened. Pastor Munson entered, a smile on his face.

"I came in because Bonnie said the flower girls are revolting in the nursery. She ran out of cookies." His smile turned watery as he took in the sight of his daughter in white. "I've never seen a more beautiful bride, Anna. Not since your mother."

"Well, no one needs sugar-crazed flower girls," Colleen said with a laugh. "You two share a father-daughter moment and we'll go rescue Bonnie."

Walking across the parking lot from the parsonage, Jenna noticed a few men wandering around. *Jake's men.* There were squad cars out front as well for the purpose of directing traffic. Anyone would have to be daft to attempt something with so many law enforcement officers present.

Even inside, men in suits opened the doors for them. Jenna recognized a few. She couldn't help but scan the area for Jake. She spotted him whispering to another man and motioning to the doors. *Probably strategizing.* She caught his attention and he gave a slight smile and nodded his head.

"They're coming over!" Ellie announced from the plate glass doors.

That was all Kate needed before she flew into action. "Close the doors to the sanctuary so they don't see Anna. Give the guys the nod to move to the front. We're ready!"

Jenna looked out the door to see Anna, her father, and men flanking them on either side coming towards the church building.

"Excessive?" a voice asked next to her.

"Definitely thorough." Jenna smiled at Jake.

He chuckled before opening the door for his friend.

"You look amazing, Anna," he said gently squeezing her hand.

"Jake, you better take your place up front now," Kate warned as she handed the bride her bouquet.

There was little time for much else as the wedding music started. Jenna watched her brothers and the other groomsmen scramble into place through the little window in the sanctuary doors. Michael looked as if he were going to vomit. Jenna laughed to herself. She'd never seen him that nervous before.

Dan escorted their mother and father to their pew in the front and the doors opened. Ellie went down first, then Tessa. Kate smiled back at the bride before she, too, walked down the aisle. This was it! It was finally happening!

Jenna was amazed at how seamless everything had gone so far. Anna had the reputation for things going awry quite often. They lovingly referred to it as *Anna's Law*. Yet, here they were almost down the aisle and nothing had… *Rip!*

"Oh no!" Anna whispered. "My heel is stuck in my dress."

"What? Can you get it loose?" her father asked.

"Maybe if I… Ugh! It's stuck in the crinoline. Wait! I think if I can just reach…"

Jenna stood in indecision. Kate was just about at her place in the front. It was supposed to be Jenna's cue to walk down. But then a flutter of fabric sounded from behind her. Jenna turned to see Pastor Munson reaching out to catch his daughter as she lost her footing while trying to free her shoe from her dress. Anna started falling backwards and her bouquet went airborne.

With the precision and ease of a quarterback Jenna dove for the bouquet, taking down two of the three flower girls in the process and also losing her own flowers to the floor. Little Evie started crying that her petals had fallen out of her basket. Lydia glared at her aunt and held her arm where she had landed on it. Eli, the ringbearer, laughed insanely at the sight. Yet, thankfully, the bride did not fall thanks to one of Jake's well-placed guards. Anna did, however, look about ready to lose it.

"No tears, Anna. It's fine. *You're* fine," Jenna said putting the bouquet back into her hands. "It's okay. Are you unstuck?"

"Yes. I'm ready now," Anna whispered and attempted to smile.

"Good. It's all good," Jenna nodded blowing the stray hair that broke away from her up-do in the scuffle.

Anna's niece, Livi, held up Jenna's bouquet to her. Some roses were missing and the baby's breath looked ragged, but Anna was okay. That was all that mattered.

"Eli, help your sister and cousin pick up the petals… *fast*," Jenna ordered the young boy and he dropped to the floor, grabbing fistfuls of flowers to put in the dainty baskets.

Thankfully, Anna had chosen the seven minute version of the *Canon in G* for the bridal party to walk down to. Jenna straightened the wrinkles from her dress and stepped forward as if nothing had ever happened. The doors closed behind her and she had no choice but to move forward. Judging by the faces of those before her, everyone facing the door saw what happened.

Michael smiled appreciatively. Young Sam openly laughed. Kate looked mortified. Tessa and Sean both tried to contain their amusement. Then, Jenna's eyes met those of Jake. He nodded at her with a smile that looked nothing short of impressed. Jenna forced herself to look away and she took her place in the line of bridal attendants.

The song ended. The doors reopened and the gaggle of little girls throwing crumpled petals emerged followed by Eli holding onto the little box containing the rings. Jenna held her breath as Anna and her father entered and made their way to the front. The rest of the ceremony went *without* incident.

After all the pictures were taken.. After Anna surprised Michael with the fire truck ride to the reception that he had wanted… After a catered dinner of filet mignon on a bed of rice pilaf… Jenna felt *tired.*

The party was in full swing. Everyone celebrated happily. Dan and Kate snuggled up close in a slow dance. Jenna's parents plied their grandkids with sweets while their parents enjoyed their time alone. Sean and Tessa held Evie in their arms as they posed for a family picture. Michael and Anna were oblivious to everyone in the room but each other.

Jenna found an empty table off to the side and nibbled on a piece of wedding cake as she took it all in. Kate outdid herself. The wedding barn didn't even look like a barn with the fabric drapes and lights. It was the picture of elegance. Just like Anna and Michael had wanted. Jenna was truly happy for them.

Yet, the small niggling feelings of sadness kept threatening to creep back in. She got up from her seat and went to the side door to get some fresh air. The mid-June evening wasn't warm or chilly. It was just right and the breeze was delightfully scented with the flowers that bloomed along the perimeter of the property. The stars twinkled above and Jenna found herself staring up at them wondering how far beyond them was Ben.

"Going to go two for two at catching the bouquet?" a voice startled her and she turned to see Jake as he appeared around the corner of the barn.

"Oh, you know," Jenna shrugged her shoulder with a laugh. "I think I should let another person have a chance this time around. Once is enough for today."

Jake laughed as he moved to stand near her and she caught him looking up at the stars as well. "This is a beautiful place."

"It is," Jenna agreed. "There's no other place like it."

"But you still want to move to Skennan Cove?"

She nodded. "I can't… I mean, I need to move on. I love my family, but…"

"I get it. They mean well, you know. Our families," Jake said softly. "They just don't know how to respond when someone they love loses someone *they* loved."

Jenna scrutinized the man next to her. Deep sorrow hung in his eyes as he still gazed at the heavens.

"*Our* families?" Jenna questioned. "You've lost someone, too?"

"My wife. Beth. About four years ago now."

"I'm sorry."

Jake finally looked at her and the grief was unmistakable.

"I wish I could tell you events like these get easier," he smiled gently. "But there's a reason I chose to guard the perimeter instead of being inside."

"How did she pass? If you don't mind me asking."

"Leukemia. We caught it too late." Jake swallowed hard. "She kept explaining away the symptoms so I didn't push her to go to the doctor. She hated doctors. I should have made her go sooner. If I had maybe…"

"Leukemia can be tricky even if you do catch it in time, Jake. There are subtypes and sometimes things get missed," Jenna searched for words. "You can't blame yourself."

"I forgot Michael said you were a nurse." Jake attempted a smile.

The two stood in silence staring into the heavens a moment longer until Jenna finally spoke again.

"Ben was shot helping people evacuate their homes in an area held by hostiles."

"A hero."

Jenna let out a dry laugh. "That's what people keep telling me. He died being a hero to strangers so I could die alone without him."

Jake didn't chastise her or even open his mouth to speak to offer comfort. He just listened.

"I'm sorry. I know I sound bitter."

"I get it." Jake nodded. "I thought that psychology mumbo jumbo about stages of grief was just talk. Turns out, it's valid."

"So it seems." Jenna and Jake fell into comfortable silence again as they both stared off deep in their own thoughts.

What made her do it, she didn't know. Jenna cleared her throat and asked, "Is the apartment still available? Did you rent it out to the person looking at it?"

She saw a smile spread across his face in the dim light. "Just so happened that the other renter fell through. Why do you ask, Little Sister?"

"For starters, don't call me that. Even my brothers get hit if they call me that," Jenna warned and Jake's smile grew. "Second, *if* I rent your apartment only *I* pay the rent. Got it? No half payments from my brothers or my parents. I pay my own obligations."

"Understood."

Jenna nodded resolutely. "When can I move in?"

"Any time. It's empty. You'll need to come sign the lease first."

"Can I start moving next week? I would like to be moved in before I start orientation the first week of July."

"We can work something out. I'll charge you a pro-rated amount for June's rent." Jake smirked at Jenna's gulp.

"Unless, of course, you want to change your mind about taking help from your family."

"Definitely not. I can do this. I'll be eating a lot of ramen, but I can do this."

"Good." Jake reached in his pocket and pulled out a card before handing it to Jenna. "Here's my number. Text me and let me know when you want to come sign those papers."

"Uh, Jake. I hate to interrupt, but have you checked your phone?" a man that Jenna assumed was another officer came outside.

"No. Why?" Jake pulled his phone out of his pocket and his entire countenance changed.

"Branson has been trying to get a hold of you."

Gone was the easy going, smiling Jake. He stood staring at the backlit screen, something akin to rage erupting on his face.

"Is everything okay? Jake?" Jenna asked starting to feel alarmed.

"Uh, yeah. You have my number, call me." Then he turned to the other officer. "Make sure they all get home safely. I need to go."

And with that Jake Corey was gone.

11

"Very clever, Corey," the Broker muttered as he listened to Scout recount the events of the day before.

His men had gone to the wedding venue on his orders. However, when they had arrived there were no nuptials – only a quinceañera and a banquet room full of dancing teens. The wedding invitation that they had gotten a hold of had the wrong church address and the wrong reception hall. A planted, fake wedding invitation. *Well played.*

"By the time we figured out where they might be having the actual reception, both the newlyweds and Corey had already left."

Crumpling up the wedding invitation he had been grasping, the Broker let out an aggravated laugh. The goal had been to tail the Tylers on their honeymoon and create an unfortunate accident. *It's all good. I can be patient. I still managed to get a message across to Corey.*

"And what is the word on the street about our friend we deposited at the cemetery?" he asked with a smirk.

"The cops haven't identified him yet, if that's what you mean."

That wasn't the information he desired. "Who did they call in? Was Corey there?"

"As far as we could tell, he wasn't called onto the scene. We were trying to stay far away from cops." Scout looked at his boss unapologetically and appeared to weigh his next words. "You know, Damon wants to talk to you about that stunt you pulled. He's not dumb. You had to have known he'd find out that you left the body where Corey would find him."

The Broker shrugged. "I did as he asked. I got rid of him. He never specified *where*."

"Be careful, Nick. You're more valuable to Damon if everyone thinks you're dead. Don't do something stupid to bring attention to yourself."

"Do you have anything else to report?" The Broker glared at the man. Who was he to tell him how to do his job? So what if they figured out he was alive? They'd never catch him.

"No, but…"

"You can go then."

The man nodded and left the room. Who cared if Damon wanted Nick's identity to be kept a secret? Nick very much wanted Jake to be aware that he was alive and well… and that Detective Corey would soon be lying in the plot next to his wife.

*****

Jake had seen the crime scene images. Yet, as he stood near the scene in person, his stomach twisted. The stone bearing his proper name glaring back at him. *Jacob*. The deceased man had long since been taken to the morgue, but Jake could still see him vividly in his mind. The man had a single shot to the forehead. He was lying on a tarp, posed with his arms crossed at his chest… just mere feet from Beth's grave.

Jake's stomach sank. It was all adding up. Nick's body had never been found. The timing of the body being dumped in the cemetery aligned with Michael and Anna's wedding. The placement of the body. A witness who described the Broker with a tattoo of the name *Beth* on his neck.

"You're sure this is Spencer's doing, Corey?" Sergeant Terry Branson stood next to him, surveying the lots stretched out in front of them. "You shot him in the chest. People saw him fall from that drop-off."

"Yes, Sir. I'm positive. This is Nick." Jake ticked off all the indicators that pointed to his old partner, growing in certainty.

"So what is this weird connection between him and your wife? I don't understand," Branson questioned.

"Before Beth and I got together, she and Nick dated. It was brief, but he wanted more." The words felt vile on Jake's tongue as he looked down at his wife's headstone with growing anguish.

He remembered the day Beth told him about her and Nick's previous relationship – if anyone could even call it that.

"Wait. Nick Spencer? As in Nick Spencer from my department? You dated him?" Jake asked incredulously one night at dinner. He and Beth had just decided to see

where their relationship would go, and she laid all her cards on the table.

Beth looked sheepish. "He can be a nice guy. He was going to my church and told me he was also a Christ follower, but..."

"He probably thought he could just wing it. I know I did," Jake sighed as he thought back on his own foolishness. "Thankfully, God wouldn't let me get away with that."

She smiled warmly at Jake, placing a hand on his in response.

"Still... Nick Spencer?" Jake laughed. "And how did it end?"

"He still texts and calls, but it's getting less and less over time." Beth scooted a little closer to Jake. "I told him you won my heart completely. There is no one for me but you."

Jake leaned down and pressed a kiss to her forehead, inhaling the scent of her shampoo. "We do seem perfect for one another, don't we? You understand me like no one else, Beth."

She snuggled in even closer, and the two sat in contented silence until Jake sighed. "Is that why he keeps trying to throw me under the bus for the littlest thing? It's like he has it out for me. J.T. even noticed."

"He'll get over it. He's a nice looking guy. I'm sure he'll have no trouble finding someone else."

"He's nice looking, huh?" Jake smirked and nudged her with his shoulder.

"He's nothing compared to you." Beth looked up at him with those doe eyes. He couldn't resist kissing her lips. Even in that moment of pure tenderness and love, Jake couldn't shake the feeling of doubt niggling inside him. Would Nick just simply get over Beth and move on? Somehow, that felt highly unlikely.

"If what you suspect is true, we have a real problem," Branson groused, bringing Jake back to the present. "I was just starting to feel at ease with the house cleaning we did at the department and now…"

"You think he still has insiders?" Jake knew it was a stupid question. Of course, Nick had insiders.

"It would make sense. It's the only way he would've been able to avoid being caught up until now." Branson grimaced. "Someone is helping him stay out of our line of vision."

Jake's jaw clenched. He lost many friends when the department went under investigation after the truth about Nick came out. There weren't many people left that Jake held in high regard. He felt his walls go up. It was easier to assume the worst of everyone than to feel the sting of betrayal again. As Jake left the cemetery, he reiterated the sentiment that had kept him alive to that day. *Keep your eyes open and your heart closed.*

*****

Her move in day finally arrived. Jenna had played phone tag with Jake after the wedding. His work kept him busy so he sent her the lease via email. She eagerly signed, scanned, and sent the document back in a timely fashion. Jenna was moving in just days before her orientation started at the hospital. Thankfully, her family had agreed to help her move her furniture from storage to her new home. There was only one thing left to do.

Jenna sat on the picnic blanket next to Ben's headstone and stared at his name in silence for a moment. Deep down, she knew he would tell her to go and not look back. She couldn't revert to that dark place she had lived in mentally for so long. It was time to get back into the *real world.*

"I'm scared that I'm going to forget the sound of your voice," Jenna said absently after a few moments of silence. "I play your last voicemail every so often. I saved it on my phone so I can hear you."

The night of the wedding, Jenna had gotten onto her old social media account to watch videos of her and Ben from their early years. As each day passed, she worried she was forgetting Ben. It felt as if she were abandoning him every time she felt the surge of excitement at the idea of her new job.

"New job. New home. New town. This is the first place where I'll be living that doesn't somehow tie me to you." Jenna sniffed back the emotion. "That scares me. Please don't be mad at me. My therapist says this is a healthy move… that it will help me live again instead of just *existing*."

She sat in silence again as if Ben would offer her words of wisdom, but all she heard were the birds calling to one another in the trees.

"I actually went to church this past Sunday." Jen shifted uncomfortably. "I figured it would make Mom and Dad happy since it was my last Sunday here."

At the wedding, they had all been distracted by the celebration. Going on a *regular* Sunday… well, apparently they were less distracted and could turn their focus to her. Jenna cringed inwardly at the sympathetic looks and well-intentioned words. She had wanted to hide. Clearly, everyone knew of her suicide attempt. The looks of pity were unmistakable.

Bonnie, the church secretary, crushed Jenna in an awkward hug, whispering things like "It's going to be okay" and "Don't give up on God." This was the exact reason Jenna stopped going in the first place. She didn't want to hear those things. She shook her head as if freeing her mind from the thoughts.

"Pastor Munson was quoting a passage in Isaiah 43 that I hadn't heard before. It was about how God is doing something new and clearing a way through the wilderness." Jenna gulped at an unexpected surge of emotion. "I'm not really sure what to think about God right now, but the idea of starting something new… and leaving this wilderness I've been in… that's appealing."

In a moment of contemplation, Jenna thought over the previous year. Slowly, very gradually, she had started smiling a little more. Prior to coming back to Deer Creek, Jenna could count on one hand the times she had smiled since Ben's death. To describe that time as a wilderness would be accurate.

Not that things were particularly delightful in Deer Creek either. There was a legitimate reason why Jenna wanted to move away again. Every time her parents looked at her, she saw their concern. People coddled her. Smothered her. Jenna needed space to grow. She needed to rediscover how to live… how to *want* to live.

"So I don't know if I believe that God is doing this or not, but I know I need to do something *new*. I'm hoping this move brings me back to life." Jenna sighed as she realized she had been a walking, dead woman. Alive on the outside, but dead on the inside.

"What if I fail again? What if I get there and can't cut it? I don't want to feel the hopelessness the way I did last year. I would never admit this to anyone else, but I'm scared, Ben."

Hugging her knees to her chest, Jenna cried. She couldn't allow the darkness to come back. Her counselor would say to open herself up to new relationships and friendships to keep her accountable. Maybe a new friendship would be nice. Helena seemed pleasant enough. But, as far as romantic relationships were concerned, Jenna never wanted to feel the hurt that came with losing someone ever again. She'd go and live her new life, but limit the people she allowed close.

Her phone lit up next to her and she saw that Dan had texted. They had already started off to her new apartment in the rented truck full of her belongings. "We're stopping for lunch. What time will you get here?"

Jenna checked the time and jumped to her feet, gathering the blanket up that she had spread out on the grass.

"I guess I have to go now," she said, putting a hand on his headstone. "I love you and I will make you proud, Ben."

With one last look behind her, Jenna got into her car and drove away. Deer Creek was in her rearview now. Skennan Cove lay ahead.

12

"Well look who decided to join us," Dan snarked at his sister as she pulled up to the curb outside her new home. He stood inside the moving truck, surrounded by boxes and furniture. "If you're having second thoughts, too bad, Kid. We just moved that monster bed of yours up two flights of stairs."

Jenna smiled innocently at her oldest brother. Most people shirked away from him when he got grouchy. Jenna knew he was just a sweet teddy bear, even if his growl sounded angry at times.

"I needed to make a pit stop. I knew y'all had it just fine," Jenna said sweet as sugar.

"Do I detect a hint of southern in that beautiful accent?" A man Jenna didn't know came down the sidewalk towards the truck. He was followed by Sean, Jake, and another man that she had recognized from the wedding… the one who alerted Jake to the mysterious text.

Dan glanced over at the flirting man with a not-so-friendly expression in his typical over-protective, big brotherly way. He had given that same look to Ben when they had started coming around the house more frequently as a dating couple.

"I guess the two years I lived in North Carolina have rubbed off on me a little." Jenna stepped forward to distract from her brother's gruffness. "I'm Jenna. And you are?"

"Trip. You're moving into my old place." The man smiled back at her smooth as silk, not even casting a glance in Dan's direction. His voice also held a slight hint of a southern drawl.

"Enough talk. More heavy lifting, Trip." Jake slid past him to the truck and grabbed several boxes, handing them to the man.

"I just came to drop off my old key. Why are you putting *me* to work?" Trip winked at Jenna.

"Because knowing you, you'll stay here long enough so you can get some free pizza. You gotta earn that pizza, Man." This came from the other stranger. The man turned to Jenna and smiled politely. "It's nice to meet you, Jenna. I'm Brian. Helena's husband."

Jenna smiled back at her new neighbor. "Tori's daddy."

He ducked his head with an amused chuckle. "Ahh. You've met my little girl."

"She's sweet."

"When she wants to be. Just like her mother," Brian said conspiratorially, but a voice came from the front doorway.

"I heard that, Hamilton! I'm still waiting on that tool box you supposedly went to go find. That kitchen cart isn't going to put itself together," Helena called out as she waddled her way down the sidewalk toward Jenna with a welcoming smile.

Jenna looked at her brothers curiously. Surely, Helena wasn't referring to *her* kitchen cart – the one that she bought new in the box. She hadn't asked anyone to assemble anything. Jenna was more than capable of doing it herself.

"I believe Mom is already unpacking bedding and dishes. Last I saw Dad, he was setting up your bed frame." Sean smiled at his sister, obviously reading her thoughts.

"I can… I can do that stuff."

"Yes, you can." Dan came up behind her with more boxes. "But people want to help you settle in. You have a busy week ahead. Just smile and say *thank you*, Kiddo."

With that they left Jenna standing there awkwardly and headed back inside with their loads. Someone behind her cleared his throat and startled Jenna. Jake jumped down from the truck and grabbed the boxes he had scooted to the edge. He looked as if he were reading her and Jenna stiffened, bracing for some comment on her stubbornness. Michael was still on his honeymoon. Someone had to take his place, right?

"Here ya go." He pushed the boxes into her, forcing her to grab a hold of them.

"Excuse me?" Jenna stumbled back a bit under the weight of the boxes. They weren't heavy, but she wasn't expecting to have them thrust upon her.

"If you want to set up the place on your own, the faster we get these boxes unloaded the better." Jake smiled. "Don't you think?"

He wasn't going to coddle her. It was… refreshing. With a nod, she turned toward the house, but snuck a look back at the man. He had a slight smile of amusement on his face as he grabbed more boxes, following behind her. Quickly turning to face forward again, Jenna accidently tripped over an uneven piece of sidewalk.

She quickly righted herself and said loud enough for Jake to hear, "The landlord better do something about that before someone gets hurt."

"You're right," he said without missing a beat. "I'll put up a sign for people to pay attention to where they're going."

She could hear the teasing in his dry tone and felt a small smile tug at her lips. She started up the steps when she heard, "Jake Corey, why are you letting this sweet thing carry heavy boxes up all these steps?"

Jenna looked up to see the man they called Trip staring down at her playfully. "Want me to take those for you, Darlin'?"

"Uh, it's Jenna. And I've got them." Yes, she knew she probably sounded a little sassier than she intended. Remembering her brother's words from earlier, she added sweetly, "But thank you."

Jake snorted a laugh as she continued up the stairs and breezed past Trip.

She entered her apartment and put the boxes down. Instantly, she was caught off guard to see that the once empty apartment was actually starting to look… *homey*. Her mother was rinsing off dishes as she unpacked them. Then, her father dried them as he put them in the cabinets. Brian and Helena were assembling the brand new kitchen cart she had bought. Tori played happily on the floor next to them with her police car and figurine. Jenna smiled at the scene.

The other men continued to go down to the truck and bring more items up. If she didn't start unpacking or moving things to their respective rooms, she wouldn't have any walking space. So, she started hefting boxes to their rightful places.

In her bedroom, she saw her bed linens and pillows in a neat pile on top of her mattress. She set to work making the bed. The sheets and blankets were picture perfect. Grabbing a pillow, she paused and buried her face into its softness.

Ben's scent was long gone from his pillow. She had run out of his cologne before she had moved home to Deer Creek. The only reason she knew it was her husband's was because he preferred firmer pillows. She held it tightly, desperately wishing she could share this new chapter with him.

"Oh, there you are, Sweetheart." Colleen came into the room with a box marked *"Ben"*. Her voice softened as she added, "I wasn't sure where you wanted this."

Jenna motioned to the bed and her mother placed the box down reverently. The flaps weren't sealed, just tucked. She undid the box and pulled out the triangular-folded American flag. In a moment of inspiration, Jenna walked out of the room and placed it on the mantel above the faux fireplace. She had seen flags displayed in other people's homes on their mantels and now she finally had one. It seemed right.

The room behind her went quiet. She turned around without warning to catch everyone watching her. Quickly, they went back to their conversations and tasks as if they weren't engrossed in what she was doing just moments before. Jenna rolled her eyes.

"That looks nice there," Jake said, coming to stand beside her. "We used to keep my father's flag on the mantel growing up."

"Your father was military?" Jenna asked without looking away from the flag.

Jake nodded. "Stationed in Iraq. He died in 2004."

"How old were you?" Jenna watched Jake's face mirror emotions she knew about all too well.

"I was thirteen."

"I'm so sorry, Jake. That's young to lose your father." Then Jenna paused and scrunched her brow as she did the math in her head. "That makes you *thirty-five*? Interesting."

The sentimental moment was broken and Jake looked down his nose at her with indignation. "Yeah… so what?"

"I'm sorry." Jenna smiled in embarrassment. She should have stopped there, but the words went from her mind to her lips before she could stop them. "I knew you were older, I just didn't know *how* much older."

Jake laughed loudly.

"I didn't mean…"

"Better stop while you're ahead, Jen." Sean smirked as he leaned against the wall watching the awkward interaction.

The phone in her pocket sang out, saving her from further embarrassment. "I should take this."

"Who is it?" Colleen asked curiously.

Dan, who stood nearby, looked at the screen and grunted. "It's that *Chase* guy. *Again*?"

Jenna punched him in the arm as hard as she could and answered the call.

"Chase. Hi. How are you doing?" Jenna said as she moved to the privacy of her new bedroom. She felt all of their eyes on the back of her head as she disappeared behind the closed door.

"How's moving day coming? I'm sorry I couldn't fly up to help." His voice sounded regretful, but Jenna sighed in relief.

"Oh, don't you worry about it. I have plenty of help, believe me. More than I need, in fact."

Chase chuckled. "Do I hear exasperation in your voice?"

"Maybe a little." Jenna smiled. "How are you doing? Any news on your next move?"

During their last conversation, he had told her he was waiting on his next permanent change of station assignment.

"I've heard a few places thrown around. Nothing set in stone yet."

"Are you going to be breaking any hearts when you leave? I haven't heard you mention… what was her name… Haylie, right?" Jen smirked as she listened to her friend clear his throat.

"Haylie. Yeah… she didn't work out," Chase stated matter-of-factly. "Probably for the best, all things considered."

"Are you being picky, Chase?" Jenna teased. "You start going to church and your tastes have changed?"

Chase was quiet for a moment. "I haven't gone in a while. It lost something after you left."

"I wouldn't exactly call myself a solid Christian at the moment," Jenna scowled inwardly, "But I do know that you are not supposed to go because of a *person*. You go to be close to God."

"I think He left with you." The words were spoken quietly. Then he threw in a sucker punch. "If I'm stationed up at Fort Drum, maybe you can help me find a church… and come with me."

Jenna didn't know how to respond. She wasn't the one who should be offering spiritual advice to her friend. That was always Ben's strong suit, not hers. She must've stayed silent too long because Chase rushed to change the subject.

"Tell me about your new place." His tone lightened.

"It's great. My neighbors have an adorable little girl…"

Jenna rattled on for several minutes about how wonderful the new apartment was until Chase was called away by a friend coming into his room.

"We'll catch up soon, Jenna. Maybe I can come visit you. You can show me around."

"Yeah… maybe." Jenna looked at her bedroom door self-consciously. That would not go over well with her brothers. "Chase, before you go."

"Yes?"

"Did you and my brothers talk? I mean… when I was… you know…" Jenna wasn't sure how to ask her question delicately.

"You mean while you were fighting for your life?" Chase sighed loudly into the phone. "Yeah. When I called your family to tell them what happened, I told them I pushed you too far."

"Chase…"

"We both know it's true. I see you every night before I close my eyes to go to sleep, Jenna. *Lifeless*." Chase sounded more pained than the day he told her Ben had died. "Then I remember how I kissed you. I don't regret that kiss. Maybe I should. What I regret was my timing."

Jenna felt her throat constrict.

"That's why Haylie didn't work out. She wasn't *you*." Someone in the background called out to Chase again. He must've covered the phone because Jenna heard her friend give an angry muffled response. When he came back on, his tone changed again, more playful and teasing. "You regret asking now, don't you?"

"A little," Jenna said honestly. "I don't know what to say."

"Don't say anything. Go unpack and settle in. We'll talk later."

With that the call ended, leaving Jenna unsettled. She thought they had moved past his nonsensical crush on her. *Apparently not.* Jenna grabbed Ben's pillow and held it tightly once more when someone knocked on the door.

"Who's there?" she called out.

The door opened a crack and her father poked his head in. "That Trip character brought up the pizza. If you don't come out, it'll be gone."

Jenna forced a fake smile, but her father was smarter than that. He eased his way in and sat next to her on the edge of the bed.

"Feeling okay?" he asked awkwardly. John Tyler normally left the softer things up to his wife.

"Sure. I'm just tired."

Her Dad grunted with a nod and put an arm around his little girl's shoulder. Jenna instantly laid her head against him and came undone at his tender touch. In her mind, she was five all over again with a skinned knee.

"You're okay, Baby Girl. You're tough. Maybe even tougher than your brothers." His words soothed. "Just don't be so tough that you start thinking you don't need God anymore. He's the one that will get you through this."

"He's not been my favorite topic lately." Jenna wiped at her tears.

"I noticed."

"I'm sorry, Dad." Jenna looked up into her father's gentle face. "I know I'm a disappointment."

"Now you stop that nonsense!" His voice was stern, but still loving. "There has never been a day that you – or those ridiculous brothers of yours – have ever been a disappointment to your mother or me."

"You sure about that?" Jenna quirked her lips. "Not even Michael?"

"Well... he redeemed himself by marrying Anna." He smiled playfully and squeezed her shoulders.

"I love you, Daddy," Jenna said throwing her arms around him before he got to his feet.

He hugged her back. John Tyler, the man's man, pressed a kiss to his daughter's forehead. "I love you, too. Now do your old man a favor. Distract your mother so I can grab a piece of that meat lovers pizza."

Several hours later, the truck was empty and her apartment was a maze of boxes. Trip and Jenna's family said their goodbyes, leaving Jake and the Hamiltons.

"I guess we should leave you to unpack," Helena said as Brian helped her up from the couch. "I wanted to make sure you knew you were invited to our Fourth of July cook out, Jenna."

"Oh! Thank you, Helena. I'm not sure..."

"Just think about it. I know you are busy, but you're invited. We always have fun." Helena smiled. "I make a mean potato salad and Brian grills. Then Jake takes all of us out on his boat to watch fireworks on the river. I guarantee you'll never have a better time."

Jenna's eyes sought out Jake to make sure Helena wasn't overstepping by inviting her along. He nodded his agreement.

"I'll think about it. It'll depend on my schedule at the hospital and how much unpacking I can get done." Jenna knew she wasn't going to take them up on the offer, but it was still a sweet gesture to include her.

Brian, Helena, and Tori left then. Jake reached into his pocket and pulled out a keyring with two keys dangling from it.

"Here you go," he said handing them to Jenna. "This one is for the front door downstairs and the other is for your apartment."

"Thank you." Jenna said quietly.

"Are you good?" His question caught her attention and she found him scrutinizing her.

"Why wouldn't I be?"

He shrugged nonchalantly. "You had a big day. And a big week ahead of you. I was just wondering."

"I'm fine. Just tired."

He smiled a soft smile and nodded. "Okay then. Let me know if you need anything. Goodnight, Jenna."

As soon as she closed the door behind him, Jenna turned to face her apartment. Then, it hit her. The silence. For the last year, she heard the constant bantering of her brothers and her parents. She heard the noises of the farm. At night, she heard her father watching his favorite television shows downstairs. Now, she was alone.

Jenna wrapped her arms around herself. Shouldn't she have felt happy? Wasn't this what she had been waiting for? A chance to prove she was okay and ready to move on? The same terrifying thought that Jenna had repeatedly pushed away entered her mind. What if she wasn't ready? What if her father was wrong about her? What if she wasn't strong enough?

13

Three days into orientation, Jenna's brain swam with extensive knowledge on safety protocols, hospital dress code, and HIPAA standards. Most of it wasn't anything new or earth shattering. She toured the emergency department with a few other new nurses joining the Skennan Cove Memorial team.

Jenna even made a new friend while watching a cheesy training video on giving outstanding quality patient care. Her lanyard said her name was Mara McAllister and they seemed to giggle at the exact same places during the motivational video. At one point, the facilitator cleared her throat and scowled at the two, putting a momentary end to their frivolity.

That is, until they both walked to their cars at the end of the day.

"Make sure to consistently smile… *just like this*… when caring for the unruly patient," Mara mimicked the voice over from the video while sporting a large creepy smile on her face.

Jenna chuckled. "If I got a nurse smiling at me like that I'd run far, far away."

"I think we are scheduled together over the weekend. At least they gave us newbies the Fourth of July off. No patients with blown off fingers for us." Mara held up her phone and showed the schedule. "Do you have plans?"

"Unpacking the last of my boxes. You?"

"There's a party on the pier. Let me know if you want to come. I'll keep an eye out for you so you have someone to hang with." Mara grabbed Jenna's phone and added her number to the contacts.

The invite tempted Jenna. Her therapist *did* say to socialize. Yet, Jenna didn't think she was ready to be surrounded by hundreds of people, dancing and drinking the night away. She had a momentary flashback to the night at the club with Chase and her co-workers. Still, there was something inside of her… a yearning for something. Could it be she actually *wanted* friendship?

"I'll text you if I change my mind." Jenna smiled at her new friend.

Mara smiled back at her but paused as she stared past Jenna to the parking garage behind her. "Do you know that guy? He was pacing and staring at us."

Jenna looked in the direction that Mara motioned to. A man stood in between cars, but turned away when he realized the women spotted him. He ran a hand through his hair and moved further into the garage.

"I don't recognize him. I don't know many people here though." Jenna's brow furrowed. "Maybe he has someone in the ER and just doesn't want to go in."

"Maybe." Mara shrugged it off. "Maybe I'm just jaded. This area has a crazy number of tweakers. He's probably just high."

"At least we can put one thing covered in the training to good use," Jenna said referring to the hospital's recommendation to implement the buddy system when walking to their cars in the garage. "Come on. I'll walk you to your car. Where are you parked?"

"Uh, the top level." Mara smirked. "I drive a brand new truck and I park where no one can dent it with a fly away door."

Jenna glanced where she had seen the man as they entered the dimly lit structure. Jenna wasn't one to get the creeps, but she felt eyes on them. She glanced over to the wall that portioned off the next parking level and thought she saw someone peek out.

"I'll drive you up to your car," she said as she looked back once more before clicking her key fob.

"Welcome to Skennan Cove," Mara said wryly. "It's a delightful mix of river rats, the wealthy, and the users."

"And you are…"

"Oh, totally a river rat." Mara got in Jenna's car and buckled in. "My guess is that will be you, too."

"You think?" Jenna laughed as she turned on her car and turned down the music she had been blasting on her way to work that morning. "I don't know how to swim and I get queasy easily. I don't use drugs. And I'm *definitely* not rich. Maybe I'll create a new category."

"Oh yeah? What would that be?"

Jenna pulled her car up the ramp as she thought about her response. "The *barely keeping my head above water* category."

"I like it. Count me in," Mara laughed. "That's my truck right there."

Jenna pulled behind her friend's vehicle. "Have a fun Fourth of July, Mara."

"You, too. Text me."

With that, the other nurse safely entered and started her truck, freeing Jenna to head home. As she made her way back down the ramps to the exit of the parking garage, Jenna found herself scanning the shadows for the odd man. She saw no one. If Ben were there, he'd tell her to lay off the true crime podcasts. With that, Jenna blocked the probably harmless man from her mind.

Moments later, she pulled into the driveway of her new home. She didn't see Jake's truck. The Hamilton's SUV with the car seat in the back was parked out front. *Her new neighbors*. It was oddly comforting to know there were people close by.

As she unlocked the front door and made her way up the stairs, she heard Helena's voice trying to get Tori to eat her dinner. The scent of something heavenly wafted through the hall. It was all so warm and welcoming. The differences between this apartment and her old place back in North Carolina were dramatic.

On her door was a note. *"I put in a couple air conditioners... unless you like sweating. Text me if you want them out."*

Jenna smirked. Jake was reading her independent, albeit stubborn, personality accurately. She'd overlook his overbearing gesture. The temperatures had been stifling and Jenna had found sleeping difficult, even with the windows open.

As soon as her door opened under her hand, a delightfully cool rush of air hit her. Her eyes closed in relief as she allowed it to touch her cheeks. Thankfully, Jake had the sense not to block her river view. He put the unit in a side window closer to where her dining area was. Sliding out her phone she texted a quick and simple thank you to the man.

A moment later her phone lit up with, "No problem."

A smile touched her lips. Looking around her, Jenna felt the closest thing to contentment that she had in years. The only problem? She had no one to share it with. A familiar stab of pain jabbed her heart. Jenna was lonely.

*****

"Splash. Splash. Splash."

Jake glanced up from his place next to Brian at the grill to watch Tori in the little blow up wading pool. The toddler had a bright pink innertube around her waist even though she could stand up in the meager amount of water that was left inside the pool. Helena sat with her lawn chair close enough so she could soak her feet. She jolted as a sudden splash of water soaked her shirt.

"Victoria Ann! What did Mommy tell you about that?" she scolded her daughter with no anger behind the words. "Splash in *that* direction – not at Mommy."

"Any sign of our new neighbor today?" Brian asked out of nowhere, snapping Jake's attention away from the wholesome display in the back yard.

"What? Oh… no. Not that I've seen." Jake's eyes instinctively went to the third story window. He thought he saw the curtain move abruptly and he smirked before turning his attention back to the plates of hot dogs and burgers. "Did you buy more food than usual? Are you expecting her to come down?"

Brian moved slightly closer to his friend and said softly, "Helena made me do it. Anyway, believe me, she'll join us once she smells it cooking."

Jake laughed out loud. "She's not some forest animal."

Brian smiled back. "Don't underestimate the power of a good burger. Who could resist a grilled burger?"

Jake shook his head and glanced back up at the window. It was then that he saw her. She stood there awkwardly as if she knew she couldn't dart behind the curtain again. She waved stiffly and tried to back away.

Pulling out his cellphone, Jake tapped a text. "Are you going to come down here or are you just going to stand there watching all day?"

He grinned as he saw the dots bouncing on the text screen.

"I'm not watching. I'm trying to fix the curtains."

He looked up at the window and gave her a skeptical look. Jake texted, "I hung those myself. They're fine."

Just then, he heard a muted scream from the house and Jake saw the curtains fall in their entirety. He ran inside, taking the stairs two at a time and pounded on the door. He had images of her on a stepladder, falling.

"Jenna, you okay?"

The door swung open and a wild-haired, wide-eyed Jenna pulled his arm into the apartment. "Kill it! Kill it! Kill it now!"

"Kill what?"

"That monster of a spider! I don't do spiders!"

Jake burst into laughter. "*You* are scared by harmless little spiders?"

"They aren't harmless… they bite. And *that* thing… is not little." Jenna waved and pointed to the bedroom emphatically. "Are you going to kill it or do I burn this place down?"

Rolling his eyes, he walked to the bedroom. Jenna followed so close behind him that he could feel her breath on his shoulder. "Got a shoe handy?"

"That box right there." She pointed from a safe distance away.

Jake grabbed the first one he found and she stopped him short. "Not that shoe. Eww."

"Do you want me to kill this thing or not?" he asked waving the high heel in his hand slightly irritated at the interruption.

"Fine. Just get it," she gritted through her teeth.

It took a moment for Jake to find the offending spider. He lifted the fallen curtains and rod just as a little black thing darted up the wall. He was just about to smush it when it jumped in his direction, causing him to startle and let out a surprised grunt. Embarrassed at his own reaction, he smacked the critter with a loud *whack.*

"Ugh. I'm going to be sick," Jenna groaned from across the room.

"Didn't you grow up on a farm?"

"So what? The fear of spiders is a real thing," Jenna defended herself. "And I'll point out that you also screamed…"

"Everything okay up here?" Brian's voice came from the living room.

"Yeah. Just fine." Jake called out and gave Jenna a pleading smile. "Don't tell him. I'll never live it down."

She rolled her eyes and handed him a tissue to clean up the disgusting smear left behind. "There was a really large bug."

“Ah. Helena hates bugs, too,” Brian said popping his head in the doorway as Jake put the curtains back in their place. “Well, if you’re done exterminating… dinner is served. Jenna, I hope you plan on joining us.”

“Oh. Thank you, but I was going to make myself something up here and finish unpacking,” Jenna said looking away from the men’s gazes.

“I don’t see any boxes but this one.” Jake pointed to the one from which he had grabbed the shoe.

Jenna looked caught and her shoulders slumped. “I guess I could visit for a little bit.”

“Great! Helena will be thrilled,” Brian said, turning to leave.

Jake looked over at her kitchen counter and saw a loaf of bread and a jar of peanut butter. “Don’t tell me that was the dinner you were getting ready to make yourself.”

“What’s wrong with peanut butter and jelly?” Jenna lifted her chin in challenge.

“On the Fourth of July?” Jake met her gaze head on. “I think that’s un-American.”

“Well, I need to be able to afford rent.”

Jake saw her lip curve slightly and he couldn’t resist breaking first with a grin. “Well… it’s a good thing that your neighbors invited you to eat for *free* then. Save your PB&J for tomorrow.”

"It *does* smell really good," Jenna said more to herself and Jake smiled.

Turned out, Brian was right.

14

The bright sunshine and subtle breeze made for perfect cookout weather. Jenna imagined her family enjoying the day back on the farm. They, of course, had invited her to come home for their usual Tyler family fun. However, Jenna knew Michael and Anna were back in all of their wedded bliss. As much as she adored her brother and new sister-in-law, Jenna wasn't in the mood to be reminded of what she didn't have. *So instead, you let yourself be swayed by the intoxicating aroma of freshly grilled burger. And you're still surrounded by happy people.*

It wasn't so bad. Jake had a good mix of music playing on his wireless speakers. The scent of coconut oil and suntan lotion reminded Jenna of the North Carolina beaches, only without the sand. The breeze coming off the river made it refreshing. Jenna stood staring at the water across from the house as boaters and people on jet skis cruised by.

"Do you like being on the water?" Helena asked, coming to stand next to her.

"Uh… not really." Jenna smiled at some distant memory. "I would dip in the ocean when Ben and I would go to the beach. But nothing more than that."

"Ben?"

Jenna looked over at Jake on the grill and then back to Helena. He didn't look up. She had assumed her new neighbors had already heard an ear full on her history. Apparently, not.

"My husband. He died a few years ago." Jenna braced for the dreaded sympathetic expression that would inevitably follow after she told someone she was a widow. It didn't come. Just a look of comfortable friendship. *Interesting.*

"I'm sorry." Helena sighed softly. Then she pointed to her daughter and said, "I used to love the water. Now with *this* little crazy, I find myself more nervous around it."

Tori ran and dove into the wading pool squealing loudly.

"I swear that girl has no fear. You wouldn't believe the crazy stunts she pulls." Helena chuckled.

"I guess that's a good thing." Jenna watched as Tori called to her dad, demanding him to watch. She took a deep breath, put her face in the water, and blew bubbles. "I had all big brothers growing up so I learned to do crazy things if I wanted to keep up with them."

"If Michael is your brother, I can only imagine," Brian laughed.

"You know Michael?"

"*Everyone* knows Michael," Jake added dryly.

"This one is a boy." Helena motioned to her baby bump humorously. "I hope Tori adjusts okay to him. She wanted a little sister… not a brother."

“Nah. I’m sure they’ll be close. I may have a few scars from my brothers, but they still are my best friends.” Jenna added with a mutter, “As annoying as they are.”

“Scars?” Helena quirked her eyebrow.

Jenna lifted her knee to show a small white line on the side of her calf. “This is from the time they told me I couldn’t climb the tallest tree in our yard. I got slashed by a sharp stick, but I did it.”

Lifting her elbow. “This is from the time they locked me out of their club house and I crawled through the window and got scratched by a nail.”

Brian and Helena laughed, but Jake just smirked with his arms crossed at his chest. “Sounds to me like your brothers weren’t the problem. It was your stubbornness.”

“I’m strong-spirited.” Jenna leveled him with a look that wouldn’t back down. She noticed Brian and Helena started looking between her and Jake like they were watching a tennis match. Helena’s smile nearly split her face.

“Oh, is that what kids are calling it today?” Jake laughed.

“I know in *your day* girls weren’t expected to hold their own, but times are changing.” Jenna matched his stance and tilted her chin slightly in challenge.

“Call it what you want. Stubborn is still stubborn.”

Brian cleared his throat. “I think dinner is ready. Helena, do you want me to grab the potato salad?”

"Huh? What? Oh… yes. Potato salad." Helena still seemed engrossed in the exchange between Jenna and Jake. Then, she turned her attention to her husband. "Will you come help me, Sweetheart? Tori should probably start getting dried off and changed."

He smiled down at her as if he was reading some unspoken suggestion from her benign request. Jenna immediately picked up on the scheme when she realized that she and Jake were the only ones left in the yard.

Awkwardly, Jenna started fidgeting with the hem of her t-shirt. She side-glanced over at Jake and he turned back to the grill, stoking a hot coal though nothing was cooking on top.

"One thing you need to be aware of, Jenna," he said out of the blue. "…is that Helena is on a rampage to matchmake. She's been focusing on me, but now that *you* are here…"

"You think she's going to try to put me with someone?" Jenna laughed. "But she hardly knows me."

"I know for *fact* she is." Jake nodded and laughed. "I swear she is obsessed with romance and warm fuzzies. She really is sweet. She wants everyone to have the same happiness she and Brian have."

"Ah, the proverbial fairytale ending." Jenna sighed.

Jake nodded.

"I don't think I believe that exists anymore, do you?" *Wow, Jenna! Way to kill the Fourth of July celebration!*

Jenna glanced over at Jake again and found him thinking thoughtfully.

Then he said something that made her pause. "I believe that God has our future in His hands… and whatever His plans are, I trust Him."

"I think I'd prefer Helena's plans for me than God's. He seems a little cruel lately." Her tone sounded downright venomous. If her mother were there, she'd get the tongue lashing of the century.

"I used to think that, too. Especially right after Beth passed away." Jake looked at her with a tender expression, no judgement.

"But you don't think it now?" Jenna asked curiously. She had all but given up on her faith. How could anyone bounce back from losing their one true love? "Tell me what your secret is then, because God and I haven't been in good standing lately."

"It was something I heard at a funeral, believe it or not," Jake said as he took a seat at the picnic table. Jenna followed. "My best friend JT died in the line of duty. I was still reeling from Beth's passing when I lost him. The pastor said that JT was, at that very moment, enjoying his reward."

Jenna swallowed hard. She had heard something like that, too. Ben's reward was to miss out on having children? To leave her? She felt anger rise up, but Jake continued.

"I was fuming at the time when I heard that. JT was young. Beth was young. So much to live for."

Jenna nodded emphatically as if Jake finally came to his senses. Yet still he continued.

"It took a few days of mulling over that statement. I went to my pastor with all my anger. He asked me why people become Christians at all. Is it because they want a great life here on earth? The Bible doesn't promise us pain-free lives." Jake paused, looking at Jenna thoughtfully. She looked away and out onto the river. "I came to Christ because I knew my sin would keep me from an eternity with God. He promises us abundant life here on earth, but the real reward happens *after* we leave this place. We ask Jesus to be Lord of our lives so we can spend eternity in Heaven with Him. That's our reward. So why would we act like God dealt a Christian a bad hand if that person was getting to experience joy beyond what they could've had here on earth?"

"We were going to have children. He'll never have that. Never see a birthday party or another anniversary." Jenna tried to control the eruption she wanted to direct at Jake.

He nodded. "That's what Beth and I wanted, too."

"Then how come you can trust God again? How is this better for them?" Jenna's heart raced.

"Because all of those things that we think are the greatest joys in life *here* on earth, cannot compare to what waits for us in God's presence." His words were soft, but spoken with strength and conviction. Jenna almost broke down. “We can’t imagine it because we’ve never experienced it here on earth. It’s a joy we won’t understand until we’re there with Him.”

A whole host of Scriptures speaking to what Jake said filled her mind. She had learned from an early age that Heaven was supposed to be the believer’s reward. Jenna attended funerals for grandparents and remembered believing those promises. She attended Kate’s father’s funeral and listened as her sister-in-law spoke confidently about Tom being with Jesus. Jenna watched her pastor grieve his wife’s death, but as a man with hope. The verses they – and Jenna – had clung to had meant something to her… back then. The verses hadn’t changed. God hadn’t changed. *Jenna* had.

“Well, I still think I’d prefer Helena’s plans.” Jenna tried to bring the conversation back around to a lighthearted place.

“Yeah… I don’t think you’d like that,” Jake laughed.

“And why is that?” Jenna challenged, daring him to say something… *anything*… more about God.

He laughed harder just as Brian, Helena, and Tori finally emerged from the house. He leaned in across the table and said for Jenna’s ears only, “Because I think it’s *us* she’s trying to put together.”

*****

Every so often, Jake would glance over in Jenna’s direction. She ate quietly, occasionally answering in short polite responses. He hoped he hadn’t overstepped. Jenna had asked how he was able to move forward. All he did was tell her the truth. It was clear the woman was heavy with grief. Jake knew what that was like. He felt increasingly burdened to pray for her to find peace.

“So tell us about your first week at the hospital, Jenna,” Helena requested after a slight lull in conversation.

“Nothing too exciting. Just a bunch of do’s and don’ts.” Then, as if she remembered something, Jenna asked, “Is the area around the hospital sketchy?”

Brian raised his brow. “Not overly so. Why?”

Jake paused mid-bite as he waited for her to respond. There was something that crossed her expression that he recognized in his line of work. She was weighing her words, trying to decide what she should say and what she shouldn’t.

“There was a guy in the garage acting weird. My co-worker said he was probably a tweaker.” Jenna shrugged it off and bit into her hot dog.

“There’s a drug presence like any other area,” Jake affirmed. “Are you working later shifts?”

Jenna nodded. “They have me down for three to eleven for the time being. They’ll move me to twelve hour shifts after they feel I’m ready.”

Jake and Brian exchanged glances. Skennan Cove wasn’t the worst area, nor was it the greatest. Brian patrolled that area in the evenings and he’d probably keep a closer eye out. At least, Jake would ask him if he could.

"It's fine. I prefer evenings," Jenna stated as she must've picked up on their silence.

"Do you carry pepper spray?" Jake asked.

"No." Jenna laughed. "Look, I don't need more big brothers. I can handle myself just fine."

"I'm sure you can." Helena patted her arm very diplomatically and gave a warning look to the men at the table.

Jake ignored her. "You should probably look into getting a keychain with an alarm or pepper spray if you have to work late shifts."

Jenna gave a feisty thumbs-up before turning to Helena and complimenting her on the potato salad. Clearly, she was done with this topic.

"I go swim," Tori said as she tried to scoot off her father's lap.

"We're going to go on the boat soon. Want to go on Uncle Jake's boat?" Brian asked his little girl who nodded profusely.

"Now? Can we go now?" Tori asked.

"I'm ready when you are, Stinkerbell." Tori had Jake wrapped around her finger. "You know the drill. You have to wear the life jacket."

"Okay, Uncle Jake." Tori's father finally released her and she pulled on Jake's hand. "Let's go! Let's go!"

"Will you come with us, Jenna?" Helena asked sweetly. "Please? I don't think I can do another year of being the only adult woman on the boat."

Jake rolled his eyes and cleared his throat. Helena was pouring it on thick… too thick.

"I really need to get back upstairs and finish unpacking."

"Your one whole box that's left?" Jake challenged.

Jenna raised her chin. *She has to be the most irritatingly stubborn woman I've ever met. Why is it so cute on her?* Just then, Jake decided to take a page out of her brothers' playbook. From her stories earlier, it was either when they dared her or told her she couldn't do something that she tried to prove them wrong.

"It's okay, Jenna. You go to your apartment. You wouldn't have any fun on the boat if you're too scared anyway," Jake said casually, trying to hide his smirk when she took the bait.

"I never said I was *scared*, Jake," Jenna spat out. "I said I get queasy. Huge difference."

"Sure. Whatever you say." He shrugged.

"I have something I take for motion sickness," Helena offered. "Especially being pregnant, I need to take something. Would you like some?"

Helena reached into her purse and pulled out a pill package. They all watched as Jenna deliberated. She looked up to her apartment window then back down at Helena.

"I guess I can finish in the apartment later," she conceded.

"Well, whoever is coming, meet me at the truck in fifteen minutes. I'll get the boat trailer hitched." Jake turned to head to his truck and smiled.

What was it about Jenna? Was it her feistiness? Michael had warned him about his sister. His smile faltered. *I actually want her to come with us. I like her around.* The realization unnerved him. One thing was for sure, Helena couldn't find out or she'd never give him a moment of peace again.

*****

The medicine felt as if it finally kicked in. Jenna sat on the boat's bench as Jake sped through the waves, passing other river vessels. Her life jacket felt stiff and uncomfortable, but she was not about to remove it. For the first part of the excursion, she clenched her eyes shut tightly. That is, until she heard Tori laugh at her. She would not be mocked by a two-year-old.

Tori found an United States flag and waved it wildly with glee at the people they passed as if she were on a parade float. Brian and Helena sat close together, his arm around her, as they enjoyed their daughter's excitement. Jenna concluded that she liked them.

Her eyes traveled until she found Jake at the wheel. He had sunglasses on and his hair whipped in the wind. His skin was tanned, probably from outings just like that one. Just then he glanced over at her. Was it the medicine that made her reaction time slow? He caught her staring before she could look away. She felt her face burn as she pretended to focus on Tori's patriotism.

"Want to drive?" his voice called out over the rushing wind. The boat started slowing down, and he called to her again. "Want to learn how to drive the boat, Jenna?"

"Uh, no. That's okay. Looks like you have a good handle on it." Why did she sound so shaken? "I think the medicine is messing with me. It's probably not a good idea."

Helena laughed. "It's just ginger supplements, Silly. It's non-drowsy."

Jenna flushed. Non-drowsy? She could've sworn she felt out of sorts.

"Come on. I'm not going to let you hurt my boat, believe me. I'll be right here." Jake got up and held out his hand to her, but Jenna sat still.

"What if I hit another boat? What if we sink?" Jenna said as terror rose up inside her.

Jake cleared his throat and cocked his head toward the toddler who stopped her singing to listen to Jenna.

"Oops. I mean… wow… isn't this fun, Tori?"

The little girl smiled, nodded, and went back to singing.

"Come on," Jake said, still holding out his hand.

Jenna took it as she moved unsteadily to the seat behind the wheel. Jake gave her instructions and soon the boat started moving. Her hair flew behind her as she drove the boat through the humid winds. A thrill surged as she watched the sun's last rays glisten on the water surrounding her. Jake did as promised. He warned her when to ease up and encouraged her to accelerate when they went too slow. Soon Jenna was smiling, albeit nervously.

"Okay. You can take the wheel back now," Jenna said as she slowed the boat down. She took the chair next to his.

"What did you think? Fun, wasn't it?" Jake asked as he took the controls back.

She couldn't see his eyes from behind his sunglasses. Jenna was starting to know his facial expressions enough to know his eyes were probably crinkled up at the edges as he smiled. *What are you doing? Stop it, Jenna. Stop it right now.*

"Are we heading back soon?" She finally found her voice. "The sun is starting to go down."

He smiled broader. "And miss the fireworks?"

"Oh, right." Jenna started playing with the hem of her t-shirt again from under her life jacket.

"Did you know pirates used to hide on some these islands?" Jake asked pointing to some of the land masses a little further out.

"Here we go," Brian piped up. "Time for our annual history lesson on the islands of the St. Lawrence."

Helena hit his midsection playfully and smiled. "But this year he has a new student. So… *shhh*!"

Jake continued to recount the history of piracy and the Battle of 1812 as they passed some of the islands that made the area known as the *Thousand Islands*. Jenna listened with interest and took in the rocky crags and various formations that he pointed out. Clearly, Jake loved his home.

Jenna hadn't even noticed he had slowed the boat to an area where other boats had gathered. Then a loud boom sounded, knocking Jenna off her seat. His hand shot out and steadied her. He tried to stifle his laughter.

Above them lights flashed and appeared in red, white, and blue. Tori started crying, proving she wasn't completely fearless.

"They're just fireworks, Baby. They won't hurt you from over here. Look how pretty," Brian soothed.

Another flash sounded and Jenna sat staring at the sky, transfixed at the sight. From somewhere on the coastline, patriotic music played loudly. *Oh, Ben. You would've loved this.* Then a thought hit Jenna from her conversation with Jake earlier.

Was Ben seeing and experiencing something better? If the Scriptures were true, the man-made fireworks – as stunning as they were – couldn't compare to the lights of Heaven. The thought was oddly comforting and left a stirring in her heart she hadn't felt in a very long time.

15

"Just got some news that may interest you, Broker," Scout said as he walked into the makeshift office set up in an old warehouse on the outskirts of town.

"Oh?" Nick didn't bother looking up from the screen of his phone. His mood was foul after the lethal warning Damon issued earlier that morning. If Nick wasn't careful, his days as Broker were numbered. Just as *he* had killed for his title, so would the next guy in Damon's good graces.

"Someone *new* moved to Skennan Cove."

The Broker finally looked up at the man with a glare of annoyance. "Spit it out. Your theatrics are wasted on me."

"It's the little sister of Michael Tyler. Anna Munson's sister-in-law and… get this… Jake Corey's newest tenant."

Now that is interesting. Nick sat back in his chair and let out a long sigh. "What do we know about her?"

"Her name is Jenna. I'm still getting intel in, but so far we know she is a nurse at the hospital. We're still trying to pin down her schedule, but I've been keeping an eye on her car in the parking garage."

"Does Damon know you are using *his* resources for this? I don't need any more heat from him."

“What Damon doesn’t know won’t hurt him. I’m still selling my usual stock. The Boss doesn’t need to know I’m multitasking.” Scout’s smirk almost caused Nick to relax slightly, but he resisted.

There was no such thing as friendships in their line of work. Scout was most likely jockeying for position. The Broker was not stupid enough to think the man wouldn’t turn around and betray him the very next day if it suited him.

“You’d better not be messy. Keep your mouth shut if you get caught.”

“We were doing this long before you joined us, Nick.” Scout knew the error of his ways as soon as the words left his lips.

“I’m sorry?” Nick rose to his feet. “What did you call me?”

“Broker. My mistake, Sir. Won’t happen again.”

Scout scurried from the room like the rat that he was and Nick took his seat again. Pulling his laptop open, he started delving into Michael Tyler’s little sister.

“Jenna…” He said her name and paused as he typed in her last name. “Tyler? Unless you got married...”

He searched online and came up with mostly old FFA articles on Jenna Tyler. No marriage notices. She was listed as an honor student in the Deer Creek local paper. In an article dedicated to graduating seniors, he saw her image and where she had planned to go to college. He zoomed in at her picture. She was fair-complected. Light colored eyes that he assumed were blue despite the black and white image. Longer wavy, brown hair. *Cute sister, Tyler. Maybe I'll have to pay her a visit.*

*****

Mara and Jenna did everything in their power to make sure their breaks overlapped on the nights they were scheduled together. They bonded over novels they were reading and played innocent pranks on one another in between the busyness of their patients' demands. In the short time they had started working together in the ER, they had developed a silent language. One look could communicate what the other was thinking. The staff dubbed them the *Twins* and for obvious reasons. Both were similar in appearance and were often called by the other person's name. Yet, they'd answer nonetheless.

The two walked into the break room with the pizza that had just been delivered and laughed over something one of the snobbier doctors had said.

"I swear that man thinks he's God's gift to this hospital." Mara made a disgusted face. "I've worked with some self-obsessed idiots before, but he has to be the worst."

"What makes it so bad is that he really is a good doctor. He knows his stuff as much as I hate to admit it." Jenna took a slice of her Hawaiian half of the pizza and sat down at the empty table.

"Eww. One of your pineapples crossed over to my pepperoni side." Mara plopped the yellow blob onto Jenna's plate. "That's just gross."

Jenna smiled as she took an exaggerated bite from her slice. "Mmm. Yummy."

"Don't talk with your mouth full." Mara joined her at the table. The two enjoyed their dinner for a moment before Mara asked, "So when can I come see your apartment?"

"Whenever neither of us are sleeping and don't have to go to work."

"So… never?" Mara chuckled. "How about Saturday? Looks like we're both off."

"Sure. Bring dinner and it's a date." Jenna smiled at her friend. She hadn't been great at grocery shopping since moving into her own place. She had been doing a lot of food delivery lately. Helena had noticed and dropped off some pork chops and rice leftovers from their dinner the previous evening. A kind gesture, but it made Jenna feel too *seen*.

"Deal. So…" Mara leaned in closer and quieted her voice. "Any new texts from the Action Figure?"

Jenna rolled her eyes. "He has a name."

"Oh, right. Any new texts from Chase?" Her friend's look was maddening, but Jenna just shook her head.

"He's been pretty quiet since he told me he still had feelings for me. Just the occasional funny picture or check in," Jenna said as she reached absently to check her phone.

Maybe it had been a mistake to tell Mara about Chase. The two had gotten into a conversation about men in real life versus the dreamy heroes in their novels. Jenna had shared how Chase had been looking out for her after her husband's passing and Mara instantly gushed as if it were so romantic. It definitely got worse after she showed her a picture of Chase in his army fatigues. He was then dubbed the *Action Figure* by Mara and there was no stopping her from that moment on.

"What about you? What happened to that guy you met at the party?" Jenna asked, happy to divert the spotlight away from her life.

"He ended up being a jerk. Shocker, right?"

"I'm sorry, Mara," Jenna said empathetically. "I wish things really did work out like they do in our books. Meet a cute guy in a coffee shop, fall in love, live happily ever after…"

"Uh oh."

"What?" Jenna asked wiping away the pizza sauce from her mouth.

"You sound… *wistful.*"

"Pfft. Stop it." Jenna waved her friend away.

"Ha! No, it's true." Mara smiled playfully. "You know… I could fix you up if you want me to."

Jenna laughed out loud. "No, thank you! After everything you've been telling me about the guys you meet? Are you kidding? I don't need a jerk in my life."

A code came over the intercom and the two knew their break was over. So was their conversation. Several injured came in from a multi-car crash and the rest of the night passed quickly as they assessed patients.

It was when Jenna approached the room of her next patient that she noticed a heavy police presence at the door.

"Hey, Jenna. I wondered if we'd run into one another eventually," Brian greeted her as she entered the room.

"Hey, Darlin'," Trip called out while checking the restraints on the man in the bed.

Mara, who had been walking by the room, must've caught the familiarity and sent Jenna a quizzical look. Jenna returned a warning glare.

"What do we have here?" Jenna asked pulling her attention back to the business at hand.

"We'll need a blood draw to determine alcohol level," Brian answered. "The warrant was just issued."

"Is this the driver?" Jenna asked as she took in the man on the bed.

Trip nodded grimly.

The suspect was handcuffed to the side-railing, but she doubted he was going anywhere. His eyes were shut and he only grunted at her when she asked him questions. It was when Jenna started poking and prodding while getting his IV line in that the man came to life.

"Get off of me," he slurred and called her a derogatory name.

"Watch it." Trip growled at the man. Brian moved a little closer in case he was needed to settle him down.

"Sir, are you hurting anywhere?" Jenna asked loudly to break through her patient's stupor. Vapors of alcohol emanated from the fellow and Jenna knew the bloodwork was nothing but a formality.

"Don't you touch me. I know my rights. You can't hold me here. You can't take my blood."

"We have a warrant that says otherwise," Trip said casually.

Jenna sighed and looked from Brian to Trip with a small sympathetic smile. They were trained for those types of situations, but it didn't make it any easier. "I'll get this bloodwork in. Let me know if you need anything. Dr. Hayward will be in shortly."

Jenna didn't get to see them much after that. Other patients sustained more serious injuries needing her attention. Broken bones. Lacerations. And one fatality. It was quite the night. As soon as the suspect sobered up a bit he was given a ride to jail, with not a scratch on him.

Mara and Jenna walked out together after their shift ended. Both were solemn and quiet at first as each of them processed the events of the evening. The patient who had died wasn't Jenna's, but the weight of it still clung to her like an albatross. She heard the weeping family and it had been all she could do not to weep as well. Mara broke the silence.

"You're holding out on me," Mara said as they walked to the garage in the humid evening breeze.

"What?" Jenna looked at her with confusion.

"Who were those fine police officers that seemed to know you by name? He called you *Darlin'*! That's adorable!" Mara said with a cheesy smile.

"He's annoying. The other one is married and also my neighbor. So..." Jenna let her sentence hang to bring home her point.

"Maybe they can introduce us to other cute cops," Mara said nudging Jenna with her shoulder.

Jenna felt some of the pressure release from her shoulders as they reached their respective cars at the top level. They had coordinated their parking spots so they could walk out with one another at the end of their shifts. "You're hopeless, Mara."

Her friend smiled and shrugged as she got into her truck. Jenna waited until Mara turned on the ignition before getting into her own car. As Jenna drove home, she blared her music to drown out her thoughts. Some nights it worked well. Others... not so much.

Pulling into the driveway behind her neighbors' vehicles, she saw a light glowing from behind her landlord's curtains. Jenna sighed. Several nights in a row, either Brian poked his head out of the Hamiltons' apartment or she'd find Jake sitting on the bottom step of the stairs when she got home from work. Jenna was getting the feeling they were keeping tabs on her.

She closed the door to her car and sighed. Jenna decided to take a stroll on the walkway next to the water rather than turn in for the night. If someone waited up for her, that was *their* problem. She never asked them to do that and the moon looked particularly bewitching that night over the river. It beckoned to her, offering a moment of peace that she truly needed at that moment.

She made it to the walkway and just stared up at the bright moon. Despite the slight haze that glazed over it, the light still illuminated the sky beautifully. The waves lapped against the rocky boundary of the banks. There was something about the sound of water that Jenna found relaxing. Wandering down the path a little way, she paused.

A man appeared to be walking up the sidewalk towards her from the opposite direction. His paced slowed when she looked at him head-on. Between the light of the moon and the interspersed street lights, she could see he was wearing a hoodie. *It's summer. Why would you wear a hoodie zipped up to your chin?*

She looked over her shoulder back at the house wondering if she had gone too far. Maybe walking after midnight near the banks of the river wasn't her best idea.

He stopped short and the two awkwardly faced one another with a distance of several feet between them. In the dim light she saw him smile and turn towards the water.

"It's beautiful tonight, isn't it?" he spoke up.

"Uh... yes."

The moonlight wasn't bright enough to see many features of the person speaking to her, but he moved into the path of the streetlight for a split second before backing away again. His forehead had some type of heavy crease. Maybe a scar?

"I live down the street." The man motioned to the row of houses. "I like coming out here when I can't sleep."

Jenna just nodded.

"What about you? Do you live near here?"

Jenna turned her head to glance back at the house once again to make sure she was still close enough to make a run for it if needed.

She regretted the action, because the man then asked, "Is that your place? Nice. Great view of the water."

"A friend lives there." Jenna tried to make up for her error.

"I didn't think you looked familiar. I know just about everyone on this street." The man's teeth gleamed in the night as he smiled at her. "Well, you have a good night."

Jenna nodded as he started walking back the way he had come from. She watched carefully wanting to see which house he entered, but the sound of a door opening nearby, followed by someone clearing their throat, distracted her. *Jake*.

She made her way across the street, glancing back to where she had last seen the stranger. Jenna could no longer see the man in the hoodie. Entering the house, she paused only slightly as she passed Jake. "You're up late."

"Were you talking to someone out there? I thought I heard voices," he questioned, pausing her steps on the stairs.

"There's a medication for that, you know," Jenna teased. "Yes, I met one of our neighbors."

"A neighbor? Did this *neighbor* give you a name?" he asked.

"No. It was just someone out for a walk. Just like I was trying to do." Jenna shrugged. At least, that was what she hoped he was doing.

"After midnight..." Jake's tone was droll and clearly skeptical. Jenna imagined the suspects he interrogated got to experience this side of him quite often. *Well, I'm not a suspect. I'm a tenant. And I don't need to answer to him.*

"There are a lot of people who like to walk at night. It's quiet. Do you know what kinds of people like to take quiet walks after everyone else goes to bed?" Jenna came back down the steps to stand in front of her landlord. She resisted the urge to poke a bony finger into his chest to drive home her point. "Those of us who have had a long night that we'd like to forget about... that's who."

Jake didn't say anything in return right away. He just looked down at her and sighed. Then, he nodded. "I'm sorry you had a crazy night. I heard on the scanner there was a pretty wicked car accident. I imagine you saw some of the victims as patients."

Jenna gulped back a surge of emotion. In the past, she handled the sights and scenes of the emergency room in stride. However, one of her patients was a five-year-old girl, bruised from her seatbelt all because of the belligerent, drunken man in handcuffs.

"I saw some of them. I'm fine though." Her feistiness dissipated at the look of empathy on Jake's face. She knew in his line of work he probably saw horrific things. Michael would tell her terrible stories of things he had come across as an EMT and fireman. Obviously, Brian and Trip got front row seats to it as well. "I'm sorry I got … *testy*… with you just then. I'm just really tired."

A grin spread across Jake's face. "I get it. Still, Jenna… maybe don't take late night walks alone from now on?"

"You know, I don't need more over protective brothers." Jenna folded her arms across her chest, trying to sound in control, but she couldn't help the small smile tugging at her lips. "I have three and I moved *here* to get away from them."

His grin faltered. Clearly, his mind was pondering on something.

"Did you recognize the neighbor? Have you seen him before on the street?" he asked.

She thought about her answer before giving it. "No, but that's not saying much considering the hours I work and the fact I just moved here."

Jake just nodded and turned to lock the front door.

"Hey, Jake?"

He turned and looked up at her as she reached the top of the steps. "You and Brian need to stop waiting up for me. Okay? I'm a big girl."

And there was that grin again!

"I'm not making any promises. Goodnight, Jenna."

16

The next day, Jake sat at his desk at work distracted. His jaw twitched as he watched the previous night's surveillance video on his phone for the hundredth time. He saw Jenna get out of her car, go toward the water-walk, and meander briefly until stopping short. No matter how he tried to zoom in, the other individual stayed off camera by a fraction of an inch. He watched as Jenna looked towards the house. *Something about the person made her uncomfortable.*

He had planned on dropping the subject with his newest renter, not wanting to agitate her. However, something in his gut made him want to press the issue. Was it the lack of sleep he had as a result of pouring over the video feed from his security cameras until the wee hours of the morning? Or was it the way Jenna got under his skin? Why should he care if she went for a walk after work? *Because Michael is my friend and I told him I'd keep an eye on her.*

No. There was something more to it. Jake had a long history of looking out for friends, but thoughts of them never consumed his mind. Not like this. He worried about her coming home so late. Worried about her laisse fair attitude of the world around her. *She's careless and stubborn. She'll end up in real trouble someday and I don't want that on my conscience.*

His mind should have been on his work like the others sitting at their desks, tapping away on their keyboards. However, his mind wouldn't rest. Jake reached for his cell phone to text her. He needed to know more details about who she saw on that walkway.

"What can you tell me about the neighbor you saw last night? How were they dressed? Was it a man or woman? Was there anything that stood out to you?" he texted.

A moment later, her reply came.

"Hello to you, too." The bouncing dots followed and he waited until another text came through. "It was a guy in a jacket. That's all I remember."

A thought struck Jake. He knew she might think he was odd asking it, but he needed to know. "Did you see his neck? Was there a tattoo?"

"No tattoo. But he had his jacket zipped up really high."

Jake sat back in his chair with a sigh. *A jacket in temperatures in the upper seventies?*

"Did he make you feel uncomfortable?"

"Everyone makes me feel uncomfortable, Jake." He smirked at her response.

"More than normal I mean."

"It was late at night… near a river, so yeah… kind of."

Jake reached down to one of his desk drawers and pulled out a file. He opened it, preparing to take a picture of his former partner to send to Jenna. Nick's face looked up at him, pausing his movements. Even before he went rogue, Nick had a smug smile and a condescending countenance about him. His way was right and anyone who differed or crossed him was labeled the enemy. Yet, Jake never would've thought Nick Spencer was capable of the horrible things he had done. Jake wished he could rest at night with the certainty that the people he cared about were finally safe. But *if* Nick was the new Broker… no one was safe.

"Corey, we've got a body in a field just off of 81. Appears to be a younger woman," Branson said coming up behind Jake abruptly, cutting into his thoughts.

Jake nodded and tucked the folder back into the drawer, locking it. With a sigh, he grabbed his keys and went to the crime scene. Questioning Jenna would have to wait, but he wouldn't let too much time pass. He needed answers.

Ten hours later, Jake pulled into the driveway with his shoulders slumped and heart heavy. All afternoon, he had the image of that teenager in his mind. Arm covered in scars and track marks. She had been awfully young to be such a hardened user. Way too young.

Jake got out of his car and took a good look up and down the darkened street before heading up to the door to unlock it. Then he paused and turned slowly back towards the driveway. Where was Jenna's car? The time was well past two in the morning. He didn't want to be overbearing and text her, especially if she stayed later at work. Yet, if Nick had approached her…

Quickly, he entered the house and locked it up tight before settling on his couch. He pulled out his phone. He typed several texts but deleted them all.

"Hey, where are you? It's late." *Deleted.*

"Wanted to see you before I turned in for the night, but you're not here." *Deleted.*

"I hope you're not on some late night drive…" *Deleted.*

Why did he sound so desperate to know where she was? He had never questioned Brian, Helena, or Trip like that. *Keep it cool… friendly. Not so severe.*

"Just getting in and didn't see your car. Still working?" he texted.

No response came so he started getting ready for bed. From the bathroom he heard his phone chime. With a toothbrush dangling from his mouth, he looked at her message and smiled.

"Picked up extra hours. I have to pay my landlord. He's kind of a pain."

"He sounds annoying. I hear there's an availability at the *Regency Apartments*… if you don't mind roaches."

Her response made him laugh and he brought the phone with him to the sink so he could rinse out his mouth.

"Did I mention my landlord thinks he's *funny*, too."

"When do you get off work?" Jake regretted hitting send the moment it went out. *What happened to playing it cool, Corey?*

"Not until seven. Keeping tabs?"

"Never. Get back to work. Your landlord's dog needs a new bone."

She didn't respond back and Jake second guessed whether he should have been *that* easy going. He was acting like a junior high school kid.

"What's wrong with me, Goose?" Jake asked the German Shepherd curled up at the foot of his bed.

The dog snorted, but didn't even lift his head.

"Why am I acting like this? I haven't felt this insecure since…" Jake stopped talking and heaved a sigh as the realization hit him like a ton of bricks. *Since I started falling for Beth.*

*****

"So what do you have to drink around here?" Mara asked as she took in Jenna's apartment.

"Energy drinks or water." Jenna winced.

Clearly, she had not inherited her mother's hospitality skills. Wearing a baggy pair of sweats and an ancient t-shirt she'd had since high school, she knew she *looked* unwelcoming, too. In her defense, she had pulled her first swing shift at the hospital and had just woken up half an hour before Mara arrived. Jenna would've still been in bed if Mara hadn't called her to ask what she wanted from the Thai restaurant she stopped at on her way.

"I guess water it is then," Mara chuckled as she made herself at home laying out the food on the table. "Where do you keep your glasses?"

Jenna motioned to the cabinet near the sink and grabbed paper plates and plastic forks. "Sorry it's not fancy."

"Girl, stop. You worked two shifts yesterday. I'm surprised you're still up to this." Mara smiled graciously as she brought two glasses of ice water to the small dinette table.

The two ate in comfortable silence until their bellies felt full. Then they chatted like school girls about their current novel and who they thought the main character would end up with at the end of the story.

"It has to be James. He's the more handsome of the two," Mara pointed out.

"How do you know that? The book doesn't say that explicitly. She describes him as blonde and blue eyed. That's it." Jenna laughed at her friend.

"But I *like* blonde and blue-eyed." Mara smiled dreamily.

A knock sounded on the door and Jenna froze.

"I hope we weren't being too loud," she said in a hushed tone. "My neighbors have a little girl."

"You pay rent here just like they do." Mara scowled. "If you live in an apartment building, you'd better expect noise from neighbors."

Jenna ignored her friend and opened the door, bracing for Helena or Brian to ask her to simmer down. When the door opened, however, it was Jake.

"Oh my…" Jenna heard Mara mutter under her breath.

Jake's eyes went to her friend who still sat at the table with a half-eaten plate of Pad Thai in front of her. He was holding a folder tightly in his hands and shifted on his feet slightly. "I'm sorry. I didn't realize you had company."

"It's okay. You can come in." Jenna held the door open wider.

"Yeah… it's okay if you come in," Mara repeated daftly.

Jenna shot a warning look over her shoulder at her friend.

"Mara, this is my landlord, Jake. Jake, this is my co-worker, Mara."

"It's nice to meet you, Mara." Jake smiled politely before turning to Jenna. "I can come back later. I had knocked earlier but didn't get a response."

"Yeah, I was sleeping pretty heavily. Sorry about that." Jenna started fidgeting. "What was on your mind?"

"Oh… yeah. It can wait." Jake shook his head and turned as if he were about to leave.

"Don't be silly. It's just us in here. No better time than the present. Unless you're evicting her, that is." Mara jumped right in and joined the two at the doorway.

Jenna elbowed Mara in the side before moving out of the way for Jake to enter. As soon as he walked past them, Mara gave Jenna a wicked grin and whispered, "He's better than the Action Figure!"

Jenna mouthed the words, "*Knock... it... off*!"

"I won't keep you." Jake opened the folder, turned it to face Jenna, and waited until her eyes landed on Nick's face. "I just wanted you to look at something and see if you recognize the person in this picture from the other night."

"You mean the neighbor?" Jenna furrowed her brow as she scrutinized the picture of a man in a police officer's uniform. He had a scar on his forehead like the man from the previous night. "It looks like that guy… only he has longer, scruffier hair. But he definitely had that same scar above his eyebrow."

Jenna felt relieved at the thought of the man being an officer just like Jake and Brian. She smiled at Jake expecting him to relax as well, but surprisingly, he didn't.

"So, you *do* recognize him? This was the man you saw?" he asked.

"I mean, it was dark, Jake." Jenna sighed and leaned to look closer at the picture. "But if I had to say whether it was this guy or not, I would say yes. Is *everyone* on this street a cop? I feel a little bit better now knowing that he wasn't a creeper."

Jake swallowed hard and the intense look he had on the night of the wedding returned.

"This is no cop, Jenna. Not anymore."

*****

Jenna's friend finally left and Jake tapped on the Hamilton's door. Helena opened it and greeted him.

"Hey, Jake." Her smile faltered as she read his expression accurately. "What's wrong? Come in. I'll get Brian."

"Is Tori in bed?" he asked, not coming inside.

"Yes. We just put her down. Why?"

"I'm going to grab Jenna. We need to have an emergency meeting."

"Oh… this isn't good, is it?" she asked.

Helena looked nervous, much like she had the last time they had a meeting. Ironically, that one involved Nick Spencer as well. He wished he could ease her tension, but they all needed to be on alert.

"I'll be back with Jenna."

Helena nodded and Jake heard her muffled voice alerting Brian to the impromptu gathering. Jake didn't have to go all the way up the stairs to Jenna's door. She was already standing on the middle step looking down at him perplexed.

"Is this like a family meeting or something? Ya'll do that here?" she asked from her spot.

"When we need to." He gave her a reassuring smile and motioned for her to join him.

She descended the steps, her face etched with concern. *Good. She needs to take this seriously.*

Jake sighed and tapped on Brian and Helena's door once more and it opened right away.

"Come in," Brian invited.

All of the curtains were closed tightly. Helena nervously started picking up toys off the floor.

"Helena, there's no need for cleaning. Sit down before you go into early labor," Brian said gently as he rubbed his hand down her arm.

She swallowed hard and nodded. "This isn't like last time, right? I don't think I can handle that again, Jake."

He sighed. "I don't know, Helena. I really hope not."

"Have a seat, Jenna," Brian motioned for Jenna to take seat before nudging his wife to a recliner. "What's going on, Corey?"

Jake filled everyone in the room on the events of the past month. The new Broker who resembled Nick with the tattoo of his wife's name. The graveside crime scene. And now, a possible encounter with Jenna right in front of their home. Helena reached over and grabbed her husband's hand. Brian squeezed it, but maintained the same look he sported while on duty. Jenna was… *Wait. Is she laughing?*

"Is this amusing to you?" Jake asked incredulously.

"You're basing all of this cloak and dagger stuff off of my two minute chat with a man I could *barely* see? Jenna raised her eyebrows. "Jake, I'm lucky if I remember what *I* look like half the time. What if I'm wrong?"

"There's enough here to warrant some new rules even if it wasn't Nick you spoke to that night," Jake pointed out and Brian nodded in agreement.

"New rules?" Jenna asked.

"Rule one: We keep each other in the know about our schedules so we can watch out for one another," Jake said raising a finger.

"Wait, wait, wait." Jenna laughed. "This is silly."

Jake put up a second finger. "Rule two: Keep alert and report anything out of the ordinary or anything that feels off to me or Brian... *immediately*."

"Or we can just dial 9-1-1." Jenna rolled her eyes.

"No." Jake shook his head. "Rule three: We don't tell anyone… not even another police officer or detective about this. I mean it, Jenna. *No one*. Not even your friend."

"He still has help on the inside?" Brian's question was more of a realization, but Jake gave his friend a curt nod.

"Branson and I think so."

"What about Michael and Anna? Are they going to be okay?" Jenna finally asked a reasonable question.

"Don't worry. I'll fill your brother in so he and Anna can take the right precautions," Jake assured her.

"Brian, maybe this time Tori and I should go to my parents' house," Helena suggested.

"But what if you go into labor?" Brian asked.

"*This* time? This has happened before?" Jenna looked at her new friends with concern.

Jake sighed. "I forgot that you were living in North Carolina at the time everything went down."

"I think there's a lot my brother didn't tell me." Jenna scowled.

"To protect you." Jake forced a smile. "I promise you… all of you… I will do whatever needs to be done to end this."

17

Sunday definitely lived up to its name. Bright sunbeams filtered through the thin opening of her curtains, gently beckoning Jenna from her restless sleep. It had been a long night. Maybe her sleep schedule was skewed after working an overnight shift the evening before, but sleep just would not come. Jenna found herself mulling over the *meeting* in the Hamiltons' apartment over and over in her mind until four in the morning.

Everything in her wanted to make light of the current events… to tell her friends they were overreacting. Yet, something in her gut twisted as she remembered their grim expressions and Jake's stern declaration of protection. It reminded her slightly of Ben's countenance when he had told her they wouldn't be able to talk for a while right before he left on that fateful mission. Why couldn't the people in her life just be teachers or accountants? Why did they have to choose such dangerous occupations? *What did you get yourself into, Jenna? If you had taken the stupid roach apartment, you wouldn't have to deal with any of this.*

Reaching for her phone, she saw that a group text had been initiated with her, Jake, Helena, and Brian. The chat had been named *House Buds*. Obviously, Helena started the group. Jenna couldn't fathom Jake or Brian naming it that. She chuckled as she scrolled through the conversation.

"Really, Helena? *House Buds*?" this came from Jake.

"You said start a group, so I did. When you start your own group, then you can name it."

Brian posted a laughing emoji.

"Jenna, we're all heading to church. You're more than welcome to come along. We leave in fifteen minutes. If not, we'll be back at noon." Helena had sent the invite at nine that morning.

Jenna checked the time. It was currently 10:25 AM. *Oops*.

Something stirred inside of her. The last time she had gone to church was the Sunday before she moved to Skennan Cove. And that was only to appease her parents. Yet, in the back of her mind she wondered if she should give it another try, especially after the conversation with Jake at the cookout.

Her Bible sat on a shelf, untouched. Every so often a verse would float back into her mind and she intended to go look it up. Then something would get in the way and distract her. Or she'd shrug it off as inconsequential. There was an ache inside of her that had re-emerged. It was as if she was missing something. Or maybe it was a *Someone*, she concluded.

Since Ben's death, she did not attempt to hide her anger at God. How could she miss a God she *hated*? How could she crave a relationship again with Someone she resented? Yet, there was a small yearning tugging at her heart. It reappeared every time she overheard Helena talk to her husband about a verse she had read in the Bible. Jenna had the *stirring* the night Jake said those comforting words on Heaven. He had found his way back to God. Maybe she could as well?

Jenna's stomach rumbled. *I need food.*

Shuffling out to the kitchen, Jenna squinted against the bright sunlight pouring in through the large windows facing the river. There were boats and water-skiers enjoying their weekend, basking in the mid-summer goodness. Maybe she could call Mara and hang out with her on some river bank. Her stomach growled once more. *Nope. Priorities, Jenna. You need groceries.*

Sure enough, she opened her cabinets and her shoulders slumped. There was a lone can of tuna that she referred to as her *very last resort.* Jenna whimpered. She could've sworn there was at least half a bowl worth of cereal left in a box on the lower shelf. Then she remembered. After she came back from their meeting, she stress-ate the last of the Crunchy Clusters. *There's no milk anyway. I really need to go to the store. Tuna for breakfast is not my idea of a good time.*

Quickly, she put on more appropriate clothing. Then Jenna grabbed her wristlet, keys, and phone before heading out the door. She remembered the group text. Was she supposed to tell them where she was going? That would be annoying. However, once in the car she pulled out her phone and tapped out a simple statement letting them know she was going to the store.

Jake responded.

"Just keep alert. Lock the door behind you."

"Okay, Dad." Jenna grinned when Helena responded with a laughing emoji.

She could imagine Jake rolling his eyes or sighing one of his loud exaggerated sighs that she was coming to expect. An image flashed into her mind of Jake sitting in church wearing nice jeans, a button-down shirt, smirking down at her text, and looking so handsome. *Stop it, Jenna! Stop this line of thinking right now!*

The grocery store seemed pretty busy for a Sunday morning. Vacationers, boaters, and fishermen grabbed snacks, beer, and ice to refill their coolers. Even though some of the junk food items looked amazing to her empty stomach, she was determined to fill her cart with fruits, vegetables, and necessities. No more eating like an unmonitored toddler.

Jenna double checked the list she had hastily scrawled on the back of a *Taco World* receipt she had scrunched in her car's cup holder from a previous night. It didn't take her long before she was ready to check out when something caught her eye. She had made herself pledge to stick to the list, but some things were worth the splurge.

*****

"What's she doing now?" The Broker asked the man he had positioned on surveillance. If the moment presented itself, he'd have Scout bring her in and the fun would begin.

"Uh… she's getting tacos from the same place she did the other night."

How could such a petite thing eat so much junk food?

"Is it crowded? Can you grab her coming out of the restaurant?"

"She's in her car going through the drive-thru," Scout sounded annoyed. "Look… I know how to do my job, Sir. I will let you know if an opportunity presents itself."

"We need to move quickly. You don't know Corey like I do," the Broker asserted. "He won't let her out of his sight for very long."

If the other night was any indication, this girl was on Jake Corey's radar. Maybe she was just a tenant, but the fact that his shadow had been standing at the curtain of his window during Nick's exchange with the woman was telling. When the front door had opened and Jake let his presence be known, Nick could see even over the distance that Corey was poised to pull his gun. His stance hadn't changed in the years he had last worked a case with Jake Corey. If Nick knew the man at all, his weapon had been tucked under his shirt in his waistband just out of sight, so not to scare the sweet young thing.

"She's headed your way, Broker." Scout's voice snapped him to attention.

"I'll take it from here." Nick turned the ignition on and waited until he saw her car pass.

Pulling a few car lengths behind her, he looked for the perfect opportunity to tap the back of her car with his. Just enough to cause her to swerve off the road. However, there were more cars on the roads than normal with the perfect July weather. He checked the clock on his dashboard. Corey stayed at church until a little after noon most Sundays. The Hamiltons normally had lunch with church friends after service. If he could be quick, maybe he could snatch Jenna before they got home.

She turned onto the street and Nick took his foot off the gas slightly. He checked his rear view. The street looked empty for the most part. That is, until they drew closer to the house. The Broker slammed his hand on the steering wheel and stopped his pursuit. Jake's truck was parked in the driveway and as soon as Jenna's car touched the blacktop, Corey was filling the front doorframe.

Cursing under his breath, he backed into a random driveway to turn around and drove off. Jenna wasn't going to be as easy to lure away as he thought. His best opportunity would be after her shift at the hospital if he could separate her from that other girl. He had more planning to do, but he wasn't going to give up. Once he had Jenna, he'd have the newlyweds and Corey right where he wanted them.

*****

"I thought everyone wouldn't be home until noon," Jenna said, getting out of her car and opening the back door to retrieve her groceries.

Jake shrugged with a slight smile.

"You left church early to check up on me, didn't you?" Jenna let out a sardonic laugh before leaning against the car with her arms crossed at her chest. "*Really*? Is this kind of babysitting *truly* necessary? You have some repenting to do, Corey, because you obviously weren't paying attention to your pastor's message if you left the service early just to make sure I was here."

Jake's expression remained cool and calm when he finally spoke. "Are you done?"

Jenna tilted her head and raised her chin ever so slightly.

"Goose needed his pill." Jake breezed past her to grab one of the grocery bags, but his eyes were scanning their surroundings.

"His *pill*?" Jenna asked in an uncertain tone. She watched in slight admiration as Jake single handedly grabbed all three of her bags.

"Yup. I forgot to give him his medicine this morning like I normally do. Didn't want to come home to a mess on the floor." Jake nodded to the front door. "Want to open that for me?"

Jenna turned away quickly towards the front door, trying to hide the embarrassed blush that crept across her face. She ran up the stairs and fumbled with her keys to unlock the door quickly. After dropping her keys several times, she opened it and turned around to see that Jake was smiling.

"Jake, I'm sorry I accused you of..."

"Being an overbearing creep?" He laughed.

"Well, after last night's talk I felt a little… *concerned*… that my freedom would be infringed on." Jenna tried to sound as calm as possible, but his eyes… those intense, blue eyes… had her feeling unsure of what she was saying. "I'm an independent woman, you know."

"Oh, I'm well aware." Jake nodded, still grinning. "I'm not trying to annoy or smother you, Jenna."

He put her groceries down at the landing in front of her door.

"Well, I appreciate that. I don't enjoy being annoyed and smothered." Jenna sounded flustered, even to her own ears.

"*However*," Jake's expression turned serious. "The threat is real and, yes, I will be keeping my eyes out for you. Just like I do for Helena and Brian… or even Trip when he was here. Because that's what friends do."

Jenna stood transfixed for several moments, staring directly into his eyes. He had these little flecks of gold closer to his pupils that she had never noticed in anyone before. His eyes started to crinkle at the corners. He was smiling again. No, he was chuckling… because she was *staring* at him. Not moving. Not saying a word. Just staring at him… and it was getting awkward. *Snap out of it, Jen!*

"So, uh… here's your bags. I'm going to go check on Goose," Jake said as he finally pulled his eyes away from hers to look down the stairs toward his own apartment.

"Yes. Check on Goose," Jenna stammered as she tried to break out of her weird funk. What was her problem? If Mara were there she'd never let Jenna live this down. Then all of the sudden she remembered something. "Jake, wait!"

He paused halfway down and looked up at her. She dove into her grocery bags until she found what she was looking for. Jenna pulled out a large dog bone.

"Here. Catch," she said as she tossed it down to him.

He caught it and looked at her in confusion. "What's this?"

"It's a bone. *Duh*!" Jenna smirked. "You said the landlord's dog needed a new one, so…"

Jake's laugh was a pleasant sound to her ears. "Well, then. *Goose* thanks you from the bottom of his heart."

Jenna stood still, watching as he descended the rest of the stairs. She was acting like a schoolgirl with a crush. Hadn't she vowed that there would never be another for her but Ben? This had to stop. She could not think of Jake like this. She blamed Mara and those stupid romance novels for putting these ridiculous thoughts in her head.

Just then the door below opened and the Hamilton family entered.

"Oh good. You're both here." Helena smiled. "Tonight is *Hospitality Sunday* and it's our turn to host life group. Can I count on you both to come?"

"Uh…" Jenna hemmed.

"I'll be there," Jake said with an easy smile, then looked up at Jenna with a challenging gleam in his eyes. They all waited for her response. "What do you say, Jenna?"

Her heart thudded in her chest. Hadn't she just considered getting back into church earlier that morning? Here was her opportunity. Yet, she froze. Maybe she wasn't ready yet.

"I thought we were being more cautious about things. Should we be opening up the house to just anyone off the streets right now?" Jenna questioned.

"We know everyone in our life group," Brian assured her. "And *if* someone new comes they're probably a guest of one of the other members."

Jenna nodded. She knew how life groups at church worked. The only way anyone knew the times and locations of the groups was if they had attended church services. She really didn't have an excuse not to go.

"I'm making homemade pizza," Helena said enticingly in a sing-songy voice.

Do it, Jenna. Stop fighting with God. If it was the Holy Spirit's prodding, He took on Ben's voice in her mind.

"Sure. Why not?" Jenna finally shrugged at her friends below. They looked genuinely pleased… and a little shocked. Especially Jake. "I'll be there."

Helena clapped her hands together happily. "Awesome! What is your favorite kind of pizza?"

"Hawaiian. Hands down the best pizza ever!" Jenna laughed at her friend's reaction of disdain.

Jake laughed loudly and pointed at their friend. "See? I *told* you it was amazing! You made me think I was the only one who loved Hawaiian pizza on the planet."

Then Jake looked up at Jenna with a wide smile. "She told me she would never make a Hawaiian pizza for the group until there were at least *two* people who like ham and pineapple toppings!"

"Hmm…" Helena lost her disdain over the pizza and took on a look of fascinated interest. "I will happily make a Hawaiian atrocity if it means Jake has met his match."

With that, the Hamiltons went into their apartment. Brian flashed them an almost apologetic smile, leaving Jake and Jenna staring at the closed door. *Wait... what just happened?* Jenna pondered as she watched Jake scurry inside his apartment. *Ugh, Helena and her matchmaking! And I'm walking straight into her trap.*

18

Jenna paused at the door but didn't attempt to knock or enter. She listened to the cacophony of voices coming from inside. An occasional high-pitched laugh rose above all other voices. Someone was enjoying the fellowship. She brought her hand up to knock, but froze. Did she really want to do this? What was happening to her? Jenna didn't *socialize*.

For the last several years, she had isolated herself so much that she wasn't even sure she could function in a group of people anymore. Yet, in the previous weeks, Jenna had started talking more. She had invited Mara over and joined her neighbors in their Fourth of July celebration. Maybe she was ready to get back out in the world.

It's okay to move on... to heal. That's what everyone had been telling her in the years since Ben's death – since her suicide attempt – but was she ready? Did she want this? Did she want to be surrounded by strangers and laughter?

"They're only strangers until you get to know them," a voice said from behind her.

Jenna spun on her heels as Jake approached. How had he made it up the stairs so silently?

"You look pretty deep in thought. You okay?" he asked softly.

"It's just that…" Jenna didn't know how to word what she felt. She tried to recall Dr. Crenshaw's emotion wheel, which listed all the various emotions to help her put a name to her feelings. "I feel *uncertain*… anxious."

Jake nodded. He didn't attempt to negate her. Many people – though trying to help – often said things like, "Don't feel that way" or "That's silly. You'll be fine." No, he just leaned against the wall and let her think out loud.

"It's been a while since I've…" Jenna motioned to the door as if that explained what she was thinking. "… done *churchy* things. It never felt right after Ben died."

"Did you use to enjoy it?"

"Oh.. yes. Ben and I had a great group of friends at our church in North Carolina." Jenna smiled wistfully. "And at my home church in Deer Creek as well."

Her smile fizzled out as she realized that most of the people she was picturing in her mind, she had lost contact with. Jenna shut them all out after Ben's death. She had learned to live without their presence, and it wasn't until that moment that she realized just how much she missed them.

"Well, I'm not going to say these people are as awesome as those friends were," Jake smirked. "But they have definitely been there for me. Some of them are… *interesting*, but they mean well."

Jenna smiled slightly and moved back from the door to let Jake enter. "I'm keeping you."

He pulled out his phone to check the time. "They never start right away. There's no hurry."

Just then, the door opened. Brian stood there, a smile growing on his face as he looked between Jenna and Jake. "I thought I heard voices out here. Pizza is ready. Come on in."

Jenna sighed and entered the crowded apartment. People of mixed ages formed a line that went around the dining room table. Little Tori played contentedly under the table with her police car, apparently used to people in her space. Guests filled their plates with a variety of pizzas and an assortment of other things laid out for the taking. Jake had already joined the line. Jenna knew she must've looked silly standing on the outskirts, so she quickly picked up a plate and joined him.

True to her word, Helena made Hawaiian pizza. She caught Jenna's eye from across the room and smiled warmly. Everything about Helena was warm and inviting. Her hospitality. Her countenance.

Jenna sat in a chair tucked away in the corner. She had been in the apartment the night before, but she hadn't really observed much about it with all of the activity going on at the time. Now, as she wanted to focus on just about anything other than socializing with strangers, Jenna took in the décor around her.

Helena's tastes were simple. If Jenna could sum up her neighbor's main themes, they would be faith and family. Above the couch, a family portrait hung of Brian, Helena, and Tori. The young mother was clearly pregnant in the photo, so Jenna knew it had been taken recently. Other framed pictures around the living room and on bookshelves gave snapshots of the Hamiltons' story through the years. Their wedding. Tori's birth. Places they've traveled to.

In the dining room, a wreath made out of grapevine and various wildflowers hung surrounded by Scriptures. So many Scriptures. Jenna smiled. It looked like Helena had the whole Bible on her wall. To a small degree, it reminded her of her parents' home in Deer Creek. Colleen had cross-stitched her favorite verses or sought out calligraphy renderings to hang. In many ways, Helena felt like a younger version of her mother. What would it feel like to be friends with another Colleen Tyler?

As if she knew she was in Jenna's thoughts, Helena waddled over and took a seat next to her. "How's the pizza?"

"Amazing. I hope it didn't put you out too much."

"Nah. I'm just glad you came." Helena gave Jenna a playful nudge. "I wasn't sure if you would."

"Why wouldn't I have?" Jenna laughed although she knew there were ample enough reasons to think that way.

"You looked like you were about to run as soon as I asked you to come," Helena said wryly. "But I promise, these are great people."

A loud giggle sounded over every other voice and they looked to see the source. A woman sat on a kitchen chair, scooted as close as she could get to Jake. He looked miserably over at Helena.

Clearing her throat and turning away from Jake's gaze, Helena tried to hide her smile.

"Who is that? What am I missing?" Jenna asked as she watched Jake smile politely at the woman next to him.

"That is Chantille. She really is sweet. Just a little socially awkward at times." Helena sounded defensive and Jenna knew there was a story there. Thankfully, Helena spilled the details. "I tried to put Jake and Chantille together. It kind of… backfired."

Another giggle. Another scowl from Jake.

"Chantille begged me for a long time to set her up with Jake. I told her he wasn't looking to date and that he was still grieving Beth, but she kept pushing." Helena kept her face turned towards Jenna and spoke so quietly that Jenna struggled to hear her. "Then one day he surprised us and said he thought he might be ready to date again. So, I set them up. It didn't go so great. She's crazy about him, but…"

Jenna looked over at her landlord and resisted the urge to laugh. He looked like Goose had on the day she spotted Jake giving him a bath outside. Disgruntled, but trying to hold it together. Just then, Chantille placed a hand on Jake's arm and kept it there. She smiled sweetly up into his face.

"How many times have they gone out?" Jenna asked, unable to take her eyes off of Chantille's well-manicured hand on Jake. It bothered her, but she couldn't – or wouldn't – determine *why*.

"Just once, but I think she thinks there's more there than what there really is." Helena sighed. "I can't even look. Is Jake shooting daggers at me?"

Jenna brought her eyes from Chantille's hand to Jake's face and swallowed hard. He was staring right at *her*, his expression unreadable.

"If you haven't gotten seconds, now's the time," Brian called out. "We'll get started on our Bible study in five minutes."

Someone knocked on the door and an older couple entered. "Sorry we're late, Brian. We were at my granddaughter's birthday party."

"We're glad you could join us. How was the honeymoon?" Brian smiled warmly.

The woman blushed and the older man laughed and said, "It was a good time away."

"*Honeymoon*?" Jenna asked Helena.

Helena smiled warmly. "They got married a couple of weeks ago. The sweetest couple you'll ever meet. It's Constance's third marriage. Tom's second."

Jenna looked at the couple with renewed interest.

All of the sudden, Jake got to his feet. "Constance, take my chair."

"Aren't you always the gentleman, Jacob?" the woman gushed.

"Don't you get designs on my bride, Son," Tom teased.

"I wouldn't think of it, Mr. Holloway," Jake smiled as he grabbed another chair for Tom and placed it next to the one he had just vacated.

"Smooth." Jenna smirked as she noticed Chantille's disappointed expression. To Chantille's credit, she hid her frustration behind a cheery smile when Constance turned to greet her.

Jake took a seat on the floor with his back against the wall next to another man since all of the seating options were taken.

"He's a good guy. Don't you think so?" Helena nudged Jenna playfully.

"Stop it, Helena. Learn your lesson," Jenna warned.

"We're on chapter twelve tonight. The topic this week is despair and disillusionment with God," Brian began from his place in the recliner, Bible and study book open in his lap. "I bet no one in this room has ever battled either of those things, right?"

A few people chuckled at his apparent sarcastic comment.

"I think if we were honest, we can all remember a time we felt abandoned or hurt by God. Maybe it was a season we found ourselves in. A prayer that went seemingly unanswered. Does anyone want to share one of those times with the group in a testimony?"

Jenna squirmed. All of the sudden she remembered about one hundred things she could be doing in her apartment at that very moment. She tried to find a discreet way to excuse herself, but Tori had wandered across the room and now stood in front of her, arms outstretched.

"Up," she requested.

"Tori, let Ms. Jenna listen. You can sit on *my* lap," Helena whispered to her daughter.

Tori looked at her mother's lap and furrowed her brow. There wasn't much room in Helena's lap with her pregnant belly.

"It's okay," Jenna said quietly. "Come here, Tori."

The toddler climbed up into Jenna's arms and settled in with a book she had pulled from a shelf. *Great. Looks like I'm stuck here.*

"I went through a time after I lost my first husband. We were so young," Constance spoke up. "I thought my life was over. Little did I know that I had so much more time left on earth. Sixty-two more years to be exact. God took Harold sooner than I had wanted, but He was telling me to take the *long* way home."

Jenna stopped breathing. Sixty-two more years. Jenna couldn't wrap her heart and mind around it. She didn't want sixty-two more years without Ben. Jenna felt dizzy and forced herself to let out her breath, blowing a few strands of Tori's hair.

Constance continued, "And if God hadn't allowed me to take this long way home to Heaven, I never would've married my Cliff. I wouldn't have experienced the birth of my children. And now... I get to experience joy in my golden years with Tom. God's been so good to me."

Tom leaned in and planted a sweet kiss on his wife's cheek. "I second that."

A few others shared stories from their lives of harrowing circumstances that made them wonder where God was. Yet, each person that spoke was able to point back to God and still praise Him. Still look at Him as a *good* God. A *loving* God.

Her eyes burned and Jenna had to remind herself to blink in addition to breathing. She could not lose it here. She was trapped under the now sleeping toddler in her arms.

"There are several verses throughout the Bible that offer comfort when we get down. What is your go-to verse that you use to encourage yourselves?" Brian asked the room.

Pages flipped as people started looking up their passages to share. Jake spoke up from his place without even looking up a reference.

"Psalm 27:13 says, '*I will see the goodness of the Lord in the land of the living.*'" He cleared his throat. He did not look in her direction, but continued to speak. "I did not want to live after Beth died. And even though I wasn't going to kill myself, I also wasn't living… if that makes any sense. I was a dead man walking for so long. When this verse came to me, I was reminded that I *can* see – *will* see – and *have* seen the goodness of the Lord in the land of the living. I don't have to wait until Heaven to see His goodness. It's here. I just need to look for Him harder sometimes."

Was that for her benefit? How dare he? What did he know about her situation? Then Jenna froze. He *did* understand. He'd been there, too. Many of the people in that room knew what it was like to feel lost and lifeless. Struggling to want to wake up every day. Struggling to wake up and actually *want* to live.

Jenna didn't hear much else spoken. Brian read from the book they were studying and then closed in prayer. Jenna remained in her seat. Tori's sweaty hair stuck in the crook of her arm. She stared down at the peaceful little girl so as not to make eye contact with any of the people who had just shared their hearts earlier.

"Are you okay?" Helena asked softly.

Jenna nodded, watching Tori's eyes move under her eyelids. She looked like an angel. *Will I see you in the land of the living, God? I wanted to be a mother so badly. I wanted to be the mother of Ben's children… not someone else's. It might've worked out for Mrs. Holloway, but that's not what I wanted. How can I see your goodness when you took so much away from me?*

A lilting laugh floated across the room as Constance showed the gushing ladies her new wedding bands. Tom looked so proud, so in love. Constance turned to her new husband and the expression of pure joy in her eyes brought tears to Jenna's. *I don't understand. How? How can I move on?*

Tori's eyes fluttered open and she started whining.

"Here, Jenna. Let me grab Tori from you," Brian said softly as he stepped forward and lifted the whimpering child into his arms. Instantly, Tori calmed and laid her head on her father's shoulder as he walked her to her room. The sight made Jenna's heart stir, but she didn't want to examine the feeling. She was free to leave.

Jenna quickly rattled off a goodnight to Helena and left the apartment. It had gotten quite stuffy inside and the hallway was refreshingly cool. She took several deep breaths before climbing the steps to her own home.

She had almost made it to the top when she heard her name.

"Jenna…"

She turned and looked behind her to see Jake.

"I thought maybe…" Jenna couldn't imagine Jake Corey anything but cool and in control, but in that moment he looked awkward. He held out the study book to her. "I thought maybe you'd like to take this. I can get another one. Even if you don't come to another life group, it's a pretty good book."

"I don't want to take your book. What will you use?" Jenna stared down as he continued to hold it out to her.

"No. It's okay. We have a few at church still. Please."

She took the book from his hand and nodded a thank you.

It was later that night as Jenna tried to fall asleep that everyone's stories and scriptures replayed in her head. She attempted to pray.

"I don't know how to do this. To live. To move forward without Ben. I know I'm functioning in some capacity, but this is hardly living. I'm going through the motions of living, but I am nothing but a dead woman walking."

Jenna rolled onto her back as tears slid from the corner of her eyes into her hairline.

"Is it possible to live again, God? Not just to go through the motions.... but *really* live? I want to see Your goodness again. I used to see You in everything. But I haven't for so long. I stopped looking for You. Don't leave me. Please, God. Help me see You in the land of the living."

19

"Are you arguing with me, *Broker*?" Damon's eyes were no more than slits, his tone menacing.

"Not at all, Sir." Nick shoved his hands in his pockets to hide his clenched fists. "When do I leave?"

"I have an associate waiting to escort you to the plane now." Damon looked down at his phone. "I want to move our operations down to Florida by the end of next month. While you are there, you will secure the next shipment and do a little *networking*."

"Networking, Sir?"

"My suppliers and allies don't like you. They don't trust you." Damon sat back in his chair taking in Nick Spencer from head to toe. "You go there and build their trust… whatever it takes."

"Are you kidding me? I've been at this for several years and you're just *now* concerned about how *they* feel?" Nick's pulse beat wildly in his neck. "Haven't I proven myself enough to you?"

"You've been *distracted* lately. Do you deny that?"

How could he? If he went against anything Damon said, the man would kill him instantly. He remained silent as Damon continued.

"Repeatedly, I have told you to let go of the past, but you refuse. And now I hear from some of my men that you continue to pursue that reporter and your former partner." Damon shook his head.

"Sir, I'm doing it for *you*… for our clients. That reporter knows too much," Nick defended. "I have her sister… we can use her to bring her out into the open."

"Ah, yes. Scout's little pet." Damon rolled his eyes.

Nick froze.

"You thought I didn't know about her? I've kept quiet about it because he seems so happy. I'd hate to ruin that for him." Damon looked amused, like a cat toying with a mouse.

"Anna Tyler can put your organization in the ground with what she knows," Nick said through gritted teeth. "She and all of those who helped her need to die."

"She knows only what I *want* her to know, Broker." Damon got to his feet, raising his voice. "She's of little to no consequence to me or my business now. Yet no matter how many times I tell you this, you keep going behind my back and pushing your own agenda."

Damon's eyes flashed fire. "It's *you* that will put my organization under. It's *you* who are being sloppy with your side-quests. It's *you* that will draw unwanted attention going after a harmless nobody instead of carrying out the jobs I give you to do."

"*Harmless*?" Nick's anger flashed, making him feel braver than he should've.

Damon laughed. "I don't need to explain anything to you. *You* are my employee. Replaceable. Or have you forgotten your predecessor?"

Nick took a calming breath before he said something that would've signed his death certificate.

"You see? This is exactly why my colleagues don't trust you." Damon's demeanor calmed as he took a seat at his desk once more. "This is your last chance, Broker. You are going to go earn their respect and you won't come back until they feel comfortable with you. Understood?"

His eyes continued to bore into him until Nick finally nodded.

"That's better." Damon smiled coldly. "You're dismissed."

Once out of earshot, Nick called the only man he trusted.

"Damon has me going on a field trip. While I'm gone, grab the nurse and hold her at the warehouse until I return. Report everything to me and to me only. Understand?"

"Understood," came the other man's response. "I'll put your new recruit on it since I can't get too close."

"I think it's time to put the sister to use. Let's use her as bait and see if we catch ourselves a nurse." Nick grimaced. He knew he was crossing a line that he would never come back from, but ultimately he always knew he would take this vendetta to its logical end.

"I'll have her go in and ask for the usual pain meds. Tell her to ask around for the nurse, maybe?" the other man brainstormed.

"Let her know if she talks, her sister is dead. I don't even want Scout aware of what we're using her for." Nick's heart rate picked up. "I don't want this getting back to Damon."

The other man agreed and ended the call with a promise to keep Nick apprised.

Nick sighed and tried to gain control of his racing thoughts. He put his burner phone back in his pocket – the phone Damon didn't know about.

Ultimately, he didn't care one bit about Anna Tyler or what she knew about Damon's business. Jake Corey was his target. Nick wanted to see that man suffer and brought down. If it meant killing his friends one by one, Nick would do it. With or without permission from Damon.

*****

In the weeks following the Bible study, Jenna made a point to look harder for God's presence in her day to day life. She began attending the Sunday evening studies. Every morning, she woke up with the exact same song playing in her head. It was a praise song that she had listened to on repeat all the time after she and Ben had gotten married. The words had encouraged her when she had been homesick. Was that God's way of reaching out to her?

There were other things that started popping out at her. Friendly conversations with Helena in the hallway that made her smile. Jake replaced her tail light when it went out. Tori gave her a random hug and told her that she loved her. Sporadic little events that blessed her. Then there were the various Bible verses that came into her mind throughout the day when she needed them most. Jenna was starting to think God really was there. He really *was* trying to point her attention back to the *land of the living.*

"So, you're telling me this group gets together to talk about *God*? For, like, *hours*?" Mara asked with an amused smile. "Girl, if you're that bored, just call me. I know a ton of things we can do on a Sunday night."

Jenna sighed. "I'm not bored. I actually like it. The more I'm getting to know them, they're all really nice."

"Are you sure it's not a cult?" Mara's brow knit as she tried to wrap her mind around what Jenna was telling her.

Everyone had invited her to try an actual church service, but she still held back a little. However, that upcoming Sunday, Jenna intended to go.

"It's not a cult." Jenna laughed. "Have you ever *tried* to go to church? Maybe when you were a kid?"

"Why would I do that?" The look of disdain on Mara's face spoke volumes. She checked her phone and saw the time. "Our break's over. Hey, tomorrow is Friday and we both have off. How about you let me take you out and show you what you've been missing?"

"Maybe," Jenna smiled at her friend as they walked back into the hospital's corridor. "I'll think about it."

"Sure you will." Mara rolled her eyes playfully. "You know, I think you like this little life group because of a certain landlord that goes to it. Tell me I'm wrong."

Mara stopped and put her hands on her hips, flashing a challenging smile. Jenna's mouth dropped open. She had every intent to set her friend straight, really she did. However, the nurse manager breezed by saying, "Get back to work, Ladies. We're getting slammed tonight."

Conversation ceased. Jenna was headed to the room where a new patient had come in by ambulance. Nothing could've prepared her for what she saw... *who* she saw. The EMT rattled off the patient's vitals and details, including that the woman showed signs of withdrawal. The patient had fallen and passed out on the sidewalk when a good Samaritan called 9-1-1. She regained consciousness when they started the IV enroute to the hospital.

"She says her name is Alex. We haven't gotten a last name yet," the paramedic stated. "She's asking for you specifically."

Jenna nodded in shock and took in the pencil thin woman laying back against the pillows. The EMT's left and Jenna's eyes went right to the gold bracelet that Alexis fidgeted with on her wrist. A very familiar bracelet with a golden heart charm. *Just like Anna's.*

"Alex? Alexis Munson?" Jenna asked in disbelief.

The shaking woman paused her fidgeting and looked at Jenna. It was her! Anna's sister. Pastor Tim's daughter. Jenna was several years younger than Anna and Alexis, but she remembered Alexis being a stunningly beautiful young girl that had captured the attention of every boy at church. At one point, even her own brother, Sean, had been close with the pastor's prodigal daughter.

In a trembling voice she asked, "Jenna Tyler?"

It felt like Jenna was gaping at the woman for an inordinate amount of time before she answered.

"Yes. I'm Jenna Tyler." Jenna used her maiden name, knowing Alexis couldn't possibly know her married name. "They said you asked for me… how did you know I worked here?"

Alexis shivered, but didn't respond. It didn't matter. Alexis was alive – and while she wasn't exactly *well* – she was sitting in front of Jenna. Anna would be so relieved – *if* she could tell her, that is.

"We missed you at Anna's and Michael's wedding," Jenna said as she went to the closet, pulling out a gown and spare blanket.

"Sure you did. I bet you all had a moment of silence for me." Alexis smirked despite obvious signs of withdrawal.

Clearing her throat, Jenna checked the IV the EMT's had already put into the woman's terribly scarred arm. "What happened tonight, Alex?"

"I don't remember," the woman muttered. "Hey, are you going to give me something for pain?"

"Where are you experiencing pain?" Jenna tried to keep her thoughts and emotions out of her expression. This woman didn't appear to have many teeth. Her skin hung off her bones making her tattoos look like deflated balloons. Her eyes looked dull, glazed over. Lifeless.

"I fell… so I hurt all over," Alexis said in a tone that insinuated Jenna was dumb for even asking. "Just give me something and I'll go home."

Jenna's brow tightened. "Let's see what Dr. Smith wants to do first, okay?"

Alexis let out a loud sigh and turned her head away from Jenna, giving her a profile view of her face. As Jenna checked her vitals, she also found herself scrutinizing Alexis Munson's appearance. Her nose was crooked as if it had been broken and never reset. Her temple had a small cut with dried blood, possibly from where she had fallen earlier. There were older bruises on her cheekbone in various shades and stages of healing.

"Anna misses you, Alex. So does your father," Jenna said the words softly. She wasn't sure if Alexis even heard them until she reached down to her wrist where the gold bracelet hung. "You know, Anna has the exact same bracelet."

"She bought us matching bracelets when I was in rehab," Alexis murmured softly. "Then I messed up again."

"It's never too late to start again. You have breath in your lungs, right?" Jenna urged.

"Don't waste your breath on me, Sunshine. I'm too far gone."

"That's not true. You did rehab before. You can do it again." Jenna pressed gently. "You are so loved and missed."

Alexis let out a mocking laugh. "Let them think I died. They're better off without me."

"That's not true. Anna talks about you all the time. So do your kids and your father."

Alexis sniffed loudly. "I bet the wedding was something. I wish I could've been there."

Jenna pulled out her phone. She showed her a few pictures of the wedding, including a few of Alexis' children in their fancy finery. Tears pooled in Alex's eyes before she snorted and looked away.

"Like I said, they're better off with me gone." Alexis' tone went cold. "How about those pain meds, *Nurse*?"

Defeat washed over Jenna as she backed away. "Please change into the gown at the foot of your bed. The doctor will be with you shortly."

Jenna didn't like the tightness in her chest as she left the room. Anna had been worried sick over her sister.

They hadn't heard from Alex in months. She had disappeared without warning. Anna said her sister was on the road to true recovery before she vanished. If Anna saw her now… well, she'd be devastated. What could Jenna do? Could she tell her that her sister had been in to the emergency room? No, of course not. There were rules and laws protecting Alexis' privacy.

From the nurse's station, Jenna watched Dr. Smith announce her presence and speak to Alexis before exiting a few moments later. She wrote something down in the file and called to Jenna with the orders she'd been expecting. A CT scan of her head. Blood work. And a simple over the counter pain medication. Nothing shocking.

Jenna came back into the room with her caddy and a little paper cup with Tylenol.

"What's this?" Alexis asked when she grabbed the cup, not caring that the hospital gown she had put on was falling down her shoulder, almost exposing her.

"It's medicine for your pain, as requested." Jenna tried to keep her tone even. "Do you want me to help tie your gown for you?"

"I *want* you to get me real medicine or let me go home. I can't be here much longer." Alexis' voice was a mix of anger and fear.

"Dr. Smith wants you to get a scan of your head and I will need to draw some blood," Jenna said calmly. "It's best if you lay back and rest. Would you like the TV on?"

Alexis grabbed Jenna's hand, not in a violent or angry manner. More desperate, pleading. She enunciated each word emphatically. "You don't understand, Jenna. I have to go."

"Alexis…"

"No! I *have* to go. He'll be home and if I'm not there…" Terror replaced the numbness Jenna saw earlier.

"Who? Is someone hurting you, Alex?"

Alexis shook her head vehemently, communicating that she was done with the conversation. She began pulling her gown down and off. Jenna ran to the privacy curtain just in time before the people walking down the hall got an eyeful.

"Alex, stop."

"I'm leaving… *Now*!" Alexis didn't seem aware of the fact her IV was still in place and Jenna rushed forward to ensure the catheter didn't pull out of her arm.

"Are you refusing medical treatment?" Jenna tried to sound unflustered.

Alexis turned to look at her as if to say, *Duh.*

"If you are refusing care, there is a form you have to sign before you leave here. Do you understand?" Jenna said holding the taped IV in place.

"Get the form and let me go. Please, Jenna."

Jenna sighed. "Can I trust you to stay put until I get it?"

Alexis nodded curtly. Jenna went to inform the doctor and grab the necessary paperwork. Upon returning to the room, the IV had been removed and Alexis was back in her street clothes. A trickle of blood made its way down her hand, most likely from the pulled catheter.

Grabbing the paper, Alexis reached for the pen in Jenna's scrub top pocket and hastily scrawled something akin to a signature.

"I'm sorry, Jenna." Alexis appeared to be sincere. "I'm so sorry. This was a mistake."

"Alex, I'm worried about you."

"Forget you saw me. It's better for you if you forget I ever existed."

Alexis started to stumble towards the door, when Jenna impulsively touched her arm to stop her.

"Wait! Alex, we can't lose you again. There is hope and I want to help you." Quickly, Jenna pulled out a slip of scrap paper and wrote her number on it. She swallowed hard, hoping no one was observing or walking by the door at that moment. She didn't want to field any questions. "Here is my number. Call me if you need out of whatever situation you are in right now."

Alexis took the paper and stared at it as if Jenna had handed her a live bomb. She shoved it inside her bra and left the room, dodging the people in the hall like someone was chasing her. All Jenna could do was watch as sadness and a whole host of other emotions bubbled up inside of her.

"Sometimes they just come in for the drugs. Can't help them, Clark," the nurse manager said as she came to stand near Jenna. "You'll get used to it."

"I… I don't feel well."

The older nurse looked at her suspiciously.

"I think it was something I had at dinner. I feel like I'm going to throw up." It wasn't a complete lie. The encounter had made Jenna's digesting food turn and churn inside her gut.

After actually losing her dinner, Jenna was dismissed for the night. She went to her locker and pulled her keys from her purse. She sent Mara a quick text telling her she was leaving early before making her way to the parking lot. Jenna had almost made it to the garage entry when she heard her name.

"Jenna…"

She turned around and saw a police cruiser inching up closer. Squinting against the headlights, she strained to see who was in the driver's seat.

"Where are you off to?" It was Brian.

"I'm not feeling great so I'm heading home." Jenna moved to his window. "What are you doing here?"

Brian looked sheepish. "My normal patrol."

"You drive through the hospital on patrol?" Jenna asked skeptically.

"Jake asked me to make sure to hit the parking garage a few times a night." Brian chuckled.

Surprisingly, Jenna didn't hate the thought.

"Need a lift to your car?" he asked and motioned to his passenger seat.

"Actually, that would be great." Jenna's shoulders relaxed and she got into the front seat of the cruiser.

"Where are you parked?"

"Top level, furthest from the elevator."

Brian cleared his throat. "You know that's probably one of the least safe spots to park, right?"

Jenna smirked in the dark. "It's where Mara likes to park. Keeps people from scratching her truck."

"Yeah… well. Don't tell Jake."

Just then, a man stumbled across the ramp and Brian hit the brakes hard, calling out the window, "Watch out, Man!"

The man paused and looked at Jenna in the front seat, an odd expression on his face. Then he realized he stood in front of the police cruiser and disappeared into the rows of cars.

"Do you know him?" Brian asked.

"No, but we've had a lot of addicts through tonight." Jenna sighed as she remembered her encounter with

Alexis. "Brian, do you know much about treatment centers? Which ones might be better than others?"

Brian rattled off a list that popped into his head. "I don't know if one is better than the others. I think that depends on the person… if they want help."

If they want help... That's just it, Alexis might have been turning Jenna's offer of assistance down, but there was something in her eyes. Desperation. Loneliness. Terror. Did Alexis *want* help? Jenna desperately wanted to give it.

It was later that night after Jenna drove home and sought the solace of her bed that she cried. It felt silly to cry over someone she didn't really know all that well. Then again, there was something else about that encounter that made Jenna unable to finish out her shift.

Surrounded by balled up tissues, she stared up at the ceiling rehearsing the conversation with Alexis over and over. The words she had said… they were the same words that *Jenna* had uttered in the not so distant past. *God, is this one of those things that points to you being present? Please help Alexis. I have to believe you can help her. Because maybe... just maybe... if you can bring Alexis back to life, you can do the same for me.*

*****

"Did you see her? The nurse?" the man asked after finally catching up to Alexis on the street.

"No."

"Are you lying?" the man checked Alexis' jean pockets, just as they did every time they sent her into the hospital for heavy pain meds. She hoped he wouldn't check her bra. "You know we'll find out if you are. Then both you and your sister are as good as dead."

"They gave me Tylenol. Scout told me not to waste time if they're only going to give me Tylenol."

The new guy the Broker brought in was called *Crow*. Probably because his voice was annoying like a crow's caw. And he wasn't kidding. It was only a matter of time before they killed her, she knew. If she could stay alive a little longer, maybe she could keep her sister safe. And now Jenna. What could they possibly want with *her*?

When they told her what she was supposed to do that night, she wished they had just put a bullet in her head and ended it right then and there. Instead, they banged her around to make her look like she had hit her head and posed her on a street corner. Then, called an ambulance.

"Remember… you weren't in there for Scout. You were doing a job for the Broker," the man growled. "I'll ask again… did you see *her*?"

"I didn't see her, okay? I got some old lady."

"When you get back, you don't tell Scout a thing about this. Understand?" Crow grabbed her, shoving her into a van.

"But what if he asks where I was? He'll hit me."

"That's not my problem." Crow shrugged.

Alexis remained silent and he muttered under his breath as they drove away. She had to get out of this. The wadded up paper close to her chest scratched her, but she didn't do anything to draw attention to the fact it was there. If she called Jenna, she could put everyone she loved in danger. *But what if she can help? What if she can get me away from them? Stop it, Alex. You don't have the luxury of hope.* Yet, a still small voice whispered, "*But, what if...*"

20

On Friday, Mara texted Jenna as promised, ensuring a night of fun and dancing. For the first time in a while, Jenna was relieved to say she was working a Friday night. It gave her the out she needed without hurting her friend's feelings. She had taken the extra shift to smooth things over for leaving the previous evening. Even if Jenna weren't working, she would've turned Mara down. Crowds of people and dancing had never been her scene. If Mara had asked for a night of reading and discussing their latest book… well, that would've been a whole different story.

"Jenna, are you sure you are feeling better?" the nurse manager asked as she came up on her at the nurse's station. "You seem distracted."

"I'm fine." Jenna lied.

The woman just gave her an unconvinced look before walking away.

Jenna shook her head. She needed to get out of her thoughts and feelings. Ever since Alexis had come into the ER, Jenna had been looking at her phone hoping to see a call from her. She had been worrying about the woman and wondering where she was. All through the night, Jenna had lain awake thinking about the words Alexis had spoken. *Let them forget I ever existed. They're better off without me.*

Jenna had expressed many of those same things before she had tried to take her own life. Some days… if she were being honest… she *still* felt those sentiments. Not for the first time since she moved away from Deer Creek and her family, Jenna noticed the absence of calls and texts from her family. Even Chase had gone silent. *What do you want from them? You complained they smothered you when you were there. Now that you're away, you're hurt that they are giving you space?*

It wasn't as if her mother hadn't tried to get her to come home for the 4th of July celebration. Jenna made the choice to stay away. She couldn't blame them. Yet at the same time, she felt lonely. The life group had helped her feel a part of a community, but they didn't know her. Not the *real* Jenna. Not the hurting Jenna trying her hardest to find God again. *Stop feeling sorry for yourself and get back to work!*

She made it through the shift. It felt odd not walking out with Mara. Knowing her friend had the day off, Jenna parked on the first level as close as she could to the entrance. Thankfully, another co-worker was on her way out as well when Jenna was leaving so she didn't have to walk to her car alone.

Jenna checked her phone one last time in case Alexis texted before pushing the button to start the engine. First came a click followed by a labored whirring noise. Jenna turned it off and restarted the car. The same thing happened again, but the engine turned over and she was able to pull out of her space. Now was not the time to have a car repair. She didn't know who in the area was a trustworthy mechanic. Her father and Ben had always taken care of those things. Maybe it was just the battery. Those were easier to fix. She definitely didn't want to put out the money when August's rent was due.

She was relieved that her car made it home. She pulled into the driveway and determined to seek out a new car battery the next day. Maybe one of her new neighbors knew a thing or two about installing one. Her father surely had shown her when she had just learned to drive, but Jenna's attention span had been severely limited to Ben and fun back in those days.

Speaking of the neighbors... Jenna got out of the car and looked towards the house. Jake's tall stature filled the frame as the door opened.

"I thought we agreed you'd stop waiting up for me." Surely, her smile would betray her words. Without fail, he had been there every night when she pulled in from her later shifts.

"I never agreed to anything." He returned the smile.

"You're home! I'm so excited!" A female voice came from inside and Helena pushed Jake out of the way as she waddled out. "Did you hear on the news? We might be able to see the northern lights tonight."

Jake sighed. If Jenna didn't know any better, she could've sworn that he rolled his eyes. Yet, when she looked at him he just appeared to be glancing up into the night sky.

"I was born in the North Country and I never remember seeing them," Jenna commented looking up as if she'd see them appear magically.

"They only come out when there are magnetic storms and solar winds. Apparently, this year the sun has been active," Helena spoke excitedly. She pulled out her phone and queued up a compass application to find true north. "It's behind the house. Come on, you two."

Jenna looked at Jake. He smiled and shrugged, but motioned for her to go ahead of him.

"So I guess we're in the all clear? No more house lockdown?" Jenna smirked into the darkness.

"Never said that."

"Then why are we out here in the open unarmed?" Jenna looked up at Jake and saw he, too, smiled into the darkness.

"And what makes you think I'm unarmed?" was his reply. Jenna stopped herself from looking to see if he was, indeed, packing heat. Speaking of heat. Her face flushed when he looked back at her, catching her unaware.

"Look! I think I see something!" Helena called excitedly. She had her phone pointed into the sky and a light green hazy line appeared on the horizon of the screen. "See?"

Jenna moved away from Jake and stood next to Helena, crowding around her phone screen. She didn't want to hurt her friend's feelings, but it didn't look all that impressive. Not when her feet hurt and she'd had a long day.

"We just need to give it time. These things are unpredictable," Helena pointed out.

Jenna took a seat on the back steps of the house, looking up into the sky. Jake sat a step down from her and leaned back on his elbows. Helena continued to scan the sky with her cellphone.

"It's not a big storm so you have to look through your phone. I doubt we'll see with just our naked eyes," Helena instructed. "Come on, Jenna. Try it."

Not wanting to be impolite, Jenna pulled out her phone and looked through the screen. A slight line of green and something white rising from the center appeared.

"You caught a pillar," Jake said as he glanced over.

"I did?" Jenna laughed.

"Mm hmm. Right here. See?" Jake leaned a little closer and magnified her screen, giving her a better visual of the phenomenon she had caught.

His cologne carried on the breeze and Jenna shivered. The darkness gave her enough cover to truly observe Jake without being noticed. His profile was strong. Masculine. Yet there was a sweetness about him… a tenderness in his eyes.

A window from above opened and Brian called down, "Babe, can you come up here for a minute?"

Jenna jumped as if she had been caught ogling Jake, but brought herself back under control before anyone noticed.

"Coming!" Helena called back. "You two keep looking. I'll be back."

Helena squeezed past them on the steps and into the house.

Jake shook his head. Even in the dim light coming from the house, Jenna saw his illuminated expression of mirth.

"What is it? What's funny?" she asked.

"I literally just sat here watching her texting on her phone. How much do you want to bet that she told Brian to call her in?"

Jenna guffawed. "No way. How do you know she was texting Brian? Maybe she was sending her northern lights picture to someone."

"Maybe." He said the word with a slight nod, but the same smile was still in place. "We'll see if she doesn't come back out right away."

"You still think she's trying to set us up."

Even in the darkness, Jenna could see his cheekbones rise. "Yup."

"That would be silly though." Jenna laughed a little too breathlessly. "Wouldn't it?"

Jake shrugged and reached for his phone putting it up into the sky. He caught another image with brighter greens and more white lines that he had called *pillars*.

"Not bad." He showed her the image he had caught. "I was wondering if this was going to be a *Linus* waiting for the *Great Pumpkin* kind of thing."

Jenna laughed softly. "Impressive. Have you seen the northern lights often?"

He nodded. "At my cabin. There's less light pollution there. When there's a good solar wind, you don't need your phone to see them."

"Really? You can see them with your eyes?"

Jake smiled again. Jenna was growing quite fond of that smile. "Up at the cabin, I can see *all* the colors. Greens, pinks, purples… and the white pillars."

"Sounds lovely."

A few moments passed with the two of them just looking at the sky in silence. It was reminiscent of Michael and Anna's wedding. It wasn't strained or awkward. Jenna felt calm… comfortable. *Too comfortable.*

She cleared her throat and asked, "So, you still think there's a risk? That your old partner is out there somewhere?"

"I do."

"It's been several weeks and nothing has happened. Do you think maybe you were overreacting?" Jenna leaned over and nudged him slightly with her elbow. "Maybe you can stop asking Brian to drive by the hospital on patrol? I'm sure he has *real* bad guys to look for."

"I stay alive by keeping aware and alert. The bad guys stay alive by biding their time and hiding, Jenna." Jake sat up straighter and looked back at her. "Don't get too comfortable and complacent. Keep your eyes open."

The light shining from inside the house hit Jake's face and Jenna once again couldn't fight the intrusive thought. *He is maddeningly good looking.* And he was genuinely concerned for her safety. No one demonstrated that level of concern for her except for Ben. Well… and Chase.

Jenna sighed audibly and racked her brain to find a way to change the topic and her thoughts.

"Do you know anything about cars? Car batteries to be specific," she asked in a rush.

He blinked as if he were trying to register the change of topic. "Uh, yeah. Why?"

"My car was acting funny. I think it might be the battery. I can figure it out myself, I'm sure. But Ben and my father have been the ones who always helped me with that stuff," Jenna prattled on. "But I can pull up a video and figure it out."

Jake's smile lit the night. "Would you actually accept my help if I offered?"

"Of course. I'm not *that* stubborn." Jenna guffawed and he laughed all the more. A deep laugh that caused goosebumps to rise on her arms.

"Of course you're not. We should probably go in. I don't think Helena is coming back out." He stood up and offered her his hand, but Jenna pretended not to notice, getting up on her own. Slowly, Jake dropped his hand to his side. "I can take a look at your car tomorrow if you want me to."

"That would be fun. I mean… great. Thank you." Jenna stumbled over her words. How many times had she rolled her eyes and laughed at her friends when they flirted with guys. Then it hit her like a ton of bricks. *You're flirting. Knock it off, Jenna.*

Without warning she turned and opened the back door to the house, holding it open for Jake. He didn't move.

"You go on in." He smiled at her and turned around to walk the perimeter of the yard. He appeared to be scoping the area. That was when Jenna saw it. There on his side. His shirt caught on the gun holster, revealing his weapon.

Slowly, Jenna made it up the stairs. She waited to hear him come in – to know that he was safe inside. By the time she made it to her door and unlocked it, she heard him below locking up and entering his own apartment. What was she doing? She had vowed that no one would ever gain access to her mind and heart again. If Jenna wasn't careful, the danger wouldn't be the ghost of some past shady cop… it would be the very much alive man that lived on the first floor.

21

The car made several clicking noises without turning over and Jake's gut twisted. The clock worked and the lights on Jenna's dashboard lit up like it was Christmas. The battery was not the culprit. Just to be sure, he grabbed the voltage meter from his toolbox. The battery was just fine. He checked the connections to make sure nothing had corroded. They, too, were fine. How was he going to break it to Jenna that she was looking at a major car repair?

Goose, who had been lying in the shade of the oak tree in the yard, lifted his head all of the sudden. Jake followed his alert gaze and saw the front door of the house open. Jenna stepped onto the sidewalk with a bowl and a bottle of water. Jake couldn't stop the smile from creeping across his face.

The night before, he had thought she looked cute in her hospital scrubs. It was Saturday morning and she padded down the sidewalk with oversized possum slippers on her feet. She wore a pair of plaid, baggy pajama pants and an oversized t-shirt sporting the *Deer Creek High School* logo. Her hair was piled on top of her head in a messy bun. *Adorable.*

Instantly, Goose left the shelter of the tree and took off like a nut after the stuffed possums on Jenna's feet. Jake's momentary trance was broken as he watched his massive German Shepherd dart in her direction.

"Goose, *heel!*" The former police dog paused, cast an agitated glance back at Jake, and plopped his rump in the grass. Jake knew that at any moment Jenna's slippers were done for.

Jenna smiled as she took in Goose sitting at attention, leaning his body in her direction while keeping his hind quarters planted on the grass. Goose tested his boundaries and inched a little closer.

"Ah. Ah. Ah," Jake warned and Goose harumphed, staying put.

"Why can't he come to me?" Jenna asked as she scooted closer to her car in the driveway.

"Do you want to keep those slippers and your toes on your feet?" Jake asked, keeping a stern eye on his dog.

"Oh! I wasn't thinking." Jenna smiled shyly as she looked down at her slippers.

"Do you always wear animals on your feet?" Jake asked and hid his smile behind the safety of her open car's hood.

"These were a Christmas present from Michael," she said as if that explained it all. Oddly, it did. They looked exactly like something Michael would get his sister.

Jake shot a glance over at his dog to make sure Goose was behaving and felt content to see the big baby had taken to rolling in the grass.

"I brought Goose a drink. It's hot out here today," Jenna said, unscrewing the cap off the bottle and pouring it into the bowl.

Jake peeked around the hood at her. "Yeah, he's slaving away in the sun. Poor thing."

He rounded the corner and took the bowl from her hands in case she thought it was safe for her to get near Goose with those things on her feet. He took it to his dog, put it down in front of him, and messed with his fur in playful affection before returning to the car. He wiped his hands on his jeans and looked at her with a half grin.

"You didn't think that maybe *I* might need water?"

Jenna held out the bottle in her hand, matching his smirk with a mischievous smile. "There's still some in there for you."

"Gee, thanks." He took it and guzzled the remainder.

"Here." Jenna laughed, reaching into what must've been cavernous pockets in her lounging pants to pull out another bottle. "Do you think I'm that insensitive? I just didn't have enough hands."

Something in Jake's chest flipped, jumped, then tightened. Her shy smile. The way she awkwardly shifted from foot to foot. The blush creeping into her cheeks. It was a feeling that had laid dormant for years. The desire to pull someone into his arms and hold them there. Jake had thought that emotion was long gone. When was the last time he had felt anything remotely like that? *Not since Beth.*

"How's the battery? Do I need a new one?" Jenna pulled him from his revelation and he cleared his throat.

"Battery is fine."

"Oh, good! Whew! I thought for sure it was the battery." Jenna slumped against the car in visible relief. Jake's chest clenched.

"It's your starter." He waited for the words to register and a pitiful whimpering noise escaped her throat.

"That sounds expensive… and something I can't go online to learn how to do on my own," she mourned to herself.

"Yeah, I'm sorry, Jen."

"Is it at least drivable? Last night it started eventually. Do you think I'll be safe to take it to work tonight?" She tried to look hopeful.

Jake ran a hand through his hair as he tried to figure out how to word his next comment. "It's no longer starting. And if it *did* start… there's no guarantee it will start again later."

Her shoulders fell, but then as if rallying herself together she squared up and looked him in the eye. "Who do you recommend in the area for repairs? Who do you take your truck to?"

Jake laughed. "I have trust issues. I do my own repairs."

Jenna sighed.

"But… I'll be happy to work on your car." Jake couldn't believe he had just offered. Where would he find the time? He'd make time… for Jenna. "I mean, it won't be done today. I'll need to see if the part is in stock and go get it. It might take me a couple days."

Jenna nodded and then added sheepishly, "Do you know what you're doing?"

Jake laughed loudly, getting Goose's attention. "I've replaced a few starters in my time."

"I didn't mean to sound like I was doubting you." Jenna blushed. "I'm sure you're amazing."

She looked stunned as if she hadn't intended on offering such a glowing compliment.

"I can go get the part now, if it's available, and work on it tomorrow after church." Jake shut the hood with a thud. "Were you planning on coming tomorrow? I remember hearing you and Helena talking about it."

Smooth, Corey. Now she thinks you're listening in on her private conversations.

"I was going to come, but…" Jenna looked at her car as if she were willing it back to life. "Maybe I could hitch a ride with Helena and Brian."

Jake made a face.

"What?" she asked as soon as she caught it.

"You might get put in the back of the van. Brian just installed the other car seat in the center row. Helena's due date is just a month away." Jake knew he was purposefully preparing her to accept the offer he was about to make. "You could… if you *wanted* to… come in my truck."

"I don't want to put you out." Jenna looked down at her possum-clad feet. "You're already doing so much."

"It's nothing. I'm glad you're coming."

The two fell into an odd silence... not wanting to speak, but not wanting it to end either.

"I should probably go get this part," Jake finally said.

"How do I pay you for it?"

Jake flashed her his most alluring smile. "Want to come along?"

Jenna froze.

"I mean, an auto parts store isn't terribly exciting, I know. But if you want to pay for the part…"

"Let me get changed," Jenna said suddenly, smiling.

Jake was still processing the fact that she had actually *wanted* to come along when he forgot about Goose. Jenna started running towards the house in her ridiculous slippers. The stuffed possums proved too much of a temptation for Goose, who now was in full pursuit of Jenna's feet. It was too late to call out to the mutt.

Thankfully, it appeared that Goose latched on to the possum's head which was just a ball of stuffing. He yanked with his strong jaw and brought Jenna down on her thigh. He tugged the possum free from her foot and ran wild with it, shaking it in his teeth.

"Jenna!" Jake ran to see if she was okay, threatening his dog under his breath. Relief washed over him as he reached her. Jenna lay on the ground laughing so hard that tears streamed down her face.

Jake tried to hide his own amusement when she quickly took off the other possum, just in case Goose returned. "Are you okay? I'm so sorry. Goose is going to get it when I get my hands on him."

Hearing his name, the large dog came prancing back proudly with a torn possum in his mouth. He sat close and allowed her to put her arms around him in a tight hug. *Who is this woman? She passed the Goose test.*

As if reading his mind, Goose leaned his muzzle into Jenna's hair. He snorted with playful approval before stealing her other slipper from the grass next to her. Jake tried to scold him, but Jenna held up her hand to stop him. Her smile was… *stunning*. He'd never seen her laugh. It was a beautiful thing.

She tugged at the possum in the dog's mouth and Goose dropped it in anticipation of what he thought might happen next. Sure enough, Jenna took the slipper and threw it as far into the yard as she could, sending the big oaf after it like he was a puppy.

"Your slippers are ruined. You know that, right?" Jake laughed. Jenna was still amused, sitting in the grass watching the dog run wild. "I'm so sorry. I'll get you a new pair."

"Nah. No worries," Jenna said as she accepted Jake's hand to get to her feet. She shot Jake an irresistibly cute face and said, "I don't remember the last time I laughed like that. It was well worth the lives of my possums."

*****

Jenna was finishing her shift and still grinning. *Years*. It had been years since she laughed that hard. Looking back on the scenario, she supposed it wasn't really terribly funny. Jake probably thought she had lost it. Yet, in that surprising moment, something was loosened inside of her. Something that had been sealed tightly. It was joy. *I will see the goodness of God in the land of the living.*

Was it the way Goose took her by surprise? Was it the adorable way his ear quirked and he lowered onto his haunches at the thrill of Jenna preparing to throw his new *toy*? She had always loved big dogs. Or was it something more?

Jake's face floated through her mind, bringing another small smile. The two had spent a good portion of the day in search of a new starter for her car. They had stopped at two different auto parts stores until Jake found what was needed. She should've been *unhappy* at the cost. It was an unplanned item to her budget. The inconvenience of being without her car should have made her cry, but Jenna shrugged it off and reasoned that it was a temporary inconvenience. *This is huge and Dr. Crenshaw will be very pleased to hear how I'm handling it all.*

It could've been the impromptu lunch at the little diner in town that tempered whatever frustration she felt over the car repair. Jake treated her to a burger at his favorite restaurant. It wasn't a fancy place. It was simple and quaint. The two laughed over Goose and chatted over greasy burgers and fries. Jake told her stories of growing up as the only child. He certainly got away with a lot as a young boy. She shared tales of being the thorn in her brothers' sides. Jenna realized that when Jake wasn't so intense and looking over his shoulder, he was actually quite enjoyable.

Maybe too enjoyable, Jenna thought to herself as a twinge of guilt tugged at her heart causing the smile to die on her lips. *What about Ben? He was enjoyable, too.*

Jake had offered her a ride to and from work since she was without a vehicle. With as fast as Jenna found herself falling under his spell, she decided she needed distance. Especially, if she had already accepted his offer to take her to church the next day. Mara was more than willing to swing by to pick her up on the way to the hospital.

"You've been wearing that goofy look all night. What gives?" Mara asked on their way home from work.

"Nothing."

"Pfft. Liar." Her friend laughed. "Your new church friends better watch out. They have a fibber in their midst."

Jenna rolled her eyes.

"Spill it, Jenna."

After a few moments of contemplation, Jenna asked her friend, "Do you think people can fall in love multiple times?"

There was instant regret after the words left her mouth. *Love? Whoa, slow down! You had a burger and he's fixing your car. You knew Ben your whole life. Jake... you hardly know.*

"Of course, I think you can fall in love multiple times. My mom loves my stepfather very much. I myself have fallen in love with many... *many*... guys." Mara snickered.

Jenna sighed. She didn't love Jake. That was preposterous. She wasn't a fairy tale princess swooning over the first man to come to her rescue. She was a modern woman. Independent. Devoted to her beloved Ben.

"Do you think your husband would want you to be lonely until you die?" Mara said as they came to a stop at a traffic light. She looked at Jenna with the glow of the red light illuminating her uncharacteristically serious face. "He sounds like he was a great guy... like he'd want you to find happiness again."

Jenna opened her mouth to answer a rebuttal when her phone sounded. A number she didn't recognize.

Jenna answered. "Hello?"

"I need out, Jenna. Help me... *please*." The words were no more than a whisper, but spoken in a trembling voice.

"Who is this?" Then Jenna remembered. "Alexis?"

“Please. I have to get out.”

“Give me your address. I’ll come right now.” Jenna’s adrenaline spiked.

“No!” Alexis’ voice rose slightly. “If you come now, he’ll see you. He’ll kill you. Kill us both.”

“Alex…”

“Tomorrow. He’s supposed to meet someone at two o’clock. I’ll be ready to go.” Alexis spouted off an address and Jenna tried hard to memorize it.

Then the phone clicked and Alexis was gone.

22

Jenna tried to pay attention to the sermon. She *really* did. However, there were so many competing thoughts fighting for her focus. Even the delicious cup of coffee that Jake bought for her on the way to church that morning couldn't keep her mind fixed on one thought at a time. No, Jenna's mind raced in so many directions all at once.

Was Alexis okay? What would Jenna be walking into later that day? Why was that Chantille girl shooting daggers at her? Why did Jake always smell so good? When was Helena due? She looked ready to pop. These were all of the questions demanding answers while the pastor spoke from his place up front.

The church felt similar to her home church back in Deer Creek. The pastor had kind eyes much like Pastor Munson's. He was speaking on the prodigal son and the theme felt like it hit too close to home for Jenna. She was, after all, a prodigal daughter. Hadn't she walked away from God the minute He took Ben? *I'm here now though, Lord. I'm trying. Help me.*

The service ended and Jenna caught sight of the cute, older couple from life group. What were their names? Oh, yes. Constance and Tom. The *newlyweds*. Constance's words from that very first group meeting that Jenna attended still replayed in her mind.

Excusing herself from Jake and the Hamiltons, Jenna quietly made her way to the older woman.

"Jenna! You came! What did you think?" Constance smiled warmly. "The people here aren't so scary, right?"

"That remains to be seen," Jenna said without thinking and slapped a hand to her mouth. Constance's laughter lilted into the air. It was a pleasing sound. "I'm sorry. I've always been told I tend to talk and act without thinking."

Constance's eyes twinkled. "I've been told that a time or two myself."

Jenna stood awkwardly with a forced smile on her face, working up the nerve to ask the question she had been stewing over for weeks.

"Is something on your mind?" the older woman asked quietly and tugged Jenna's arm to lead her further away from the noisy crowd of people.

"You said something the other week…"

"Uh oh. Do I need to apologize for something?" Constance looked concerned.

"No. Not at all." Jenna ran a hand over the front of her dressy shirt and slacks, smoothing out imaginary wrinkles. "You said that God was taking you the long way home. Do you think that's because He had other things for you to do first? Or…"

Understanding lit Contance's face and she patiently waited for Jenna to get her tortured thoughts together.

"I lost my husband a few years ago. I'm trying to figure out if the reason God is making me stay here on earth is because there's more for me … or is it punishment? I tried to join him… Ben. Obviously, it didn't work, but… am I being punished? Is that why I am still here?" Jenna fidgeted, not making eye contact. Oh, how Jenna hated vulnerability. She sounded like an awkward child, not an adult woman, as she fumbled to put what she was feeling into words. "Never mind. That sounded silly even to my own ears."

Jenna turned to walk away when Constance's hand gently touched her arm.

"I know what you mean." Her response was soft. "After my first husband died, I felt my life ended with his. I didn't want to continue and every day felt like a punishment… a curse."

Jenna swallowed hard, unable to speak or move. She slowly brought her eyes up to Constance's.

"Then I met my second husband. He and I went on to have a family until the Lord took him home as well after a hard fought battle with cancer." Constance looked wistful momentarily before continuing. "As long as you have breath in your lungs, Jenna. You need to believe that means the best is yet to come for you. God is not done with you. No matter what is going on around you."

Jenna's throat tightened but she dared not move or look away from the gentle gaze of the woman in front of her.

"Who would have thought that God would still have a purpose… for *me*. At my age?" Constance chuckled and pointed to her groom, Tom. "But that man over there…

he needs me. Do you know this morning he tried to wear suspenders? Who does that anymore?"

Jenna burst into laughter.

"And maybe, you might just be a part of someone else's story that God's writing," Constance said, lowering her volume. Then, all of the sudden, she looked past Jenna at someone behind her. In a cheerful greeting, she said, "Hello, Jake! Are you waiting for this sweet young woman?"

He cleared his throat. "I don't want to interrupt anything."

"Not at all. I will see you both tonight at life group."

Constance smiled and squeezed Jenna's arm once more before moving away to find Tom. He stood off to the side beaming as she approached. Maybe Jenna's *long road home* was also a scenic route… allowing her a second chance at love as well. Did she want that? The thought was bittersweet.

"Are you hungry?" Jake asked once he and Jenna were seated in his truck. "There's a restaurant I've been meaning to try."

"Do they have a dollar menu?" Jenna grinned. "I just bought a starter for my car, remember."

"My treat."

"Again? You paid for my lunch yesterday."

"I don't mind. I like being with…" Jake snapped his mouth shut and his cheeks took on a deep blush. Then, he recovered. "You're not so bad to be around. Michael made you sound a lot worse."

Jenna laughed. "Oh, really? And what did Michael say about me exactly?"

His grin spoke volumes.

As much as Jenna wanted to keep saying things to make that grin reappear, she saw the time on the dashboard. "I really would love to grab something with you, but I'm meeting someone."

The grin faltered. "Oh. Anyone I know?"

How did she answer that? Did Jake know Alexis? He probably knew *of* her at the very least. How much could she… *should* she share with him? Jenna opted for keeping Alexis' plight private. The woman might not want the world to know of her struggle.

"Just someone I know from the hospital," Jenna stated casually. "She needed my help with something."

"*She*?" The relief with which Jake said the word brought a slight thrill to Jenna's chest. Had he thought she was going on a date?

"Yes. She is definitely a she." Jenna smirked and looked out her window, but not before glancing at Jake. He sighed quietly and a small smile still remained on his handsome face.

"So, it's a no to the restaurant, but how about drive thru? Any preferences?" he asked, changing the topic back to food.

"There's a taco place down the road that you can get three for…"

"Yes, I know the place very well," Jake chuckled. "Tacos it is."

*****

Jenna shifted uncomfortably on the back seat of the car. She'd never used a rent-a-ride service on her phone before. She had never *needed* to. Her car wasn't finished, but Jake assured her when they got back to the apartments he was going to work on it that day. She was grateful that he was still in his apartment changing clothes when her ride arrived. She didn't want to entertain questions or commentary about jumping into a stranger's vehicle. Now as the car turned towards a less than desirable part of town, Jenna fidgeted. The tacos churned in her gut. Maybe she *should've* asked Jake to get involved… with Alexis' consent, of course.

Brian had given her a detailed list of treatment centers and Jenna had made calls the night before to narrow down who would take Alexis in. However, Jake could have probably moved obstacles if any happened to arise. At the very least, his presence would've been calming for her. *That's odd. He does have that affect on me. That was something only Ben could do in the past.*

"Are you sure this is the place, Lady?" the voice from the driver's seat startled her. Jenna saw his concerned look and furrowed brow in the rearview mirror.

"Uh, yes." Jenna said looking out her window at the house numbers. "590 Crane Street."

The street was filled with one story bungalows, many in bad shape. People sat on their porches fanning themselves in the oppressive August heat. A cool snap was due to hit in the next day, hopefully bringing rain with it. The lack of precipitation made the small yards appear brown and lifeless.

"Do you think you can stay close by?" Jenna asked bringing her attention back to the man who looked at her in the mirror. "I'm bringing a friend out and we'll need a ride away from here."

The man looked shocked that she'd even asked him to remain. "*Here*? You want me to hang out and wait for you ... *here*?"

"Please. I'll pay you extra for any inconvenience."

The man sighed. "Go on the app when you're ready to leave. I'll keep an eye out for your name, but I'm not staying parked here."

It wasn't exactly what Jenna wanted to hear, but it was better than nothing. She nodded and told him, "Hopefully it won't be longer than ten minutes. Please don't go far."

He growled and pulled away from the curb as soon as she shut her door. Surely it was her imagination, but it felt like there were at least a dozen pairs of eyes on her as she walked to the beat up old house. Jenna rallied her courage and knocked boldly.

The door burst open and a pair of hands pulled her inside. Jenna tripped over her feet but managed to right herself before she landed on the ghastly carpet stained by who knows what. The scent in the living room reeked of a few things she could pinpoint and some she could not. Her eyes flew to the one who opened the door.

"I wasn't sure you'd come," Alexis said nervously. Her hands trembled violently.

"Are you ready to go, Alex? The driver said he'd try to stay close, but I need to request him now if you're ready." Oh, how Jenna hoped she was ready!

Alexis stumbled and limped towards the back of the house to a bedroom. There were new bruises on her arms and face. Jenna couldn't be sure, but there seemed to be a large patch of hair missing from the back of Alexis' head. Had it been that way the other night?

"Alexis, please tell me who is hurting you," Jenna said softly.

"A bad, bad man." She grabbed a grocery bag and pulled clothing from a hamper in the corner of a disheveled room.

A mattress lay on the bare floor, stained just as badly as the carpet. Bed sheets, blankets, and pillows were strewn all over. There were holes in the wall, making

Jenna wonder if a fist had caused them or someone being thrown against it.

"Is the *bad man* your boyfriend?"

Alexis paused and looked up at Jenna as if she were out of her mind. "There's no love and romance here. He uses me. He tricked me to get to Anna. And I stay to make sure she stays safe."

"Anna? What does she have to do with this?" Jenna dared to move further into the room.

Alexis' shoulders slumped and began shaking as she started to sob. Regret filled Jenna. This had to wait until they were somewhere safer to talk freely.

"Alex, please forget I asked. Let's just go," Jenna said helping the woman shove whatever clothes she could into the grocery bag. "We'll talk in the car on the way out of here, okay?"

"Have you told my family you saw me? Do they even *want* to see me again?" Alexis asked between fits of tears.

"I didn't. You told me not to, remember?" Jenna pulled her phone out and looked up the app to get a hold of the driver. *Please let him be nearby, God. And please let Alex be ready to go.*

"Maybe this is stupid. They won't want me back. Not after… everything." Alexis dissolved into more tears and Jenna felt panicked.

"The pastor was talking about the prodigal son today in church. Do you remember that from the Bible?" Jenna pulled Alexis upright to look her in the eye. "The son thought the same thing, but remember what the father did? He ran to meet his son when he came back. Alexis, if you are serious that you want to change, you will."

"Shh." Alexis hissed suddenly and pulled Jenna further into the room, shutting the bedroom door behind them. She had her ear against it and a panicked look on her face. "He's home! Why is he back so soon?"

"Who?" Jenna's heart pounded in her chest.

"Scout thought I had used and passed out, but I just *pretended* to use. If he finds you here… we're both dead."

"I've got to call Jake. He'll help us." Jenna switched functions on her phone. "He's a cop. A detective. Anna knows him. He helped her and Michael. Did she tell you about him? Jake Corey? He can help us, too."

"No! Cops can't be trusted." Alexis hit Jenna's phone out of her hand. "Get in the closet! *Fast*! I'll try to get him away from here so you can leave."

"Alex!" Jenna begged through clenched teeth and tried to resist being shoved into the crowded closet. However frail Alexis may have looked… she still had enough strength to force Jenna inside and shut her in.

Between the slats on the door, she saw her phone. Alexis, in a quick move, covered it under part of the blanket. She moved to the door just as a man entered the room. His eyes scanned every corner, landing on the closet momentarily. Jenna held her breath.

"I thought you were going to meet Damon?" Alexis tried to sound casual, but her voice quivered.

"He cancelled. Why do you care all of the sudden?" he asked, his eyes looking around the room for anything out of place.

Alexis slumped against him and pulled his face down towards hers.

"Maybe I missed you." Her voice was slurred. It hadn't been that way moments ago. Was she acting?

"I'm surprised to see you awake. Maybe you need more? Maybe something stronger?"

"No. I need *you*." Alexis reached up and pulled the man's head down in a kiss. Jenna felt her taco threatening to come up her throat. "Let's go out. I'm hungry, Baby."

The man seemed to be buying it and started following her out the door. Just as Jenna thought she could breathe again the man turned one last time to look around the room.

"Hold on! Hold on!" His voice grew loud and Jenna held her breath, clenching her eyes shut. She opened one eye to see him lifting the grocery bag of clothes Alexis had been stuffing. "What's this? Did you think you were going somewhere?"

"What? That? No!" Alexis said in a panicked tone. "I was hoping you'd take me to the laundromat. I didn't want to take the whole basket."

"You lying to me? You know what happens when you lie to me," the man shoved her out of the room.

"Scout, no!"

Then came another man's voice. Smooth. Calm. Eerily familiar.

"Now, Darlin'. I know you know better than that. Do we have to re-teach you this lesson?" That voice! Where had she heard it before? *Darlin'.*

Jenna didn't get time to put the voice to a face. What followed next were screams and begging coming from the living room until the front door opened and slammed shut. Then, there was the sound of a car peeling away from the house, the motor vibrating the windows of the house. It vibrated Jenna, as well. Or was that her trembling in terror?

Silence. From somewhere outside Jenna heard the sound of children shouting to one another. A car horn. Laughter from a woman. Music blaring from a stereo. Jenna's heartbeat pulsating in her ear muffled all other sounds.

Jenna didn't know how long she stayed in stunned stillness inside the closet, but she knew she had to get out… and fast. She opened the door slowly. It was when she turned around to look at the place she had sheltered in that she saw an arsenal of weapons that normal citizens would not possess. *Jake, help me.*

23

The ride-booking app said all drivers were unavailable. The taxi service in the area told her she'd have a waiting time of at least forty-five minutes. Time was not a luxury Jenna possessed. That left Jake. How would she explain this to him?

She called and got his voicemail, but hung up. Jenna was not going to wait for Alexis and her abusers to return. She definitely couldn't wait around for Jake to get his messages. Slowly emerging from the bedroom, Jenna looked around the small house carefully for her best route of escape. What if they were still close by? They might see her leaving from the front door.

Going to the back door, Jenna eased it open and saw a small back yard abutting an alley of gravel that went behind the other buildings. Many of the houses had privacy fences so maybe she could get away from the house unseen. Stepping out into the yard, Jenna heard the voice of each of her brothers – plus Jake – in her head yelling that this was a crummy idea.

Dialing Jake once more, she walked briskly towards the graveled alley and pretended she belonged there. *Don't let fear show on your face. You're a bold, confident woman. Just keep moving. Act like this is your street. Don't make eye contact.*

"You've reached the phone of Detective Jake Corey. I am unable to answer right now. Please leave your name and number…"

"Ugh. Jake Corey! Answer your stupid phone!" Jenna said through gritted teeth.

Apparently, she had been unaware that she missed the sound of the beep. Jenna's message had been recorded and sent.

"If you'd like to leave another message, please hang up and…"

"No, no, no!" She slid her phone back into her jean pocket and walked a little quicker.

The alleyway spilled off onto a street and Jenna turned onto a sidewalk that looked like it led to businesses. She saw a convenience store ahead and made that her goal. Just as her foot touched the parking lot her phone vibrated.

"Jenna, what's wrong?" Jake asked with concern in his voice. "I got your message. I'm sorry I didn't answer. I just finished with your car and took it for a test drive."

"Um, could you pick me up?" Jenna tried to keep her volume down as someone walked past her into the store.

"Of course. Where are you?"

Jenna strained her neck to look at the sign above her.

"Gentry's Convenience Store."

Silence.

"Jake, did you hear me?" Jenna asked.

"Uh... yeah. And why are you *there*?" His tone shifted slightly. It reminded her of her oldest brother Dan's tight, clipped tone. The tone he reserved for displeasure. Normally, Kate was the recipient of it.

"It's really a long story and this place is making me feel ... weird. So can you just come please?"

"Text me your exact location and stay put," he said. In the background, Jenna recognized the dinging sound that his truck made when his door opened. "I'm on my way. Are you inside the store?"

"No."

"Get inside and stay in there, Jenna." Jake sighed. "And when I get there... be prepared to tell me how you landed in *Broker* territory."

He hung up and Jenna stared at her phone in disgust. "How dare you... you bossy... *jerk*!" *Who did he think he was? Even my brothers would get a fist in their gut for ordering me around like that!*

A man walking by glanced over at her and smiled. He had been walking towards the store, but changed direction and came to stand directly in front of Jenna.

"You lost, Little Girl?" he asked and reached his hand up as if he were going to touch her hair that was draped over her shoulder.

Jenna took a step back and the man's grin broadened.

"Did your mother ever tell you it's rude to ignore people when they're speaking to you?" He took a step closer.

"I'm… I'm not lost. I'm waiting for someone," Jenna said as she turned and walked quickly to the store's plate glass doors. The iron bars on the door and windows were a giveaway that crime was clearly an issue in that area.

The man was hot on her heels.

"Who are you waiting for? You looking to score a hit?"

"No."

The jingle of the bells on the doors caught the attention of the man behind the register and Jenna sent the attendant a pleading look. However, the man looked disinterested and went back to whatever he found intriguing on his phone screen. Thankfully, the other fellow started browsing the store, but Jenna could feel his eyes on her. Out of the corner of her eye, she could see him watching her, circling her like a shark ready to attack.

She grabbed a pack of gum, a soda from a refrigerator, and pretended to browse what appeared to be elaborate vases in a glass case.

"You looking for a bong?" the clerk called out to her finally.

"What? *No*!" Jenna said in shock. "I… I'll just take these, please."

The man shrugged and rang up her purchases. Jenna's relief was palpable when a large truck pulled into the parking lot and the driver's side door opened. Jake jumped down, his sunglasses hiding whatever emotion he was feeling at the moment. His clenched jaw, however, indicated that he wasn't pleased. The man who had been trailing her seemed to have disappeared. *Good.*

"You okay?" Jake asked, holding open the truck's passenger door for her.

"Yes. Thank you for coming."

Jake gave a curt nod and grunted. Jenna lifted her chin in defiance at his irritation. It was hard to maintain an edgy look as she attempted to climb into his truck. Her brothers inherited all of the Tyler family's height. Unfortunately, Jenna had been given her mother's stubby legs. It wasn't helpful that she had to accept Jake's hand to get herself seated, especially when she was trying to maintain a sense of independence.

Shutting her door once she was safely inside, he visibly clenched his jaw again. Jenna could've sworn she also saw the side of his eyebrow twitching, but his shades hid it well. She watched him walk around the front of the truck to the driver's side, turning his head to look in the direction of the dispensary before taking his place at the wheel. *Here it comes. He's probably going to lecture me on all things safety... like I don't know anything about the big, bad world.*

Silence.

"Are you going to say something? I know you're dying to," Jenna said after the prolonged silence finally got to her.

Jake sighed and reached into his jean pockets, pulling out a set of keys.

"Here," he said, handing them to her without taking his eyes off the road. "Your car is fixed."

"That's it? *Your car is fixed*?" Jenna looked at him waiting for him to say something… *anything*… more. "You're not going to tell me how stupid it was to come here alone? Or that anything could have happened to me because no one had a clue where I was?"

"Nope."

There was a huge difference from their easy going banter at the taco restaurant earlier in the day to that moment. The cab of the truck was filled with tense silence. Why did Jake's one word answer bother Jenna so? Why was he so quiet? Was it because he cared about her and she had worried him? Or maybe he *didn't* care at all and he was put out by driving there to pick her up. There were no answers forthcoming and Jenna instantly remembered why she never wanted to date anyone ever again.

*****

Help me hold it together, Lord.

Jake prayed all the way to Jenna's location for her safety. Then, he prayed all the way home that he wouldn't say something he would regret later. He had been taking Jenna's car for a test drive when her calls had come through. When he pulled into the driveway at home and listened to his voicemail, he felt his blood run cold.

He hadn't let his guard down as far as being alert, but Jake had eased up on harassing Jenna about Nick Spencer and the potential for danger. Then, he found out that she was stranded… in the heart of known Broker territory. His friends in the police department are dispatched to that very same store at least twice a day. What was she doing there? She said she had been helping a friend from work. Where was her friend while Jenna sat unprotected? Jake needed answers, but he had to calm down before asking them.

The truck came to a halt in the driveway behind Jenna's newly fixed vehicle. He opened his mouth to speak, but Jenna opened the truck door and slid down to the sidewalk. Resisting the urge to acknowledge how cute it was that she couldn't reach the running board, he called to her.

"Jenna, wait."

She paused at the door of the house and turned to meet him head on. *Why is she angry? She's the one who put herself in that situation, not me.* Hands on her hips, Jenna's head was cocked to the side as if expecting him to defy her. Jake felt a small tug at the corner of his mouth. *I could kiss that pout right off of her.*

"Is something funny?" she asked in a rush. Her cheeks were flushed and he pictured her as a little girl holding her own against her three older brothers.

He removed his sunglasses and looked down at her, trying to school his obvious attraction. "Do you mind telling me what you were doing in that area? Who were you trying to help?"

"I don't think that's any of your business."

"That area is a known crime area, Jenna. No one goes there to *hang out*." Jake's smile disappeared. "You said you went to help someone… what kind of trouble are they in?"

Jake wasn't a detective in St. Lawrence county for nothing. He read people better than most. Many called him a human lie detector. There was a flicker of something in Jenna's expression. It was the same look criminals made when they were trying to give just enough truth without divulging too much.

"Let's start with a name. How about that?" Jake pushed when she remained quiet. "What's your friend's name?"

There it was again. The corner of Jenna's eye twitched. Something was off.

"I can't…"

"Can't or won't? There's a huge difference between the two," Jake bit out.

"Stop it, Jake. You're grilling me like I'm a criminal. I don't have to tell you anything." Jenna turned and entered the house.

He followed right behind. "There's a lot of things at play right now that you don't understand, Jenna. I don't want to see you in the middle of something that can get you hurt."

“Look, Corey! This is a sensitive situation,” Jenna spouted off. “And I don’t need another overprotective brother watching over my shoulder.”

Jake vaguely heard the door to the Hamilton’s apartment open, but he paid them no mind. Thankfully, they remained silent. Her foot landed on the first step of the staircase and he reached out, spinning her around so they were face to face... or close enough. His hands gently rested on both of her arms.

“I can’t protect you if I don’t know where you are or who you are dealing with, Jenna.” He tried to keep his tone even, but his pulse was racing in his ears. *Cool off, Corey. Slow down. You’re going to scare her away.*

His eyes lowered to her lips and he noticed how they trembled ever so slightly. She looked vulnerable for a moment, but as if catching herself, she shook her head.

“But I’m not yours to protect,” she said in a pained whisper.

Just then, someone above them on the landing cleared their throat at the same time as the front door flew open. Life group members started filing in. Jake instantly dropped his hands and took a step back from Jenna.

“I was wondering if you two remembered it’s our night to host life group again.” Brian looked apologetic at the interruption, but Jake knew it was a good thing. Jenna was right. She wasn’t his.

*****

"The Broker returns Tuesday. Where are we with that nurse?" the man asked Crow over the phone before getting into the passenger seat of the van.

"Maybe closer than we realize," he answered in amusement. "I think our fish bait has been lying to us."

"Explain."

"My contact said they spotted someone who looked out of place wandering around Scout's street just now. Real close to his house." Crow sent the image his friend had taken. "They followed her to *Gentry's*. Does she look familiar to you?"

The image was grainy and blurred, but Jenna Tyler was unmistakable to him. And so was the truck she was getting into. He sighed. *Jake Corey*.

"Sounds like Scout's little *pet* has been working behind our backs," Crow stated.

He glanced over at Scout. He was an ugly man covered in pot marks and tattoos that he, no doubt, received in his many stints in prison. He sat unsuspectingly at the driver's seat while Crow unloaded the goods on Scout's precious Alexis. The Broker didn't want Scout involved, but they'd have to tell him something to explain why his favorite junky had to die.

He ended his call and turned to Scout.

"It seems your woman has been reaching out to people she shouldn't, Scout."

The man swallowed hard, but didn't respond.

"Not only that, but she reached out to someone connected to Jake Corey. A nurse at the hospital." Scout didn't need to know that that had been the plan all along. He'd use this to their advantage. "The Broker already knows you've been talking to Damon so this isn't going to go over well at all."

"I'm not a snitch," Scout said through gritted teeth. "I've done nothing but try to help the Broker. I know my place."

"Good. Because you're going to have to prove your loyalty to him. Kill *her*," the man said nodding in the direction of the woman crumpled behind him on the SUV floor. "I'll have to have Crow grab the nurse. She knows too much now and you don't want that getting back to Damon, do you? Damon will kill you for sure if he thinks your *girlfriend* put his operations at risk."

Thankfully, Scout bought it.

"She's outstayed her welcome, Scout. She's led Corey right to our doorstep… the very thing Damon didn't want."

Scout swallowed hard. "I'll do what I have to do."

"You'd better. I want her gone *tonight*." He got out of the car, but sent a quick glance over at Alexis. Hopefully, Nick wouldn't be too upset over the loss of his bait. Alexis was a liability now. *Oh, Darlin'. What have you gotten yourself into?*

24

The promised cold front arrived Monday, bringing with it thunder storms and torrential rains. Many people were relieved by the drastic cool down and moisture for their yards, but Jenna found the day gloomy. It went along with her current mood. A very cranky Jenna tore her apartment apart looking for her favorite cardigan. Her hospital badge was clipped to that sweater and it was nowhere to be seen. She was still new enough to the hospital to be uncertain how serious they viewed something such as that. At the previous hospital she had worked in, she would've gotten a lecture at the very least.

Sinking onto her couch with a thud, she decided to give herself time to sulk and ponder the events of the day before. After her verbal back and forth with Jake, Jenna had no intentions of going to life group. She didn't want to sit across the room from him and pretend everything was okay. It wasn't!

Ever since she uttered those blasted words, nothing felt right. *But I'm not yours to protect*. It was true. Jake had no reason to claim any protective tendencies towards her. He was not her brother. Not her father. Not her love. Then why did it irk her so?

"Because I *want* to be his."

The words were painful to admit and they didn't bring a sense of relief or realization with them. Just loneliness and emptiness… with a stab of guilt. What would Ben say? Jenna was acting like a lovestruck teenager over the man. *If Ben were here…*

"But he's *not* here," Jenna cried. "He's enjoying Heaven and basking in the glory around him. And I am *here*… lonely. Why? Why, God?"

Jenna's mind drifted to life group. She had sat stone-still next to Helena all night and pretended not to watch Jake out of the corner of her eye. Every so often, she thought he glanced at her as well. However, she must've been mistaken because Chantille ended up engaging him in a lengthy conversation and he paid Jenna no mind. Not even when she finally excused herself as soon as the closing prayer was uttered.

"Why would you let me go through this, God? Why didn't you just let me die." The words sliced at Jenna's heart. She had been healing well… or so she had thought. Was this a momentary pity party or was she going backwards into the pit she had just escaped? Jenna couldn't afford to go back.

"Help me, God. I don't want to be lonely, but I don't know how to move forward without Ben either."

Jenna thought about Constance's words and how she pointed out Tom's need for her. Jake didn't *need* her. She didn't foresee him ever needing anyone, especially someone as messed up as herself. Dr. Crenshaw had given Jenna less frequent appointments, noting that Jenna progressed nicely in her healing. *Maybe I need to call her and schedule a maintenance appointment.*

"Now quit feeling sorry for yourself and find that sweater and your badge," Jenna scolded herself as she realized time was getting away from her.

She had searched her apartment up and down. Could it be in her car? No. She had gotten rides to and from work because her car was acting up. Just then, a thought hit her. She grabbed her phone and texted Mara.

"Did I leave my sweater in your car Saturday? It has my badge."

Mara's response came quickly. "Yes. I have it. But to get it back you have to spill the tea on what happened this weekend. I've been waiting to hear and you never called."

Mara had a front row seat to Alexis' call Saturday evening. She had asked all kinds of questions after Alexis had hung up abruptly and Jenna had promised her answers when she had them. Now she didn't know what she would tell her. Alexis was still out there, hopefully not hurt… or *worse.*

Jenna finished readying for work, relieved that at least she knew where her badge was. Hopefully, Jake had already left for the day. She didn't want any awkward run-ins on her way to her car.

She slid into her driver's seat of her car relieved… and slightly disappointed… that she hadn't seen him on her way out. His truck was already gone. Out of the corner of her eye, she saw a brown paper bag with a note taped to it sitting in the passenger seat.

I'm not good at wrapping. Hope these fit. I took a guess on shoe size. These should be Goose-proof. -Jake

Curiously, she opened the bag to see a pair of grandma style slippers, very pink with a solid inch of rubber on the bottom. Jenna burst into laughter. Maybe Jake *would* be the kind of guy who'd try to wear old man suspenders to church, after all.

When had he put the slippers in her car? Before or after his rescue? Jenna decided to put forth the olive branch.

"Thanks for the slippers," she texted.

A moment later his response came and she bit her lip with a smile.

"They looked comfortable."

She shook her head as she responded with, "I will never slip and fall. They're very … sturdy."

It took a moment for him to respond and Jenna hoped she hadn't sounded ungrateful.

"Why do I feel like that was a slam? Are they not your style?"

Jenna openly laughed out loud. "In about thirty years they just might be."

He sent her a frowny face emoji, but then the dots reappeared as he continued writing a text.

"I'm sorry I was overbearing yesterday. I protect people… it's my job. It's hard not to be protective."

Jenna sighed. *It's my job,* he said. He didn't say, "It's because I like you, Jenna" or "I have feelings for you and I don't want to see you hurt." She needed to let this go now. He was a friend… a *protective* friend. Because it was in his nature to be protective… because it was his *job*.

"I forgive you… don't do it again," she texted and threw her phone back into her purse.

The clock on her dashboard alerted her to the fact that she was now running late to work. Jenna shook her head at her own ridiculousness. *You're wasting so much time on thinking these stupid thoughts about Jake Corey. What's it getting you? Late for work, for starters. Dr. Crenshaw would have you reframe your thoughts. So, reframe your thoughts about Jake.*

"Jake is too old for me," Jenna said out loud. "How old is he? Thirty-five? Yeah… that's *way* too old for me."

A few moments of silence passed and Jenna burst out with, "And he wears cologne that would draw too many other women. Like that Chantille girl. Women can be like mosquitoes drawn to blood with the right cologne on a good looking guy."

She sighed loudly as she pulled into the parking garage at work, swerving to avoid hitting a reckless van as it sped out of the opening.

"*AND…*" she shouted out as if the realization that hit her was the nail in the coffin for her romantic thoughts on Jake Corey. "His job is too dangerous. What would you want with another man that could end up leaving you again too soon. He could die in this line of work… just like Ben."

Funny… When Dr. Crenshaw took her through the reframing exercise, it had always had a more positive effect on Jenna. Now she just felt… *sad.*

Pulling into the spot next to Mara's truck, Jenna realized her friend probably had to enter the building rather than wait for her to hand off her sweater and ID. Jenna was five minutes late for work thanks to her nonsensical crush on Jake Corey. It had to stop.

*****

Jake slipped his phone back into his pocket after checking to see if Jenna had sent any further texts. He enjoyed the playful back and forth bantering with her, but there was an uncertain feeling underlying their chat that distracted him. And Jake could not afford to be distracted by his blue-eyed, firecracker of a tenant.

A call had come in from a family that was fishing at the river's edge just outside of Deer Creek. They were on a family vacation, trying to get the last moments of summer fun in before school started in September. Their campground was located in the same area where Jake had fired off the shot that killed Nick Spencer… or so he had thought. Normally, he didn't get calls in that region, but this one required the attention of both him and his Sergeant.

Thanks to the drought, the father and son had been able to stand on rocks that were normally covered by the moving waters of the river. It afforded them an opportunity to explore a little and what they found confirmed Jake's worst fears. A Kevlar vest with a bullet lodged right in the front center. Jake had a vest identical to it. Most detectives and law enforcement officers did.

"We were just playing around in the dried out part of the riverbed that we don't normally get to see. I saw this sticking out from a cluster of rocks." The father held up the muddied bullet-proof vest.

Branson sighed and leaned over to Jake. "How much do you want to bet that Spencer's name is on that vest somewhere?"

Jake's jaw tightened. He reminded himself that this just confirmed his suspicions. It didn't change anything else. It wasn't new information. He had been correct to tighten up security at the apartments. Stories of the new Broker resembling his old partner, now confirmed the clear truth. Nick Spencer was not only alive, but he was the Broker.

Jake excused himself and pulled out his phone. He had to make sure precautions were taken, especially for the accident-prone key witness.

"Michael. How's married life?" Jake asked his old friend as he took a seat in his truck.

"It's great. I don't know why I fought it for so long. There is no such thing as a boring day with Anna." His friend sounded truly happy. No doubt, Anna kept things lively with her penchant for trouble. And Michael would've had it no other way.

Jake felt a stab of pain. He had loved being married. Loved waking up every morning to the same sleeping angel. Loved coming home to the lights on in the apartment. Loved embracing and feeling the closeness of his wife. *Oh, Beth.*

"Please tell me you're not calling to tell me my sister is acting up," Michael laughed. "Remember… I warned you she is stubborn. Maybe you can tell her to call home once in a while? Mom is doing her best to give her space."

"Yeah. Jenna is… *something*… all right."

"Uh oh. That doesn't sound good." Jake could hear the smile leave Michael's tone. "Is she okay? She's not relapsing is she?"

"No. Nothing like that," Jake assured him. "But she did have an encounter with someone we both thought was long gone."

Michael stayed silent and Jake continued.

"Nick Spencer isn't dead, Michael. Call Cal and get a plan in place for Anna's safety. He's not trying to hide and that tells me one thing… he *wants* us to know he's coming."

*****

Crow looked over the picture of the nurse from his phone. He'd been sitting there on the top level of the parking garage for over an hour, early enough to ensure that he wouldn't miss his target. The picture he had been staring at wasn't the best quality. Just a brunette getting into a truck.

Just then, a truck pulled into a parking spot. It seemed to resemble the one in the picture. An attractive brunette jumped down from the driver's side pulling out a gray sweater from inside the cab. Crow reached for his binoculars and zoomed in to the badge dangling from her cardigan. *Jenna Clark.*

He got out of the van quietly pulling the side hatch open. He grabbed the syringe he'd prepared earlier and followed behind the woman at a brisk pace. She wasn't in a hurry to get inside the building. In fact, she seemed to be waiting for someone… giving him the perfect opportunity to get close enough to inject the needle into her arm.

He pretended to talk to her as if he knew her in case the cameras picked up the exchange. Then he led her carefully to the van and shut the side door as she lay motionless on the floor. *Smooth, Crow. We'll see if I don't get promoted by the Broker before the week is out.*

*****

Jenna's stomach twisted. No one had seen Mara at all that day. She wasn't answering calls or texts. The nurse manager was angry at Mara for skipping work and less than pleased at Jenna for losing her badge. The first part of Jenna's shift was spent arguing with the woman, trying to tell her something had to be wrong with Mara.

"Her truck is parked in the parking garage. She said she'd meet me to give me my ID, but I was running late," Jenna explained. "She wouldn't just disappear. She needs this job and wouldn't jeopardize it."

"Right! Because Mara is the picture of responsibility," the woman rolled her eyes. "The two of you joke around and act like this job isn't all that important to you. If we didn't need nurses so badly…"

Jenna cringed at what her next words might be.

"Just go to HR and get another badge, Clark. Don't lose this one please." With that, the nurse turned and walked away.

A little while later, Jenna re-entered the Emergency Department hoping to find that her friend had just pulled a not-so-funny prank on her. However, there was still no sign of Mara. Jenna had convinced the ER security guards to send someone out to Mara's truck. The nurse manager continued to give her the stink eye, and Jenna knew she had to get to work. She prayed the security guard would find out where her friend had wandered off to so she could put her mind at ease.

Risking the further wrath of her co-workers, Jenna disappeared into the break room. Maybe now was the time to let Jake's over-protective ways get involved.

His phone went to voice mail.

"Nice to know I can count on you in a pinch, Corey," Jenna muttered under her breath before calling the only other person she could think of.

Hopefully, Brian was still working.

"Brian Hamilton's phone." A familiar voice answered, but it was not Brian's.

"Who is this? Where is Brian?" Jenna asked growing nervous.

"Jenna!" The voice sounded surprised. Shocked, in fact. There was an uncomfortable pause before the man spoke again. "He's away from his desk. How can I help you, Darlin'?"

Brian's partner. What was his name? Flirty. Slight southern accent. Kept calling her... *Darlin'*.

"Trip?" Jenna swallowed hard as she recalled the voice of the unknown man at Alexis' house. Could it be? Surely not. *It has to be a coincidence. Right?*

"Wasn't expecting to see your name pop up on Brian's phone." Something in his tone changed slightly.

"I'll call back later," Jenna said in a hurry and hung up.

She began pacing and wringing her hands. There must be a mistake. Jenna had to have heard wrong. A lot of people call women *Darlin'*, right? The door to the lounge opened and Jenna jumped.

"Jenna, you were right," Henry, the Emergency Department guard, burst into the room. "I had the head of security pull the video feed from the garage. Someone grabbed Mara. We called the police. They're on their way."

*****

"You idiot!" Scout yelled at the top of his lungs for the hundredth time at the man tied to the chair. Trip had called him in a rage to alert them to the fact they grabbed the wrong Jenna Clark. Then he demanded that Crow be dealt with immediately. "How hard is it to grab *one* woman?"

"She's the one from the picture," Crow tried to reason coherently with several missing teeth. "Her badge said…"

Scout pointed to the woman curled up in a fetal position on the floor, "*This*… is not Jenna Clark. Now, thanks to you, I have to dispose of *three* bodies before the

Broker gets back… *and* grab the correct nurse. If Damon finds any of this out…"

"*Three* bodies?" One of the other men presiding over the punishment asked.

Scout swallowed hard. "We can't leave witnesses now, can we? Take care of the woman and this idiot."

"And who's the third, Sir?"

"None of your business," Scout scowled.

It hadn't been his intention to develop a fondness for his captive, but it was Alexis' life or his at this point. He couldn't bring himself to kill her the night before. She wasn't even coherent from the beating anyway. He'd wanted one more night to say his goodbyes before taking her out.

Maybe he'd show her mercy and mix up a lethal concoction. She'd started trusting him in the months he had kept her… or maybe she had just become too dependent on the drugs he gave her. He could count on her to inject herself. She wanted them so badly, he no longer needed to do it. Technically, he wouldn't be the one killing her. She'd kill herself by accepting the needle he offered. She'd never see it coming. She'd assume it was just him giving her the next hit. Alexis never turned down a good high.

25

It was the shift that would never end. The police were called. A detective – *not Jake* – showed up to question Jenna and any other possible witnesses. Jenna found herself unsure of who to trust. Jake was the only one she thought she could talk to without fear of giving information to the wrong person. A group of police officers also showed up to aid in the search for Mara. Among them were Brian and Trip.

Jenna tried to busy herself so she wouldn't have to speak to them. Was Trip the man she heard talking at Alexis' house? Jake had warned her that the Broker had inside people on the police force. Surely, Brian wasn't one as well. No. That didn't feel right. Yet, Trip… he gave her a bad feeling in her stomach.

"Jenna…" Someone called her name and she turned to see Brian coming towards her. Trip was not far behind.

"Oh… hey!" Jenna said awkwardly.

"I'm sorry about your friend. Are you okay?" Brian asked, genuine concern written all over his face.

Jenna had sat under his Bible teaching. He prayed and spoke with conviction and a true love for the Lord. He and Helena were safe people. She tried to relax, but her eyes kept shifting from Trip and then to the ceiling.

"I'm… fine. I'm sure she's okay."

"Detective Riles said you were supposed to meet Mara here early?" Brian asked, gently pushing. "Why?"

Trip stood just slightly behind Brian, head cocked and listening intently to whatever she had to say.

"I... I already told the detective everything."

Brian furrowed his brow at her, sensing her hesitation. "I know, but sometimes talking about things can open up something you might've forgotten."

"I need to get back to work, Brian. I'm sorry." Jenna was about to turn away from the officers when a glint in Trip's eyes caught her attention.

Trip's expression of interest and concern shifted to something akin to anger and frustration.

"Why don't we sit down for some coffee, Darlin'," he said moving forward. "Clearly, you're upset. You can talk to us."

He reached out his hand as if he were about to touch her and Jenna jumped back in fear. Her action took both men by surprise. Trip quickly pulled back and pulled his phone from his pocket.

"Excuse me, Hamilton. I need to take this call," he said as he moved only slightly further down the hall.

"Jenna?" Brian's gentle voice brought her eyes back to his. "What aren't you saying?"

"I don't know who to trust." She sounded shaky to her own ears.

Her insides were quivering. What if she was wrong? What if Trip wasn't the man she had heard at Alexis' house? She could accuse an innocent man – a police officer – of something criminal and vile.

"You know you can trust me… please. Tell me what has you upset," Brian urged.

Jenna looked past him down the hall to where Trip stood with the phone at his ear. Something told her that he wasn't talking at all, but listening intently to see if she was going to say something. Jenna looked up at Brian and he turned to look down the hall towards his partner. Did he figure out why she was hesitant? Did he suspect Trip, too?

"Okay, Jenna. I'm going to call Jake. Either he or I will be here when you're done to follow you home. Understand?" Brian's tone was no-nonsense. "Under no circumstance are you to leave this building until one of us are here. Got it?"

Gone was the independent, self-sufficient woman of the day before. Jenna just nodded like a compliant child and moved away to finish her shift.

*****

"Tell me this is getting fixed!" Trip seethed into the phone. "Of all the stupid…"

"It's getting handled. Relax." Scout's anger matched his own.

"Don't tell me to relax!" Trip's rage was at epic heights and about ready to spill over. "That … *junky*… you adopted has made a mess of everything. Somehow, Jenna knows I'm a part of this. The only way she could've known is if your little *toy* told her I was involved."

"And I said I was taking care of it!" Scout yelled into the phone and Trip covered his end with his hand so no one could hear.

Glancing towards Jenna and Brian, the pit in his stomach grew. She kept looking his way and talking in hushed tones, but he could barely hear what they were saying. He didn't need Brian digging where he shouldn't.

"Is she dead yet?" Trip asked in a cold tone. He was done with this conversation. Thankfully, he and Nick went way back. Surely, the Broker would show loyalty to Trip before he would to someone like Scout.

"Yes." Who knew one word could be spoken with so much pain and anguish? "Happy?"

"Delighted." If Trip had been a nicer person – maybe in a different time or a different place – he might have felt bad for the idiot. *Oh well.* "And what about the other woman?"

"She's gone. She tried to run, but Turk shot her. Problem solved," Scout told the man on the other end.

"I need all available resources at my disposal before Nick gets back. Send everyone to the location I am texting for an emergency meeting." Trip sent Scout the location. "You dump the nurse in the woods behind the marina storage units. Your girl can go in the river. Put our guy in the pit with our other fallen brothers. Call me when you are on your way."

"*By myself*? I guess I'm not included in this *meeting* of yours?"

"Yes, by yourself. It's your fault the job had to be given to an imbecile. All because you couldn't keep your girlfriend under control." Trip could gaslight with the best of them. He tried to keep his voice down as a handful of people passed by. "Am I clear, Scout? No more mistakes."

Scout's reply was an angry grunt as the call ended. Trip checked the time. As soon as his shift as an officer ended, he'd have to focus on his *other* job. But first, he'd have to see what – if anything – sweet Jenna told his *partner*.

*****

Alexis lay still on the floor of the van as it bounced over potholes and train tracks through the darkness. Next to her a woman lay in a puddle of blood, motionless. The fresh gunshot wound to her chest bled profusely, but with Scout so close by she knew she couldn't help her. Still, Alexis thought she saw her chest rise and fall in shallow breathing.

"Hang on. Just a little longer," she whispered to the woman.

Without moving too much, Alexis shifted slightly to see Scout at the steering wheel. He mumbled something angrily under his breath. He repeated her name several times as if he were grieving Alexis. Slowly, she reached for a cloth that she had been laying on. Carefully, she pulled it out and reached over to the woman.

She had seen on a television show once someone had applied pressure to a gaping wound. Would that work for a gunshot to the heart? She'd try it regardless. She doubted the rag was clean, but the two ladies were fighting a losing battle anyway. What would it hurt at this point?

Scout believed *her* to be dead as well, so he wouldn't expect Alexis to be moving around behind him. He had trusted her too much. At some point, Scout had stopped injecting her himself and assumed she was addicted enough to inject her own arm with his so-called *special cocktails*. Alexis had stopped injecting herself with the full amount in the needles days ago, slowly tapering from the fentanyl-laced drugs and disposing of the remaining liquid in the syringe onto the floor. This last needle... well, she wasn't dumb. She knew by the way he spoke to her and handed it to her it was probably meant to kill her.

When Alexis saw Jenna in the hospital that day and had been offered a way out, she knew it was time. She had to try to get free. She recalled the lessons she had learned through various treatment centers. She remembered her children. She used the bracelet her sister, Anna, had given her as a reminder of who and what she had to live for. Alexis *had* to survive. She'd live... or die trying.

Movement at the front of the van made her hold her breath. Scout made a phone call and instantly started fighting with that southern demon again. Alexis could hear him yelling on the other end. She knew his voice well. It haunted her nightmares. Trip's voice sounded menacing to her, even muffled and from a distance.

Jenna had wanted to call the cops for help just the other day. If only she knew that there were monsters given the task of protecting the city. Alexis had prayed in earnest that Jenna managed to get away. She thought they had gotten her until they brought *this* woman in. They called her Jenna, but this was not Jenna. It took them a while before they realized their mistake. Did that mean Jenna made it away safely?

The conversation grew angrier and Scout hung up and threw his phone down in a rage. It bounced off the middle console and hit her on the head. A small smile lifted her lips. If she could pocket his phone, she'd be able to call for help. *What was the name of that detective that Jenna trusted? Corey something.*

The van came to a sudden stop and Alexis' eyes flew to the other woman. Scout opened his door and slid out of the van. Taking the cloth away from the wound, Alexis tucked the cloth back under her body to conceal it.

"Hang on," Alexis repeated. "I'll try to get you help."

The sliding door opened and Alexis put her face down into the carpet of the van's floor, holding her breath. Scout needed to believe she was dead for this plan to work.

"Come on. Let's get this over with," Scout said as he lifted the bleeding woman in his arms.

Alexis wondered if the woman had died already. She was growing sallow in color with each passing moment. Maybe it was too late after all. Alexis chanced a quick peek and relaxed when she saw the woman's pinky finger move ever so slightly. Was she playing dead, too?

Scout carried the woman out of view. Now was Alexis' chance. Grabbing the phone that had fallen, she pressed 9-1-1 and slowly started moving to the edge of the van's open door, dragging herself through the puddle of sticky blood. Alexis resisted the urge to wretch and pressed on. She saw him carry the woman to a wooded area on the side of the road. While his back was to her, she made her move.

Vaguely, she heard the dispatcher ask what her emergency was. Hopefully, Scout was so engrossed in his job that he didn't hear as well. Alexis made it to the opposite side of the street before bringing the phone to her face.

"Help. There's a woman with a gunshot wound to the chest. We're on a road behind Skennan Marina's storage buildings," Alexis said as she took in the large metal buildings used to store boats during the colder months.

"Ma'am, what is your name? Do you know the address? Are *you* okay? Do you see any other landmarks?" the person on the other end asked questions in rapid fire succession.

"Can you track this call? I'll leave the phone on and drop it here. Please hurry. She's not going to make it."

Alexis placed the phone face down so the light wouldn't catch Scout's attention. Slowly, she began backing away into the trees and ran as fast as she could towards the lights of the town. Behind her she heard the angry yell of the man who had held her captive and the sound of the van coming back to life. The headlights were approaching and Alexis did the only thing she knew to do. She went flat on her belly in the overgrowth and prayed with all that she had left.

*****

It was almost eleven o'clock when the ER received word that a gunshot victim was incoming via ambulance. Everyone was on high alert, nerves still raw over what happened to Mara. The tension had been palpable all evening and Jenna wanted to fall onto the floor in tears. Maybe she needed to go back home. Not her apartment. Her home in Deer Creek. She yearned for her mother's arms around her. To hear her father say it was going to be okay. She'd even put up with her brothers' nonsense without complaining. Maybe she'd allowed too much distance to form between her and her family over the past months.

The doors opened and a collective gasp rippled through those standing ready to jump into action. *Mara!* The EMT that ran alongside the stretcher spouted off her weak vitals. She was barely hanging on, but she was alive. Jenna couldn't move. Everyone bustled around Jenna, doing their respective jobs. Yet, Jenna stood transfixed, staring at her blood-soaked friend.

"Clark!" The nurse manager's voice broke through the chaos as she grabbed Jenna's arm. "Jenna, go home. Clock out."

The words were spoken sternly, but there was a hint of kindness to them. The older nurse's expression looked as terrified as Jenna felt inside.

"I want… I want to stay here with her."

"No. You know you'll just get in the way. Go on. We'll talk tomorrow."

Jenna didn't know how she was holding it together. She got her things from her locker and walked to the exit of the Emergency Department. She did all of this without breaking down. Yet, when the doors slid open and she saw Jake leaning against his truck waiting for her, she dissolved.

He moved towards her and she fell against him, sobbing into his chest. His arms came up and encircled her and she felt his warm breath on her hair.

"I called you. You're really bad at answering your phone," she whimpered into his shirt.

"I'm sorry. I got called away." He just held her for a moment, letting her soak his shirt with her tears. Jenna would've pulled back, but he soothed her and she really needed his embrace a little while longer.

"Shh. It's going to be okay. Brian told me what happened." Jake's voice resounded with deep emotion. "I'm so sorry."

She felt his hand on the back of her head, cradling her gently. She didn't know if she truly believed it was going to be okay, but in his arms she felt safe… cared for… protected… *His*.

26

There wasn't enough coffee in the state of New York to satiate Jake Corey's need for caffeine that Tuesday morning. His head spun with random pieces of information he had been given the night before. After getting all of his tenants under one roof Monday evening, Jake pulled Jenna aside to hopefully shed some light on what was going on.

It had taken some prodding, but Jenna finally opened up about Alexis. Jake could see her go back and forth in her mind about whether or not she should divulge Alexis' situation. However, she finally decided it was worth the risk if it saved the woman's life.

Jake tried to keep himself in check as Jenna told him how she had gotten a ride to the house Alexis was being kept. She told him she was forced to hide in a closet filled with, what she described as, "big guns". And if that weren't enough, someone stalked her around the convenience store. Maybe Jenna had sensed his growing displeasure, because she became tightlipped rather quickly when he had asked about the men she encountered at Alexis' house.

"Hey, what's that scowl?" Brian asked showing up at Jake's desk. The two often had lunch together when time allowed.

"Just thinking about last night," Jake answered as he opened the side drawer of his desk and grabbed his wallet.

Brian nodded in understanding. "Let's go talk. I have some *concerns* myself."

With a sigh, Jake let his head drop. Of course he did. Jake had sensed his friend was holding something back as well the previous night, but with Jenna present he didn't share.

"What do you have for me, Hamilton?" Jake asked as soon as he sat in Brian's passenger seat.

"No burgers first? No fries? Just right to the tough stuff, huh?"

"I like getting the negative out of the way. Then we can find a solution over the burger and fries." Jake smiled.

With a curt nod, Brian began. "I noticed something off about Jenna last night that has been bothering me. She was holding something back when we came to talk to her at the hospital."

"Well, her friend *was* kidnapped. Could it have been her concern over Mara?" Jake played devil's advocate, but he knew there was more to it.

"She wouldn't have acted that way with me. I'd like to think we've developed a friendship over the past couple months with her living in the apartments and attending our life group." Brian shook his head as he talked. Then he sighed and said what was really on his mind. "I think it has something to do with Trip."

"Trip? What about him?" Jake furrowed his brow. Jenna hadn't acted oddly the day she met Trip at the apartment… the day she moved in. Had he missed some interaction between the two of them?

"When I saw her at the ER, she looked sad and worried for her friend… like I'd expect her to be. However, when she looked over at *us* her whole face changed," Brian said pulling into the drive-thru line. "It was as if she was *scared*. Not just scared for her friend, but scared of *us*."

"Still… it could be just her processing what happened to Mara."

"Well, I thought so, too. But then Trip left to take a call and she visibly relaxed. She kept looking behind me at him as if she didn't want him to hear."

"Is Trip acting any weirder than he normally does?" Jake smirked. Trip was a lot of things. Goofy. Obsessed with the ladies. But he wasn't a criminal. When the department investigated and purged all of the threats, Trip remained. He never raised any flags.

Brian ceased talking long enough to order their food before continuing. "When we were home she acted just fine around me. I'm telling you… something about Trip has her shutting down."

Jake digested Brian's words as they collected their food from the window. "Trip can be a flirt. Maybe he went too far after they met? Maybe he tried calling or texting her? Jenna is … *reluctant*… to date again. If he pushed her too far that might explain her reaction to him."

Brian burst out laughing despite the seriousness of their conversation. "*Reluctant*? And how would you know she's *reluctant* to date again, Corey?"

"Leave it alone, Brian. Just pray for the food," Jake ordered. His friend blessed the meal and the car was silent momentarily as they enjoyed their first bites.

Yet, Brian kept smiling like a fool. "If what you think is true... maybe Jenna's *reluctance* of Trip is because her heart belongs to someone else?"

"Yeah. Her deceased husband." Jake shot him a look.

"Hmm. But what if..."

"But what?" Jake glowered. This conversation was taking an unwanted turn.

Brian threw up his hands in amused defeat. "Nothing. Never mind. *Geesh* are you touchy or what?"

Jake sighed and brought his mind back to the topic at hand.

"When we get back I'll try to catch Jenna before she heads in to work. Maybe she'll talk a little more today now that she's rested," Jake decided. Trip had been their neighbor and friend for years. If he was somehow involved... Jake's gut twisted at the thought. He'd been betrayed before, but with each occurrence it was getting harder and harder to bounce back.

*****

No one would let her borrow their phone. She had begged for help… for food… water… *anything*, but was met with sneers and hurtful comments. Some threatened to call the police on her. Most just gave her a side-eye and walked on by her. Alexis didn't blame them. She was wearing dirty clothes smeared with the blood of the woman from the van. It didn't matter that she had found a gas station bathroom to wash her skin free of the crimson streaks, she still looked horrific. People avoided her.

After sitting through sermon after sermon given by her father on topics like the *Good Samaritan* and loving one's neighbor, she found herself doubting that humanity had the capacity for compassion at all. She couldn't go to her usual places for help, like soup kitchens or the women's shelter. Desperation set in.

Guilt stabbed her as she remembered how she found an unlocked car containing a zippered hoodie. She had to disguise herself as best as she could. Scout and those evil monsters that he worked with had eyes everywhere and she had to stay in the shadows. Hidden. Concealed. So, she stole the hoodie from the car along with a bottle of water and loose change that she found in the console.

It took her all night and most of the next day to make it to the police department where Anna's and Jenna's friend worked. How would she find him and not run into Trip? Trip's face floated into her mind and she shivered. That southern drawl must charm the women. Sweet as honey, but poisonous like venom.

Alexis had once given up on the miraculous, but it was nothing less than a miracle that she had managed to hide in the woods from Scout. She had sobbed tears of relief when the van pulled away from her location. Maybe God could spare her one or two more of those miracles. How was she going to find this Corey guy?

She leaned against the brick wall of a building across the street from the police department. Despite the late summer heat, Alexis pulled the hoodie up over her hair to conceal her face as best as she could. The minute she walked through those doors, she would be walking into enemy territory. *Please, God. I can't do this on my own.*

Her hands shook violently as the withdrawal symptoms attacked her. She had gone over twenty-four hours without one of Scout's injections. Even though she had been weaning herself over the past several days, she was not prepared to go cold turkey. If she didn't get help soon…

A car pulled up and parked on the sidewalk in front of her. The car doors opened and two men got out, sending her slinking a little further into the crevice between buildings. One of them made eye contact with her and she quickly looked away. He didn't give her a look of disgust or loathing. There was a hint of concern. Tenderness, with a kind smile.

"Alright, Corey. You call Jenna and see what is going through her head," the other man said. "Maybe you'll have better success than I did finding out what has her so freaked out."

Did he say *Corey*? Alexis wasn't sure if her crazy next move stemmed from her raging withdrawal or if it was boldness, but she called out to the men.

"Corey? Do you know Jenna… and Anna?"

Both men looked up at her, startled. She had been around a few cops in her day to know they were ascertaining whether she was a threat. The one dressed in uniform had his arm raised slightly at his side as if waiting to see if he needed to reach for his taser. The man dressed in regular clothes just looked at her curiously.

"And you are?" His eyes were still kind, but he was definitely scrutinizing her.

Alexis looked to the other man and nodded in his direction. "Is he trustworthy? I know one too many of you cops that aren't good people."

To her surprise, the other officer's posture relaxed and he forced a pleasant smile. "How can we help you?"

"Jenna told me to find someone named Corey. Is that you?" Alexis felt her legs growing weak under their gazes. Surely, they could see her tremors.

"Yes, *I'm* Jake Corey." The man moved closer and Alexis considered darting down the alley as he approached. He must've sensed her trepidation because he paused and raised his hand as if he approached a cornered animal.

"Is Jenna safe?" she finally managed to ask. "They didn't get her, did they?"

Corey's face softened even more. No wonder Jenna said he was one of the good guys. It radiated off of him.

"She's safe, Alexis. She's been worried about you."

"You know my name. She told you about me?" Alexis felt a lump in her throat rise to the surface.

"Both she and Anna have. Your family misses you very much. How can we help you?"

"And… and… that other girl? Is she alive? I called the police, but I don't trust all of them." Alexis flicked a glance at the other man who stood still.

"What other girl?"

"The girl!" Alexis voice raised slightly as desperation started winning over her composure. "You know, she was shot. I called the police. Is she okay? They thought she was Jenna."

"She was alive last time we checked in." This came from the other man. "You're the one who called? You saved her life!"

Alexis felt tears burn her eyes. "She's alive."

Both men nodded. But the man named Corey was the next to speak. His face took on a look of fear. "Alexis, you said they thought the woman was Jenna. Who are they?"

"Scout… Trip… All of them." Her head hurt and she brought her hands up to try to rub the pain away.

"Did you say *Trip*?" the other officer asked quietly from his place.

"They can't get to Anna. I can't let them."

"Hey, Alexis." Corey took a chance and came to stand right in front of her. She tried to look him in the face, but her eyes couldn't seem to focus on one spot. "Will you let me get you help?"

"What… what kind? What if they drag me back? They'll kill me this time. They'll kill my family. They said they would." Of course, she wanted help, but what if she messed it up again? What if she failed? "I want to go home… back to my family, but I can't."

"No. We'll make sure you are safe, okay? Let me call in a few favors. Do you trust me?" Jake Corey's voice seemed to break through the chaos in her mind.

"I don't think I have a choice."

Jake gave her a gentle smile. "My truck is around the corner. Brian, can you give us a lift to my truck?"

"Of course."

She nodded and let him move her away from the alley and to the car. Alexis had two choices: trust that they were as good as they seemed or run for her life. If she ran, she was as good as dead. Scout or one of the others would find her eventually. One choice offered her hope, the other certain death. If she was wrong, she'd be dead soon anyway. Alexis chose to hope again.

*****

He hadn't eaten. He hadn't slept in days. If he did sleep, the nightmares assailed him. Nick moved his body wrong and his ribs felt like they might burst through his skin. If not for the binder that he wore, they probably would've. His other wounds, covered under adhesive bandages, kept catching on his clothing or chest hair.

Yet, Nick walked down the rollaway steps at the small aircraft's door and did his best to look composed, despite the rage festering inside of him. He could feel the eyes of the man behind him, boring into the back of his skull. They let him live. Nick surmised he was supposed to be grateful for that. *How gracious of them.*

Damon fed him to the wolves. He supposed the vacation of torture was to teach him a lesson. Oh, he had learned a lesson, but probably not what Damon had intended. From now on, Nick was on a single mission and loyal only to himself. He was done.

"They're unloading the cargo into the trucks from your trip, Broker. Any further instruction, Sir?" This came from Scout. His tone… His demeanor was off. Nick cast him a glance and noticed he looked sketchy as well.

"Where's Trip? I want filled in… *NOW*!"

"Yes, Sir. He's waiting for you in the car." Scout paused, causing Nick to pause as well. Nick cast him a questioning look. "About Trip, Sir…"

Scout's voice went low and Nick braced for whatever Scout was about to tell him.

"He's going to tell you that I did not do my part while you were away. It's a lie. He was trying to take over… like he thought he was *you* or something."

The back door of the SUV opened and Trip emerged.

"Welcome back, Stranger. We have a lot to discuss," he said under his breath as he slid in to the middle, allowing Nick the window seat.

Scout moved to the front seat to sit next to the driver that Damon had sent.

"Join us, Scout," Nick said menacingly. "There's plenty of room."

Both Scout and Trip looked uncertain, but dared not voice it. Nick was grateful for the cover of his sunglasses. His bloodshot, twitching eyes would give away any façade he tried to portray. Scout reluctantly moved to the side of the car and squeezed in next to Trip. Both men were clearly displeased at being so close to one another.

"Scout, you go first," Nick ordered as soon as the car pulled away from the air strip. Trip opened his mouth to protest, but the Broker made a point to pull out his gun – that Damon's men finally returned to him – and rested it on his lap.

Scout began telling Nick a horrible story of botched jobs and mistaken identities. When Trip tried to interject, all the Broker had to do was snap a finger and he went quiet. He evened out his breathing before returning to Scout.

"Let me get this straight," he said, clearing his throat. "Trip gave *you* one task to complete and you couldn't see it through? And now she's running free somewhere? And what about Jenna Clark … did *either* of you finally get her? Is she waiting for me at the warehouse like I had asked?"

Trip held his breath from his spot in between them. Nick would deal with him next.

"No… *but* …" Scout stammered.

"Trip, sit back."

The man complied. Nick pulled his gun and shot directly into Scout's chest.

"Pull down this road," Nick told the driver who looked at him quizzically from the rear view. "*Now*!"

The driver pulled down a road that was no more than gravel and trees.

"Stop here," Nick barked.

Trip nonchalantly wiped at the sleeve of his shirt that now was marked by crimson splatter. "You couldn't have pulled over first and taken him outside, Nick?"

"Shut up. Open the door and get him out."

Trip complied without delay. Good thing or the Broker would've put one in his chest as well. The day was still young. After Scout was rolled out of the car and left on the side of the road, the driver waited for the order to get back on the main thoroughfare.

"You better tell me something to make me smile, Trip, or I swear you are next."

"Don't worry, Nick. I've got a plan."

Trip started to spill the details, but Nick held up his hand to stop the conversation. His eyes darted to the driver, then back to his old friend from his police department days. Under his breath he uttered, "Later. After we get some place secure."

Glancing back at the man behind the wheel, Trip nodded in understanding. The rest of the ride was quiet as Nick tried to control his breathing. Nick was well aware his days were numbered and that was fine with him. Somewhere in the back of his mind, he knew this obsession of his would be a suicide mission and end in his death. And he didn't care, as long as Jake Corey joined him.

27

Jake texted Jenna, asking her to take off of work. That wasn't going to happen, not if she wanted to stay in the hospital's good graces. Then he asked her to stay put until he or Brian was able to see her safely to work. He didn't go into detail as to why. However, after the events of the past several days, she concluded a ride to work wouldn't hurt. Mara had been taken in broad daylight from the parking garage.

Jenna agreed to the overprotective measures, until a friend from work called and told her that Mara had stirred and said Jenna's name. She'd asked for her. Understandably, they couldn't give her any details of Mara's condition over the phone. Her only option was to go in to the hospital early.

She had texted Jake several times and surprise, surprise, surprise… no answer. Was she supposed to just sit and wait for him to show up? What if she missed her opportunity to talk to Mara before her shift began?

Jenna knocked on the Hamiltons' door.

"Hey, Jenna. Come on in. I was just getting ready to sit down and have some tea," Helena said warmly.

"I would love to join you, but I need to get to work early. Have you heard from Jake? Or has Brian mentioned anything following me to work?" Jenna asked in a rush.

"No. I know they were going to have lunch together today, but I hadn't heard anything else." Helena furrowed her brow. "Is everything okay? Did something happen? You seem anxious."

"Mara woke up, and if I am going to get to see her before I start work, I need to leave now. But Jake told me to wait for one of them to take me in or follow behind me, just to be safe." Jenna threw her hands up in frustration. "Now I'm regretting agreeing to it. Him and his blasted overprotectiveness!"

"I'm so glad to hear your friend woke up! We sent out a prayer request within the group. We didn't give details, I promise," Helena assured. "Just that it was an emergency."

"Thank you for that," Jenna said sincerely. "All I know is that she woke up briefly. I won't know her condition until I get there."

The two women stood in indecision for a moment. "I'd give you a ride myself, but I just put Tori down for her nap. Do you want me to text Brian?" Helena asked apologetically.

"No. Don't worry about it." Jenna shook her head and glanced down at her phone. "I may just risk making Jake mad and…"

Jenna froze, gaze still on her screen.

"And what?" Helena asked when Jenna remained silent for a few moments. "Jenna? Are you okay? I really think you need to wait for Jake."

"Um, I think I have a solution." Jenna couldn't believe her eyes at the text she had just received.

It read, "I hope this is the right house or someone is going to call the cops on me. I'm pretty sure that's your car. I know I should've called, but I wanted to surprise you."

Chase!

"Excuse me, Helena! I have to go!" Jenna flashed her friend a smile and flew down the stairs to the door, throwing it wide open.

There, just a few feet away, stood her and Ben's old friend dressed in military fatigues and sporting a cheesy grin on his face.

"Chase! What in the world are you doing here?" Jenna didn't know what to feel. Part of her wanted to strangle him for his silence. The other part wanted to hug him because seeing him reminded her so much of Ben… then other memories started flooding back. She stood on the porch in indecision. "You know I hate surprises."

"I know, but I couldn't resist." He moved closer carefully as if he was taking her in, assessing her overall condition. "You … you look amazing, Jenna. Lighter than when I saw you last, that's for sure."

Jenna sighed and nodded ever so slightly. "Well, come on up. I'll give you a quick tour, but then I have a massive favor to ask of you."

"I've been here all of five minutes and already you're proposing?" Chase teased as he came in the front entry. "Fine. I accept. I *will* marry you, Jenna Clark."

Jenna rolled her eyes and tugged on his arm. Then she noticed Helena still at her door. Her face was slightly amused, but also apprehensive about the stranger climbing the steps.

"Helena, this is Chase. He is a dear *friend* of mine and Ben's." Jenna introduced, enunciating certain words over others. "And, Chase, this is Helena. She and her husband Brian are my *new* dear friends. She makes the best Hawaiian pizza."

"I will try not to hold that against you." Chase nodded politely. He seemed to have lost some of his excitement, however. "It's nice to meet you."

Helena returned the smile and looked at Jenna curiously.

"We'll talk later. I promise." Jenna gave her arm a squeeze, knowing that her friend would pepper her with questions as soon as an opportunity presented itself.

Jenna led Chase to her apartment and showed him the main living area. "What do you think? Not bad, huh?"

He let out a slow whistle as he moved to the large windows overlooking the river. "You weren't kidding about the view. Very nice, Jenna."

"Thank you. Now, what are you doing here? And why didn't you call?" Jenna slapped his arm in reprimand. "I haven't heard even a hello from you in … forever."

"Not forever. Weeks," Chase corrected.

"A month, at least."

"I'm sorry. Things have been moving rapidly and I was busy in trainings." Chase looked sheepish. "I meant to call you as soon as I made it to Fort Drum, but…"

"Fort Drum? You're stationed *here*?" Jenna wasn't sure how to feel about that. Just then she noticed the shoulder sleeve insignia on his uniform sporting the two crossed bayonets.

"Well, quite a drive from here, but … yeah. Definitely closer than North Carolina." His tone took a soft, hopeful lilt. "Are you happy to see me?"

"Of course I am." Jenna hoped the words didn't sound as uncertain as she felt.

Chase opened his arms wide, inviting her to enter into an embrace. Awkwardly, Jenna gave her friend a side lean and patted his midsection.

"Is Fort Drum feeding you okay? You seem smaller than I remember," she chuckled nervously before pushing away.

The hurt was evident in his expression. This was not the reception he had hoped for, clearly. Jenna had wondered so many times what it would be like to be near Chase again. Would her platonic feelings for him change?

Could she get past the past and explore something new with Chase? Now she knew. She couldn't. However, it wasn't Ben's face floating into her mind this time causing her to falter.

Chase sighed, cleared his throat, and seemed to gather his composure. "So, you said you had a favor? What can I help you with?"

Jenna realized how uncomfortable things had become in a matter of minutes, making her request feel wrong to even ask. "Never mind. It wasn't anything important."

"Jenna, you're forgetting I know you pretty well." He smirked. "Just ask. I'm fine. I promise."

She looked at him, uncertain, until he finally burst out laughing.

"Ask it already, Woman!"

"I needed a ride to the hospital. I have a shift that starts soon and…"

"A ride? That's it?" Chase smiled as he started fishing the keys from his pocket.

Jenna nodded, biting her lower lip apprehensively.

"Sure. No problem. Let's go. We'll finish catching up on the way."

"Chase, are you sure? You drove all this way to see me and…"

"I'm sure. Now, move it before you're late. Move. Move. Move." His voice was authoritative like he was ordering one of his soldiers to action then finished the tirade with a playful smile.

Jenna rolled her eyes, grabbed her work bag, and left her apartment. She was locking her door when she heard the downstairs apartment door open. Helena peeked out.

"Are you okay?" she asked. "I heard loud voices."

"Yes. I'm fine. Chase is giving me a lift to work. I'll call Jake on the way to let him know… *if* he answers, that is."

She could tell Helena had more she wanted to say, but to her friend's credit, she stayed quiet. Chase, however, shot his questions in rapid fire succession as soon as they were on the road.

"So, who is Jake? Why doesn't he answer his phone for you? Why the weird cloak and dagger looks between you and your friend? Do I need to have a chat with this guy?"

Jenna just shook her head. "He's my landlord. I've told you about him."

"The old guy?"

"He's not old," Jenna chuckled softly. Then she addressed his other queries. "He's a cop, so he's busy a lot. That's why he doesn't answer his phone. And what *cloak and dagger* looks?"

"Oh, I see how it is." Chase let out a chagrined laugh.

"What?"

"You *like* him." Chase shook his head. "It's obvious. That goofy smile on your face. That weird way you just said *he's a cop and that's why he doesn't answer his phone*."

"Whatever, Chase." Jenna rolled her eyes as she pulled out her phone and started calling Jake.

"Is that his contact picture? Let me see…" Chase glanced over momentarily at her phone and shook his head. "I didn't stand a chance, did I?"

"Turn left here." Jenna instructed before adding, "What in the world are you talking about?"

"It's all over your face. You're blushing," Chase observed. Then, he sighed and bowed his head as if resigning himself to the truth. "So, tell me about this guy. Is he worthy of you?"

"Is he worthy of me?" Jenna snorted as she repeated his question. How did she explain the complexity she found herself in? Should she even try? "It's not quite like that, Chase. Turn right at the light."

Chase complied and waited for Jenna to continue her explanation.

"It's… *complicated*. And there is enough on my mind right now that I don't want to go there, okay?"

Chase shrugged. "Fine, but if he hurts you..."

Jenna called Jake and sent Chase a warning glare for him to stay quiet.

"Hey, Jenna." Jake answered at the first ring.

"You actually answered. It's a modern day miracle."

"Well, I changed your ringtone in my phone settings to know when it was *you* calling over some other mere commoner," Jake explained.

Chase heard the exchange and made quiet gagging noises from his seat, earning him another swat on the arm from Jenna.

"You did that?" Jenna tried not to gush and turned her face and phone towards the window, away from Chase's view.

"Yeah… *Flight of the Bumblebee* seemed fitting." Jenna could hear the amusement in his voice as she felt a tiny stab of disappointment.

"Ha! That's a good one," Chase laughed out loud.

Jake cleared his throat. "Who is that?"

"Uh… that is Chase. Remember me telling you about him?" Jenna motioned for Chase to pull into the hospital parking garage. "He surprised me with a visit and I got him to take me to work early… so you're off the hook."

Jake went silent momentarily and then cleared his throat. "I was hoping we could talk. There are some new *developments*."

"Did you hear that Mara woke up? Is that what you're referring to? She's been asking for me. That's why I'm going in early."

"She woke up? That's great!" Jake sounded sincerely surprised before he went back to his usual guarded tone.

"But there's a couple other things we need to talk about. Are you already at work?"

"I'm in the parking garage as we speak, getting ready to go in. Can it wait until later?"

Jake sighed. "That depends, are you actually going to wait for me to pick you up this time or are you going to get a ride with someone else?"

Jenna's mouth drew into a tight line. Normally, she could tell when Jake was teasing. This didn't sound humorous. He sounded *irritated*… at *her*. Glancing over at Chase she saw his eye brows were raised in curious amusement.

"Forgive me if I couldn't wait for you all day, Jake Corey." Jenna tried to control her rising ire. "Mara was asking for me. If Chase hadn't shown up I would've driven myself… regardless of what we had agreed on."

Jake didn't respond so Jenna continued, "I will also remind you that I am perfectly capable of taking care of myself."

"I'm well aware, Jenna. We'll talk later," was Jake's clipped response.

With that the call was over and Chase let out a slow whistle.

"What?" Jenna snapped at him.

"It all makes sense now."

"What does?" Jenna asked as she gathered her things.

"The two of you… you're in love. He's jealous."

Jenna burst into sardonic laughter, trying to read Chase's face to see if he was serious.

"No. You have no idea what you're talking about. It's nothing even close to that." She shook her head vehemently, but inside she wasn't so sure. "Like I said … it's complicated."

"Oh, I'm sure it is." Chase smirked. "Relationships always are."

"Thank you for the ride, Chase," Jenna said softly. "And I'm sorry we haven't gotten a chance to talk."

"It's my fault for not calling ahead. I'm glad I got to see you. It's put my mind at ease."

Jenna just looked at him. "How so?"

"You're cared for. Even if it's not by me, I can step back now." His words were spoken resolutely, but sadly.

"Chase, I'm…"

He smiled at her and waved her on. "Get to work, Nurse Clark."

Jenna smiled softly at him and gave him a pretend salute. "Yes, Sir."

"Jenna," he called out before she shut the door.

She paused and looked at him.

"If he screws up, I'm next in line."

*****

Jenna paused at the entry of the glass walled room in the ICU wing. Machines beeped. Wires were everywhere. And there in the middle of it all was Mara, pale except for the heinous bruises all over her face and arms. She looked tiny against the mountain of pillows behind her. An oxygen mask covered her face.

The scene before her unnerved Jenna. The bullet had just missed her heart and they had been able to remove it. However, Mara still had a long road a ahead. How did one just bounce back after something like that?

"She's in and out of consciousness, but each time she wakes up she asks for you," the nurse said warmly. "Go ahead in. It's okay."

Reluctantly, Jenna obeyed and took a seat near Mara's slightly turned face. She reached her hand out and rested it on her friend's arm, causing her eyelids to flutter. They parted revealing sluggish, swollen eyes.

"Jenna…"

"Hey, Mara. You really have a way of scaring people, you know that? If you wanted the day off there were better ways to go about it." Jenna tried to tease, but she knew her tone and the tears falling from her eyes betrayed her. Was this how her parents and brothers felt standing above *her* all those years ago? Regret and guilt stabbed Jenna in the heart.

Mara was weak, but she seemed insistent on talking.

"Jenna…"

"Shh. I'm here. You're safe."

Mara shook her head and tried to form words.

"Mara, save your energy. I know the police will want to talk to you. Don't waste it on me."

Just then, Mara used what strength she had to grab Jenna's hand and squeeze.

"Not… safe."

"I promise you are. No one can get to you here." Jenna hated the terror in her friend's eyes. What had she endured at the hands of her captors?

"You… Jenna. They want… *you*."

28

Trip pulled up to his former home. Was he taking a chance? Yes. Could this little mission backfire on him? Most definitely. Trip was banking that Brian and Jake hadn't caught on to his involvement with the Broker. Jenna's countenance when he and Brian arrived at the hospital had unnerved him, but Brian did not act as if he had picked up on it. One thing was for certain, Trip needed to know what if anything they did know. And there was no time to play around.

A plan was formed. Now he just needed to put it in place. He *could* go right into the building with the keys he had copied from his old set. He had handed the originals back to Jake, but not before making a spare in case he needed them, assuming Jake hadn't changed the locks yet. The problem was… Helena and her little girl. They were *always* home.

Thankfully, in the years he lived in the top apartment, Helena had adopted Trip as a baby brother. His visit might not be viewed as suspicious to her. Especially, if he came bearing gifts. He pulled out his phone and dialed.

"Hello?" the soft spoken voice answered.

"Helena? Hey, Darlin'. It's Trip." He waited with bated breath to see how his call would be received. Helena wore her emotions out there for everyone to see. If she was nervous around Trip, he would know right away.

"Trip! Oh, my word! I was just thinking of you the other day. I made peanut butter cookies and I know you love those," Helena's voice made him smile. "I meant to send some with Brian for you, but pregnancy brain strikes again."

He knew a moment of guilt. Brian and Helena had always been like family to him. He could do without Jake and his overbearingness, but the Hamiltons were good people. He wouldn't hurt them. He'd just use them as a means to an end. Trip needed the money more than he needed friends at that moment.

Jake had given him *some* grace when it came to rent, but, when he got several months behind, Jake had insisted he find a new place to live. The Hamiltons offered to loan him the money to catch up, but Trip had played it off like moving was what he had wanted to do all along. He even let Jake think there were no hard feelings… that they were still friends. Then Nick approached him and promised him more money than he'd know what to do with. Enough to pay off the men he'd gotten entangled with. All he'd have to do was betray Jake.

Pushing the unpleasantness of guilt away, he walked to the front door with a bouquet and a brightly colored gift bag.

"Do you have any of those cookies left? Because I happen to be downstairs at the door and would absolutely love one."

"You're *here*?" she laughed. "I think Brian ate the last of them yesterday."

Through the thin curtain on the window, Trip watched as there was movement at the top of the stairway. Helena stood there waving at him just as friendly as ever.

"I brought a little something for Stinkerbell. If I remember correctly her birthday is next week." Trip laid it on thick. He held the gift bag up so Helena could see.

"Give me a minute," Helena chuckled and ended the call.

Trip watched the very pregnant woman make her way down to the door and tucked his phone in his pocket. As soon as the door opened, Helena gave him a touched expression and said, "Aren't you just so sweet?"

"Aww, well. You know me… sweet and awesome." He handed the bag to Helena and she peeked at the teddy bear inside.

"She'll love it. Thank you, Trip." Helena smiled warmly. "I'd invite you up but she's asleep and Brian isn't home yet."

Then, it was as if a light went off in her head. "Aren't you and Brian working together today? You could've just given this to him to bring home."

"I took today off. I was out doing errands when I realized Tori's birthday was coming up. I figured I would drop it off on the way to my appointment."

Helena nodded showing no concern at all.

"Anyway, have you *met* your husband?" Trip laughed. "How much do you want to bet that this would be in the back seat of his car for a week before he remembered I handed it to him?"

She laughed in agreement causing him to relax.

All of a sudden, Helena's face became mischievous. Her eyes landed on the bouquet that Trip still grasped. "And those flowers? Are those for Tori, too?"

"No, Darlin'. These are for Jenna. She had a rough day yesterday. Is she here?"

"No. She has already left for work, but I'm sure she'll appreciate those when she gets back tonight." Helena smiled.

"Oh, well… I was hoping she could put these in water right away. I'd hate for them to wilt." Trip feigned concern.

"I'll take them up to her apartment and put them in a vase. She won't mind." Helena accepted the roses. Trip hoped that the little bug he inserted inside one of the blooms would stay in place.

"Alright then. Thank you for taking those up. Give Stinkerbell a hug for me," Trip said as he took a step backward and prepared to leave. Then Helena said something that caught his attention.

"Jenna will really appreciate these. Especially after what happened to her friend. Praise God, she woke up! I know Jenna was really worried sick."

Trip almost fell over the step on the porch.

"Her friend? The one we had gotten a call about? The kidnapped nurse?" His throat felt dry. "She's okay?"

"For the moment, she is. That's why Jenna went in early. Her friend was desperate to talk to her," Helena said with a concerned face. "Who would do that to someone?"

Trip tried to school his features. "It's a cruel world, Darlin'. You better get back up to your little one and lock the door behind you."

Helena smiled and waved goodbye to Trip as he moved to his car. The other girl survived… and she was talking. If Scout weren't already dead, Trip would've killed him. Nick would not like this one bit. He drove a little further down the road to a children's play park and opened his laptop. If his plan was successful he'd soon have audio.

Almost immediately, the sound of little toddler giggles came over his speaker.

"Look, Tori. Look what Uncle Trip brought for you!" Helena soothed.

"Bear! My Bear!"

The sounds became muted and Trip assumed the bear's mic was probably crushed against the chest of the innocent little girl. He pulled out his phone and dialed Nick.

"Hey, Boss. We're up and running with audio."

"Good. Keep on it and report if anything interesting comes up."

Trip paused. "Uh… Nick… we have another loose end from Scout that needs fixed."

"What loose end?" Trip could hear the seething in Nick's question.

"The nurse. She's alive and talking."

"Fix it."

"Nick, you know I can't just walk into a hospital and…" Trip shook his head. He was in a precarious position, having one foot in the police department and one foot in Nick's world.

"I said, fix it."

Trip felt rage starting to creep up inside of him. This was not what he had envisioned. Nick had promised to get him vetted to work closely under Damon… that hadn't happened yet. What was worse, his creditors still weren't paid.

"What's in this for me, Spencer? When will I get that windfall of money you promised?"

"What's in it for *you*?" Nick's laugh made Trip's blood run cold. "You get to live… unlike Scout."

There was no room for argument as Nick ended the call. Trip weighed his options. Nick was becoming more and more unhinged. Not for the first time, Trip wondered how he had gotten himself tangled up in this mess. More importantly, how was he going to get himself out of it?

*****

Jake sat in his truck processing the events of the day. Tuesdays were supposed to be boring… uneventful. Not *that* Tuesday. Jenna's call unnerved him. The *man* in the background unnerved him. He tried to rationalize that his mood stemmed from the fact she wasn't taking her safety seriously enough. In truth, it was the fact that Chase showed up.

Chase had all but disappeared from her life. She hadn't mentioned him much at all over the past month. The calls she had felt the need to take or the texts she had to return had all but stopped. Then Chase showed back up… out of nowhere… randomly, at the worst possible time. Michael wouldn't like this one bit. Jake had listened intently to the brothers talking about how they felt Chase led to Jenna's suicide attempt.

Jake didn't know if he would put that much blame on the man, but he didn't like his reappearance. Not when Jake was trying to keep Jenna safe from Nick and who knows what else. Would Chase stick his nose in their situation and offer input on her safety? Then it hit him. *You're jealous. You're scared he's going to take Jenna's attention away from you.*

"That's ridiculous," Jake said out loud in the quietness of his truck. But the more he sat there thinking over the previous months that he'd known Jenna, the more he realized that somewhere along the way he started… enjoying her... *liking* her. Could he see himself starting to *love* her?

He sighed into the darkness of the night. *I can't love her, God. Can I? That would be a cruel joke. Don't let me fall for someone after all this time just to have her reject me. What if she isn't ready to move on from Ben?*

His phone rang, interrupting his thoughts.

"Hey, how did things go with Alexis?" Brian asked quietly. Judging from the background noise, his friend was still at work and was attempting to talk discreetly. "I'm getting ready to head home and I didn't see you at your desk. I wanted to catch up before I got to the house."

Jake had asked Brian to look into Trip's activities over the past week covertly. Alexis called Trip out. While he was with her at the hospital, she gave a full account of the man and described him down to his freckle on his wrist. It made Jake not only filled with rage at another friend turned traitor, but he was heartsick. Trip had gone camping with him and Brian not that long ago. How long had he been working with Nick… the Broker?

Forcing himself back to the question at hand, Jake smiled back at the events of the afternoon. In the middle of the negative, there was redemption.

"Alexis is safe and on her way to recovery, hopefully," Jake said leaning his head against the seat rest.

He decided, for Alexis' safety, he'd take her to a facility two towns over from Skennan Cove. He stayed with her until her father arrived. The man must've dropped everything to get there because he made it in record time coming from Deer Creek. Alexis had been worried her father would reject her, but the man sobbed like a baby when he saw his daughter in the hospital bed.

They'd treat her for severe dehydration and the withdrawal symptoms overnight and in the morning she would be on her way to another treatment center closer to her family. Pastor Munson said he wouldn't leave her side after Jake gave him a heads up about the current situation his daughters both faced. After leaving the room, he also alerted Michael.

"That's good. I'm glad to hear that. Praying she sticks with it this time." The background noises turned into the echoey garage and the sound of Brian's engine starting.

"Did you find anything on Trip that I can take to Branson?" Jake asked, knowing Brian was able to talk freely in the safety of his car.

"Nothing obvious. I keep hoping Alexis was mistaken," Brian said. So had Jake, but his conversation with her earlier dispelled any hope.

"He was off on Sunday while Jenna was playing hero. He *could've* been there. Maybe that explains Jenna's reaction," Brian surmised. "But when Mara was taken, he was with me the whole time."

"Doesn't mean he wasn't involved. We don't have a way of knowing where Nick was and it appears he has quite a few men doing his bidding, according to Alexis." Jake rubbed his temples.

"So, what now? I have to work with Trip like nothing ever happened?"

"That's exactly what you do. Until we have more than Alexis' story to go on, tell no one. Act like everything is fine. We don't know how bad this is yet." Jake heard a text come through that halted any more conversation with Brian.

Jenna. He said a hasty goodbye to his friend and read her words. "Can you talk? It's important."

He didn't get a chance to respond. A melodic tune filled the cab of his truck. He smiled briefly. Jake had told Jenna he had changed her ringtone to an annoying song to alert him she was calling. But it wasn't an annoying tune at all. It was sweet and beautiful... like Jenna.

"What's up, Jenna?"

"Can… can you come to the hospital… now?" She stuttered.

"What's wrong?" Jake felt his chest seize.

"There's a detective here… and another man in a suit… they're going to call you." Jenna sounded like she was on the verge of hyperventilating. "Mara… Mara said…"

"Jenna, I need you to breathe. Slow down," Jake tried to soothe her as he started his truck and peeled away from his parking spot.

"Mara said… it was me. They're after me." Jenna hiccupped a sob. "This was all my fault, Jake. Mara almost died… because of *me*."

29

Jake listened attentively to every word Branson and the detective assigned to Mara's case told him. Yet, his eyes kept resting on the silent woman who stood at the end of the ICU hall, staring in at her fragile friend. Jenna looked pale and childlike as she wrapped her arms around herself protectively.

"The phone found at the sight of Mara's dumping ground is still locked. I have people working to unlock it. I'll let you know if there's anything tied to Spencer," Detective Riley promised. "You'll get me Alexis Munson's information?"

Jake hesitated and looked at Branson. His superior nodded slightly. A secret conversation was spoken in mere seconds. Branson deemed Riley trustworthy.

"She's gun shy as you can imagine, Riley. Proceed carefully," Jake stated as he texted the other detective the information about the hospital she was staying in.

The man nodded and reached for his phone as it rang. His brow furrowed as he listened and didn't ease even when he hung up. "A male body was found near the air strip. What's going on in this town?"

Detective Riley left to attend to the next matter at hand, leaving Sergeant Branson and Jake.

"Who are you going to post at Mara's door, Sir?" Jake asked suddenly.

Branson threw out a couple names and Jake nodded. "I take it there's a reason you're asking. Want to fill me in, Son?"

Did he? Hopefully, Alexis would tell Detective Riley everything she had told Jake about Trip, but Jake couldn't be sure she would trust him. He filled Branson in on everything he knew. There was a moment of panic as Jake prayed whether or not Branson was still to be trusted. He had done nothing but help Jake up to that moment. Then again, so had Trip.

The man looked pained as he ran a hand over his balding scalp. "Looks like another sweep is in order."

"Yes, Sir. Unfortunately."

"And about this young woman," Branson nodded in Jenna's direction. "I'm assuming you've been coming up with a plan to keep her safe?"

Jake gave a curt nod and looked down the hall at Jenna, who still had yet to move from her spot. "Yes and I don't think she's going to like it."

*****

"*Absolutely* not." Jenna shook her head and shot daggers with her eyes. Were they seriously suggesting that she take a *vacation*? She'd only just started working at the hospital. They were going to get her fired. If she lost her job, what then? Move home again? Become the family pity case once more? "It's not going to happen."

"Ms. Clark, I understand your hesitation," the man Jake referred to as Branson was speaking. They had pulled her into a small waiting room reserved for grieving families. "I hope you can see the seriousness of your situation. You heard Mara recount her experience. The men who did this to her will not hesitate to do worse to you. They want to lure your brother and sister-in-law out in the open. Now that they don't have Alexis Munson to do that… you are the target."

Jenna's breath caught in her throat. "Alexis? Is she…"

"She's fine. Safe," Jake reassured her. "That's where I was earlier today. Her father is staying with her."

Her father was with her! Something released in Jenna's chest and she felt tears sting her eyes. "She's alive."

Jake nodded. "And we need to make sure *you* stay that way as well."

"What do they even want with me? I don't know anything!" Jenna's voice rose. "This isn't fair. I'm just getting started here. I can't lose my job, Jake. I can't…"

"Ms. Clark, you continuing to come in for your shifts, under the circumstance, could put more people in danger than just yourself," Branson spoke bluntly. "They took your friend in broad daylight from the hospital's parking garage."

The thought registered in Jenna's mind. Mara had been taken because the one watching thought it was Jenna. When they realized their mistake, they discarded her like she was trash on the side of the road. Would they try again? Who might get hurt next time? Would they come into the hospital? Jenna shuddered at the thought.

"But I'll lose my job," she whispered barely audibly.

"Point me in the direction of who I need to talk to," Sergeant Branson's face took on a paternal expression.

He reminded Jenna of her own father. She could really have benefitted from her father's presence right then. A hug from her mother would've been welcomed as well. Maybe if she got fired and went home, it wouldn't be so bad. She could try to get her old job back. Her parents wouldn't turn her away. Her room was probably just as she left it. But she would be leaving her new life. Her new friends. *Jake.*

I'm a failure. I didn't even make it two months on my own.

She was spiraling. It had been a while since she had felt unhinged. Even when she had been terrified at the house Alexis was held in, she had kept it together. But Jenna had a purpose then… to help Alexis. What was her purpose now? To stay alive? *Where is the goodness of God in this situation? Where are you, God?*

She felt tears threaten to surface and got to her feet before Jake could notice.

"What am I supposed to do? Where do I go?" she asked.

"You stay in your apartment. We go into lockdown and as soon as it's safe, you come back to work." Jake made it sound so simple.

"And if I get fired and can't pay rent?"

Jake sighed. "We'll cross that bridge when we get to it, okay?"

"Who said you were going to get fired?" Branson got to his feet as well and gave a lopsided grin. "I have a way of talking to people. Show me who I need to talk to. I bet they will be more than willing to give you time away under the circumstances."

"Starting when?" Jenna asked Jake.

"Immediately. The sooner we get you somewhere safe, the better."

Jenna nodded, resigned to her fate. *Then that's all there is to it. It's the end of my new beginning.*

*****

The ride home started out in excruciating silence. Jake tried to fill Jenna in on Alexis' bravery and her hope for a fresh start. To her credit, Jenna responded genuinely relieved for the woman. However, she slumped back into her despondence.

"Jenna, if Branson said your job is safe, your job is safe. You can trust him, I promise."

Jenna sighed. "I can't shake this feeling…"

"What feeling?"

"That I… that I'm going to go back to the Jenna I was before I moved here. I can't, Jake. I can't go back to that version of me." Jenna's admission was painful.

"Then don't. Who said you have to go back? You didn't lose your job. This isn't done yet, Jenna."

Another sigh.

"Are you hungry? The taco place is still open," he suggested.

"No, thank you."

"Are you sure? Well, do you mind if I grab something? I'm starved." It wasn't a lie. That Tuesday was the longest day he had encountered in quite some time. It felt like days since he had eaten, not hours.

Jenna shrugged slightly in response.

Jake pulled into the drive-thru and ordered enough food to feed an army. He sent the Hamiltons' a quick text alerting them that they needed to have another family meeting and that he'd bring dinner. While he was waiting for the food, he also sent a text out to Michael and Anna to make sure they were safe. Michael texted back that, between Detective Jenkins in Deer Creek and his brothers, they were well protected.

"How's Jen?" Michael texted.

"Not liking her new arrangement. Probably hating me right now. Turned down a taco."

Michael's response was instant. "That's serious. She loves tacos."

Jake chuckled quietly.

Then he realized Jenna was watching him on his phone. He cleared his throat and slid it in his pocket before receiving the order from the lady in the take out window. Placing the bags behind them in the back seat, he pulled away towards home. Moments later, the sweet melodic tune of Jenna's ringtone sounded.

Jake snapped his attention to Jenna, who had her phone to her ear and a small smile on her lips.

"You're calling me?" he laughed, relieved to see a glimmer of humor – albeit small – in her eyes.

"It's rude to text when you're with someone sitting right next to you… especially if you're texting my brother about me."

He smiled and nodded. "You're right. I apologize."

There was silence for a moment until Jenna spoke. "I thought my ringtone was *Flight of the Bumblebees*."

Jake smiled without saying a word as they pulled into the driveway. They entered the house and Jenna climbed the stairs to her apartment, when Jake called up to her.

"Meet down here in five minutes, okay?"

She nodded and let herself into her door with her key. Jake had just gotten his own door opened when she came back to the top of the stairs looking down at him with a puzzled expression.

"You got me roses?" she asked. "Why?"

Jake started up the stairs. "I didn't."

Was that disappointment on her face? He made a mental note to get her flowers sometime in the near future if she liked them so much.

"Then who? There's no card." Jenna picked up the vase from her table and brought them out to show him. Then as if the answer hit her, she sighed. "Chase. He must have come back after dropping me off."

"That's nice of him," Jake hated how irritated he sounded. If he didn't do something quick, Chase would be the one buying Jenna flowers permanently.

"Why did you say it like that?" Jenna asked giving him a side eye glance.

Thankfully, the door below them opened and the Hamiltons came out onto their landing. Brian, who held a wiggling Tori, motioned to the food bags Jake still held in his hand. "Are we going to eat or what? I'm starved."

"Do you like your flowers, Jenna?" Helena asked when she spotted them. "I didn't know what to use for a vase so I used your pitcher. I hope that's okay."

"That's fine. I'm surprised he did this. So sweet." Jenna returned the vase to her table and rejoined her friends.

"So… who brought you flowers?" Brian asked curiously and gave Jake a sly expression.

"Chase," Jenna answered as she came down the stairs.

"Who?" Helena asked with a chuckle. "Oh, that guy that was here earlier? No, it wasn't him. It was *Trip*."

Everyone froze there on the stairway between their respective apartments. Except for Helena, that is.

With exasperation, she gaped at them. "Are we going to eat or what?"

*****

Across town, Damon seethed after dismissing his driver – turned informant – from the room. His cousin was dead. Discarded on the side of a no-named road near the airport. The same airport that the Broker landed in earlier from his field trip. Apparently, the object lesson he had been given wasn't heeded.

Scout wasn't particularly bright. He was never going to make it through the ranks of Damon's other men, but he was family. As if killing his man wasn't enough, the Broker still pursued his ridiculous preoccupation with yesterday's concerns.

If the Broker wasn't stopped, the deal Damon had made with the powers-that-be would be breached. Then, his livelihood *would* be affected. His agreement to guarantee the safety of that journalist and all involved was the only thing ensuring his clean escape to Florida, no questions asked.

The only one standing in the way of Damon's plans was the *Broker*.

30

"What's everybody looking at?" Helena asked with her hands on her hips staring at her husband and friends as they continued to stand in the hallway in between the apartments.

"Trip was *here*?" Brian asked with urgency in his voice.

Jenna looked up the stairs at her apartment and shuddered. Apparently, she hadn't been crazy after all regarding Trip. Jake affirmed her fears in the truck when he told her that Alexis named Trip as one of the men keeping her at that house, drugged and compliant until they needed her to grab her sister, Anna.

"Yes. Why is that so crazy?" Helena reached over to grab one of the food bags from Jake's clenched hands. "He remembered Tori's birthday was coming up and brought her a gift. And he said you had a rough day yesterday and brought you the flowers, Jenna."

The way Helena shrugged off the encounter chilled Jenna to the bone. She had no idea the danger she and Tori had been in.

"Where is this gift he brought?" Jake asked.

"Tori's bed. It's a cute teddy bear." Helena sighed in frustration. "Is someone going to fill me in on what's going on?"

Jake motioned for everyone to follow him to his apartment. Brian, who still held Tori in his arms, began filling his wife in on their *friend.* Jake took Jenna to the side of the room. Goose had greeted them all as they entered, but leaned against Jenna's legs as Jake spoke to her. He was either desperate for attention, eavesdropping, or he sensed there was a need to stay vigilant.

"Can I go into your apartment to look at the roses?" he asked.

"Y… yes. But why? They're just roses."

He forced a smile, probably to keep her calm. "I just want to be sure."

Jenna nodded and began unpacking bags of food while Helena let reality sink in. Trip had been their friend. Someone who lived under the same roof. Someone they trusted and loved like family.

"You honestly think he would do something like that? *Hurt* someone? *Betray* us?" Helena held her pregnant stomach and sank into a chair at the table.

"That is how it's looking." Brian rubbed her shoulders lovingly.

Jenna helped Tori into a chair at the table and opened up a plain burrito for her. Goose sat attentively next to the youngster, hoping she would drop him a treat onto the floor.

"You're sure you heard *his* voice at this woman's house?" Helena asked Jenna with grief on her face.

Jenna nodded. "He's got a very distinctive way of talking. And Alexis even named him, Helena. I'm so sorry."

"But he was talking to me like everything was normal between us. He didn't act … crazy… or anything like that. You all have to be mistaken," Helena said with tears starting to stream down her cheek. "He wouldn't use a gift for Tori to betray us, would he?"

Brian sighed. "You said it is on Tori's bed? I'm going to go look it over. Eat something, Helena. You'll feel better."

Brian left the apartment. Jenna heard Jake's voice in the stairwell and assumed the two were going into police mode. She turned her attention back to Helena who was now nibbling on a quesadilla.

"Are you going to be okay? Stress is the last thing you need right now. Your due date is coming up pretty quickly, isn't it?" Jenna, even in her current state of affairs, noticed that Helena's belly looked lower than it had been the day before.

"Yeah… we're pretty close. I lost my mucus plug today," Helena said as she took another bite of her food.

Dropping her taco back onto the table, Jenna looked at her friend in shock. "Today? And you didn't think to mention this? Did you call your obstetrician? Does Brian know?"

"Yes to both. We're not worried. With Tori, I lost my mucus plug *a whole week* before going into labor."

Helena then smirked at Jenna. “Sorry for the TMI. This isn’t exactly dinner conversation, is it?”

“I’m a nurse. There’s no such thing as TMI with me, Helena.” Jenna smiled, but she was still not ready to drop the topic. “Have you had any contractions?”

“Nothing consistent. Just those ridiculous Braxton Hicks. They go away if I rest.” Helena reached over and took Jenna’s hand. “I’m fine. Really, I am. Other than wanting to go into mama bear mode and hurt a certain smooth talking hoodlum… I’m fine.”

The men reentered the apartment and took a seat silently at the table. Too silently.

“Well?” Jenna asked as Jake opened a taco and took a massive bite.

“They’re both bugged,” he said with little emotion.

“Bugged?” Jenna and Helena asked at the same time.

“Bugs! Ew!” Tori repeated, pretending to slap an imaginary bug on the table.

Jake smiled softly and ruffled her hair.

“What are we going to do?” Jenna felt her hands start to shake. This wasn’t her life. She wouldn’t say she was boring. After all, she worked in the emergency room. However, she wasn’t the kind of person that got *bugged.*

“Nothing. Not until I talk to Branson. This might be something we can use to our advantage.” Jake took another bite of his taco before reaching for another.

"*Nothing*?" Jenna watched him eat as if he had two heads. "You mean I'm supposed to live in my apartment with him watching me like a sitcom?"

Jake chuckled. "It's an audio bug, not a camera, Jenna."

"And how do you know that? What if you missed something?"

"I have a scanner that looks for hidden cameras and bugs." Jake shrugged. "It's just a bug."

"Of course you have a scanner." Jenna sighed in annoyance. "Maybe it's just a bug to you, but I am not okay with pretending he's not watching… I mean, listening to everything I do."

"You don't have to be. You won't be staying up there," Jake said matter-of-factly as he balled up the taco wrapper and put it in the empty food bag. "After you finish eating, you are going to go pack a bag and then we are all leaving."

"Leaving? To go where?" Jenna couldn't believe what she was hearing.

"At this time of night?" Helena glared at her husband looking for a better explanation.

He just shrugged and muttered, "I swear this is the longest Tuesday ever."

Jake nodded. "And it's going to be a little longer still. The cabin is about an hour's drive."

"Cabin? Your cabin?" Helena questioned Jake. "That toothpick fort you have in the middle of no man's land?"

"That's the one." Jake smiled smartly as he got to his feet. "Pack for at least three days. There's a lake if you want to swim. I want to leave here in twenty minutes."

Jenna and Helena exchanged glances trying to make sense of what they were just told.

"I can't even pack my lunch in twenty minutes," Jenna whined.

"Then I suggest you cram that taco down real fast and get moving. We can't stay here tonight," Jake said as he opened his refrigerator and started putting things into a bag.

"We have locks. And you are both cops." Jenna got to her feet to argue.

"Trip might have a key," Jake said quietly.

"You mean… you never changed any of the locks after he moved out?"

"No, Jenna. I dropped the ball," Jake said in a tired and testy tone that made Jenna hush.

He sighed and turned to her.

"There wasn't much time between his moving out and you moving in. Then I got busy and… *distracted*."

"Distracted with what?" Jenna didn't know why she asked.

"*You*. Okay? I got distracted by you," Jake admitted in frustration. "It was a stupid mistake, but I *trusted* Trip. We all did. Another stupid mistake. And I cannot afford to make any more of those from here on out."

Out of the side of her eye, Jenna saw Helena's mouth fall open. Brian eased her out of her chair and they ushered Tori towards the door as if not wanting to interrupt Jake and Jenna's conversation. Too late.

"When you go up, talk like normal. Act like you are putting Tori to bed," Jake instructed. "Helena, make a point to tell Brian about Trip's visit and the bear. Brian, you play it up. Say something about how kind that was of him to do. We can't let him know we know."

They agreed and scooped an already sleepy Tori into their arms, leaving quietly.

"I distract you?" Jenna asked as soon as the door closed behind them. "Like, in a good way?"

Jake ran a hand through his hair. "Does this feel good to you? My mistake let a traitor into our house."

Jenna swallowed hard. Did that mean he was going to pull away from her? She didn't want that.

"It's not your fault, Jake."

He brushed past her into his room, returning moments later with a duffel bag that he was shoving clothes into.

"We don't have time for you to comfort me." Jake didn't look like he was in the mood to talk. "Go pack. Turn music on or the TV. Anything to cover up the sound of you rustling around. You're down to ten minutes, Jenna. Go."

Jenna left hesitantly, a little hurt and a little curious. She *distracted* him. So, she hadn't been the only one feeling something between them… right? She sighed as she made her way up the steps and into her apartment. It had been so long since she had worried about what a guy thought of her. But there she was… worrying that Jake would see her as a liability instead of someone to have a relationship with. It didn't feel good. Ben had always made sure she knew he was crazy about her. Jake wasn't Ben.

"Snap out of it, Jenna. He didn't say he loved you. He said you were a distraction," Jenna muttered.

Then she realized what she had said… out loud. Clenching her jaw tight she walked to the TV and put it on loudly, glaring over at the deceptively beautiful roses. The clock on the wall reminded her that Jake gave her ten minutes. With the frame of mind he operated in, Jenna had little doubt he meant it. What would he do? Leave her behind?

In a mad dash, Jenna took a suit case and just grabbed whatever she could from her drawers, stuffing things into the case haphazardly. *Makeup*! She ran into the bathroom and grabbed an armful of cosmetics and toiletries. *Think, Jenna. What else will you need?*

Phone charger. Her latest novel. A bathing suit. Towel. Sunscreen. Sun glasses. Like a whirlwind she dashed through the apartment, occasionally eyeing the flowers wondering if Jake was correct about there not being a hidden camera. She stuck her tongue out at it just in case.

She turned around and saw Jake standing in her apartment, silent and smirking.

“Wh…” she began until his face turned serious.

Jake put a finger to his lips and shook his head. He mouthed out, “Where is your bag?”

Jenna went back to the bedroom and returned with her rolling suitcase, bulging at the seams, following right on her heels. He scowled, shook his head, and took it out the door, motioning her to follow. Doing a once over, Jenna grabbed her purse and phone, silently shutting the door behind her as the TV blared the nightly news.

“The body of a man was discovered earlier today near an isolated area behind the Skennan Cove Airport…”

*****

The Hamiltons were already loaded into their SUV, waiting patiently as Jake and Jenna exited the house. With the house locked behind him, Jake quickly opened the back door to his truck and hefted Jenna’s suitcase up next to Goose on the backseat. The dog instantly started sniffing every inch of it. Probably a throwback from his working days sniffing for drugs.

“Old habits die hard, Buddy?” Jake ruffled Goose’s hair before taking his seat behind the wheel.

It didn't take long for Jenna to barrage him with questions.

"How do we know they aren't going to follow us?"

"We don't. That's why I have Brian leading so I can look for anyone suspicious behind us," Jake said as he watched the Hamiltons pull out onto the street.

"What if they try to break in while we're gone?"

"Then the security cameras I have running will catch them and I'll call the police." Jake kept one eye on his rear view and one on the road ahead of them.

"You talked to Sergeant Branson? What did he say? What's he going to do about the bugs in our apartments? Do they have enough evidence to arrest Trip?" Jenna's eyes were wide. There was fear there, but Jake surmised that her anxiety was coming from her lack of control more than anything.

"Yes, I talked to Branson. He has a plan. That's all I am going to say right now, Jenna. Can you please just try to trust me?" Jake looked over at her. She looked tired… exhausted. So was he, for that matter. "Look, we have a long drive. It's late. Try to doze off for a bit, okay?"

"Am I distracting you?" Jenna rolled her eyes.

Of all the cheeky things to say! Jake smiled in the darkness. "Yes, actually. You are. Go to sleep."

He thought the matter was settled as she attempted to get comfortable, but then she sat up straight.

“What’s the matter?” he asked looking all around in case she saw something he had missed.

“I forgot my pillow.”

Reaching one arm behind him he fished around until he found what he was looking for. He handed her his pillow. She took it and mumbled a shy *thank you.* She turned her back to him, maneuvering into a comfortable position.

Finally, in the silence, Jake could ponder on Branson’s call. Riley got a report back on the phone found where Mara had been dumped. Numerous calls could be traced back to Trip’s phone. Incriminating texts not only placed Trip in the center of the mess, but he appeared to give orders. The dead man found earlier that day was suspected to be the owner of that phone, possibly killed as punishment for the botched kidnapping.

Jake glanced over at Jenna. He doubted she was truly asleep. She was wired too tightly. What was he going to do about her? Maybe he should’ve sent her back to Deer Creek to be under the watch of Detective Jenkins along with Michael and Anna. The thought caused his chest to constrict. No. He needed her close. Not just to protect. Not just for purposes of the investigation. God was using her to bring him back to life. There was no way he could let her go now. *Now we just need to convince her of that, God.*

31

Jenna clutched Jake's pillow tightly to her chest as she stared out of the window. The lights of convenience stores and shops slowly morphed into isolated stretches of treelined roads and dark forest. She cast a glance over her shoulder at Jake. His eyes were glued to the road and occasionally to the rearview mirrors, telling her that he was still making sure they weren't followed.

The air conditioning was on a little too high for her liking, but she remained quiet with her attention focused on the quickly changing scenery. In the silence, Jenna had a lot of time to think. She thought about Mara, still clinging to life. She thought about Helena and how this trip wasn't a great idea for her friend's pregnancy. She thought about how she hated rustic camping and hoped this cabin was less primitive than she was imagining. Most of all, she realized how terrifying her situation actually was. Her stomach twisted into knots.

All of the sudden, Jake pulled the truck into a hard left and Jenna thought for sure he was crashing into trees. There was no road! She grabbed the side of her seat and the door, letting out a gasp. Then she realized, there was indeed a type of road… if one could call it that.

"Oh, you're awake." She could hear the smirk in his tone. She turned to face him and sure enough, she could see his face. There it was illuminated by the dashboard lights… a slight grin.

"Where are we?" Jenna sat up straighter and pried her hands off the door.

"We're very close to the cabin. Soon you can actually get some *real* sleep," he said as he followed the dirt road.

They turned abruptly at a tree with a bright pink strip of reflector tape tied around the tree's trunk. He stopped the truck, got out, and removed it from the tree before getting back in and continuing down another path. This path was even more overgrown than the previous. Finally, they came to a stop next to the Hamiltons' parked SUV.

"Stay here until I come back out, okay?" Jake instructed as he slid out of the truck once more.

Brian also emerged from his vehicle and the two, with Goose at their heels, followed their flashlight beams to a dark, foreboding structure. Jenna watched as their lights went across the old windows. Finally, a softer glow radiated from inside the cabin making it look less like a scene from a horror movie. The men came out and began unloading the truck and SUV.

"Can I help?" Jenna asked as she watched Brian retrieve a fold-up playpen and blankets from the back of his car.

"Sure." Jake smiled warmly. "Want to bring the food bags in?"

Jenna jumped out to help and breathed in the clean late summer air. There was no light pollution to hinder the amazing view of the Milky Way and Jenna paused a moment to take it in. That is, until she caught a glimpse of the interior of the cabin.

Her stomach sank as she slowly approached the rickety steps. Three bowed beams of wood resting on cinderblocks made up the stairs. The stoop outside the door felt like it could give way under her weight. Inside, the warm light that initially comforted her turned out to be kerosene lamps, emitting a pungent odor.

"Put the nonperishable food in that container." Jake pointed to a storage bin as he helped Helena bring in a sleeping Tori. He laid her in the playpen that her father had set up in one of the rooms off of the main room.

Jenna saw a refrigerator and opened the door only to realize it was not on.

"It's not working," Jake said with a chuckle. "Not unless I get the generator going and I don't think that's likely."

"But … what about the other food?"

Jake went out onto the porch and brought in a cooler that he must've had in the bed of his truck. "For now, we'll use this. Tomorrow I'll need to run to town and grab more ice. I emptied both the Hamilton's icemaker as well as my own before we left."

Jenna turned away after nodding numbly. She was a farm girl. She had gone camping as a kid. She'd gone fishing with her brothers and didn't need them putting the worm on her line. She held her own when it came to chores and tackling the less pleasant aspects of farm life. Staying in a cabin without electricity shouldn't have been so daunting to her. But it was.

"Did you tighten that lid on the container?" Jake asked as he went to double check and added something heavy to place on top of the lid. "We don't want the mice to get into it."

"*Mice*?" Jenna shuddered.

Jake smiled sympathetically, patted her on the back, and moved back outside to grab more things to bring inside. Jenna watched him leave and glanced over at Helena coming out of the room where Tori slept. They exchanged displeased expressions.

"Maybe you should lay down, Helena," Jenna said. "I'll help them get the other things in."

Her friend smiled faintly, but motioned to an empty wooden platform bed in their room. "Thank you, but there's no laying down in here until Brian blows up the air mattress."

As if on cue, the men reentered with folded up vinyl mattresses and a battery operated air compressor. Helena quickly shut the door to where Tori slept so the noise wouldn't wake her. Sadly, the cries of the little one sounded over the machine. Helena whimpered in frustration and went in to her daughter.

"Here we are. Bed number one." Jake slid the large sized mattress to Brian who took it into the room where Helena tried to get Tori back to sleep. "Yours is next, Jenna."

"Maybe I can sleep in the truck?" she suggested, but the look on Jake's face told her that was not going to happen.

He blew up the other mattress and slid it onto the wooden platform in another room, smaller than the one the Hamiltons occupied.

"I don't suppose you brought bedding," Jake surmised.

"I had ten minutes," Jenna said dryly.

Jake nodded in understanding and spoke gently, "It's okay. You can have my sleeping bag."

"Wh...what about you? Where are you going to sleep?"

Jenna's eyes followed to where he pointed, an old faux leather loveseat. "Goose and I will be just fine out here."

"But you're at least six foot three. How are you going to..."

"Worried about me?" His grin was cheesy, yet slightly endearing.

She was about to make a funny comeback when she realized something important was missing from the structure. The cabin consisted of two basic bedrooms, a wooden table and chairs, a vintage fridge with an extension cord plugged into nothing, the ratchety couch, and a wood burning stove. Jenna looked around the cabin for something more.

"What is it?" Jake asked noticing her sudden panic.

"Where's the bathroom?"

A smile split his face and Jenna felt her stomach sink even further. "No. Tell me it's not outside."

"Okay… I won't."

"Really?" Jenna whined. "Mice… no electricity… outdoor plumbing…"

"*Plumbing*?" Brian laughed as he entered the room.

Jenna shot Jake a pleading look. "Please tell me there's a bathroom."

"Kind of." He smirked and nodded for her to follow him outside. He grabbed his flashlight and led her to the side of the cabin and what resembled an upright coffin.

Opening the door, Jenna whimpered. It was nothing more than a wooden platform with a potty seat placed over a hole dug deep into the ground.

"How will we brush our teeth? *Shower*?" Jenna asked quietly as the reality of the next several days sunk in.

"Bottled water for teeth brushing and the lake for bathing."

She wanted to cry.

"And you come here… for *fun*?" Jenna asked in shock.

"Well, I don't normally have company when I come," Jake chuckled as he shut the door and started walking her back to the cabin. "I come here to think… get my head straight when I need it. To pray."

She tried to look at the cabin through Jake's eyes. Maybe she could see the draw for a man like him. He was definitely the rugged type. Ben had been adventurous, but she couldn't fathom him enjoying the great outdoors to *that* extent.

"It's okay, Jenna. Hopefully, everything will get taken care of quickly and we can go back to the house," Jake tried to comfort her.

"I'm sorry. I know I must seem ungrateful." Jenna paused Jake's steps with a hand on his arm. "This… the last couple of days… it's just all been too much. I'm overwhelmed."

She dropped her hand back to her side and let her shoulders slump in defeat. Jenna wasn't expecting Jake to lift her chin gently with his finger. She looked up into his face and for a moment she forgot how to breathe. She couldn't see every detail in the late night darkness, but she felt his tender gaze. He seemed like he wanted to say something. He opened his mouth, but shut it again.

Then finally he spoke as he stepped back from her.

"You're exhausted. Let's get your bag so you can get to sleep."

At the truck, he handed Jenna a sleeping bag before lifting her rolling suit case down from the back seat. It wouldn't roll over the branches and rocks so Jake carried it into the cabin, placing it just inside her tiny room. After she had rolled out the sleeping bag, he handed her an extra flashlight.

"If you need to go out to the toilet, wake me. It's too dark out there to be wandering around… even with that." Jake nodded at the flashlight she clutched.

Jenna shuddered and wrapped her arms around herself at the notion of going outside in the middle of the night. How long could she safely hold in the urge to go?

"Are you cold? It gets chilly here at night… even in August," Jake said as he looked over at the wood burning stove. "It can get into the forties. I can start a little fire and put it out before I go to sleep. It'll be enough to take the chill out of the air."

"I'll be okay. Goodnight, Jake."

Jenna slid backwards into the room and closed the door. The darkness was both comforting and overwhelming. It was comforting *not* to see her surroundings. Her imagination came up with all types of horrible scenarios, probably from the scary movies she shouldn't have watched over the years. The darkness consumed everything without even a small window to let the moonlight in.

As she hurriedly readied for bed and got settled inside the sleeping bag, she heard Jake tap on the door of the room next to her. She heard the men mumble to one another followed by the sounds of Jake putting wood into the stove. Moments later a scent reminiscent of a campfire wafted through the opening at the bottom of the door and Jenna fell asleep.

Jenna was trapped in the closet. Through the slats in the door she could see Alexis being beaten badly. Trip was there smiling and laughing, but Jenna stood frozen. She couldn't do anything to help the woman… all she could do was watch. If she so much as breathed, they might find her hiding there.

Then the door of the bedroom opened, causing the scene before her eyes to morph and change. Mara walked through the men beating on Alexis as if they were illusions. Mara looked like a ghost. Her face emotionless... pale. Her chest and clothing were covered in blood as she moved through the room... heading straight to Jenna's location.

The door opened, but Jenna was no longer in a closet. She was in the parking garage at the hospital.

"This is your fault. You killed me, Jenna," Mara accused. "I didn't deserve to die... but YOU do."

Jenna started backing up slowly as Mara kept walking closer and closer.

"No, Mara. No. I'm sorry."

Her body hit something behind her. Turning, she saw Ben standing there. His smile was warm and loving. His arms came around her.

"Help me, Ben."

Then what had been a comforting embrace, turned into a tight crushing grip. Ben's face distorted from the handsome, loving man she had married to a hideous rotten corpse. A man resembling Jake stepped out of the shadows, but made no effort to help.

"Protect me, Ben," he mocked and mimicked. "Why should I, Jenna? You unfaithful, cheating, backstabbing..."

Jenna couldn't hear anymore. She pushed away, trying to run, but he caught her. He grabbed her, bringing her to her knees. His hands on either side of her face opened her mouth as pills went down her throat.

"You were supposed to die!"

She couldn't breathe. The pills were being chased down her throat with some type of acidic liquid. She gagged and sputtered until she managed to call out, "Help me, Jesus!"

There were hands on her shoulders, shaking her. Her eyes were open, but the room was so dark. She felt trapped. What surrounded her? *The sleeping bag.*

"Shh. Jenna, it's okay. You were having a nightmare," a familiar groggy, yet masculine voice came from nearby.

"I can't see."

"Close your eyes for a minute," Jake instructed and she complied. Gradually, Jenna opened them after hearing the click of his flashlight.

A flicker of light illuminated the small room and Jenna's eyes finally landed on the man sitting on the edge of her bed. At the door, Brian and Helena stood, concern etched on their faces.

"You're okay," he soothed. He brushed a tear away with his finger before it fell into her hairline. "It was just a dream."

"I'm sorry. I'm so sorry. Did I wake up Tori?"

"She's fine. She goes back to sleep easily." Helena came further into the doorway. "Are *you* okay?"

"I'm fine. Go back to sleep." Jenna forced a smile, but doubted it looked convincing. "I'm sorry. I'm okay now."

Brian and Helena sighed and gave Jenna sympathetic smiles before going back to their room. Jenna heard Tori's little voice asking for juice and she felt a new wave of guilt wash over her. How long would it take them to get their daughter back to sleep… if at all? Then she saw Jake, still sitting at the edge of her bed. His expression was one of great tenderness and concern.

"I'm okay. Go back to bed."

He checked his phone. "The sun will be up shortly. Want to come with me to town and get coffees for everyone?"

Another tear escaped as Jenna nodded. He must've known there was no going back to sleep after that. It had been a long time since she'd had such a painful nightmare – especially one that left her feeling dark and hopeless. She knew it was a dream, but the undercurrent still remained. The hellish words that the *real* Ben never would've uttered kept replaying in her head. They latched into her brain like a fishing hook embedded in the mouth of its victim. *You were supposed to die!*

32

"Want to talk about it?" Jake asked, glancing over at his silent passenger.

Jenna shook her head and wrapped her arms around her chest.

"You know you are safe, right? I'm not going to let anyone hurt you, Jenna."

A tear slipped down her cheek and she swiped at it angrily. "Can you save me from myself?"

He wasn't sure if he heard her correctly, but when he looked at her he saw a frightening mix of anger and despair.

"Care to explain that?" he asked as he pulled into a small diner's parking lot.

The sun was just breaking over the tree tops. The two had been driving for fifteen minutes or so. When they set out, the sky had been pitch black, and as they sat staring straight ahead, pink and orange streaks illuminated the sky. The dawn was Jake's favorite time of day. It reminded him that after the loneliness of night, the sun never failed to rise, chasing away the darkness. He hoped Jenna could draw comfort from it now.

"I don't think I can explain," Jenna whispered. "I'm sorry. I'm just tired and cranky. I'll be fine."

She forced a smile, but he saw through it. He used to do the same thing… comfort his friends before engaging in some type of behavior that would hurt him.

"Why don't you try?" Jake returned her smile. "I'm a great listener and I may understand better than you think."

Jenna looked up into the splitting sky and sighed before telling him every graphic detail of the night terror. It was when she got to the part about Ben that she struggled to get the words out.

"And then Ben…" Jenna stopped and Jake swallowed hard. He was well acquainted with guilt dreams. After Beth's diagnosis and death, he had them quite frequently.

"Go on. What about Ben?"

Jenna swiped at a few more tears and shook her head. "It sounds stupid to speak it out loud. I know he would never have said anything like that."

"Like what?"

She hiccupped on the words. "That I should be dead."

Jenna let herself have a moment and Jake waited patiently, almost scared to move lest she stop talking again.

"It's like I had even failed at dying. I mess everything up." Jenna smirked angrily before proceeding. "I couldn't get Alexis out of that house safely. Mara was carrying my sweater and badge. It was supposed to be me that night in the garage. And Ben… *I* encouraged him to join the military. I never thought they'd send him somewhere that…"

Jenna left her sentence hanging and it was Jake's turn to sigh.

"You know that none of this is your fault, Jenna. Don't you?" Jake spoke softly, reaching over and turning her face towards his with a finger under her chin.

Her eyes said it all. All of the crimes and evils of the world balanced right there on her shoulders as if she had some power to stop them from happening.

"Mara and Alexis are victims of the bad guys, Sweetheart… not you." His thumb brushed away another tear. "And from what I have heard about Ben Clark from your brother and from you… he was a hero. I highly doubt even you and your stubbornness could've stopped that man from doing what he had to do."

Another tear fell.

"This may surprise you, Jenna, but you can't stop the bad things from happening in this world. You're only human. You don't have that much control."

"I do like control," Jenna sniffed with a small, watery smile.

"Really? I couldn't tell." Jake grinned and moved his hand away from her face before getting serious again. "As for failing at dying…"

Jenna put her hands up in defense. "I know, I know. Please don't tell my family that I said that. They already think I'm crazy."

Jake shook his head.

"No, they don't. Michael told me you're the strongest person he knows." Jake ignored the look of disbelief she gave. "You didn't fail at dying. God succeeded in intervening. He still has a plan for you. People to help. Things to accomplish. A future."

A future with me... Please, God. He kept those last sentiments safely tucked away in his mind, but continued to look into the blue pools that were Jenna's eyes. The heaviness had lifted from them and he could've sat there staring forever. Thankfully, his phone sounded before he made things awkward.

Jake remembered the real reason he needed to drive to the small town that morning. Branson was going to fill him in on next steps regarding Trip. The cabin made his phone useless with no bars or reception. Any communication needed to be timed just right for when Jake made it to the little strip of civilization. That road only boasted a gas station/mini mart, a roadside produce stand, and the small diner.

"Branson, can you hold on a moment?" Jake then put his hand over his phone and turned to Jenna once more. "If I give you my card can I trust you to get the coffee and maybe a few donuts? Don't go buying everything on the menu… I'm not rich, you know."

Jenna rolled her eyes and grabbed the card that he offered. "I'll try to control myself."

Jake watched with a hint of a smile on his lips as Jenna entered the diner. Through the windows, he could see her as she talked to the woman behind the counter and pointed out the pastries she wanted.

"Corey… you there? You know this isn't a *real* vacation, right?" Branson's voice brought him back to reality. His boss was right. This was no time to let his guard down. He had people to protect. And if he wanted to pursue any type of future with that blue eyed, sassy nurse who just snuck a bite of a donut thinking no one saw her… he needed this to end. Quickly.

"We picked up Trip. He's being detained for questioning. His number popped up several times in the dead guy's phone. Some enlightening texts as well. Figured you'd want to talk to him, too."

Jake let out a slow breath. Oh, there was plenty he wanted to say to his former friend, but that's not what Branson meant.

"I'll be there as soon as I can," Jake said in a restrained tone.

"Remind Helena we still need her to make a formal statement regarding Trip bringing the bear and roses over. Our guys went to your place and retrieved them after our talk last night," Branson stated. "Stop in the evidence locker and sign out the *gifts* he left for show-and-tell time on your way up. He's pretending to be quite puzzled over everything."

Jake gritted his teeth. "I'm sure he is."

"I'm keeping him as far away from prying eyes as I can. If we play this right, we might be able to use Trip to our advantage." Jake hoped Branson was right.

The call ended and Jake caught up on texts and checked the alerts on his phone. A few caught his attention, but Jenna was walking back to the truck, laden with a tray of coffees and a sack of donuts. Jake got out and helped her with the drinks and opened the door for her.

"Did you finish your top secret conversation?" Jenna asked.

Jake forced a smile. "Yes. And I'll be heading out as soon as I drop you back off at the cabin."

"What? Why?" Jenna probably didn't mean to look so worried, but her guard was temporarily down. Tiredness could do that to a person. "Where are you going?"

"Hopefully, to get some answers."

Jenna just nodded silently, not even trying to hide her concern. He smiled softly at her before pulling away from the diner and back onto the road.

"Not a cloud in sight," he said, looking up into the morning skies. "If it stays this nice, I may have a surprise for you tonight when I get back."

"You'll be gone *that* long?" Jenna said quickly. Then, she caught herself. Heaven forbid that she admit she wanted him around. "I mean… what surprise?"

He didn't answer. He just smiled as she rolled her eyes once more and looked out her window. He sent a prayer that what he had seen on the weather app on his phone was true. It would be nice to see Jenna awestruck instead of worried. Hopefully, Trip would talk and Jake could get back in time… because he could use a little awestruck wonder himself.

*****

True to his word, Jake stayed at the cabin only long enough to change clothes and pull Brian to the side to discuss something. Whatever they were speaking about must've been intense, because both men scowled and tried to keep their backs to Helena and Jenna.

"Do you know what that's about?" Helena sauntered up close to Jenna and asked quietly.

Jenna shrugged. "Mr. Branson called him and Jake asked me to go get the donuts and coffee while he talked to him."

"Figures. He's being too secretive." Helena sighed and rubbed her baby bump. "I hope we can go back home today. That air mattress killed my back last night."

"I'm sure I didn't help waking everyone up screaming this morning. I'm sorry about that." Jenna couldn't look her friend in the eye.

"Stop." Helena nudged her playfully. "It's normal to have bad dreams after the week you've had. Any word on Mara?"

"My friends from work said she's still groggy, but she's alive," Jenna said. "Her vitals are getting stronger."

While Jenna had waited for the coffees and donuts at the register, she checked her messages and was happy to see one of her coworkers had kept her updated on everything. Jenna hoped Mara didn't think she ditched her. First she almost gets the woman killed, then she abandoned her without even saying goodbye.

Jake and Brian finished talking.

"It might be a good day to S-W-I-M at the lake," Jake spoke quietly so as not to get Tori hyped up. "I'll be back as soon as I can. There are hot dogs in the cooler."

On their way back from the donut shop, Jake ran into a small minimart to grab a few extra bags of ice and food items.

"How long will you be gone?" Jenna knew she sounded overly eager and tried to play it down. "So I know how many hot dogs to cook tonight."

Helena didn't miss a beat. She let out a little lilt of a giggle and pretended to be interested in the picture Tori colored on at the table. Jake must not have missed Jenna's interest either because he smiled that sideways smile that made her toes curl.

"Are you going to miss me?" he said in a teasing tone, clearly amused at Jenna's sudden discomfort.

"For Heaven's sake, Branson is waiting, Corey," Brian interrupted, slightly amused but also slightly put out. "I want to get my wife and daughter home sometime before my second kid graduates college."

Jake's smile broadened and he winked at Jenna before heading to the door. "Go ahead and put two dogs on for me. I plan on being back before dark."

With that he was gone and the truck's engine came to life. Goose wandered to the door and paced nervously, wondering why he wasn't invited along on the outing.

"Okay, you're holding out on me." Helena's face was one of pure delight. "Last night he admitted to being distracted by you. You're acting like his leaving is the end of days. What is going on?"

What could Jenna say? She didn't even know. All she knew was that Jake did all the things Ben had once done: made her smile, gave her goosebumps, made her think of a future. And now, he managed to do something that Ben had never needed to do. He pulled her back from the brink of losing herself again in the darkness.

*****

Trip looked awful. They had picked him up sometime overnight, meaning Trip was on little sleep despite the coffee, sodas, and waters they offered to keep him pliable. Jake stared at him from the other side of the small window in the door, clutching the clear evidence bags containing the flowers and bear that he had gotten from the evidence locker. As he waited to confront the man, something in his chest tightened.

Trip had been like a kid brother to him. The betrayal Jake felt in that moment ignited a mix of rage and hurt. It far exceeded any type of pain over Nick's actions. Trip had lived under his roof. They watched football together. Went fishing together. He had been a pallbearer at Beth's funeral. And he dared hurt those closest to him, using a toy to betray Tori. He dared put Jenna in danger and possibly plotted her demise. He needed to pray before he entered that room.

Before he could utter one word to God, Branson spotted him and motioned for him to enter. He opened the door slowly and watched as Trip sat up straighter.

"Jake, man! I am so glad you are here. Whatever this is… it's all wrong." His voice broke with intense emotion. "Please, you have to believe me. You're my family, Jake!"

"Then what's this?" Jake said as he came further into the room. He threw the items he had crushed in his grasp onto the table.

Trip looked at the bear and roses, a glimmer of defeat followed by rallied cluelessness. "I… I don't know. What is it?"

Jake let out a hard laugh and shook his head. From his chair, Branson, too, let out a disbelieving sigh.

"You are going to try to tell me you don't remember coming to give this to Helena?" Jake asked incredulously. "You're not an idiot, Trip. You know I have cameras putting you at the house. I have the conversation right here."

Jake held up his phone, the condemning video already queued and ready to go.

"I gave Tori a bear and brought flowers for Jenna because she was having a bad day. So what?" Trip looked offended. "What are you accusing me of?"

Jake shook his head. The level of denial Trip was touting was either insanity or stupidity… or both.

Branson motioned to someone outside the door and said, "Bring in the laptop."

Trip sat up.

"I was waiting until you got here to play this card, Corey," Branson stated as he took a laptop handed to him by another officer. "This is your laptop, correct? We retrieved it from your car when we served you with the warrant."

He opened it and pulled up a file.

"There's nothing on there, Sarge," Trip pleaded.

"Just like the texts and phone conversations between you and a known criminal were nothing," Branson said without looking up from the computer screen.

"I already told you, that phone was planted. Someone must've put those things on there."

Jake shook his head. If he believed there was an ounce of truth to Trip's words, he'd beg him to stop talking. To get a lawyer. Trip was a cop. He knew better than to incriminate himself, but at that moment, Trip was like every other criminal brought in. He still thought he could outsmart the police holding irrefutable evidence. Sadly, it was a level of arrogance and insolence Jake had seen in his younger friend before. He truly believed himself to be untouchable.

"Mm, hmm. And the testimony of the woman who pointed at your picture and said you were one of her abusers?" Branson finally looked up when he was satisfied he had found the file he needed on the laptop.

"Do you know how many druggies and shady people I put away? You don't think someone wants to see me accused of something like this?" Trip started laughing at Branson as if it was the Sergeant who was out of his mind.

He laughed until Branson turned the computer screen around and pressed play. The innocent voice of Tori filled the room as she sang to the bear. Helena was in the background speaking to her doctor on the phone. Jake's jaw clenched as he leveled Trip with a glare.

"But wait," Branson said, holding up his hand. "There's more. Look at all of these images, Corey. See anyone you know?"

Jake moved to look at the screen. Images of women.... So many women in compromised situations. Then Branson highlighted a few pictures for Jake to notice. Pictures of Jenna. Walking to and from her car at the house. Pictures of Jenna in the hospital garage... at the taco place... with *him* on the way to church.

Jake's knuckles started cracking and Branson closed the laptop.

"You're in a tough spot here, Trip," Branson said finally.

Gone was the contrite, pleading friend who was claiming his innocence. In his stead, was a hardened, emotionless man refusing to meet anyone's gaze.

"Here's something to think about. You're going to jail. I don't have any doubts about that. I want you to think about the people who you'll be rubbing shoulders with."

The vein popping out of the side of Trip's temple indicated that he had already thought about that.

"I also want you to consider this..." Branson's tone went ice cold. "The man you are hitching your wagon to... the Broker... Nick Spencer..."

Trip's breathing quickened.

"I hear his reach goes well beyond the bars of a prison cell. And then there's the people he works for..." Branson pointed out. "You're quite the loose end, Trip. We've seen what happens to loose ends before."

"Or..." Jake spoke up after Branson gave him the nod to offer the deal they had agreed to beforehand. "You can help us get Nick. Before anyone else gets hurt… including you."

Trip shuddered.

"Do the right thing, Trip. You got caught up in this somehow…" Jake sighed. "… and I want to believe you're the same guy that Brian and I trusted. You were like a kid brother to me."

Trip stayed silent, but his eyes were turning red and watery as he listened.

A moment passed.

"I think I need to call a lawyer," he finally spoke with an uncharacteristic quiver to his voice.

Branson shook his head and let out a sardonic laugh. "You think, Son?"

Trip swallowed hard, but said nothing more so Branson continued.

"You can lawyer up. That's your right," Branson said as he rose and put both hands on the table and looked directly into Trip's face. "Or you can think about it overnight. Help us and help yourself. You have until tomorrow morning at nine."

33

Jenna was starting to think that maybe she could see what Jake saw in the cabin, after all. The breezy August day slowly turned into a comfortable summer's evening as the wearied campers reclined by the fire, waiting for Jake's return. Jenna had made many realizations that day, making her reconsider Jake's statement about the cabin helping one to think better. Was it the environment? The peaceful woods? The scenic lake? Or maybe it was because Jenna almost drowned. Funny how an event like that can open a person's eyes.

It started after everyone readied for a swim at the lake. Brian thought he was so covert, hiding a gun under his t-shirt and telling the ladies to go ahead and swim. He'd rather read, he had said. Clearly behind those sunglasses he was not looking at the book in front of him. She rarely saw a page turn, but she did see his head rotate every so often as if scanning the perimeter of the area.

Helena stayed close to Tori at the edge, not wanting to go past ankle deep water level. They threw rocks into the lake and watched the ripples. Tori shouted with happy enthusiasm each time her stone broke the surface. The water shimmering in the sunlight was breathtaking and Jenna stood mesmerized.

She decided to wade in a little deeper. She had never learned how to swim, but she felt bold. Maybe she would find someone to teach her. If she was going to live so close to the water, it might be nice to be able to enjoy it. Jenna went out a little further still. The water was past her chest now and she dipped her shoulders under to get relief from the blazing sun above.

"Jenna, be careful. I think there is a drop off somewhere…" Helena's voice called out, but was suddenly cut off when Jenna lost her footing on the slippery rocks.

She was plunged under water, eyes opened and arms flailing. Her legs went out from under her and she couldn't find the rocky bottom. The drop off was deeper than Jenna knew how to maneuver. Little fish swam by her face. They were like the ones she and her brothers put on the ends of their fishing hooks to catch bigger fish. *Funny the things that pop into your mind when you're dying.*

Dying? Drowning? No! She didn't want to. She couldn't breathe. The water stung her nose and throat. Panic set in and she thrashed for what felt like a lifetime until she felt a hand reach down and grab her arm. She was pulled up and then pulled along, her face above water.

"Are you okay, Jenna?" It was Brian's voice. "Jake would kill me if something happened to you."

She coughed up the water from her lungs and tried to get her legs under her once more.

"Are you steady? You okay?" Brian asked, his face etched with concern.

"I'm… I'm okay," Jenna managed to get out, in between coughing fits. She was standing on her own legs in the knee-deep water. Then, it hit her.

She *was* okay. The panic that struck her when she couldn't breathe… when she couldn't get her face above the water… she didn't want to die at all. She could have if she really wanted to. She could've let herself go deeper into the lake… pulled back her hand that reached out for help. But that was just it. Jenna didn't *want* to die. She wanted to live. Hadn't she prayed to want to *want* to live? And she did *very much* want that. *When had that happened? Thank you, God.*

In between coughing up more water, she laughed. She knew she must've looked ridiculous. How could she explain this to someone who had never wanted to die? She would look like an idiot. Crazy. Indeed, Helena was clutching her chest with one hand and her daughter's hand in her other. Brian looked uncertain as to whether Jenna was safe to leave alone in the lake.

"Are you sure you're good?" he questioned again.

"Yes, I'm sorry I scared you," Jenna said after she could finally catch her breath. "I'm good. I promise."

"I should've told you about that drop off sooner, Jenna." Helena still looked concerned. "I went under in the same spot the other year, but *I* know how to swim."

"I swim… I swim…" Tori pulled against her mother's hand to go back into the water.

"Uh, I think we should dry off and go back to the cabin, Stinkerbell," Brian said as he retrieved the weapon he had concealed under his book on the beach chair. He had hidden it there when he had to go into the lake for Jenna. "Who's ready for hot dogs?"

Helena gave him a look and nodded at the gun he put back in his waist line. "Is that thing necessary?"

"Would I have it out if it weren't?" He dropped a kiss on her forehead and waited for everyone to start moving back towards the cabin.

Jenna's next realization hit just as poignantly as the first. The fire in front of her flickered and filled the air with the scent of burning wood. They had already eaten dinner, saving a hot dog or two for Jake on a paper plate wrapped in foil. Tori had gone down to sleep willingly, tired from her splashing and swimming. The door of the cabin was propped open so they could hear if she awoke.

Across from Jenna, Helena leaned against Brian on the wooden bench. He rubbed her back and spoke softly to her. Occasionally, the two would giggle and Brian would talk to the baby who apparently was making Helena constantly have to reposition. The scene was heartwarming. Beautiful. It made something in Jenna ache. She wanted that. After Ben died, she gave up on ever having it. However, she wanted it now more than ever.

Constance had told Jenna that maybe she still had this in her future. Could that be true? Jenna had always wanted to be a mother. To know what it felt like to have life growing inside of her… a life created out of deep love between her and her husband. *A husband. A family. Is that even possible for me, Lord? I don't want to be jealous, but I want what Helena and Brian have. Do I even dare to hope?*

The darkness was split by a flash of headlights and the low roar of a motor. Brian eased Helena over and stood up, just to make sure it was who they were expecting and not a trespasser. His shoulders eased as the truck pulled up and parked. Jake waved from the driver's seat. Goose ran to the door of the truck to greet him and Jake gave him some love before joining everyone at the fire.

"You're late," Brian teased.

"I had a few things I needed to do," Jake returned. His eyes landed on Helena. "Are you okay, Helena?"

"Just tired." The woman sat up a little and Jenna noticed not for the first time that day, she looked very uncomfortable. "Can we go home now?"

"Not quite yet." Jake looked apologetically at Helena and Brian before his eyes landed on Jenna.

"We saved you some dinner." Jenna retrieved the plate and handed it to him. "It's probably cold now."

All of the sudden she felt uncomfortable under his scrutiny. While he was gone, she decided she wanted to live… and to have a husband and family. Unsurprisingly, it was *his* face that floated into her mind when those desires surfaced. How did she express those thoughts to him? Should she even try? What if he wasn't thinking the same? Would it scare him away?

"Something on your mind?" Jake asked as he attempted to pull the plate free from Jenna's grasp.

She let go when she realized her death grip kept him from taking it. "Oops. Sorry."

"Did something happen while I was gone?" Jake asked the group, clearly sensing something.

Brian and Helena simultaneously looked at Jenna, throwing her under the bus.

"Nothing. Everything is fine." Jenna stumbled with the words. "But I think I need to look into swimming lessons."

Brian snorted with a wry smile. "That's an understatement."

Jake's brow furrowed, but Brian saved the day by getting straight to business. "What's the update on Trip?"

Jake took a seat on the bench near Jenna and divulged the information he had. Trip was in custody and they gave him until morning to decide whether he would redeem himself by helping them get the Broker. Only then could they all go home safely.

"So, what now? We wait on Trip to all of the sudden have a conscience?" Helena asked, suddenly close to tears.

Jake nodded, clearly feeling the pressure to get everyone home safely.

"I stopped by the hardware store and replaced the locks at the house," Jake offered. "I updated the security system. When we do get home, we'll be in good shape."

"What if I take Helena and Tori to my mom's house?" Brian suggested. "No offense, but we're not necessarily the main targets here."

His tone wasn't mean, just clearly concerned for his family.

Jake nodded. "You're right. As long as you aren't at the house right now, you should be safe."

"Your mom's house?" Helena shifted on the bench to face her husband. "Are you out of your mind?"

"Fine, we can go to *your* mother's place."

"In *Ohio*?" Helena asked incredulously, holding her stomach as if the mere thought made her ache.

"Then we'll go to my mother's."

Helena let out a harsh laugh. "Ugh… no."

Jenna and Jake looked on in silence as the couple tried to hash out a plan.

"If they leave, we'll need to find a place for you to go as well," Jake said to Jenna while their friends continued discussing. "The best option would probably be in Deer Creek with Michael and Anna. They're under Detective Jenkins' watch. He's a good guy and you'd be safe."

Jenna snapped to attention. Home? In Deer Creek? She hadn't been with her family since she moved to

Skennan Cove. It wasn't as if it had been years. In truth, it was only a couple of months since she and her family were together. Yet, it *felt* like years. So much had happened. So much had changed in Jenna. She wasn't the same. Could she go back home now? Wouldn't they still look at her with pity and concern?

"I know!" Helena got to her feet, once again holding her very low hanging belly. "Constance and Tom! They are our emergency plan for Tori if I go into labor. Maybe we could stay there?"

Brian considered it and nodded. "I can give them a call in the morning."

"Then its settled." Jake's tone and demeanor seemed almost sad… defeated.

"*Is* it settled?" Jenna muttered under her breath. There Jake went again, deciding for her where she'd be safe. She would make that call… not him. Home was the most reasonable plan, but *if* she went it would be *her* idea, not his.

He gave her a side glance that spoke volumes. Jake looked spent. Too tired to argue.

"Why don't you all try to get some rest. Pray hard that Trip will do the right thing," he suggested wearily.

"I think that sounds like a good idea. I do feel like I need to lay down," Helena said, slightly stumbling.

Brian caught her arm and steadied her. "Are you sure you're okay, Sweetheart?"

"Yes, I was just on my feet too much playing with Tori at the lake. My back hurts," Helena said, arching her back to find relief.

Jenna checked her phone to see what time it was. She didn't tell Helena she had been doing it, but Jenna had been seeing if her complaints were following a pattern. So far they seemed far enough apart and not consistent. Yet, Jenna had an uneasy feeling. Maybe it was for the best that the Hamiltons found more comfortable lodging. Helena could go at any time. Even if it meant, she, too, had to find an alternative.

Brian and Helena slowly eased into the cabin, shutting the door behind them. Jenna rose to follow, but she felt the warmth of a masculine hand hold on to hers, bringing her back down to the bench. Her arms broke out into goosebumps as she looked down at her hand and watched as his covered hers so perfectly. Slowly, she brought her eyes up to his face. She did not want to argue with him about going home. Jenna wanted to enjoy the warmth of his touch even if just for a moment.

"I promised you a surprise," he said softly.

That's right, he had! Jenna looked up into his face as they sat there in front of the fire and her mind raced. Heart thudding in her ears, she nodded slowly.

"Yes, you did."

He smiled at her and then looked up at the canopy of trees above them. "Do you trust me enough to go for a little walk?"

“I… guess?” Jenna let him pull her up to her feet and he doused the campfire with the water bucket that had been sitting next to them.

After he was content the embers were dying, he held out his hand for her once more. Jenna hoped he couldn’t sense the slight trembling in her fingers as he led her down a dirt path that went back past the cabin and into the woods.

“Um, should I be concerned?” Jenna was only half teasing. After everything she had seen and experienced over the past several months, she never knew what to expect.

She heard Jake chuckle.

“We can turn back if you want, but I think you’ll want to see this,” he said, still holding her hand and still moving forward.

“See what?”

“Be patient. We’re almost there.” His flashlight guided them along the forest trail and Jenna could not see a logical destination in front of them.

Her nerves gnawed at her stomach and she looked for anything to talk about to distract her from her racing thoughts.

“Do you think Trip will help you? Or will we have to find somewhere else to go?” Jenna could almost see his shoulders slump in the darkness.

"I wish I knew, Jenna. I know I don't trust him," Jake sighed. There it was again. His tone. The sadness. It sounded like defeat. "I don't know how I missed it."

"Missed what?" Jenna almost tripped on a branch trying to keep side by side with Jake. He slowed down when he realized she stumbled.

"Trip. I didn't see it coming," he pondered quietly. "I can normally read people really well. That's my job. He's been my friend for years. How did I miss it?"

Jenna stayed quiet, allowing him the space to talk, but gently squeezed his hand.

"Nick Spencer… somehow his betrayal wasn't a complete surprise. There was always something about him that I couldn't get comfortable with." Jake let out a hard laugh. "Even before I found out he and Beth had dated briefly."

"Well, he sounds pure psycho. Who tattoos another man's wife on his neck?" Jenna shook her head. "Trip was slippery."

"To say the least," Jake muttered.

"Do you think Brian and Helena will be safe if they leave?" Jenna took a chance in asking the question. She saw Jake's reaction when Brian mentioned it.

Once again, Jake sighed.

"I sure hope so. It's not what I would recommend, but I understand why they need to. It's just that…"

There was a silent pause and Jenna looked over at his dark silhouette.

"What?" she prodded.

He let out an ironic laugh. "Let's just say, I guess you aren't the only one with control issues."

Jenna thought back to their conversation they had shared earlier that morning. "You too, huh?"

He smiled in the darkness and nodded slightly. "Yeah. If you hadn't noticed."

It was Jenna's turn to smile.

"I can't keep the people I care about safe if you're scattered all over the place." His admission came out quiet and nearly stopped Jenna's legs from moving forward.

"You care about… *me*?"

He stopped and looked at her. She wished there was better lighting. Was he laughing? Was he serious? Not knowing what was going through his mind drove her crazy.

"I thought that was obvious," came his soft response.

"Well… I mean… of course. I'm under your roof, right? You care about your tenants. Or do you mean… more?" Jenna floundered. "Like a friend? Or… *more*?"

Was this what it was like to be her sister-in-law Anna? They used to laugh at how flustered and tongue tied she became around Michael, but now it all made sense. Jenna had lost all her faculties. *Great job, Jenna. Jake probably thinks you're like a smitten little girl now. Prepare to be friend-zoned.*

Maddeningly, he chuckled and pulled her forward on the path ahead. His phone came out and he opened his compass.

"Perfect. We're going in the right direction," he said.

"Yeah… perfect," Jenna muttered. How dare he leave her hanging like that!

"Did you say something?"

Did she hear *amusement* in his tone? Did he not realize that she could punch just as hard as any man?

"No." Jenna glowered in the dark. "Are we almost there?"

"Yup. Right through here. Watch your step," he said as he moved his hand from hers to her upper arm. He led her through an opening in the trees.

There were boulders and rocks looming in the slight clearing and he motioned for her to sit. She hadn't felt like they were walking on an incline, but they appeared to be higher up on a hill overlooking the lake in the distance.

He sat next to her, shoulder to shoulder, and gave her a slight nudge.

"Look up," he said quietly.

Out of the corner of her eye she saw him turn his face upwards to the sky and she followed suit.

Jenna rarely gasped. Nothing really took her by surprise anymore. She had seen and experienced it all… or so she had thought. Above them, looming massive and commanding, were white pillars standing like sentinels of Heaven. In between them ribbons of color danced in shades of green, pink, purple, and red.

Just when she thought one color had faded, another replaced it in a choreographed movement of beauty. There was no end to it. They arched across the sky and rhythmically swayed as far as her eyes could see. Neverending. Vibrant colors of joyful creation.

"I will see the goodness of the Lord in the land of the living," Jenna whispered as her heart exploded at the sight of God's glory before her.

She didn't know why the sight undid her, but she felt the tears spring up and she let them fall freely. Jenna had felt God's presence before. In times of intense worship at church. Even in her darkness when she was in pain. But His presence was *there*… in *that* place. Little Jenna – as broken and screwed up as she was – sat under the banner of the throne room of God in that moment. Her eyes closed and she could imagine the sound of thousands upon thousands of angels singing to God in worship.

"Is this what Beth and Ben are seeing in Heaven?" Jenna asked as she looked over at Jake, who also sat in stunned reverence, staring at the sky.

He shook his head slightly. "No. What they're seeing and experiencing is even *better* than this."

His hand found hers once again. The two sat in silence, staring at the wonder above them. When the lights started fading and disappearing from sight, Jake gave her hand a squeeze.

"I more than *like* you, Jenna. Not as a tenant or as a friend," he said, returning to their earlier conversation.

Jenna turned to look at him and found his eyes were fixed on hers.

"I need to know if I have a chance here," his voice broke slightly and Jenna felt her heart skip. "I know we both have loved others… deeply… but I want to see what God might have for you and me…together… as a couple. I know it's quick and I'm taking a risk that you'll think I'm reckless, but I …"

"I'd like that too," Jenna rushed to say.

"Yeah?" His cheeks rose as he smiled, his face illuminated by the remaining starlight.

"Yeah." Jenna smiled right back as his hand moved to her face. His thumb stroked her cheek and she leaned her forehead in to rest against his.

"I may already be in love with you, Jenna. Does that scare you?"

"No," Jenna whispered. "Because I know that I'm already in love with you."

"I'm going to kiss you now," he warned and Jenna rolled her eyes.

"You're taking too long, Corey."

"Wow, you are bossy." His words were cut short as Jenna brought her lips to his. She may have initiated the kiss, but he was making sure she never doubted his intention again.

34

"Psst! Jenna, wake up."

Jenna groaned and buried her face further into the pillow. The scent of Jake's cologne on the pillow he had let her borrow brought a small smile to her face. Was it a dream? The northern lights. His hand on hers. His kiss. He loved her! *Please don't let it be a dream, God.*

"Jenna, I kind of need you!" It was a female voice, panicked yet familiar.

"Helena?" Jenna rolled over and looked at the door of her small room. A flashlight blinded her instantly.

"Ooh, sorry." The light moved away from Jenna's eyes and when they adjusted she saw her friend.

Helena leaned against the doorway, slumped over a bit. Her breathing seemed rapid. *Oh no. Helena is in labor.*

"Are you having contractions? How far apart?" Jenna sat straight up and threw back the sleeping bag.

"Oh, I think we're well past timing things," Helena said through gritted teeth.

"Has your water broken?" Jenna went through a mental checklist in her mind of what to ask.

Of course, they had covered labor and delivery in nursing school and she had even done some shifts in the maternity unit back in her early years. But never…

never… had she delivered a baby. The only relief she had was that labor could take hours. All they needed was enough time to get Helena to the hospital.

"I think it broke while I was asleep." The woman clenched the wood of the doorway and put her forehead against the jam. "When I stood up I noticed I was already wet."

Jenna groaned inwardly.

The main door to the cabin opened and shut, and both Brian and Jake entered looking frenzied.

"We called for an ambulance," Jake assured them.

"How will they… find us out here?" Helena said through what Jenna recognized as Lamaze breathing.

"I'll go back out to the main road and lead them in," Jake said quickly. His eyes met Jenna's and she saw the concern and doubt there. "Jenna, can you… do you know how to…"

Jenna nodded hesitantly. *Could* she? *Did* she? She helped move her friend further into the room. "Helena, can I check you?"

Helena agreed and allowed Jenna to guide her to the bed. In a moment of quick movement, Jenna threw the air mattress to the side and spread the sleeping bag out. No pregnant woman wanted to navigate the bounciness of an air mattress. Helena screamed in agony as she lay down.

Jenna turned to the men. "Did they say how long until the ambulance arrives?"

"They're coming from Skennan Cove." Jake looked like he was going to be sick. *As far out as we are – even at high speed – that could still be a half hour or more.*

Jenna groaned and shut the door to give Helena privacy. Tori's cries sounded from the other room, followed by a shaky sounding Brian trying to soothe her.

"You'll be just fine, Helena," Jenna said with confidence she did not possess as she pulled up Helena's nightgown to check her friend's progress. "Babies take a while to deliver. You'll be settled at the hospital with an epidural before you…"

The words died on Jenna's lips.

"Wh.. what? What's wrong, Jenna?" Helena's nails dug into the side of the wooden bed frame.

Throwing the door open, Jenna called to the men.

"She's going to deliver this baby before that ambulance gets here. Brian, get in there with her." Jenna pointed him into the room. "Jake, you're on Tori duty."

Jake took the weepy toddler from Brian and tried his best to comfort the scared little girl.

"What do we need to do? What do you need, Jenna?" Jake asked, rocking Tori and patting her on the back.

Another scream came from the bedroom, followed by Brian calling out, "*Jenna*!"

Both Jenna and Jake ran into the room, but Jake instantly stopped short when he saw way more than he had bargained for. "Whoa! I'll just stay out here."

"Good idea," Jenna said as she looked through her purse for something… anything… that would help. She found two hair ties and put them on her wrist before yelling out to Jake. "Do you have a pocket knife or scissors?"

"Uh… yeah. My hunting knife." His face instantly turned green.

"Gahhh! My knitting bag! I have scissors," Helena yelled.

Jenna tried to think quickly of everything she'd need. This was a primitive labor and delivery unit, to say the least.

"Do you have one of those suction bulbs in Tori's diaper bag?"

"The snot sucker?" Brian asked, proud of himself for knowing what she meant.

"Sure... that. Do you have one?" Jenna felt genuinely nervous about bringing a baby into less than sterile circumstances.

"No. Is that important?" Brian looked terrified.

"We'll be fine. It's fine." Jenna wasn't sure if she was talking more to her friends or to herself.

Jake ran into their room and started rooting through the various bags until he and Tori returned with the scissors.

Perfect! She would kiss him later for finding what she needed, but for now…

"Can you boil the scissors in water, please?" Jenna asked as she positioned herself at the base of the bed. Thankfully, Jake must have started a fire at some point to boil water for coffee. He'd have to wait for his caffeine fix. "Helena, does your smartwatch take heart rate?"

Helena nodded and Brian helped pull up what Jenna needed.

"Brian, keep an eye on that for me." Jenna moved Helena's legs and positioned her where she needed her. Sending up a prayer, Jenna began instructing her friend. "Do you feel ready to push?"

"What do you think?" Helena yelled.

Brian's eyes turned into saucers and he mouthed the words "I'm sorry" to Jenna.

"Okay, then. When I say go, give me a nice long push until I say stop." Jenna looked at Helena, who nodded back at her. "Go. Push, push, push, push… keep going. Keep going. Okay, stop and take a breath."

"You did so good, Sweetie. Keep up the good work!" Brian said as he kissed the top of her head.

"Don't…"

"Don't leave? I'm not going anywhere. I'll stay right here by your side," Brian said, taking her hand in his lovingly.

"Don't… *talk.*" Helena bared her teeth. The grip she had on Brian's hand must have been something because he looked down at his hand that was turning white in her grasp.

"The next contraction, just start pushing as you feel it, okay?" Jenna asked, trying to sound upbeat. This went on for some time. Pushing, followed by a moment to breathe, before pushing again. The baby's head was crowning.

The door to the cabin opened and closed, followed by the sound of a car engine. Jenna assumed it was Jake going to find that ambulance. They couldn't get there fast enough. Jenna occasionally glanced at the elevated heart rate on Helena's watch and grew concerned. *Please let them get here quickly, Lord. Keep Helena safe.*

It took a few pushes until the little head came oozing out into Jenna's hands.

"Brian, go get the scissors from the water. Does Tori have extra blankets? Preferably clean? I'll need a few."

He raced out and returned with what was needed. When he re-entered, his eyes landed on the top of his son's head.

"Oh, wow. That's him! That's my little boy."

"Jenna… I have to…" Helena raised up on her elbows, and it was once again time to push.

"Keep going. You're doing great, Helena," Jenna encouraged. "He's almost here… and… he's out! Rest."

The baby slid out the rest of the way easily and Jenna almost fumbled to secure him. He came out angry and vocal, exercising his little lungs. Relief flooded through Jenna at the sound. She used the blankets to clean his face and took a moment just to stare down at the wrinkly, red baby. *He's so beautiful.*

"He's okay?" Helena cried.

"He's perfect," Jenna gushed.

Brian handed her another blanket and she wrapped the baby before turning her attention to the next steps. Jenna broke off both of the hair ties from her wrist and knotted the cord in two sections.

"Do you want to cut the cord, Dad?" she asked Brian. "Cut right in between the two ties."

Brian did his part, and Jenna laid the baby on his mother's chest, skin to skin. She pushed gently on Helena's belly before telling her, "We just need to finish delivering the placenta. Can you give another push?"

Jenna helped the placenta out with a gentle pull, and that was that. She had delivered a baby. She sat back in awe at the scene in front of her. Helena began feeding her baby. Brian praised his wife and kissed his boy's head.

"I'm sorry I was so mean to you," Helena whispered to him.

"I have no idea what you are referring to," he smiled.

"Good answer." Helena smiled back tiredly.

"What is his name? Jenna asked.

"Brian Elliot Hamilton." The pride in both Brian and Helena's faces spoke volumes.

Just then the door burst open and Jake entered followed by EMT's with a stretcher.

"You did this?" one of them asked.

"She's one of the ER nurses," said another. "Good job, Clark."

Jenna spouted off pertinent details and they loaded Helena onto the stretcher with the baby content at her breast.

"Momma!" Tori called out from Jake's arms.

Brian took her and held her up so she could see her baby brother.

"Look, Tori. It's baby Brian," her father said. "That's your brother."

The little girl didn't look impressed. Brian leaned her down so Helena could kiss Tori's cheek.

"Here are your car keys. I borrowed your car to go to the main road to flag down the ambulance since I needed Tori's car seat," Jake said, handing Brian the keys. "I also called Constance and Tom. They said their house is open and they are excited to have everyone."

"Thanks, Man. It means a lot that you did that." Brian looked near tears, which made both of the manly men uncomfortable.

"If you put Tori's car seat in my truck, Jenna and I will get her to the Holloways' house," Jake offered. "I assume you're following Helena to the hospital and I don't know anything about those car seat contraptions."

It finally was too much for Brian, and he reached over and hugged Jake with his free arm. "Thank you, Corey."

Jake just cleared his throat and nodded.

"And people think women are schmaltzy," Jenna teased.

"I think we're ready to go," one of the EMT's spoke up. "Let's get you and little man checked out to make sure there's no infection. They may keep you overnight."

"Brian, grab our things!" Helena called out as they started wheeling her out the door.

"I'll be right behind you," he called back.

Brian held on to Tori a while longer while he set about packing. She was clingy as would be any toddler who had her throne usurped by a bald headed newbie. Jenna cleaned off in the lake as best as she could and changed into new clothes, but she craved a real shower. By the time she made it back up to Jake, Brian had already left and Tori sat sniffling over a donut at the table.

"So," Jake said moving in closer. "You delivered a baby. Is this just another day for you or what?"

Jenna smiled. "Definitely a first for me."

"You're amazing, Jenna. There are no words." Jake looked at her adoringly and Jenna melted.

He leaned in and kissed her gently, but it ended much too soon. He looked apologetic. "We need to get going. Branson has probably been trying to get a hold of me."

"Of course." Jenna hated moving away from him, but he was right.

Trip's deadline came and went. The cabin still needed packed up and cleaned before they left. They needed to hurry. Walking back into what had been her room, Jenna saw the chaos left over from their eventful morning. "Uh, Jake, about your sleeping bag…"

****

After a brief stop to throw away the sleeping bag and the cabin's trash in a dumpster, the truck headed back to Skennan Cove. Tori settled into her car seat and, thankfully, dozed off. Jake was grateful for Jenna's way with little ones. He adored Tori, but he wasn't used to her being so distraught.

He had tried all his tricks and none of them worked. Even having Goose next to her in the back seat wasn't enough to soothe her. It took Jenna singing the most ridiculous songs and the juice cup she produced from thin air to cause Tori to calm down. Not for the first time since meeting Jenna Clark, Jake concluded she was pure magic.

As soon as they got a little distance from the cabin, his phone rang out with all of the missed texts and voice mail notifications. He sighed, sending up a prayer that whatever was being said on those messages was good news.

“I’ve got to call Branson,” Jake informed Jenna. Normally, he would pull over and wait until he could conduct the call in private, but time was of the essence.

Jenna nodded in understanding as Branson picked up on the first ring.

“Where in the world have you been, Corey?” the sergeant demanded.

“Well, Hamilton’s wife delivered their baby this morning so…”

“Understood,” Branson said in a more reasonable tone. “Is everyone healthy?”

“Yes, Sir. As soon as we got on the road all of your texts came through. I haven’t had a moment to read them,” Jake stated. “Where are we with Trip?”

“He decided to be compliant.” Branson sounded as relieved as Jake felt inwardly. “He has a lot of demands, but the DA didn’t seem too worried… as long as we catch the bigger fish.”

“Do we have a plan in place yet?” Jake asked as his mind formulated next steps.

“One is coming together, but I would sure appreciate your thoughts.” Branson let out a wry laugh. “I imagine you have one in mind as we speak.”

“Yes, Sir.” Jake tightened his jaw. He felt Jenna’s curious eyes on him. He didn’t need her privy to what he was thinking. “Do we have someone available that can watch over Jenna and Tori, Sir? Until Nick is brought in…”

"Say no more," Branson said easily.

Jake spouted out the Holloway's address and avoided making eye contact with Jenna. The night before, he had mentioned her going back to Deer Creek, but he didn't have time to ensure she was safely delivered. If she were at the Holloways' house, at least he'd know where she was and that she'd be taken care of.

Once, Jenna had shrugged off his protection, saying that she wasn't his to protect. But, as far as he was concerned, their kiss the night before changed everything. He not only professed his love for her with that kiss; Jake made a promise that she would have the life she thought was impossible after Ben's death. And, if God willed it, she would have that with *him*. But first, he needed to clear the obstacles.

35

"I'm sorry. Exactly *when* did we decide where or *if* I was going anywhere?" Jenna asked Jake as soon as he got off the phone with the sergeant.

"The Holloways' house is the safest place for you right now under the circumstances." Jake didn't even look her way. He just kept driving, which made her even more irritated. It was as if he had made the decision for her and that was that. "I don't have time to get you safely to Deer Creek or I would. This is the next best thing."

"I can drive myself, you know."

Jake shook his head emphatically. "And risk having Nick follow you? Grabbing you? No way."

Jenna remained quiet as she thought through what he was saying. She had played down the danger once before. Then, Mara was kidnapped because they thought she was *her*. Her strong will recoiled at the notion of giving in, but Jake made sense. Of course, he couldn't risk losing the opportunity of catching Nick to drive her home to Deer Creek. And the longer they were out in the open, the more they ran the chance of being seen by Nick or whoever was working for him. She didn't like it, but it was wise to stay at the Holloways'.

Jake glanced at her quickly and smirked.

"What?" Jenna questioned him.

"No fights? No pushback?"

Jenna rolled her eyes and looked out the window.

"I imagine it would be wise to stay close by for Tori's sake. You know, until Helena and Brian get home," Jenna said nonchalantly.

"Ah. For Tori's sake." Jake smiled. "That's very considerate of you."

Jenna bit her lower lip to keep herself from smiling.

"Was there someone else that maybe played a part in your decision to stay around?" His tone was clearly fishing for acknowledgement.

"Maybe." Jenna smiled back at him. "Someone needs to make sure Goose is okay. He got pretty anxious when you left the cabin yesterday."

Jake forced his eyes back on the road and his smile faltered.

Surely, he knew she was being playfully coy. Just in case, she added, "I guess I wouldn't want to be too far from you either."

He sighed and reached over to hold her hand.

"What I said last night, I meant every word. I want a future with you." Jake swallowed back emotion and Jenna gave his hand a squeeze.

"Me too," Jenna reaffirmed.

"And I know I can come across as …"

"Overbearing, bossy, and high-handed?" Jenna supplied with an innocent smile.

Jake chuckled softly. "I was going to say over-protective and cautious."

"Hmm. I like my words better."

"You need to know that I am *protective* of you because I love you." Jake's words took the playful quip Jenna was planning, wadded it up into a ball, and threw it into a trash can. "I will not let anything happen to you, Jenna. I'll do whatever it takes to keep you safe. I won't fail again."

The last part was said so faintly that Jenna wasn't sure if she even heard correctly.

"I know, Jake. And I love you, too." Jenna gave his hand another squeeze. "And I know you will be the best guard the Holloways have ever had protecting their house. Probably the only guard they've ever had, but you get my point."

An expression crossed his face that Jenna was unfamiliar with. It unsettled her. His expression was a cross between resolve and something hidden. He lifted her hand to his lips and kissed the top of her fingers before letting go. She wanted to probe a little to see what he was thinking, but Tori started to stir and asked for her mommy. When they got settled at Constance's house, she would question him more.

There was so much about Jake she didn't know. To others on the outside, it would look insane how fast they fell for one another. But there was something about Jake that reminded her of home. Not her home in Deer Creek. Not her apartment. Not even the home she had once shared with Ben. It wasn't a place, but a distinct feeling that he was quite possibly why God let her live… to give her a second chance at love and a future.

*****

Jake tried not to rush away too quickly after getting Jenna and Tori safely inside Constance's house. However, he had no time to stay and chat. Especially, if Jenna got wind of what would be involved in catching Nick Spencer. Before going into Branson's office, Jake sat down at his desk and wrote out his plan in the form of a script for Trip to read on the phone with Nick.

There was so much that could go wrong. Trip wasn't exactly trustworthy just because he agreed to help. They were dealing with a traitor. He had betrayed Jake once, he could do it again. In addition to Trip's sketchy character, what if Nick suspected a set up? Trip had been locked up. Surely, Nick picked up on his absence. Fear stabbed at Jake's chest and he rubbed it as if that would somehow soothe it. *I can't fail again, God. Please.*

"Corey, when did you get here? Were you waiting for a special invitation, Son?" Branson asked, coming out of his office.

There was no time to waste. Jake gave the sergeant a rundown of his idea and let him read what he had in his hand. The older man gave a curt nod of approval and had Trip brought to the interrogation room.

"Before I agree to anything, Boss," Trip started right away with his demands. "I need to be reassured that our deal is in place. I go to a different state to serve my time and my charges are reduced. Did I leave anything out?"

"You were here when the DA agreed. I'm not repeating myself." Branson looked like he wanted to vomit as he said the words. Jake, too, felt sick to his stomach that Trip wouldn't get the full penalty of his crime. But if they could get Nick… well, maybe it would be a necessary evil.

Jake stepped forward and handed the script to Trip. "Read this to him and say nothing more. Understood?"

Aggravatingly, his old friend held the paper and took his time dragging his eyes over every word. Finally, he sighed and leaned back in his chair.

"You want me to tell Nick that you invited me to fish with you and Brian at the lake?" Trip questioned as he looked up from the paper.

Jake nodded curtly, pinning the man with his glare.

"I mean, I guess this could work. I can sell anything," Trip said, followed by that smug smirk that Jake wanted to thrash off his face. "He'll get suspicious if he goes and doesn't see me and Brian there with you. So, I guess we're going on a road trip? Just like old times?"

"No way. You are staying here behind bars where you belong," Jake said through clenched teeth. "We'll have someone there that resembles you."

Trip shook his head. "See… you think Nick is dumb. That's the problem. He's unhinged and crazy, but not dumb. You don't think as soon as I tell him the plan he'll be double checking on my whereabouts to make sure I'm heading to the lake like I said?"

Branson cleared his throat. "Just get acquainted with that script, Trip. Corey, let me see you in the hall."

Trip smirked one last time at Jake as the two men left the room.

"He's not wrong," Branson said almost immediately.

"We can have decoys. They can wear sunglasses and fishing gear to hide their identity," Jake reasoned, but inside he hated to admit Trip had a point. "Brian can't join us. He's on paternity leave. You want me out there alone with *Trip*? Do you trust me that much that I won't hurt him?"

"I know your character enough to know you won't, Jake," Branson said in a parental tone that he pulled out only on rare occasions – a tone Jake missed hearing from his own father. "This is almost over. Just go along with it so we can put Nick away once and for all."

"But it's going to take forever to get the clearances we need to let Trip out to…"

"Let me handle that," Branson smirked.

"We'll need time to get our guys in place. We can use my cabin as base. I can drive Trip and Brian's decoy in the morning to the lake from the cabin, but we'll need guys already out there in place."

"Don't worry. This isn't my first rodeo, Son." Branson smiled.

"I'm sorry, Sir. It's just that…"

"No need to explain." The sergeant held up his hand to cut Jake off. "I know you're invested in this for many reasons, but I need you to trust me."

They re-entered the room and Trip looked up at them with the same arrogant smile as before. "Is it show time?"

Branson rolled his eyes and produced Trip's cellphone from a manila envelope retrieved from evidence. He turned it on and several messages proceeded to ding one right after another. Mostly women.

Trip grinned as he scanned them over, but Jake kicked the legs of his chair to get him to straighten up.

"You think this is a game, Trip?" Jake seethed.

"No, Sir." Trip mock saluted and picked up the script once more. "I may need to add a little here and there for this to sound believable. I don't talk like a robot."

"Keep to the script or our deal is gone."

"Don't worry, Jacob," Trip said rolling his eyes and sitting up straight. "I won't ruin your little plan."

Jake's jaw clenched. His chest tightened into that pain again. It took him a few moments to realize he was holding his breath. How was he supposed to trust this lunatic sitting in front of him? After what he did to Alexis? After what he would have done to Mara? And to *Jenna*? *Please let this work, Lord. Let this nightmare be over.*

With each ring, Jake's heart thudded that much harder. Finally, on the third ring Jake heard *his* voice and his stomach lurched.

"Where have you been? I've been calling and texting you!" Nick's voice was hard like flint.

"*Tsk. Tsk. Tsk.* Don't be jealous, Baby," Trip teased, winking at Jake. "I've been preoccupied."

"With what exactly?"

Trip chuckled. "If you must know, I met a girl. I've been with her the last couple evenings."

"Spare me the details. From now on when I text, you answer. Understand?" Nick sounded tired to Jake. He didn't sound like the evil mastermind he had anticipated on hearing. "Damon has kept me close by. I haven't been able to get away from him or his guys long enough to see if there's been movement at the house. What have you heard?"

Jake stepped closer and slid the paper closer to Trip, tapping it with his index finger. Trip responded by sighing and rolling his eyes like a reprimanded teenager.

"They're planning a trip. Jake has a place near a lake that he goes to every summer. Guess who he invited to come along fishing?"

"Where? When?" Jake relaxed slightly, hoping Nick was genuinely taking the bait.

"I don't know the exact location. It's in the boonies," Trip supplied. "I'll text you the location when I know."

"Will Jenna be with him?"

The question caused Jake to hold his breath again.

"Uh… probably at the cabin," Trip supplied. "Why?"

"Imagine the irony," Nick sounded almost amused with himself. "He watched his wife die a slow painful death and did nothing. Now he can watch his new girlfriend die right before I put him out of his misery. He can die crying like the coward he is."

Jake's chest constricted even more as he clenched his fist at his side. He felt Branson's hand on his arm and looked over to see the warning in his eyes not to react. Jake let his breath out slowly and quietly.

"I'll text you the location as soon as I know anything," Trip said ending the conversation as instructed.

Branson took Trip's phone, powering it down and putting it back in the evidence envelope. He and Jake went back into the hallway.

"Go rest. Get your head clear," Branson ordered. "I'll keep you up to speed on the plans."

Jake got in his truck, reliving each painful word Nick spoke, plus a few words he had repeated to himself over the past several years. He drove out of town, far down a country road. When he was far enough away from civilization, he parked. For a moment, he sat there in silence, just trying to regulate his breathing. Then, as the images and condemning thoughts filtered into his mind, Jake screamed. He screamed loud and hard enough to hurt his throat and when he couldn't scream anymore, he sobbed.

Time was slipping away from them. Beth had wanted to die at home, surrounded by Jake and Goose. She wanted to go looking out over the river. He had moved a bed close to the window so she could see out, but Beth didn't even have the strength to sit up anymore. He would often sit behind her, letting her rest against his chest just long enough to see the sun shining on the waves. She would doze off and he would hold her there, pressing kisses to her head.

But that day, Beth would leave him. Her breathing grew more labored and Jake hurt for her, watching her work for each gasping breath.

"I'm so sorry. I should have made you go to the doctor. I should have insisted you take the chemo," Jake cried silently next to her sallow colored face. Her eyes were opened halfway, but not seeing. Those beautiful eyes that could make him do just about anything, now were glazed over. The life light in them was slowly dimming. "My job was to protect you. I failed you, Beth."

She couldn't answer him even if she were aware of his words. He knew she would argue. She'd say the words she had voiced every time he dared suggest he was somehow at fault.

"That's not how I want to go out, Jake. Let me go peacefully... on my terms. Let me just be with you until... I'm not. And then let me go home. Let me fly to Jesus where I belong."

He could still hear the raspy sound of her death rattle followed by that long drawn out exhale in his head. Jake sat there bodily in his truck, but his heart and mind were several years back in time by her side. Nick was right. He should've done more. Maybe he could've forced her into the truck to take her to that radiology appointment. He should've convinced her harder... begged her... *anything* at all to get her to live a little longer. To be with him a little longer.

A melodical tone rang out in the silence of his truck cab. *Jenna.* He picked up the phone, wiping his tears on his forearm.

"Hey! You answered!" she quipped. After a few heartbeats of silence, she asked, "Jake? Are you there?"

"Yeah... sorry." He took a breath to get himself back under control. "What's going on? Everything okay over there?"

"You left without saying goodbye. I came downstairs from putting Tori down for a nap and Constance said you left." Jenna sounded as if she wanted to scold him, but thought better of it. "Is everything okay?"

"You were busy with Stinkerbell and I needed to get to the office. Everything is fine," Jake comforted with a certainty he didn't feel. "I'm on my way back now."

Jenna let out a rush of air and gave a nervous laugh. "Oh good. I thought you were going to go save the world and just leave me here."

Jake sighed. How was he supposed to tell her that was his plan exactly?

"I love Tori, but she can be a bit much." Jenna sounded a little apprehensive. "I think seeing you would help her… a lot."

A smile lifted the corner of Jake's lips. "*Tori* needs me, huh?"

Jenna tried to sound nonchalant. "And Constance wants to know if she's supposed to cook dinner for the guys you have sitting out front."

"I'm sure they'd like that." Jake pulled away from the side of the road and pointed his truck back toward Skennan Cove.

"And you? Will you be here for dinner?" Jenna asked timidly. "Just so we know how many places to set at the table."

"I guess that depends on what she's making?" Jake tried to lighten his mood and tone.

"Lasagna. It smells delicious."

"Well, then. I'll be there in fifteen."

Their call ended and Jake realized he was smiling like a fool. How could he be so torn apart one moment and then, with one call from Jenna, turn into a pile of mush?

When Jenna Clark agreed to take that apartment, he'd had no intention of engaging her… befriending her. Her living there was supposed to be a favor for Michael, nothing more. Jake hadn't bargained on falling for anyone so quickly. Yet, there he was, not only interested in dating again, but wanting to go full force into a relationship with Jenna Clark. He didn't care how fast it seemed. She brought him life after so much darkness. And she could call him every derogatory name in the book, but he was going to protect her whether she liked it or not. Even if it meant his death.

Jake quickly called Branson.

"I want the officers stationed with Jenna doubled. You heard Nick. He will use her to get to me if he finds out where she is."

"I agree," Branson said wearily. "I'll send them over this evening. We'll head out to the cabin at three. Get some sleep, Corey. This is going to get intense before it gets better."

36

"You seem distracted, Broker," Damon said flatly from his place at the head of the long table. Nick sat to his immediate left and quickly raised his head to meet the man's eyes.

He had been checking his phone occasionally for any communication from Trip, but nothing showed since their last conversation. Damòn was getting suspicious and he knew he had to watch his back. Even when he had dismissed himself to take the call, Nick noticed an uncomfortable glance exchanged between Damon and one of his men.

Undoubtedly, the fact that Nick decided to go to his car to talk to Trip rather than stay within the building spoke volumes to his boss. The distrust was mutual. It was a matter of time before Damon put a bullet in his brain. To be honest, Nick couldn't care less. As long as he accomplished his purpose first, that is.

"I'm sorry, Sir. You have my full attention." Nick forced a compliant smile.

"Good to hear," Damon said with little sincerity. "As I was saying, I want you to handle the shipment tomorrow night. It's *precious* cargo."

"Tomorrow night, Sir?"

"Yes. Is there a problem with that?"

"Uh, no. Not at all." Nick looked around the room and saw no one else surprised by the request. "It's just that this isn't your usual night for deliveries."

"Scout is my man for these things, but he seems to have gone quiet. I don't suppose you've heard from him?" There was something challenging in the man's eyes. Nick resisted the urge to swallow. *He knows what you did.*

"Nothing yet, Sir."

"Well, then…" There was an evil gleam in Damon's eyes. "I'll need you to take Scout's place. Unless he reappears, of course."

Nick clenched inwardly. *Just agree and shut up, Spencer. It's not like you'll be there to accept it anyway.*

"I'll be happy to receive the shipment, Sir."

Damon nodded, seemingly pleased with his response. Ever since returning from his little *excursion* that Damon sent him on, he had to try to stay off his boss' radar as best as possible. It would all be over soon and Nick would be free of it all.

The rest of the meeting was nothing but background noise. Nick had things he needed to accomplish. Thankfully, he had been gathering his important papers and writing down all of his information to pass on to his sister. That morning, in fact, he had put it all in a manila envelope and addressed it to her most recent address. Hopefully, she wouldn't have a heart attack when she saw who it was from. Nick Spencer was supposed to be dead.

However, if she followed his instructions, she'd inherit a decent sum of money after his *real* death.

The men started leaving the room and Nick dismissed himself as well. It didn't take a genius to see that Damon suspected him of some foul agenda. Damon and one of his goons whispered to one another quietly as Nick exited. He'd be surprised if Damon's random shipment wasn't actually an ambush sent to take him out.

Sending Trip yet another text, Nick quickly made his way back to his apartment. He spent little time there, so there was nothing to become emotional over. Everything he valued was either ready to mail to his sister or in his car. He grabbed the envelope and something to eat before heading out the door once again.

As was his plan, he made it to the post office just before they closed and mailed his sister everything she would need to claim his money. Also included was a hastily scrawled note apologizing for his absence in her life and for what a horrible brother he had been. His parents had already died. Thankfully, they never saw what he had become.

Nick drove to Beth's resting place and waited for Trip's text. While he passed the time, he made sure his guns were loaded and that he was ready to finish out his mission.

"You once told me that you had hope that I would turn my life around," he said sitting up against her headstone. "I'm sorry I disappointed you. There was never hope for me. I know you spoke of God and I swear I tried it your way."

Nick laughed coldly into the early evening breeze.

"That stuff wasn't for me, Beth. I know it gave you comfort while you suffered so I guess it had a purpose."

Nick sat in silence for a moment.

"If you were here, I wouldn't need to die." His throat constricted. "I loved you so much more than he did. You know he's moved on right? That's how much he loved you, Beth. Acting like you never existed."

Angrily, he pulled at a clump of grass beside him.

"I'll take care of it, Baby. Just know that I would've done everything to keep you alive. I love you, Beth."

He pressed a kiss to his fingertips and placed it on her name as he got to his feet. Then he reached into his pocket to pull out a few cards and pictures that he had saved from his short time with her. He laid it on the ground in front of her headstone and walked away for the last time.

*****

Jenna pulled out the garlic bread. It was an insignificant task, but her handiwork looked exactly how garlic bread should look. Toasted golden brown, glistening with butter, and smelling like an Italian delight. She stood staring at the tray of bread slices with pride when the door off to her side opened and Jake stepped in.

Even exhausted, the man looked handsome. She stood awkwardly staring at him for a moment, before motioning to the tray on the stove.

"Just in time." She grinned at him. "I've been laboring all day to make this garlic bread for you."

He returned her smile.

"Is that right? Well, it looks amazing," he said, with his eyes not once glancing at the bread. He inched closer and planted a kiss on her cheek. He might have lingered a little longer if Constance's voice hadn't drifted into the room from the hallway outside the kitchen.

"Did I hear Jake?" Constance asked as she came into the room, clearly in all her glory to be hosting so many in her home. "I'm so glad you're back. Now this one can stop checking out the window every two seconds."

Jenna was about to deny the claim when Constance said, "Go wash up while Jenna and I get the food on the table."

Jake smiled smoothly at her as he disappeared towards the small washroom.

"I was *hardly* looking out the window every two seconds," Jenna scolded her older friend.

Constance winked at her. "Fine. Every five seconds then."

"Let's bless the food and Jake can take some of this out to his friends," Tom instructed as the tray of bread and lasagna were put on the table.

Jenna settled Tori into a high chair and handed her a sippy cup of apple juice. Jake came in and claimed the seat next to Jenna's. Tom blessed the meal and Constance cheerfully put a healthy portion onto disposable plates for the officers outside.

"Would you tell those nice gentlemen they can have more if they'd like, Jake?" she asked as she handed him the plates.

"Of course. I'm sure they will be thrilled." Jake smiled warmly and disappeared through the front door to take the food down to the officers parked at the opening of their driveway.

Jenna watched him through the dining room window as he handed them the food and remained a little longer to discuss something. She wondered what they were talking about. Couldn't they leave now that he was back? Wasn't their presence overkill?

Moments later, Jake came back in and took his place at the table. "They send their thanks, Constance."

"I'm delighted to have company. Aren't you, Tom?" Constance gushed.

He nodded while taking another bite of lasagna.

"Our kids are always so busy. It's nice to feel needed and I'm glad we can help." Constance smiled. "We had a video call this afternoon from Helena and Brian. She showed us the baby. He's adorable."

"Oh? How are they doing?" Jake asked. "Are they okay?"

"They're keeping Helena and baby overnight and sending them home tomorrow," Jenna supplied. "Helena's blood pressure was elevated, but it sounds like it's coming down nicely."

"That's good to hear." Jake nodded.

"I know there is not a lot that you can tell us about what is going on, Jake," Constance began. "But please know you are all welcome to stay here as long as you need to."

Jake smiled and nodded. "Thank you both for your generosity and hospitality. I hope this is over very soon so everyone can go back to some normalcy."

"So who's after you? Someone you put away in jail or something?" Tom asked bluntly. Constance must have kicked him under the table because he jumped and gave her a look. "What? I think that's a valid question."

Jake looked over at Jenna and smirked.

"It *is* a valid question," Jake agreed. "For now, I will just say that you're not far off the mark. In fact, I hate to further impose…"

"Anything you need. Anything at all," Constance reaffirmed.

"I requested to double the officers guarding the house." Jake said the words so bluntly and matter of fact that it caught Jenna by surprise. "Please don't be startled if you find more people outside wandering around tomorrow."

"Why more? Now that you are here, isn't that enough?" Jenna asked.

Jake looked like he wanted to melt at her words, but he cleared his throat. "I appreciate that vote of confidence, but I will need to leave in the morning. I'll feel better knowing you all are well protected."

"*Leave*? But why?" Jenna furrowed her brow. "I thought you said it was safer for us to stay here?"

"For *you*, yes," he said the words softly. "I need to end this. I have a job to finish, Jenna."

The table grew momentarily quiet and Jenna forced herself to cut Tori's food into tiny pieces. The little girl looked up into Jenna's face and smiled the most cheesy smile. For a moment, it kept Jenna from telling Jake Corey what he could do with his job.

"Helena and Brian will be coming tomorrow. The officers won't keep them from coming in, will they?" Constance asked.

"No. They are familiar with Brian and I will remind them," Jake assured. "Tom will be free to go to and from work as well."

Jenna sensed him looking at her from the corner of her eye, but she wouldn't meet his gaze. Why were men so … so… *ugh*… she didn't know the word. Macho? No, Jake wasn't macho… not in the obnoxious sense. He was protective. Caring. *Heroic*. Well, she was tired of the men she fell in love with being heroic. Why couldn't someone else be heroic for once? Heroic actions often led to death.

The thought caused Jenna to shudder.

"Are you alright?" Jake nudged her with his shoulder, trying to get her to look at him.

"I'm just peachy."

The rest of dinner consisted of small talk or entertaining Tori. When Constance got to her feet to begin cleaning up, Jenna followed.

"You and Jake go ahead and visit in the living room, Dear." Constance took the tray of bread from Jenna's hands. "Tom and I have a good system in place. He'll help me clean up dinner while I get this saucy little angel cleaned up."

Tori beamed up from her seat with a red beard.

"I can help get Tori washed up at least," Jenna offered.

"Stop. Go talk to him. He's worried about you," Constance said softly, taking her hand before nodding her in the direction of the living room.

Jenna let out an exasperated sigh. She didn't want to talk to him, not if he was going to tell her that she had to stay at that house and wait for everything to be over.

"Can we talk?" Jake asked coming up behind her and reaching for her hand.

She made the mistake of looking into those electric blue eyes. What was she thinking? With very little thought she allowed him to take her hand and lead her into the living room.

"So, Constance told me she taught you some granny hobbies today. How did that go?" Jake grinned.

Jenna couldn't resist chuckling and pulled a little embroidery hoop from a basket next to the couch. Without a word she handed it to him.

"Oh, wow! It's… uh… the state of New York?" He was clearly trying not to hurt her feelings.

"It's a deer head." Jenna bit her lower lip to keep from laughing.

"No… really?" He laughed.

She snatched it back. "I just haven't put the antlers on yet."

"Oh, well then. That will make it better," he teased.

"I guess I wasn't cut out to be a Victorian homemaker embroidering samplers. I'm a nurse. I can stitch up flesh wounds," Jenna said as she tucked her creation back in the little sewing box. "Let's just hope I don't have to stitch *you* up before this is all said and done."

"Jenna…" Jake pulled on her arm gently, bringing her into his embrace. "Say what you need to say."

"I don't want you to go. Let someone else do it." Her words were muffled against his shirt and she knew she probably sounded like a child.

"This is mine to finish."

Jenna pushed away and gave him a glare. "Why does it have to be?"

"Sit down. I'll tell you what the plan is so you at least know what is going on."

Jenna complied. Jake proceeded to fill her in on everything from Trip's call to Nick and the threats made against her. He informed her of the decoy Brian and the mock fishing trip. Jake was emphatic that there was a whole team being brought in, including a sniper that would be in place way before Nick Spencer showed up.

"We're taking every precaution. The goal is that everyone walks out of there with little to no harm," Jake assured her tenderly. "It's just that some of us will be in hand and feet shackles at the end."

Jenna didn't respond to his little joke so he nudged her and added, "That's supposed to be Trip and Nick, in case you didn't get that."

"Yeah, I got it." Jenna glowered.

"Talk to me, Jenna." Jake sighed.

"So what? We're just supposed to trust that Nick is going to give up willingly?" Jenna looked doubtful. "We're supposed to trust *Trip,* of all people?"

"No, we're supposed to trust *God.*" Jake rubbed his face with his hands. He looked tired and a whole host of other things that Jenna had missed while wallowing in her own emotions. "I really could use a little encouragement here. I'm scared, too. This *has* to work. I *need* this to work."

Jenna pushed aside her fear and anger at the guilty parties to lay her head on Jake's shoulder.

"You're right," she whispered. "I'm sorry."

He straightened up and put his arm around her, bringing her close.

"It's just that..." Jenna had a sudden image float through her head of those men in their dress blues approaching her door that fateful morning. "I'm still learning that I can trust God... even if the worst happens. I don't want the worst to happen again, Jake. I don't know if I can take it."

A tear slipped over the rim of her eye and onto his shoulder.

"We can't control the outcome, Sweetheart." Jake pressed a kiss to her forehead. "God already has that planned out. And we need to trust that if He already has it planned out... *no matter what it is*... He will get us through it."

She knew his words were true, but she didn't want to talk about it anymore.

"This is tomorrow's worry. Let's not think about it right now, okay?" Jenna begged. At least maybe they could enjoy a night with friends and pray together after breakfast in the morning before he left. For that moment, they were safe.

37

"Oh… my… word, Helena!" Jenna gushed over her phone screen at the little baby boy sleeping contently in his mother's arms. "I can't wait to hold him."

Helena beamed through the video call. "I will gladly let you hold him if it means I can take a nap."

"You've got a deal," Jenna chuckled. "How's Brian?"

Her friend rolled her eyes and turned her phone to show Brian asleep soundly in the recliner in Helena's hospital room. "He's just fine."

Jenna smiled. "When are they discharging you?"

"As soon as the doctor comes in in the morning. I miss my own bed," Helena said wearily.

"I know. If everything goes as planned tomorrow, we can go home. We can go back to normal." Jenna tried to reassure her friend, but inside prayed that what she said was true.

"Oh, I don't think things will be normal." Helena smirked. "Don't think I didn't notice you and Jake being all cute and new coupley."

Jenna's smile illuminated in the light from her phone. She was tucked in the guest bed, trying to keep her voice down as Tori slept in her crib a few feet away.

"He really is amazing, isn't he?" Jenna gushed. "I never thought I would even look at someone new."

"Jake is rare. Fiercely loyal. I wasn't sure he'd find anyone after Beth. I never thought I'd see it." Helena smiled warmly. "It makes me happy. There aren't many good guys left like him and Brian. Grab him and don't let go."

"I'm scared. The way I feel about him is... well, it's just crazy. I shouldn't be in love this fast, right?" Jenna asked.

Helena raised her eyebrows in interest.

"I always laughed at the girls in college who fell for the first guy who came along and made plans with them after a few dates," Jenna explained. "I'm dreaming of children and a future. This time last year, I was sure I'd die alone."

"How did you know you loved Ben?" Helena asked quietly.

"Well, he was my best friend. I had so much fun when I was around him. He looked out for me... thought about me above himself. Pointed me to Jesus."

"Does Jake do those things? Has he... in the time you've known him?" Helena's smile told Jenna she already knew the answer.

"Yes." Jenna felt tears stinging her eyes as she thought about it in detail. "And then some."

"Well then." Helena's smile was serene. "I think that people who have loved deeply in the past know faster than anyone else what the *real* thing is when they see it."

"What if I lose him too?" The stubborn tear finally fell over the rim of her eye and down her cheek. "He's going out there with decoy Brian and Trip to face Nick alone… what if he doesn't come back?"

"Who is decoy Brian?" Helena asked, brow furrowed.

Jenna gave her friend a quick rundown of the plan Jake had recounted to her. Her fear resurfaced as she thought of the risks the next morning would hold.

"Why couldn't I have fallen for an accountant?" Jenna sighed.

Helena's face shared her concern and Jenna felt guilty. "I'm sorry, Helena. This is supposed to be a joyful time. I shouldn't have unloaded all of that on you."

"Jenna Clark! We're family," Helena said sternly, causing baby Brian to stir. "I don't care if I've known you for a couple months or for a lifetime. You are my sister in Christ. And Jake… he's my brother. No matter what the outcome is tomorrow… we'll lean on each other, okay?"

The two chatted a little while longer before Jenna's eyes grew heavy. The baby needed to be fed and Jenna needed to sleep. Tori would wake up wanting breakfast and Jenna had to be in a good mindset to see Jake off. She would pray with him… just as she had before Ben's deployment. Then she would trust God. *No matter the outcome, God. Help me trust you.*

*****

Jake flipped onto his back, staring up at the ceiling fan in Tom's den. The old couch's springs stabbed him in the most unpleasant places, but it was okay. He couldn't get too comfortable anyway. It was after two in the morning and very soon he would have to sneak out of the house. So much depended on that plan working. The familiar tightness in his chest reemerged and in the darkness he sighed heavily.

The scant amount of sleep he had gotten that evening would have to suffice. Even in the moments he had managed to doze off, his dreams awoke him, leaving him feeling rattled and anxious. The tick… tick… ticking of the antique clock on a bookshelf sounded ominous. With each tick of that clock, he drew closer to a showdown that could end badly. So, he prayed.

Lord, you already know the outcome of this day. Help me to remember that You are in control... even if this doesn't end the way I want it to. Keep Jenna and everyone here safe. I feel so drawn to her, God. I feel like she is an answer to prayer, but I'm scared to get my hopes up. I'm scared I'll make some stupid mistake and either put her in more danger or I'll have to let her go to keep her safe. I'm just... scared. I need You to go before me. The only faces out there I will see will be Nick's and Trip's... both traitors. And I will need to trust all the others... trust isn't really something I want to do right now. Help me, God.

The alarm on his phone went off. It was time to get up and leave. Jenna would wake up in a few hours, expecting to find him waiting at the breakfast table. His heart hurt as he pondered what she might feel or think when she realized he had left without her knowledge. It was for her own good. Hopefully, he would return to her unscathed and he could make it up to her. *Hopefully.*

"The replacements are here." The text came from one of the officers outside.

"On my way out," Jake responded.

Branson had been kind to get his opinion on the officers assigned to the Holloway house. Jake felt certain everyone would be fine. Still, a niggling doubt pressed in on his chest. He once felt secure with Trip as well.

He splashed water on his face, brushed his teeth, and ran a comb through his hair. His reflection looked... *old.* He smirked. Jenna had referred to him as *older* once before. Well, he was feeling it that morning. *Don't get in your head, Corey. Finish this so you can get back to her.*

Walking out into the early morning darkness, Jake made his way down the drive to the officers in their cars. The August morning felt sticky and humid. In a few hours a hazy sunrise would awaken everyone in the house, but he would already be in his position.

Once more, he looked around at the Holloways' home and felt reassured that this was the best place for Jenna and the Hamiltons. The house was on a bit of a hill and surrounded by trees. Conveniently isolated. They didn't have many neighbors and the ones they *did* have were friends. The only traffic on that road was local and the drivers were easily identified. *Leave her in God's hands. She'll be safe here.*

Jake greeted the officers Branson sent over and gave them a few instructions and reminders. The Hamiltons would arrive at some point that day. Tom would leave for work. Everyone seemed comfortable with their assignment… except for him. With one glance back at the darkened house, he got in his truck and left.

*****

"Where are you?" Nick texted Trip for the hundredth time.

Trip was a night owl. In the past, he had responded right away when the Broker had texted him. Something felt wrong. Trip's location had been turned off on his phone. Not for the first time in the past day or two, Nick wondered if he was walking into a trap.

Trip wasn't his friend. Nick didn't have any of those. Therefore, there was no trust. There was no expectation that Trip would sacrifice himself for Nick. There wasn't anything in it for Trip. Nick surely wouldn't do it for him if the shoe were on the other foot. No, he was alone in this, fueled solely by his desire to kill Jake and to be put out of his misery.

Nick's mind raced in the early morning hours. He'd slept here and there, but his car wasn't conducive to decent naps. The time for rest would come. Nick wondered if the heaven Beth used to talk about would take him still. Maybe if he pleaded. Maybe if he recounted all the good things he had done.

Nick laughed. Who was he kidding? What good things?

"Get your head out of the clouds, Spencer," Nick scolded himself. "If you wait on Trip, you'll probably be walking into an ambush."

Nick rested his head against the headrest. What were his options? He could run. *No.* He could wait on Trip. The thought was comical. What if he could figure out *where* they were convening? Jake had a dive cabin. He knew about it from when they had been partners briefly. Beth referred to it as his thinking place. She had hated it because there was no electricity. *Think. Think. Think. Where did she say it was?*

Pulling out his phone, Nick did a search of the lakes surrounding the area. There were many. Upstate New York was literally a fisherman's paradise with all of the lakes and rivers. He scanned the names, seeing if any rang a bell in his mind. A few sounded vaguely familiar, but he couldn't risk driving the wrong direction.

Nick's brow furrowed as a memory hit him. Several years back, hadn't Jake emailed invitations to the guys from the department asking them to come have some weird kumbaya Bible study at that cabin? It was shortly after he had married Beth, and Nick sneered at the idea of attending. There was supposed to be Bible study, a cook out, and *fishing at the lake*.

It was a long shot, but Nick logged in to his old email from work. Would it flag him or alert someone he was hacking in? That didn't matter as long as he got where he needed to be. He never deleted emails. Others called him messy. But if he found what he needed, the joke was on them.

"Ha! *Carson Lake*." Nick turned the key in his ignition and set the coordinates. "You failed again, Jake. This time you betrayed yourself."

*****

This cabin has always been a place of solace... peace. But now...

Jake watched armed law enforcement converge on his tiny cabin. Just the day before, he had been there with the people closest to him. A little life had been born. Jake had watched the northern lights and bared his heart and soul to Jenna.

"Does this place have a real bathroom, Corey?" someone asked.

"Around back."

The man snorted and disappeared around the corner.

Jake observed as the sniper – a middle-aged man he knew as Ellis – prepared his weapon. The *Precision .308* was ready for work, as was its handler. Ironically, Nick had been known as an accomplished sniper once upon a time. Would Ellis be the one to take him out or would Nick be taken down peacefully?

"I'm ready. Who wants to drop me off for school?" Ellis teased.

"Radio in when you're in place," Branson ordered.

Ellis nodded and left with one of the men to the overpass and the isolated section of the lake. Their plan was in motion. There was no going back now.

Branson slapped Jake on the back. "The sun's coming up. We need to get Trip where he can text Spencer."

Jake sighed.

Trip had been in the van, chained to the bench the entirety of the morning. He had changed into jeans and leisure clothes before leaving the jail, as if he really were going on a lighthearted fishing excursion with his old friends. From the time Trip would send that text, they would have maybe an hour of waiting before Spencer showed. *If all goes well.*

"Branson, we have company!" another man called out over the radio.

"We weren't expecting anyone else." Branson's brow furrowed as he and Jake stepped outside, guns holstered but within reach.

The headlights of a car flashed. An engine turned off and a man emerged. "I heard we're going fishing. You didn't think you were going to do this without me, did you, Corey?"

38

Jenna fumed from her place at the breakfast table. That morning, she came downstairs to find Goose whining at the front door, pacing back and forth. She had immediately gone to Tom's den and found the door wide open with no one inside. It didn't take a genius to see what had happened. A note rested on top of a pillow on the couch. *I love you.* That's all it said. Not an explanation. Not an apology. Just *I love you*. Words that should've made her heart flip flop instead caused it to break.

"Well, who in the world is that?" Constance said suddenly as she pulled back the curtain in the kitchen and looked out.

"Is it Jake?" Jenna asked breathlessly. Maybe she got it all wrong. Maybe his absence was easily explained. Maybe he just went out for donuts or something.

"No. It's not Jake, Sweetheart. I'm sorry." Constance looked back over her shoulder at Jenna sympathetically. "If I didn't know any better, I'd say that's Carol's car."

Jenna's shoulders slumped. "Carol?"

Constance nodded. "Yes, Carol from church. Sweet woman. Now, why is *she* here?"

Tom had already left for work, leaving everyone to figure out on their own why Jake had left so abruptly. The officers were kind and very happy to receive the muffins Constance had baked, but they gave no information in return.

"Well, she cleared security," Constance chuckled from her place at the window. "She's on her way up the driveway."

Jenna scowled. She was still getting to know the people at church and she didn't want to give anyone a wrong opinion of her. However, Jenna did not want to pretend to be social. *How could he do this to me? Why would he leave without saying goodbye?*

"Oh, my!" Constance gushed all of the sudden. "Well, that's a twist, isn't it?"

"What?" Jenna finally joined her at the window and saw the woman named Carol. She opened the back door of her car and helped out a young woman before taking out an infant car seat.

Helena! Jenna ran to the door and threw it open. Running to her friend, she threw her arms around her, being careful not to knock her off balance. Tori came bounding out of the door as well and instantly held her arms up to her mother.

"Let's get you inside, Dear." Constance took the car seat from Carol and motioned for everyone to re-enter the house.

"Connie, do you mind telling me why you have police guarding your house?" Carol asked with a look of concern. "Where is Tom?"

Putting her free hand on her hip, she leveled her friend with a look. "Well, I'm not a black widow, Carol. He's at work."

"Then who… what is…?" Carol stammered.

"I can't talk about it right now. It's top secret." Constance whispered the last part. "When it's safe… you'll be the first person I call, I promise."

"*When it's safe*?" Carol's eyes grew wide, but Constance just waved goodbye and rushed those in her care back indoors.

Helena allowed Constance to get her settled on the sofa in the living room. Tori hugged her mother tightly.

"Where's Daddy?" the little one asked with her sweet voice muffled in her mother's hair.

"Daddy is with Uncle Jake at work." Helena met Jenna's gaze and the impact hit Jenna square in the chest.

"*What?* But he's on leave!" Jenna said weakly.

Helena gave a dry laugh. "There was no keeping him down after I told him what you told me."

"Oh no," Jenna groaned. Would Jake be mad at her for giving out details when he came back? *If* he came back? Her stomach twisted. Had she just put Brian in danger?

"Like I told you last night, Jenna," Helena said with concern and worry that mirrored Jenna's. "We're family."

*****

"What are you thinking, Hamilton?" Jake wanted to throttle his best friend, but at the same time his presence soothed him.

"What am *I* thinking?" Brian's eyebrows shot up. "What are *you* thinking? A decoy Brian?"

"Jenna..." Jake shook his head as he realized she must've talked to Helena. He'd have words with her later.

"You know better than this, Brian. You can't just show up..."

"Well, I did. And unless you want me going back down that road, I'm here," Brian said resolutely. "You might as well put me in. If Nick is watching, he'll know *that* guy isn't me a mile away."

Brian stuck his thumb out towards the man who had on a fishing vest and sunglasses.

"We'll talk about this later, Hamilton," Branson growled. "Get him suited up."

Moments later, Jake and Brian watched as Trip was taken out of the van. He must've sensed Jake tense up at the sight of him because Brian whispered, "We can do this, Corey."

"Hey, Guys. Just like old times, huh?" Trip tried to sound funny, but it was clear he felt nervous and apprehensive. In another place and time, Jake would've felt sorry for him.

"Let's get this over with," Jake said through gritted teeth.

The fishing gear went into the truck bed. Brian sat in the back seat while the officers settled Trip, still shackled, into the front of Jake's truck. Branson handed Jake Trip's cell phone so they could send the crucial text.

"Ellis, report," Branson spoke into the radio, realizing enough time had passed.

"Ellis, here. Green light," the man responded.

Branson nodded to Jake. "It's go time."

With a sigh and a silent prayer, Jake climbed into his truck. Soon it would be over… one way or the other.

*****

"Ellis, here. Green light," the sniper said as he looked up at the decent tree with sturdy branches.

Nick tried not to criticize his choice too harshly. If it had been *him*… back when he had been a sniper… he would have chosen the outcropping of high boulders about twenty feet down the path and he definitely wouldn't have given the green light until he was settled. Oh well, it wouldn't matter anyway.

Dagger clenched firmly in his fist, Nick pounced. Just like the good old days, he moved silently and resourcefully, slitting Ellis's throat and letting the man drop to the ground. He dragged the body to a brushy area and covered him as best as he could in a hurry.

With a cocky smile, Nick shook his head. He got there early enough to spot the sniper being dropped off. While he was careful to look for the others who were surely taking their places, he felt confident things were landing in his favor. All he needed was a clear shot of Jake Corey.

In the distance, he heard a car go over the overpass. He could have sworn he heard twigs snapping and movement coming from the woods as he exited, but he pressed onward. Nick moved to the hiding spot he had selected for his encounter with Jake. There was a hidden crevice at the base of the bridge, neatly tucked in the concrete piles of the overpass. He was shielded by overgrown bushes and the side of the hill that the overpass merged out from.

A text vibrated his phone. Trip sent the location. A small smile spread across Nick's face. *Now I wait.*

*****

"We could try to look like we're enjoying this, right?" Trip suggested as the three positioned themselves around the water and rocks on the lake's edge. "Aren't we supposed to look like friends fishing? He'll know something is up."

"Shut up," Brian bristled as he threw his line into the water. "I don't want to hear your voice."

"I know I've blown it, but please listen to me," Trip begged. "I have problems."

Jake's jaw clenched. "Yes, you do."

"No… I mean … I got myself into something I couldn't get out of," Trip tried to explain. "I owe some very bad people money. Nick offered to help…"

"So, you sold out your friends." Brian shook his head, rage bubbling just under the surface. "Using *my* daughter as a way in."

"Don't engage him," Jake warned as he scanned the perimeter. To their right were rocks and boulders and Carson Lake. To their left was the over pass, half over the incline of the hill and half over the lake. They had gotten confirmation the other men were surrounding their position, hidden in the wooded area. Yet, something felt off… wrong. "He's trying to distract us. Keep alert."

"No, I'm trying to say… I'm sorry. I screwed up." Trip sounded sincere, but now wasn't the time. Nick could show up at any moment.

The conversation in his earpiece caught Jake's attention.

"Everyone, report," Branson ordered.

"Hamilton."

"Corey."

"Hindes," said another officer.

All reported, except for one.

"Ellis, report."

Silence.

“Ellis, report,” the order was repeated, but not returned. “Does anyone have visual on Ellis?”

“Negative,” the team responded.

Jake and Brian exchanged looks as they listened to Branson issue instructions. “I want eyes on Ellis.”

“What? What is it?” Trip asked when he noticed their silence.

“We’re too out in the open,” Brian said to Jake, clearly feeling uneasy as well.

Scanning the perimeter, Jake noticed movement just to their left, near the piling of the overpass. Before he could call it in, a shot rang out and Trip fell backwards into the water. Both Brian and Jake lunged towards him and tried to drag him somewhere safe. Yet, they were exposed.

“Shots fired. Shots fired,” Jake called out. “Trip is hit.”

“It’s so hard to find loyal friends, isn’t it?” a voice called out, shielded behind brush and concrete. “Although you wouldn’t know a thing about loyalty, would you, Corey? What would Beth say if she knew you already moved on? What’s her name? *Jenna*?”

Jake could pinpoint his location, but Nick was well concealed. “Come out, Spencer. This is over.”

Nick laughed. “Yes, it is.”

In his earpiece, Branson yelled out orders, and from his periphery, Jake saw the men trying to get a good shot at Nick. Yet, the man stayed in his concrete sanctuary. He had to draw him out. Jake moved forward.

"No, Jake," Brian hissed from his place next to Trip.

Jake thought he heard his friend mutter, "Jenna will never forgive me if I let something happen to you."

Still, he pressed on slowly... carefully... as if he approached a rabid animal. He'd need to do something radical to get Nick to give the team the opening that they needed.

"I know you loved Beth, Nick." Jake called out, despite the words turning his stomach. "What wasn't there to love about her? She was gentle and kind. Do you think this is how she would want to see us?"

"Shut up. You failed her! You killed her."

"You don't think I blame myself every day for not pushing her to get checked sooner? I loved Beth!" Jake yelled. "I didn't kill her, Nick. *Cancer* did."

"Liar! Now you'll die, too!" Nick did just what Jake had hoped he would do. He emerged just enough, the barrel of his gun trained right on Jake.

A shot rang out, followed by another. Jake fell into darkness with one last fleeting thought. *Whatever the outcome, Lord. Keep Jenna safe.*

39

Constance did her best to keep Jenna and Helena in good spirits, but Jenna was growing weary of putting on a front to make her feel better. Hours had passed since Jake left that morning and there had been no news. No texts. No calls. The officers guarding the house hadn't even given an update, though they had promised to let them know something as soon as they were cleared to do so.

"So what was that supposed to be?" Helena asked Jenna and nodded to the embroidery hoop in her hand.

"I was making a little deer for baby Brian's nursery." Jenna smirked.

"Oh… wow! Thank you… I think," Helena chuckled.

"Jake thought it was the state of New York," Jenna's smiled faltered then as she once more thought of the man who had captured her heart.

"I'm sure he's okay, Jenna. I'm sure both of them are fine." Helena gave one of her hourly peptalks. "They're trained for things like this."

Jenna nodded silently. Words escaped her as she checked the clock. The third batch of cookies she had made would soon need out of the oven. Who knew she would turn into a stress baker? All of those lessons her mother had given her in the kitchen actually paid off.

She walked into the kitchen and took the tray of cookies from the oven just as the buzzer sounded. If Jake and Brian didn't get back soon, she and Helena would get fat eating all of the things they had baked during their wait.

"You know, I bet the officers would like some fresh baked cookies," Constance suggested from the kitchen table.

Jenna scowled.

"I couldn't help but notice they seem to be moving around a little more," Constance continued. "I wonder what has them so busy all of the sudden."

Jenna looked out the window. They did seem to be a little more animated than the last time she had seen them.

Constance cleared her throat. "Might be a good time to take them cookies… and see if there's news?"

"Oh." Constance's words finally hit their target as Jenna nodded. "Yes, you're right. We shouldn't be stingy with these, should we?"

Constance smiled. "There are bottled waters as well. And for goodness sake, Jenna, smile at them. Haven't you ever heard you catch more flies with honey?"

Jenna flashed Constance a practice smile.

"Well, don't make them think your deranged, Dear." Constance chuckled as she helped put a few cookies in a plastic container.

Jenna gave her best smile and Constance smiled back, patting her on her arm. "Better. Remember, they're just doing their jobs."

Jenna nodded, taking the small offering to the officers.

"Hello, Officer. We thought you all might want some chocolate chip cookies," Jenna said kindly holding up the container.

"That's very nice of you," the one said moving closer.

"We've had a lot of time on our hands in there. Especially, with not knowing anything…"

The officer gave her a tolerant smile. "Thank you for the cookies, Ma'am."

"I don't suppose you…" Jenna's query was cut off by radio static, followed by rushed words.

"Three dead, including the suspect. Two wounded. En route to Skennan Memorial."

The officer and Jenna made eye contact, but she didn't get a chance to ask questions. He moved to his partner and asked her to go back inside the house. He *did* promise once more that they'd let them know as soon as they information to share.

Jenna did as she was told and found both Helena and Constance waiting to hear what, if anything, she had learned.

"Three dead, including the suspect. Two wounded being moved to Skennan Memorial," Jenna repeated numbly.

"*Nick* is dead then?" Helena asked, trying to piece out the information.

"And so are two others," Jenna stated, her voice quivering.

"There were a lot of men out there, I'm sure." Constance wrung her hands. "It doesn't mean it was Brian or Jake. Though, it's sad no matter who it was."

A familiar sick feeling rose inside of Jenna. Out the window, the women noticed two officers getting into their cars and pulling away from the driveway.

"They're leaving? What does that mean?" Jenna looked to Helena as if she might know, considering she was the only police officer's wife in the room.

Her friend just shrugged with the same worried sick look on her face.

"Well, I've had about enough of this," Constance said kicking off her slippers, and putting on her outside shoes.

She swung open the door and marched down to the two remaining officers at the base of her drive. Jenna's eyes widened, watching Constance's hands move excitedly as she spoke to the officers. In another place and time, Jenna might have found the scene amusing. Constance resembled an angry hen. The respectful men let her rant a moment before saying something back to her in return.

Constance listened, gave a curt nod, and started back up the path to the house.

"What did they say?" Helena asked as soon as Constance kicked off her shoes by the door.

"All they could tell me was that half of them have been dismissed. You can derive from that what you will." Constance shook her head. "They didn't have names for the wounded or the dead yet. Then, they apologized saying they knew we've had a *long* day."

A long day? A long day was working a hard shift. A long day was cleaning the house. This wasn't just a *long day.* It was *torture.* What if one of them didn't come back? Brian was a father and a husband. And Jake... Well, Jenna couldn't let her mind go there. If she lost another person she cared for...

"See those keys over there, Jenna? They go to my old Lincoln in the garage." Constance broke Jenna's train of thought.

Jenna looked over to where Constance was nodding. A set of keys hung on a hook near the door leading to the garage.

"Look, they're getting ready to do their perimeter check. I'll distract them while you take my car to the hospital," Constance instructed. "I'll smooth it over with them."

"Constance!" Jenna looked at her in surprise.

"It's not like we're prisoners here. We need answers, so go get them. Call us as soon as you know something," Constance nudged her on.

Jenna grabbed the keys and her purse from the back of a chair at the table. She sent Helena an uncertain glance before she disappeared behind the garage door. Jenna rallied her inner rebel as she got in the mammoth car and raised the garage doors. The car started smoothly enough. Making sure no one was in her path, Jenna peeled out.

She had never driven a car that large before. The seat bounced her all over the place despite the seatbelt securing her. The radio was playing what sounded like grocery store music. She tried to look in the rearview mirror to see if she was being followed, but she didn't see anything. For a split second, Jenna felt like she was living inside one of the old video games she and Ben would play back in the day.

Her phone rang. Michael! Of all the times for her brother to call!

"Not a good time, Mike." Jenna held the wheel with one hand and her phone with the other.

"I'm hearing things over the scanner. Are you okay? Have you heard anything from Jake?" He sounded just as panicked as she felt. "And what in the world are you listening to?"

"I'm on my way to the hospital to find out for myself."

"Jenna…"

"Don't start with me. This is *your* fault, you know?"

"What is?" he asked defensively.

"Why did you show me that apartment? Why did you bring Jake into my life?" Jenna cried. "He left this morning before I could say goodbye. Do you know what my last words to him were? *Don't forget to shower, Corey.* I don't want my last words to him to be that, Michael."

"Jenna Colleen Tyler-Clark!" Michael threw all of her names into the mix. "What in the world is going on over there?"

"I love him," Jenna said more to herself than to her brother. "And I can't lose him. Please tell me God wouldn't let that happen again."

There was silence.

"Mike? Are you still there?"

"You *love* him? Jake?"

Jenna was getting ready to turn into the hospital parking garage. "I've got to go, Michael. I'll call when I know something."

"Wait, wait, wait…"

But she didn't. She pulled that boat of a car into the first spot she could maneuver and made a mad dash for the door of the emergency room, praying one of her friends would let her in. Thankfully, one of the guards who had helped her the day Mara went missing saw her coming and rose to walk her back.

Jenna walked down the hall of the ER, but was met with a wall of police officers. They eyed her carefully as she got a little too close.

“Clark, what are you doing here?” the supervising nurse approached her. “I thought you were…”

“Please tell me who they brought in,” Jenna felt her throat close up as she imagined the worst.

“You know I can’t. Why are you here?” The words weren’t spoken unkindly. If anything, they were spoken with compassion that Jenna had never heard come from the other nurse.

“She’s with us,” a familiar voice said from behind her. “Let her through.”

She saw the man Jake referred to as Branson, standing at the door of one of the rooms. The men parted, but still watched her warily.

“You’re making me break rules, Young Lady,” Branson said with a sideways smile.

“Jake?” It was all Jenna could manage to get out.

“Yeah, he’s fine. So is Hamilton.” Branson pointed into the room he had just exited. “They’re in there.”

Taking a deep breath, Jenna entered the room and Branson went to go talk to his men. Brian’s arm was in a sling. Jake sat on the edge of a hospital bed, getting stitches on his forehead. Their eyes met and he kept trying to turn away from the doctor so he could see her.

"Sir, please. Unless you want a jagged line, you'd better stay still," Dr. Smith instructed.

"You're okay?" Jenna asked quietly. She moved slightly closer as she took in the wound on his head.

"I'm fine. Want to tell me why I'm getting calls and texts from the guards we put outside the house that you broke free?" Jake looked at her sternly and raised an eyebrow, but winced when it stung. Once again, the doctor sighed and paused her movements.

"How about you tell me why you left without saying a word this morning? Do you have any idea how worried I was?" Jenna had been trying to hold it together, but she was about to come undone.

"You needed to sleep and I needed to get out of there with as clear a head as possible, Jenna," Jake said. "If I had to face everything out there today with the image of you crying or upset…"

Motion out of the side of her eye caught her attention and she leveled an unsuspecting Brian with a glare.

"And *you*!" she pointed to him. "Text your wife."

"Whoa!" He put his hands up in defense. "Chill, Tiger. I already did."

"You did?"

"Yeah, probably around the same time you went joyriding in Constance's Lincoln Town Car," Brian smirked.

Jake grimaced.

"We heard there were three dead," Jenna said softly.

Dr. Smith stood back to look at her work before gathering everything up and dismissing herself from the room to offer them privacy.

"Ellis, Trip, and Nick." Jake's expression was haunted.

The name Ellis didn't ring a bell, but Jenna assumed it was another officer and sent up a prayer for his family.

"And how did this happen?" Jenna asked softly, motioning at the gash on his head as she moved in a little closer.

"Brian thought it was a good idea to play hero and push me out of the way of a bullet," Jake stated. "He *did* however cause me to hit my head on a rock."

"And your arm?" Jenna turned to ask Brian.

"He didn't go down smoothly," Brian smirked. "It's just a sprain."

Despite the relief and joy Jenna felt, there was still a heaviness in the room. Whether those who lost their lives were the bad guys or the good guys… loss of life still stung.

"Did *you* have to shoot Nick?" Jenna asked Jake, filled with compassion.

Jake sighed and glanced over at Brian. The two exchanged looks before he finally said, "No. We still don't know who did, but it was a precision hit."

"Is it over, Jake? Are we safe now?" Jenna asked and he pulled her closer to stand in front of him.

Her eyes searched his face. He looked exhausted, but there was a peace there that she hadn't seen until that moment.

"Yeah, I think it's finally over, Jenna." He pulled her in further and kissed the side of her head as she rested against him.

Brian shuffled uncomfortably. "I'll just be right out here, but I'm leaving the door open, You Two!"

Jake smiled at Jenna before bringing his lips down to hers. Jenna's heart soared. Jake was alive. He had survived and they could have a future together after all. There was so much she wanted to say in that moment, so much she wasn't sure she could express. So instead, she let herself be drawn into the kiss a little deeper.

When Jake finally broke away, he looked down at her with a smile. "So… you love me, huh?"

"What?" Jenna blushed. "Why would you think a thing like that?"

"Despite the fact you already told me?" he whispered in her ear. He smiled and reached for his phone, pulling up a long line of texts sent to him from Michael. "It must be true if you'd admit it to your brother."

"Oh! I guess I did tell him," Jenna laughed as she remembered the crazy drive to the hospital. "Poor guy. He kind of got an earful."

"I can't tell whether he's happy or if he wants to kill me," Jake sighed. "I wasn't supposed to fall in love with you, you know. He only asked me to keep an eye on you."

"Want to change your mind?" Jenna looked straight into Jake's eyes and challenged him.

"Never. You're stuck with me for good, Jenna Clark."

*****

"Is it done?" Damon asked into his phone as he watched the last of his suitcases being loaded into the SUV.

"The Broker is dead. I never even saw the man you sent in. Impressive," the man on the other line assured.

"And his friend? The one he called Trip?"

"Also dead."

Damon sighed. "Then it looks like all is in order. I kept my part of the arrangement, now you keep yours. I want to leave this place for good."

"That's wise. Can't say I'm sorry to see you go."

"And, Branson… good job. Your payment was deposited into your account. Enjoy your retirement."

*****

Jenna sighed from the driver's seat of Jake's truck. Until his head wound healed and there were no ill effects, he was at her mercy. All of the vehicles had been retrieved and Constance's Town Car, as fun as it had been to drive, was returned to its garage until its next adventure.

Jake and Jenna made no attempt to get out of the truck. They both seemed preoccupied with their respective thoughts. Jenna reflected on the visit she had made to Mara's room while she had waited for Jake to be discharged. She hadn't been sure what to expect from Mara. Would she hate Jenna?

It was a pleasant surprise to discover that Mara had been just as worried about *her* as Jenna had been about Mara. The two visited briefly until Mara grew tired. Healing would take a while, but she'd get there. She even said she'd consider coming to one of the life group Bible studies to thank them for the prayers. Apparently, several had sent get well cards. It made a huge impression on her.

"You're being awfully quiet," Jake said softly from his place in the passenger seat. "Are you okay?"

The Hamiltons pulled into their spot beside them and got out of their car. Tough guy Brian had already ditched the arm sling. He helped his little girl get down from the car and moved to take the baby's car seat with his good arm. Helena and he entered the house for the first time as a family of four.

"I'm good. I'm more than good actually," Jenna said softly. "I never thought I would be, but I am."

He held her hand and squeezed. "Me, too."

With a mischievous glint in this eye, he leaned forward, opened the side console, and pulled out a little velvet jewelry box. He handed it to her and watched as her eyes grew large.

"Jake, I know we love each other, but…"

"Just open it." Jake smirked. "I may be a fast mover, but not *that* fast."

Jenna opened it. Inside, was a door key.

"Ahh, for my new lock." Jenna smiled as she realized what she held.

"Read the card I put in there."

Jenna looked at the folded up 3x5 card still in the box.

"Sometimes taking the long way Home allows you to see more of the goodness of God in the land of the living."

Jenna's throat tightened. She once tried to take a short cut, but God showed her grace and mercy in allowing her a little extra time… a longer path full of new adventures, friends, and love. One day, she would close her eyes and be in the presence of Jesus, but until then she would see the goodness of God in her everyday life. Every morning she'd be grateful for her beating heart. She would love and be loved. And she would enjoy each moment taking the long way home.

Epilogue

Five years later…

"Are you sure your parents won't mind us tagging along?" Helena asked, getting little Brian down from the car.

Jenna looked at her friend with a quirked eyebrow. "You're kidding, right? My mother has talked about nothing else since I suggested it."

Big Brian held onto Tori's hand and Jenna smiled as the little girl watched the other kids play at the bottom of the hill. Dan and Kate's three children played tag with Tessa and Sean's only daughter, Evie. Anna's nieces and nephew joined in, making it look like a wild free-for-all as children ran every which way. The look on Tori's face was one of curiosity mixed with uncertainty.

"This is all from one family?" Brian asked, mirroring his daughter's apprehension.

"Well, family plus *extended* family." Jenna's heart swelled when she spotted Alexis helping Colleen carry food from the house. She looked… healthy. She had gained some weight and her wide smile revealed her pearly white dentures. Pastor Munson had his usual place next to Jenna's father at the grill, obvious mirth on his face over some joke the two had just shared.

The Hamiltons started heading down the incline towards the mob of Tylers and Munsons and were soon enveloped into the chaos. Jenna just stood still and took it all in. Another Memorial Day found the family gathering and enjoying one another's company. A familiar ache crept in to Jenna's heart. The loss of Ben still hurt, but it didn't immobilize her as it had in years past. With Memorial Day, came their wedding anniversary and the anniversary of her suicide attempt. Jenna referred to it as her *Second Chance Day*.

A warm hand took hers and she looked down as the sun reflected off the gold band on Jake's ring finger. In his free arm was a wild haired, blue eyed mini version of herself.

"Want to go see Grandma, Bethany?" he asked and she nodded wildly.

As soon as Jake put her down, she ran with reckless abandon down the hill, Goose on her heels. Jenna chuckled as she watched Anna hide behind Michael as the dog appeared. Laughter and warmth radiated from the front yard of the Tyler home.

Jenna sighed.

"You good?" Jake nudged his wife with his shoulder.

"Of course. Why wouldn't I be?"

"Because I heard you throwing up this morning in the bathroom. What was this… three days in a row? This pregnancy seems harder on you than Bethany's."

"Why do you have to be so observant, Corey?" Jenna shook her head in amusement. She wasn't ready to make an announcement to her family just yet. Not after her miscarriage and knowing Anna and Michael were still struggling to get pregnant. She'd wait until her second trimester to share the news.

"Being observant is my job. Especially when it comes to you."

Jenna smiled. "Ahh, yes. Sergeant Jake Corey. He doesn't miss a thing."

"At your service." He held out his arm for her to hold onto as they descended.

They made it down the hill and Michael wasted no time approaching them.

"I was wondering if you were ever going to get here," Michael bombarded. "Jake, whatever Dan tries to pull... remember you promised that you'll be my partner in corn hole."

"Did I promise that?" Jake looked at Jenna, scratching his chin. "I don't remember who I had promised that too."

"Watch it, Corey." Michael smirked. "I let you marry my sister."

Jenna rolled her eyes. "Whatever, Mike."

Jake checked once more that Jenna was okay before joining the ongoing tournament off to the side.

"I missed you this morning," John Tyler said as his daughter approached the grill and planted a kiss on his cheek.

"How was it? Were Ben's parents there?" Jenna asked quietly.

"Not this year. I think they finally took that cruise they'd been putting off." John put the cover back on the grill and turned to his daughter. "But Ben was well represented. Your mom and I put a wreath at the monument in his honor."

"Thank you, Dad."

John nodded. "Are you and Jake going to visit his grave on your way home?"

"Yes. I picked flowers from our garden this morning," Jenna said as she looked over the distance to where Jake calculated his bean bag throw very methodically.

She smiled absently, watching the scene. Bethany clung to his leg, while he threw the bean bag landing a perfect shot. Michael cheered and gloated over his older brothers.

"Now that's something I like to see." John's voice brought her back to reality.

"What?"

"My baby girl smiling."

Jenna felt tears stinging her eyes when she saw the emotion in her father's expression.

"God is good, isn't he? Through it all… the good, the bad, the joyful, the grief…" John sighed, looking over his family scattered across the yard. "When your mother and I married over forty years ago, we had no idea what to expect."

Jenna smiled and her eyes went to her mother engaging Anna, Kate, and Tessa in an animated conversation.

"Dan and Kate are training to take over this farm. Sean and Tessa are devoted to their ministry. Michael is out there saving the world while Anna writes and helps little kids learn to love books."

Nodding at her father's words, she never expected what he said next.

"Then there is you…"

"Your screw up?" Jenna laughed.

"No." John shook his head emphatically. "You were always the strongest of any of us. Independent and bold. You knew what you wanted and weren't afraid, even if it meant moving away. You faced the worst anyone could imagine and came back stronger and better than before. I'm proud of you, Jenna."

Jenna swiped at the tear falling down her cheek. "Stop that, Dad."

"Well, it's true and it needed to be said." John sniffed as he reopened the lid to the grill. Thankfully, he changed the subject because Jenna's emotions couldn't handle any more. "Saw that friend of yours. What was his name? Chase?"

"Chase? You saw him at the Memorial Day parade?" Jenna smiled.

Chase had come to cook outs at their house off and on over the past five years, but life after retiring from the military was demanding. He took a civilian job on Fort Drum, claiming he fell in love with the area. Jenna had seen less of him over the past year, but she was happy to see him finally settling down with a nice woman who returned his affections.

Her father smiled. "Chase turned out to be a nice guy, but I think you chose well. Jake is good for you."

Jenna smiled in the direction of her husband. He and Michael screamed a victory cry as their game concluded. "Yeah, I think he's a keeper."

As if sensing he was the topic of conversation, he made his way to Jenna and her father.

"We won," he said with a cheesy smile.

"I figured. Congratulations." Jenna kissed him as a reward.

She smiled serenely and Jake held her.

"What's that smile about?" he asked tenderly in her ear.

"All of this… my family, this place... *You*. It's home and I never want to take any of it for granted."

Off to the side, her brothers stood around laughing. Jenna and Jake joined them, curious about what was going on.

"You can't join the club. It's for boys only!" Eli, Dan's oldest son, told his little sister and cousins as his baby brother and Sam nodded in agreement with their leader.

The little wooden playhouse was guarded by the boys, but they didn't see what was transpiring off to the side. Jenna looked up at Jake and winked. Bethany had climbed in through the little window on the other side with the help of Tori. No one noticed until she landed on the floor inside. Pushing the boys out of the door, the other cousins cheered and entered unhindered.

"My club now," Bethany smiled.

"Well, that feels familiar," Dan laughed and nudged his sister.

"That's a whole new generation right there." Sean smirked.

"The future of Deer Creek and the surrounding areas are in for a treat." Jenna smiled at Michael's words. One thing was for certain, the Tyler family had definitely left their mark on Deer Creek and Deer Creek left its mark on them.

Dear Friends,

This series was written with the heart and desire to help women, no matter what their past or background, know that there is healing through the power of Jesus. Kate had an estranged relationship with her father, causing her to struggle to look at God as a Father. Tessa had to overcome past trauma and look to God as her redeemer and constant peace. Anna struggled with her identity, not knowing who she was or where she fit in until she discovered herself through Christ.

Then there was Jenna. Her story is one of grief, but also something that goes much deeper. Mental health is real. Depression and sadness can cripple the strongest person. Ultimately, she found her strength in God and was able to say that she "*saw the goodness of God in the land of the living*". However, many struggle to say that.

Please, if you find yourself in a dark place, seek help. Don't wait it out. Don't try to do it on your own. There are people who love you and who want to help. If you have thoughts of harming or taking your own life please reach out to a pastor or counselor today.

Suicide hotline: Call or text 988.

Just because The Deer Creek Chronicles is over doesn't mean there won't be more fun!

*****

Follow me on my D. Emily Smith - Author Face Book and Instagram pages for upcoming news and future book releases!

www.ingramcontent.com/pod-product-compliance
Lightning Source LLC
LaVergne TN
LVHW090545110826
845146LV00001B/23

* 9 7 9 8 2 1 8 8 9 8 8 3 0 *